"What do you want, Mace?" Rhett's question was soft, guarded.

She skewed her lips to the side as if trying to find the right words. "I'm just wondering where the boy I knew went."

Rhett crossed his arms. "He grew up."

"That's a pity," Macy said. "He had this amazing ability to dream big, but plan well—something this place really needs. That boy could have shaped the ranch into something beyond what his father possibly ever could have."

He clenched his teeth and reminded himself that Macy was just being Macy. She'd been known to kick a hornets' nest before—literally.

He pressed his palms against the armrests. "You finished?"

"For now, sure. Forever?" she asked. "Not a chance."

Rhett couldn't hold in a chuckle. "I don't doubt it one bit."

This was the Macy he remembered, *his* Macy—someone who would stand against the wind and glare at a coming storm. Someone who didn't flinch.

Well, not his Macy. He wasn't quite sure where that thought had come from...

Easter on
the Ranch

Jessica Keller

&

Mindy Obenhaus

2 Uplifting Stories

The Rancher's Legacy and *Their Ranch Reunion*

LOVE INSPIRED
INSPIRATIONAL ROMANCE

LOVE INSPIRED®

INSPIRATIONAL ROMANCE

ISBN-13: 978-1-335-62190-0

Recycling programs
for this product may
not exist in your area.

CONTENTS

Avid reader, coffee drinker and chocolate aficionado **Jessica Keller** has degrees in communications and biblical studies and spends too much time on Instagram and Pinterest. Jessica calls the Midwest home. She lives for fall, farmers markets and driving with the windows down.

Visit the Author Profile page at LoveInspired.com.

THE RANCHER'S LEGACY

Jessica Keller

He restoreth my soul: he leadeth me in the paths of righteousness for his name's sake.
Yea, though I walk through the valley of the shadow of death, I will fear no evil: for thou art with me; thy rod and thy staff they comfort me.
—*Psalms* 23:3–4

For the ladies in my *Psalms* 23 study. Thanks for being my sisters. Thanks for yanking me back on the path. Thank you for being there. Always.

Chapter One

"I don't know why you're here." Rhett Jarrett rested his elbows on the large desk. It was too large—too grand—and he'd never look right behind it. Never be able to fill the spot his dad had. "I mean, other than it's always nice to see you. But you know where I stand on this."

Uncle Travis pushed more papers across the desktop. "With time, maybe you'll see his reasoning."

Rhett opened a drawer and slid the papers unceremoniously inside. Rereading the will wouldn't suddenly make him appreciate the choices his father had made. All it would serve to do was remind Rhett his dad had found a way to control him after the grave.

Late afternoon sunshine poured through the wide windows filling the west-facing wall of the office. March had begun unseasonably warm, even by Texas standards.

Upon entering the office a few minutes ago, Rhett had immediately cracked a few of the windows in an attempt to banish the musty odor of too many papers and books collecting dust in one cramped place. No doubt the wood paneling lining the lower half of the walls hadn't helped his mood either. It only seemed to add to the dark heaviness that had settled on Rhett's life since his dad's sudden passing. Unsaid words, missed opportunities and apologies that would never happen weighed him down.

No amount of fresh air would clear his chest of those things.

Air gusted in, carrying with it the smells of the horses in the nearest enclosure and the cattle in the pastures beyond. They mingled with the scents of Texas Indian paintbrush, bluebonnets and red poppies. Wild-flowers quilted the fields on either side of the long driveway leading to his family's property. Spring at the ranch had always been his favorite time of year. He liked the physical parts of the ranch—the animals, the fields, the work.

Just not all the *other* aspects of Red Dog Ranch.

Not the parts his dad had cared about.

"Uncle Travis, listen. I—" Rhett started.

The door to the office clicked open and Macy Howell appeared in the doorway. With her hand resting on the knob, she hesitated for a few seconds. Her long, black hair swayed from her abrupt stop.

Rhett had known he would see his dad's office assistant sooner or later, but after the last few years of carefully visiting Red Dog Ranch only when he had been assured she was busy or away from the property…it was startling to see her so soon his first day in the office.

Macy adjusted the armful of files she clutched. Her gaze hit the floor like a dropped quarter. "I didn't realize you were busy. Should I come back later?"

But Macy casting down her eyes didn't compute for Rhett. Growing up, she'd been the girl who would spit at a wildfire and dare it to come closer. She'd hauled hay bales in the field at the same pace as Rhett and his brothers had.

When Rhett had scooped Macy into his arms after she'd been bitten by a copperhead, she had told him not to worry because the pit viper had barely kissed her. Even in that sort of pain, she'd been focused on being tough and making others feel better.

The Macy Howell he knew didn't hesitate, didn't look away.

She especially didn't look *down*.

The back of Rhett's neck prickled in a way that made him want to scrub at it. He fought the urge to ask her what was wrong. But they'd stopped asking each other prying questions three years ago. One kiss had changed everything.

Ruined everything.

And he shouldn't care.

Didn't care.

He dug his fingers into his knees.

Kodiak, Rhett's seventy-pound Chesapeake Bay retriever, lifted her giant head and sniffed in Macy's direction. The dog lazily looked back at Rhett as if to ask if this person was a threat.

Oh, she was.

With a gaze that could melt his resolve and her bright smile, Macy definitely was.

Satisfied that Rhett hadn't given a command, Kodiak let out a loud harrumph and laid her head back down. Her front paws stretched so the tips dipped into a spear of sunlight.

Despite Macy seeming to act out of character, the sight of her standing there in jeans and a flannel over a blue T-shirt still hit Rhett with the force of a double-strength energy drink spiked with strong coffee. She had a pencil tucked behind her ear. She looked like... like the best friend she'd once been. Like the person he used to be able to count on.

Like someone who hadn't rejected him.

Looks could be deceiving.

Uncle Travis's bushy gray eyebrows rose as if to ask, "Are you going to answer her, or what?"

Rhett cleared his throat, but it felt as if he'd swallowed a mouthful of summer soil that had baked in the Texas sun for weeks on end. Gritty and dry. "What do you need?"

"These are the files for the teens with internships starting this weekend. You should probably look them over. Know something about each one before you have to train them." She stepped into the room holding the pile of file jackets like a peace offering. "Brock always did."

Brock Jarrett, also known as his father.

Rhett's shoulders stiffened. "There's no one else set up to train them? Dad did it all?"

"I don't think Brock had made plans in case..." Uncle Travis's voice drifted away.

In case he died suddenly.

In case a trip to the library became his last trip.

In case one uninsured teenager sending a text while driving changed the Jarrett family forever.

Macy took another step into the room. "He usually spent the first few days with them, yes. They each get assigned to a staff member, but Brock did the bulk of the mentoring."

Rhett shook his head. "Someone else can do it."

Kodiak groaned and lifted her head, alerted to trouble by his change in tone.

Macy's wide brown eyes searched his. "Rhett." She whispered his name and, for a reason he didn't want to explore, it made his gut hurt. "Please."

Rhett let his gaze land on the painting of longhorns instead of Macy. Meeting her pleading eyes made his resolve shaky and that was the last thing he wanted. His mom had painted the picture years ago, before her mind had begun to fail her. She'd proudly given it to Brock as a Valentine's day gift.

Thinking of his mom made Rhett sit a little straighter. Her well-being depended on how he ran this ranch now. The will clearly stated Rhett was to take care of her and provide stable jobs for his sister, Shannon; Cassidy, the girlfriend of his deceased brother, Wade; Wade's daughter, Piper; and his brother, Boone, and his family. With Boone off at seminary with his wife and daughter, at least that responsibility was off Rhett's list. But the others stood.

However, so did the will's ironclad wording about the ranch continuing to serve foster kids. If Rhett put a stop to the foster programs at Red Dog Ranch, the will stated he would have to forfeit his inheritance. It was continue his dad's work or get none of it.

"Leave them on the table." Rhett jerked his chin toward a small side table near the office door.

Macy did, but she stayed in the doorway. "We need

to talk about the spring kickoff event and the Easter egg hunt."

"Put those thoughts on hold. I'm looking into cancelling programs," Rhett said as he turned back to his uncle. "Which means you and I need to keep talking."

Macy's eyes narrowed for a second. She was biting her tongue. Years of knowing her made that clear, but she backed out of the room and closed the door.

As Rhett waited for his uncle to say something, he rubbed his thumb back and forth over an etching near the bottom right edge of the desktop. His dad had made him muck stalls alone for two weeks straight after Rhett had carved the indentation. At all of seven or eight years old, it had been quite a chore.

Uncle Travis offered a tight smile. "She's the perfect one to work with to help you meet the terms of the will. You see that, don't you?"

Rhett pinched the bridge of his nose.

Of course he saw that.

It was half the problem.

Macy had always put the foster programs before everything else, just like Brock had. Before the moneymaking aspects of the ranch, before family, before friendships. She had a passion and knowledge Rhett lacked, but working alongside her would be difficult; between losing his dad, dealing with family drama and being forced to put his business on hold to deal with Red Dog Ranch, Rhett was already past his ears in difficult. He needed to start making hard decisions and taking action to mitigate losses and stress.

Keeping a wide berth from Macy was one significant way to limit stress.

"As executor, don't you have the power to change the stipulations?"

His uncle's shoulders drooped with a sigh. "We've been over this."

And they had.

Many times.

As executor, Travis's job was to make certain all of Brock Jarrett's wishes were carried out to the letter. And Rhett's father had left many…letters. Red Dog Ranch had been willed to Rhett in full—the land and his father's vast accounts. But there were conditions.

If Rhett rejected the position of director, then they were supposed to sell the land and donate the money from the sale to a charity Brock had stipulated. Even in death his dad had placed continuation of the programs offered at the ranch before his family's long-term well-being. The only other option allowed in the will was for the property to pass to Boone, but Boone had been emphatic about refusing the inheritance. He wanted to finish seminary. He had a plan that didn't involve the ranch and no one could fault Boone for putting God first.

Well, Rhett refused to remove his mom from her home, from the land she loved. Even at the expense of his own happiness. His father had effectively tied his hands, making him the bad guy if he backed out.

Rhett lifted his chin. He wasn't backing out. He would take care of his family's future, would succeed in a way his father never had.

Kodiak made a small sound in her sleep, drawing Rhett's attention for a heartbeat.

He had placed his business, Straight Arrow Retrievers, on hold after getting the call that his father had passed away. But "on hold" might quickly become "closed forever." A burning sensation settled in Rhett's chest.

It was too much to manage. Too much to juggle. There was no way he could keep his business, the ranch and the foster programs all running successfully. One of them had to go.

His jaw hardened. "I'm going to find a loophole out of the foster programs at the ranch."

Uncle Travis frowned. "Even if you could—and I'm fairly certain you can't—talk like that would have broken your dad's heart."

"He knew how I felt about everything when he chose this for me," Rhett said.

While Red Dog Ranch had always functioned as a working cattle ranch, it also existed as a place that served children in the foster system. When Rhett was young, they had started hosting large parties for foster kids throughout Texas Hill Country for every major holiday. That had morphed into weekend programs that taught horseback riding and other life skills. The final addition had been building a summer camp on the property that was free for foster children to attend.

The summer camp had been Brock's pride and joy. It had seemed as if he lived all year for the weeks the ranch swelled with hundreds of kids. His father had poured his time and energy into every single one of the kids. Often as kids aged out of the foster care system, Brock had offered them positions on his property.

Rhett cared about kids who didn't have a home.

He did.

But it would be almost impossible to carry on his

dad's mission with the same passion. He scrubbed his hand over his jaw and blew out a long breath. As horrible as it sounded, he resented Red Dog Ranch and all that it stood for. His father had cared more about it and the foster children than anything else.

Especially more than he'd cared about Rhett.

Uncle Travis clicked his briefcase closed and stood up. He hovered near the desk, though. "A gift is only as good as what you do with it."

Rhett stood. Crossed his arms over his chest. "A gift and a burden are two very different things."

But Uncle Travis pressed on. "Your aunt Pearl, bless her, she never knew what to do when someone gave her something really nice." He laid his free hand over his heart. "When I lost her and got around to cleaning out her stuff, you know what I found?"

Rhett pressed his fingertips into the solid desktop and shook his head. Once Uncle Travis got started down a rabbit trail, there was no point stopping him.

"Boxes of expensive lotions and perfumes that our kids had given her over the years." Travis fanned out his hand as if he was showing an expansive array. "She'd just squirreled it all away. Jewelry that I'd given her and the kids had given her." He pursed his lips. "All never worn."

Rhett offered his uncle a sad smile. Aunt Pearl had been one of his favorite people growing up and he knew, despite her stubborn streak, Travis missed her every day. Letting the man talk would do no harm.

"Pearl grew up poor, you see," Uncle Travis said. "I don't know whether she was waiting for a time she deemed special enough to use those things, or if she just didn't believe *she* was special enough to use them. But in the end it didn't matter, did it? All those things, those pretty things, all of them went to waste. Unused. Rotting and tarnished or full of dust. Pearl never got to enjoy them because she didn't believe she was worth enjoying them."

Rhett looped a hand around the back of his neck and rocked in his boots. "Why are you telling me this?"

"Like I said—" Travis's voice was wistful "—a gift is only as good as what you do with it." His uncle tugged on his suit jacket and made his way toward the door. "Remember, son. 'For unto whomsoever much is given, of him shall be much required.'"

It had been a while since Rhett had cracked the book. "I know the Bible, Uncle Travis."

He paused as he opened the door. "Ah, but do you know the heart of God in this matter? Have you sought *that* out, son? Because that's more valuable than a hundred memorized Bible verses." Uncle Travis shrugged. "Just a thought."

After his uncle left, Rhett fought the urge to sit back down and drop his head into his hands. Fought the desire to finally lose it over his dad's death. Fall apart once and for all. But he couldn't do that, not now. Maybe not ever.

Way too many people were counting on him to be strong.

Rhett mentally packed up every messy emotion in his heart and shoved them into a lockbox. He pretended he was jamming them down, squishing them until they were so small and insignificant they weren't worth thinking about. Or talking about or sharing with anyone.

No one would care about them anyway.

Then he clicked the lockbox shut and tucked it into the darkest corner of his mind to be forgotten.

Macy was going to pace a hole in the floorboards at the front of the ranch's office. Travis Jarrett had left half an hour ago, but Rhett still hadn't vacated his father's office. What was taking so long?

She jerked her hair up into a ponytail.

The second—the very second—he left that office he'd have to listen to her, hear her out.

She'd *make* him.

Macy paused near her desk and picked up a framed photo of her and Brock Jarrett. It had been taken at last year's spring kickoff event for Camp Firefly—the free summer camp Brock ran at Red Dog Ranch for foster kids. She traced a finger over the photo—Brock's smile.

Macy blinked away tears.

After her father walked out of her life when she was ten years old, Brock had stepped in and filled that void. And when her mom died eight years later the Jarretts had moved her onto their property. Rhett's dad had been family to her—*Rhett* had been like family to her too. Now they hardly acknowledged each other, and with Rhett's mom fading fast, Macy couldn't help but feel like she was losing everyone she cared about all over again.

"I'll keep your secret," she whispered to the image. "I promise."

She set the picture down and absently rubbed her thumb back and forth across the raised scar on her pointer finger. A nervous habit she'd tried, unsuccessfully, to break more than once. The scar was Rhett's fault. Six years ago, he had dropped his cell phone when they were out hiking and she'd crawled back over the large rocks on the trail to get it, disturbing a copperhead in her zest. Of course, Rhett had carried her to safety, rushed her to the hospital as her skin swelled and blistered and the pain intensified, and stayed by her side while she healed. The memory caused a rueful smile to tug at her lips. He had lost his cell phone after everything anyway.

She forced her thumb to stop moving.

The scar on her finger wasn't the only one she blamed him for. The Do Not Cross tape coiled around her heart was all his doing too.

Macy whirled toward the door to Brock's—no, Rhett's—office.

Enough.

She marched toward the door and didn't bother knocking before opening it. "We need to—" The words died on her lips. Rhett wasn't there.

The man must have slunk out the never-used back door like the guilty dog he was.

Macy balled her fists.

They would have to face each other—have to talk at some point—and today was as good a day as any. She hadn't been able to get a good read on Rhett with Travis there so she had held her tongue.

I'm looking into cancelling programs.

Not if Macy had anything to do with it.

She grabbed her keys, locked up the office and hoofed it out into the yard. Orange mingled with pink and gold in the sky. A slight breeze carried the chill whisper of the approaching night. The sun had dipped close to the horizon, not quite sunset yet but soon enough.

Various structures peppered the Jarrett property. The office and main buildings serving the summer camp wrapped through the front of their land, including ten camper cabins and a mess hall that was built into the side of the largest hill they owned. The barns and cattle fields took up the opposite end of their holding, and the family home rested like a gorgeous crown jewel at the end of the long driveway. Macy lived in one of the small bungalows tucked just west of the family ranch house. A handful of staff members lived on the property.

Macy passed the small corral that housed Romeo, the ranch's attention-needy miniature donkey, and Sheep, an all-white miniature horse that belonged to Rhett's niece, Piper. Romeo trotted beside the fence line as she walked, trying to coax an ear scratch out of her.

"Not now, buddy." Macy didn't break her stride. Still, his pathetic bray made her heart twist. She loved the little donkey and all of his quirks—maybe *for* his quirks. "I'll bring you apples later, deal?"

Beyond their enclosure, she spotted a horse and rider picking their way through the bluebonnets blanketing the nearby field. She squinted, trying to focus on the rider. Shannon Jarrett, Rhett's sister. Despite the fact that none of the women were related, Shannon, Cassidy and Macy had formed a tight-knit sisterhood. Especially during the last five years.

Macy climbed onto the fence and waved at her friend.

Shannon nudged her horse into a trot so she was within yelling distance in seconds.

"Did you see where your rat of a brother went off to?" Macy called.

Shannon tossed back her head and laughed. "Well, I know you aren't talking about Boone." And neither mentioned the other Jarrett brother, Wade. His death five years ago had been the catalyst that set the Jarretts drifting apart. Being Wade's twin, Shannon had been deeply affected by the sudden loss of him. She hadn't quite regained the wide, carefree grin she'd been known for as a child. Probably never would.

"I could hardly call a man training to be a pastor a rat." Macy joined in the laughter.

Shannon nodded, her short blond waves bobbing. "Rhett walks Kodiak to the lake every morning and every evening. I don't think she can last a day without swimming. Rhett says it's in her breed's blood."

Macy tipped her head in a silent thank-you and made for the lake.

Red Dog Ranch sat on over three thousand acres of gorgeous Texas Hill Country land and had multiple lakes and ponds. Some of them Macy would need a horse or one of the trucks to reach, but she guessed Rhett had stuck to the one closest to the house. Long ago, she and Rhett had dubbed the body of water Canoe Landing. It was where he'd fished with his dad and where he and his siblings had learned to swim. Macy too.

Embers of memories burned in the back of her mind. She snuffed them out. A million yesterdays couldn't help her solve the problems she faced today.

When Macy hiked over the hill that led to Canoe Landing, she paused. Rhett had his back to her. His shoulders made an impressive cut against the approaching sunset. Rhett had always been taller and broader than his brothers. The Wranglers and starched button-down he wore fit so well, they might as well be illegal. Under his cowboy hat she knew his hair would be naturally blond-tipped and tousled.

He was the kind of handsome that female country-western singers wrote ballads about, but it was clear he had never caught on to how attractive he was or how many hearts he could have broken if he'd wanted to. Rhett wasn't like that.

She fiddled with the end of her flannel.

Kodiak bounded out of the water, dropped a soggy ball at Rhett's feet and then leaned around his leg and let out a low growl. Her yellowish eyes pinned on Macy.

Rhett pivoted to see what had captured his dog's attention. His eyebrows rose when he spotted Macy. His eyes were such a shocking shade of blue and his tanned skin only made them stand out more.

I'm sorry I kissed you and ran off.

I'm sorry I never returned your calls. I was confused. I let too much time pass.

I ruined everything.

She swallowed the words rushing through her mind.

Macy tucked her thumb over her scarred finger. "You snuck out the back?"

Rhett patted Kodiak's head before he lobbed the ball in a wide arc. It splashed down in the middle of the lake. The dog became a blur of brown along the shoreline. She dove into the water, going under before paddling wildly.

Rhett crossed his arms over his chest. "I didn't know

I was supposed to check in with the assistant before leaving."

"Listen." Macy squared her shoulders and lifted her chin a notch higher to hold his gaze. "We need to come to some sort of a truce here or else work is going to become very miserable, very fast."

Unless he fired her, of course. Rhett had the power and ability to do it, so while she wanted to push him and fight with him over the foster-related events at the ranch, she needed to tread the subject carefully.

Good thing Macy had cooled down considerably since she'd locked up at the office.

Rhett shifted his line of vision to watch Kodiak swimming in circles. "I suppose you're right." He glanced back at her. "We can't keep acting like the walls of Jericho to each other if we're going to be sharing office space."

"You're...you're going to let me stay then?"

The notch in Rhett's throat bobbed. His gaze traced her face. "This is your home, Mace. You love your job." He looked away. "I don't plan on taking that from you."

"Thank you," she whispered. She tentatively touched his arm. "Rhett, I'm so sorry about your dad. He loved you a lot."

His bicep tensed under her touch. " I thought we had plenty of years left. I never thought—" A harsh exhale of breath escaped his lips. "What a stupid thing to say. No one expects these sorts of things."

"I'm here." She squeezed his arm lightly, then let go. "If you need someone."

His brow bunched as his eyes cut back to her. "We haven't spoken in three years."

"The walls of Jericho fell down." Macy slipped her hands into her pockets. "You know that, right?"

A muscle in Rhett's jaw popped, once, twice. "I'm a... I'm not looking for friendship again, Mace. Not with you. I think it's important to put that out on the table."

She knew Rhett hadn't meant the words maliciously; he was just stating reality. Rhett was a man who dealt in facts. It was his attempt at being forthright. Chivalrous even, making certain no one would get the wrong idea from the get-go.

But, wow, what he said smarted.

Not with you.

Those three words stung her worse than any pit viper ever could.

After Brock's funeral she'd foolishly hoped she and Rhett might have been able to let bygones be bygones and fall back into the easy, lifelong friendship they had once shared. A part of her had even wondered if God was drawing them close for another chance at being together in the way Macy had always wanted.

Well, consider that balloon popped and tossed in the garbage.

"Understood." She kept her voice even. If they weren't going to deal in niceties she might as well get down to business. "We need to talk about the foster programs."

Rhett let out one sharp laugh that held no hint of humor. "Which one?"

"Let's start with Camp Firefly." As if summoned by her mention, a pack of fireflies began to flit over the lake. Kodiak had noticed them too and began snapping her giant muzzle in their direction. The little bugs looped and pitched in oblong circles around each other. Encouraged by their presence Macy said, "You can't cut it."

Rhett cocked his head. "Who said I was?"

"You did." She jabbed a finger in his direction. "Mr. I'm-Looking-into-Cancelling-Things."

Rhett rubbed his finger across his lips. Was he hiding a smile? Was this a *joke* to him?

Kodiak slogged out of the water. She gave a shake, sending droplets flying, and then walked toward her master, her tail wagging the whole way.

"I can't make any promises about next summer, but with only three months left until camp it would be hard to cut it." Kodiak dropped down at his feet. She adjusted to lay her head near his boots, leaving wet marks on the legs of his jeans. "Some of the kids have already gotten letters inviting them. No matter what you think of me, I'm not heartless, Macy." He cut his gaze to collide with hers. "I promise, I'm not."

"I know you're not," she whispered into the growing dark. Rhett had never been a spiteful person. Hurt, but never hurtful.

They both stared out over the water as the sun tucked itself further into tomorrow.

"It's just…" Macy looked up into the sky as if she could find the right words somewhere in the clouds. "Your dad really cared about these programs. He cared about each and every foster kid. I'd hate to see *any* of the programs get cut."

Rhett stiffened. "My dad cared more about those foster kids than he did about his own flesh and blood." There was no trace of a smile left on his features. Only hurt mixed with a hint of disappointment. "You know I'm right."

Bringing up Brock had been a mistake, but it had easily slipped out. Brock and Rhett's relationship had been tense since Wade's death. They'd fought over blame instead of helping each other grieve. Macy had never understood how the fault of a boat capsizing in the Gulf of Mexico could belong to either of them.

Rhett tapped his thigh, causing Kodiak to rise and follow after him.

"Rhett, please," she said. "The foster programs, they're important. They were started because—" Because of you, she almost said. *Right or wrong, they were supposed to be Brock's love letter to you.* "There has to be a way to make it all work."

"It's late, Mace. We can talk about it tomorrow." He tipped his hat and walked past her up the hill in the direction of the Jarrett house.

Macy stared after him, watching Kodiak's tail bob in rhythm with Rhett's footfall—the whole time wanting to call after him, wanting to spill her secret so he could understand once and for all. So she could help him work through the hurt he felt over his father.

But she could never tell Rhett that he'd once been one of those children in need.

That Brock and Leah Jarrett had adopted him.

Chapter Two

When Rhett padded into the kitchen at the family ranch the next morning, Shannon offered him a cup of coffee with a sad smile.

He declined. Shannon consumed at least six cups of the stuff a day, but Rhett had never taken to it. That hardly stopped his sister from trying to get him to drink it whenever she could.

However, he wished he was a coffee drinker because it had been a long night.

Rhett bit back a yawn. "Does Mom walk the halls yelling like that often?"

Shannon nodded, swiping at her eyes. Then she took a long swig from her mug.

Guilt stabbed through Rhett's chest. Strong and palpable.

For the last three years he'd been gone, running Straight Arrow Retrievers, his dog-training business more than a hundred miles away from Red Dog Ranch. For his mom's sake, Rhett had made a shaky truce with his dad and had visited the ranch a few weekends a year.

It had been difficult to find days to visit when Macy wasn't going to be on property or he would have visited more often. Foolish now that he thought about all he had missed. All for stubborn pride. He had missed his mother's decline, missed so many days when he could have been spending time with her. Rhett rubbed his jaw.

He had kept in touch with Shannon, Cassidy and Piper with phone calls and video chats and they had often made the trip out his way for visits when he hadn't been able to come home.

But he hadn't been around when his mom had started showing symptoms. Hadn't gone along to the countless doctor appointments. Hadn't been a part of the discussion when her plan of care was decided. And having only been back living in the family house for three days, Rhett scarcely knew how to speak to his mother any longer.

Dementia.

Such a small word for such a life-altering disease.

Before now the extent of his knowledge had sadly been gleaned from TV ads that rattled off more about the dangers of the marketed drug than actually showing the truth of the illness. Commercials that depicted smiling elderly people watching their grandchildren play or sitting hand in hand with their equally elderly spouse.

All lies.

Rhett hadn't been at Red Dog Ranch to watch his mom's mind deteriorate, but Shannon had. Boone had too, up until he had enrolled in a divinity school last year, moving his wife and daughter out of state in the process.

Rhett opened his mouth to say something to Shannon but closed it just as quickly. What was there to say? "I'm sorry" sounded small. Too little, too late.

Six months ago Brock had hired a nurse to be with Mom during the day while he was working and he managed her care at night, but now with Brock gone…they needed to figure something out. Rhett made a mental note to pull out his mom's insurance information and check over the plan to see what it would cover. The day nurse always arrived before breakfast every morning, but Rhett needed to look into the possibility of having someone with her at night, as well.

Ever present, Kodiak followed him to the fridge.

"Not much in there," Shannon offered. "You'd do better to head to the mess hall. Cassidy does most of the staff meals there." She jerked her chin to indicate the direction of the mess hall. It was located where the biggest hills began to roll through their property. Their father had insisted on building the dining hall there so that a huge, long basement could be constructed into the hill. All the nonperishable bulk food used to cook staff meals and feed the kids who came for summer camp could be stored there in a cooler environment without wasting tons of energy. The concrete basement also served as a great spot to find momentary relief from the heat of summer. Brock had searched for a contractor who would build into the shape of the land like that for a long time. Basements were rare in Texas.

His mom shuffled into the room, her hand resting on her nurse's arm. Rhett had seen plenty of his parents' wedding photos and snapshots of their dating history to know that his mother had always been a beautiful woman and maybe even a touch regal in how she carried herself. Now in her midsixties, he thought she looked a bit like the actress Helen Mirren. Outwardly she appeared healthy, but her pale blue eyes told the real story…she looked through him vacantly. She smiled pleasantly at him, almost blandly, as the red-haired nurse helped her into her chair.

A large common room made up the heart of their home. Vaulted ceilings with exposed beams gave the house a grand bearing, and a stone fireplace in the sitting room only added to that feeling. Every stone had been mined from Jarrett-held land. The kitchen flowed directly into a dining room and the large sitting area. In the sitting area, the wall without the fireplace boasted two-story-high floor-to-ceiling windows. From Mom's vantage point, she could gaze out to the wide lake where he took Kodiak for her swims and beyond into a field of bluebonnets.

Her chair looked as if it was about to swallow her petite frame. As she gazed around the room, her eyes never really landed on anything in particular. It struck Rhett that she looked lost.

Lost and scared.

His throat felt as if someone had stuffed a bale of hay down it, followed by some of the pebbles that made up the driveway. Rhett swallowed hard, once, twice, three times before he could get any words out. "How are you this morning?"

She pursed her lips. "Do you know where Brock is? I've looked everywhere but, by the cat's yarn, I can't find him."

Rhett glanced at Shannon, who gave an infinitesimal shake of her head. *Don't tell her. Don't correct her about Dad. Don't correct her at all.* Shannon had gone over the rules with him in regard to how to deal with Mom a handful of times in the days since he'd been back. But every time Mom asked… Well, someone might as well have kicked him in the stomach while wearing steel-toed boots. And then sucker-punched him in the jaw for good measure afterward.

Their mom had been present at the wake and funeral. She'd wept with Boone and Rhett each on either side of her, holding her up. She *knew*.

But right now, she didn't. Her mind was living in the safer Land of Before.

He wouldn't lie to his mother, but he'd learned quickly there was no reason to cause her undue emotional trauma either.

Rhett cleared his throat. "I haven't seen him in some time."

True. Far too true.

His mother dipped her head. With shaking fingers she traced a swirling pattern into the armrest of her oversized chair. "He's probably off somewhere with Wade, don't you think? It feels like forever since I saw my baby boy."

Shannon's coffee mug clattered against the kitchen island's stone countertop. She braced a hand on the counter and the other was pressed against her heart. "She mentions him—" her whispered voice broke "—all the time. I can't…" Her shoulders trembled as she hurried out of the kitchen.

Rhett wanted to go after her, but what comfort could he really offer? The family had lost Wade when he was only nineteen years old. Nothing he would say to his sister could change the truth of what had occurred. Wade was gone and Rhett couldn't make the anguish of losing her twin disappear.

Grief over Wade threatened to swallow Rhett in equal measure to what he felt over losing his father. Wade had stormed off spewing hurtful words at the whole family the day Rhett had cornered him, confronting Wade about every horrible thing Wade was involved in.

You know what? Don't worry. You'll never have to see my pathetic face again. Wade's final words came back to bite Rhett. His brother had left the ranch and headed straight for the Gulf of Mexico and boarded a small party boat. When the boat capsized everyone on board had been too intoxicated to get off in time, to radio for help.

Wade had been right. They never got to see his face again.

Brock had blamed Rhett for Wade's death. Rhett shouldn't have spoken to his brother that way. Wade would still be with them if Rhett hadn't confronted him. But Rhett had shot back that it was Brock's fault for allowing Wade to flounder for so long, allowing him to go down a wrong path years before he drowned. For investing more into the nonprofit at the ranch than his own son.

Rhett and his dad had never completely patched the bridge between them after that. Rhett walking away from the ranch had only solidified the tension in the relationship. If given the chance, Rhett would have handled both Wade and his father differently.

There were things Rhett would take back if he could.

So many things.

But right now he could only move forward. Do better. Be present.

Rhett shifted from one foot to the other. "I believe you're right, Mom, about Wade and Dad being together." His voice caught on the last word and he prayed she wouldn't notice.

She folded her hands in her lap and looked toward the lake. "Just as I thought. Still…" Her voice trailed off for a heartbeat. "I'm looking forward to when Wade comes back. I long for the day you and him are in the same room together again."

"Mom," Rhett said, keeping his voice even. "Wade may never come home."

"Don't you say something so horrible." His mom met his gaze. "He will. My boy will."

Before he left the house Rhett pressed a kiss to his mom's forehead, made sure she didn't need anything else and checked in with the nurse, Louisa. He should have headed straight to the mess hall, but his boots pointed south of there, in the direction of the little white chapel his father had built soon after he started Camp Firefly.

Rhett checked his phone. He was so used to having it on silent because the ring tones and even the vibrate setting interfered with training dogs. Most of them he trained using whistles and other noises so distractions were unwelcome. He had texts from a few of his clients who had been in the middle of sessions when his dad had passed so he'd put them on hold. They'd been patient, but training built week by week and he needed to either continue with them or send them to a new trainer, or else the dogs would lose their momentum.

Rhett made a split-second decision—offering them time slots if they were willing to come out to the ranch and refunding them if they didn't want to drive so far. One client texted back immediately, confirming a time slot for the next day. They were eager because they already had their dog signed up for contests. Two more asked for refunds and referrals to other trainers.

As he approached the church, he noticed that someone had used large white stones to outline a path leading to the chapel's front door. It was set up on the hill nearest to the mess hall. A wide cross had been erected on the hill years before the chapel's creation. At the end of each camp session, his father had the kids write on rocks the last night and lay them at the foot of the cross—usually a word symbolizing something they were trusting God for.

Distantly, he wondered if they'd kept up that practice after the church had been built. Would he have to lead that ceremony this summer?

Rhett tested the door. Open. He slipped inside, slid off his hat and stooped to dodge the end of the bell rope. Sunlight streamed through the stained-glass windows, painting the dull brown carpeting with a brilliant prism of colors.

Do you know the heart of God in this matter? Have you sought that out, son?

Of course he hadn't. If he sought out what God wanted…it wasn't worth it. If the Bible was true—and Rhett believed it was—God seemed to ask for dangerous, impossible things. Rhett was trying so hard to keep himself together, he couldn't afford dangerous faith right now.

Rhett gripped the edge of a pew. He hadn't willingly set foot inside a church in five years. Not since learning about Wade's death. His father's funeral had been held in a church, but he didn't count that time. He had entered that church out of duty, not choice.

If Rhett's own father—his flesh and blood—hadn't cared enough to know about his dreams and worries, he couldn't imagine God would either. Much like Brock had been, God was busy with far more important things than Rhett and his heart. After all, God had a universe to run. Rhett's small slice of the world hardly measured up to that. And he couldn't blame God for not concerning Himself with what must be Rhett's miniscule burdens in the very grand scale of human history. But it sure made Rhett want to keep his distance.

Rhett considered himself a Christian, but he certainly didn't like to bother God.

"You may not care about me, and that's fine." A wash of embarrassment flooded through Rhett at the idea of talking out loud, but he pressed on. "But Shannon… Please…could You be there for Shannon? She's been through a lot and I don't know how to help her. And Mom, God, please. It's hard. Seeing her that way."

The weight of so many new responsibilities sagged onto his shoulders. His father's death hadn't only made the ranch his obligation, but in a very real way Rhett had become the head of the Jarrett family. A role he wasn't sure he was cut out for. Between worrying over what his mother needed and his concerns for Shannon, he already felt stretched thin.

And then there was Macy. Macy touching his arm by the lake last night. Macy saying she was there if he needed her. Macy studying him with those large brown eyes that seemed to know everything about him. Rhett swallowed hard. Working alongside her was going to be difficult because the truth was, he missed his friend.

But he couldn't forget that he'd offered her a job at his business and when she'd showed up on his doorstep it was to turn him down, to pick the ranch—to pick his dad—over being near him. Worse, when he had tried to usher her inside so they could talk things over she had grabbed his shirt and kissed him—a kiss he had never known he had wanted until that point but afterward had never been able to get out of his head.

Then Macy had run off.

Rhett had left messages for two weeks. Messages she hadn't returned.

Now he had to see her every day and it was hard to forget their old friendship, the jokes they had shared over the years. That kiss.

Kodiak whimpered behind him.

Attempting to alleviate the tightness building in his chest, he blew out a long stream of air.

It didn't help.

Macy wrapped her fingers around the mug in her hands and prayed she wasn't making a huge mistake.

From the wide bank of windows in the mess hall, she had watched Rhett veer off the walkway and head toward the chapel. Witnessed him duck inside. The minutes had ticked by and curiosity had gotten the better of her.

Patience might be a virtue, but it was one that Macy sorely lacked.

Now in front of the chapel, she rested her hand on the doorknob and sucked in a fortifying breath.

Rhett did not want her friendship—he'd made that crystal clear last night—but coworkers should be civil to each other. An employee could check and see how her boss was doing without it meaning friendship, right?

Besides, she knew him too well to ignore the fact that he was obviously under a lot of stress. Her heart went out to him. If only she could convince him to share his burdens. He didn't have to manage everything alone. He wasn't alone at all.

She opened the door and let it close with a thump behind her so as not to startle him with her presence. He swiveled around in his seat. His hair was sticking out in adorable angles, reminding her of old times when he'd been a sleepy, hopeful boy swapping secrets with her around the campfire instead of the serious man he'd grown into. An awful twinge of longing stirred through her. She missed the Rhett who had been all dreams and optimism. He had changed once he hit high school, closing up a little more with each football game his father failed to show up to. Each broken promise.

But his hair wasn't sleep mussed. The particular style he was sporting at the moment had been caused by him grabbing the tips of his hair and yanking as he thought through something. She'd seen him do it enough times to recognize the signs.

"I can leave." He rose and put his hat on. Ever beside him, the large dog stood when he did. "It's all yours."

She held her free hand up in a stop motion. "I came to see you."

His left eyebrow arched.

"Here." She extended the mug and walked down the aisle. "A peace offering."

"What are we making peace for?"

"Last night at the lake."

His large dog edged to sit a few inches in front of the toes of his boots as if the beast was concerned that Macy might try some ninja-attack move on Rhett at any second. As far as Macy could tell, the animal had appointed itself as Rhett's personal guard.

As if a man with muscles like Rhett needed one.

"Is that thing safe?" Macy looked down at the dog.

He nodded. "She won't do anything unless I tell her to."

She handed Rhett the mug. "Earl Grey Crème black."

His features immediately softened and he cocked his head as he accepted the mug. "You remembered my favorite tea?"

"Your favorite *drink*," she corrected. Unlike most of the cowboys and staff at Red Dog Ranch, Rhett had never taken to coffee. After she'd tried the Earl Grey Crème black tea that he preferred, she had to admit it was delicious. It was a perfect balance of milk, sugar, vanilla and bergamot flavors while still delivering a welcome kick of caffeine.

My dad cared more about those foster kids than he did about his own flesh and blood.

Regret formed a lump in her throat. She glanced at the light bleeding through the stained glass windows, then glanced back at Rhett. "I'm sorry. Last night when

I brought up the foster programs and your dad… I know that still hurts."

He blew out a long stream of air, looked away. Nodded to accept her apology.

A part of Macy wanted to tell Rhett that Brock had loved him and the rest of his family. Maybe Brock had been bad at showing it, but they had been his life. His passion for foster kids had bloomed from his love of family—he'd wanted to give kids without homes the same opportunities and security that his children had been afforded.

But right now wasn't the time.

With Brock gone, it might never be the right time.

Macy searched for a way to connect with Rhett, anything that could encourage conversation. She needed to establish easy communication between the two of them so they could work alongside each other for the best of the ranch. And if she was being honest, her heart squeezed at the sight of her oldest friend looking so… lost. Despite what he had said last night, she wanted to connect—wanted him to know he wasn't alone.

Her gaze landed on his dog. *Perfect.*

"So, when did you acquire your ever-present shadow?" She smiled, hoping he could see the words were kindly meant.

"Kodiak." The dog perked up when he said her name. It was a good name for her because the dog's coat was the same red-brown color of a Kodiak bear. Her fur went slightly curly near her neck and back haunches.

Rhett grinned down at Kodiak and stroked behind her ears. "She was a training failure." His voice was warm. "Weren't you, girl?"

"She looks well trained to me."

His smile dimmed when he looked away from Kodiak to meet Macy's gaze. "What I mean is, her owner brought her to me to be trained and then she bonded to me and refused to go back with her owner." He crossed his arms over his chest. "It's not generally seen as a good thing."

"Well, she seems happy with the arrangement," Macy said.

"Her breed is extremely loyal." Kodiak let out a groan, protesting at the absence of his pets. "So once they pick their person it's an almost impossible bond to sever." He relented and tapped his fingertips on her head. "The breed can be hardheaded."

"Her breed?"

"She's a Chessie." He must have noticed Macy's confusion. "Sorry, that's dogspeak for a Chesapeake Bay retriever. People hear the retriever part and think they'll be like Labs or goldens, who love everyone and everything, but Chessies aren't like that. They're affectionate with their family but are extremely protective and don't warm to strangers easily."

As if to demonstrate what Rhett was talking about, Kodiak butted her head against Rhett's knee but kept her yellow eyes trained on Macy the whole time. The dog was definitely suspicious of her.

Macy inched back a half step. "Does that happen a lot? Training failure?"

"Thankfully, she was my only one. But her owner was my first client when I started the business so failing on the first one..." He rubbed his chin. "Well, let's just say that was like a bull kick to the ego. I almost thought about turning tail and coming home." He cleared his throat. "Back here, I mean."

She'd never known he considered returning to Red Dog Ranch.

"Rhett, that last time we saw each other…" Macy said. *When I kissed you.*

Rhett held up a hand. "We're different people than we were three years ago, Mace. I don't see the point of backtracking down that road."

When her boyfriend had broken up with her, she'd driven the hundred miles. She'd shown up on Rhett's doorstep. He had thought she was there about the job he'd offered her, but she had grabbed his shirt and yanked him into a kiss. She would never be able to forget how his body had gone rigid. He hadn't returned the kiss and, when she broke away quickly, his eyes had been wide, horrified. "Why did you do that?" he'd asked. Repeated it twice.

And she had turned around and run back to her car. Too mortified to face him for months afterward. It had been the action of a woman who had read a man wrong.

So completely wrong.

Rhett had never cared for her. Not like that.

Not like she'd wanted him to.

Macy rubbed her thumb over the jagged scar on her pointer finger. "Why didn't you come back home? After Kodiak, I mean?"

He lifted his shoulder in a half shrug. "There was nothing to come back to."

I'm not looking for friendship again, Mace. Not with you.

Macy tugged her inner shield closer in an attempt to

make his words bounce off of her harmlessly, but they went around her defenses and struck the tender places left in her heart. She'd thought she had walled off the part of her that cared about Rhett—about all men—because she knew there were no romantic relationships waiting in her future. Not now, not ever. If Rhett, who had known her better than anyone in the world, could see her completely and find her lacking...could not want her...then no one would.

No one wanted Macy Howell. Not for the long haul. Not her father, not the ex-boyfriend who had started the fight between her and Rhett three years ago and not her closest friend.

Why didn't anyone ever fight to be with her? What made her not worth it?

Because something's wrong with you.

Hot shame poured through her body.

Macy took another step back and fought the warring desires to slam her finger into Rhett's chest as she gave him a piece of her mind or to turn and run so she could go lick her wounds in private. But if she wanted to help the foster kids, she couldn't do either. She needed to be able to work with him, talk to him.

Relax. This isn't personal. It will never be personal again.

She forced a long drag of air through her nose.

Macy might not matter to anyone, but she could make her life matter by fighting for the kids. By making sure Rhett didn't end up cutting the programs they all looked forward to.

She let a breath rattle out of her. "Kodiak's a good fit

here." *There, back to a safe topic.* Macy gestured toward Kodiak. "Red dog. She could be the ranch's mascot."

Rhett frowned. "She's brown."

Macy narrowed her eyes, pretending to examine Kodiak. "It's definitely a reddish brown." She wrapped her fingers over her opposite elbow.

Kodiak looked up at Rhett with such adoration.

"You were always fond of dogs," Macy said. "I guess training them was a given."

"Dogs make sense." He shrugged. "You don't have to be anyone special to gain their loyalty. A dog is simple to figure out. They only ask for kindness and time spent together."

"And treats."

He smiled. "And treats."

She hugged her stomach as she watched him walk out of the chapel, her mind roiling with so many emotions it was difficult to sort through them. But one thing was certain: it was going to be near impossible not to fall for Rhett Jarrett all over again.

Chapter Three

Kodiak snored near Rhett's chair as he sifted through the files Macy had left in his office yesterday. Each name and picture made his heart twist.

Gabe Coalfield, seventeen, wants to be a veterinarian someday.

Harris Oaks, eighteen, would be happy to do anything to have a job.

Deena Rich, seventeen, just wants to feel useful for once.

Rhett pushed the papers away and covered them with one of the financial ledgers. As he made decisions he wanted to continue being able to think of all the children involved in terms of a faceless, nameless group—not as individuals with hearts and dreams.

With ambitions in their lives he might crush if he closed the ranch's doors to them.

He pinched the bridge of his nose.

Why had he been put in this situation?

Going over the calculations in his father's books had only solidified Rhett's decision to cut programs. Brock had neglected the cattle business that went along with the ranch, among other things. While the Jarretts enjoyed the cushion of an ample bank account for now and healthy investments in a few other areas, the ranch hadn't turned a profit in years, which meant Brock had been slowly dipping into the family's savings in order to keep the daily functions of the ranch running.

Fine to do once in a while, but the records showed it had become the way of Red Dog Ranch. That couldn't stand any longer. If they kept operating in such a manner, eventually funds would run out. Money Rhett needed to pay for his mom's medical care. Funds he needed to use to compensate staff dependent on the ranch for their livelihoods.

Additionally, he wanted to be able to leave Wade's daughter, Piper, and Boone's daughter, Hailey, something someday. As well as any other nieces and nephews who might come into the family down the road.

His father may not have cared about the Jarrett legacy—about providing for the long-term future of their flesh and blood—but Rhett did.

And there was nothing wrong with that.

Rhett dug his elbows into the desktop and sat straighter in his chair.

He would not allow himself to feel guilty for doing the right thing.

One of the teenager's photos had slipped loose when he shuffled them under the ledgers. Rhett picked it up and studied it. The girl had crooked teeth; her smile appeared forced. The look in her eyes—lonely and beaten by life—gutted him. She would have an internship, but she represented so many kids waiting for an opportunity, a break. One he was considering taking away.

He turned the picture over.

A soft knock on his door. Macy, more than likely.

Rhett massaged his temples. Earlier in the chapel he had opened up way too much to Macy. How did she do that to him? They'd been around each other for twenty-four hours and his resolve to stay distant had already crumbled.

And she lived a stone's throw from his house, so even when they weren't in the office he couldn't escape her presence. They hadn't spoken in three years and yet she *knew* him. Knew how his mind worked. Knew how he ticked. It was unnerving.

He dropped his hands to his desk and studied the spot on his arm where her fingertips had rested.

Since they were little, Macy had always had a way of cutting through his nonsense and zeroing in on pieces of Rhett he thought he'd hidden from the world. Then again, he'd always been terrible at playing hide-and-seek.

When they were young, it had been one of Macy's favorite games. She'd never failed to find him and find him quickly. However, she had also possessed a knack for unearthing the most unimaginable spots to hide in. Once they were a little older it had become near impossible to ever locate her. Most times she ended up having to reveal her spot, no matter how hard he'd searched.

It would seem he was still terrible at hiding from her.

"Come in."

She opened the door, clipboard in hand. Her smile

was tentative. "Have you had a chance to go over the files I left?"

He nodded.

She took the chair on the other side of his desk. "Great. Let's decide who each of them will be placed with."

"Do you know what a liability it is having them here? Our insurance rates are sky-high with all the minors on the property." He had spent a chunk of his morning reading legal nonsense and now his head felt foggy with all the information.

"The social workers have signed off on the waivers," she reminded him.

Rhett sighed and slid the files to her side of the desk. "You can go ahead and make all the placement decisions. You've been at the ranch all this time and I'm only just back, so I'm deferring to your knowledge here on what's the best fit for each of them."

She didn't move to pick up the paperwork. Macy opened her mouth. Closed it. Looked toward his mom's painting and then back at him. "I'm more than happy to help." She spoke each word deliberately. "But your dad always wanted to be a part of the process. He said it was—"

"Mace," he cut in. "If you haven't noticed by now, I'm not my dad."

"I realize that. I should have phrased that differently." She hugged her clipboard to her chest. "No one is asking you to be a replica of Brock."

Wasn't that *exactly* what everyone wanted him to be? His dad's will had set him on a lifelong course where he'd have to hear again and again and again how he didn't measure up to Brock. If he succeeded with the ranch he'd have to hear how he was following in his dad's steps, and if he failed he'd have to hear how disappointed his dad would have been.

"Aren't they?" He hated how hoarse his voice sounded.

She offered him the hint of a smile. Her wide brown eyes studied his face. "I'm not."

Wasn't she though? After all, wasn't she the one who kept bringing up how his dad had done things?

"I really promise I'm not." She gave a small shrug. "It's just really hard to strike him from all conversations when I'm missing him."

Understandable. Talking about Brock was clearly healing for her, but the same thing opened Rhett's wounds deeper.

"Then what do you want, Mace?" His question was soft, guarded. "Because when you look at me like that…"

She skewed her lips to the side as if trying to find the right words. "I'm just wondering where the boy I knew went."

He sighed. She might as well have said she didn't like the person he'd become.

Not that it mattered. He shouldn't care about what an old friend thought of him.

Rhett crossed his arms. "He grew up."

"That's a pity," Macy said. "He had this amazing ability to dream big but plan well, stay rooted and focused—something this place really needs. He had the heart and determination to grow Red Dog Ranch into an amazing place if he'd wanted to. I think that boy could have shaped the ranch into something beyond what his father possibly ever could have."

He clenched his teeth and reminded himself that Macy was just being Macy. She'd been known to kick a hornets' nest before—literally. She'd treat him no differently. It was her nature to push and he had loved that about her.

Just…not right now.

He pressed his palms against his armrests. "You finished?"

"For now, sure. Forever?" she asked. "Not a chance."

Rhett couldn't hold in the chuckle that escaped from his lips, though it had an edge of desperation in it. "I don't doubt it one bit."

This was the Macy he remembered—his Macy—someone who would stand against the wind and glare at a coming storm. Someone who didn't flinch.

Well, not *his* Macy. He wasn't quite sure where that thought had come from.

Macy ran a slender finger down the to-do list on her clipboard. "Now, about the Easter egg hunt…"

"Wait. That's still on?" He flipped through a stack of paperwork in his dad's inbox. "I'm sorry, I'm not caught up on everything. I thought we still had time to alter things." And he had figured his father was waiting until the last minute to reach out to previous vendors like he always had. His father had possessed a huge heart, but he hadn't been much of a planner. Rhett had been considering his father's lack of planning a blessing for once because it would make the event easier to cancel if nothing had been set in stone yet.

Her eyebrows shot up. "Of course it's still on."

Rhett rubbed his forehead. "How much do we usually spend on it? In total."

She thumbed through a few pages on her clipboard. "At least ten thousand. We always have a huge turnout," she added quickly.

Some people might have thought she was estimating high, but Rhett didn't believe she was. The Red Dog Ranch Hunt had become an event that drew many foster families from far away. People booked every room at nearby hotels in order to attend. The event had taken on a life of its own, complete with his father hiring a private helicopter pilot to drop candy over the fields as the children watched. When it came to these events his father had been nothing if not excessive. They also provided a full ham supper for around a hundred people who stayed afterward. The dinner was a ticketed event that raised money specifically for a college scholarship program for foster kids. Not to mention purchasing the eggs and prizes, paying staff to run various games and do setup, hiring a company to put up and tear down decorations and seating. Renting outhouses and paying for random other items.

Honestly, she was probably guessing low.

Rhett flipped the ledger to the latest financial records and twisted the book in Macy's direction. "Tell me how we can afford to host any event with this kind of bank account?"

Macy sucked in a sharp breath. "I had no idea he'd let it get this bad." She held up a finger. "He would sometimes mention that we should cut expenses here and there and then never did it so I figured we were fine. I never pushed the issue."

"Seriously?" He cocked an eyebrow. How could she not know? She'd been his assistant.

Macy waggled her head. "I promise you, I had no idea. You know how your dad could be about these things. He managed the accounts himself. I entered the bills into the finance software and entered payroll, but I only handled submitting those expenditures for his approval. I didn't balance the accounts. I never *saw* the actual money in the account." She pulled the ledgers closer. "Oh, Rhett. What a mess."

He believed Macy. Brock had been a man who kept many things close to his chest. Judging by how she had responded, Rhett knew she had never seen these books. Hadn't realized the foster programs were draining the family's personal accounts.

Rhett pressed his fingers against his forehead. "My dad had a big heart."

She looked like she might cry. "He had a *huge* heart, but that doesn't excuse this." She gestured toward the ledgers.

Rhett nodded. "Huge heart. Not a lick of business sense."

Macy snaked her hand across the desk to cover his. "You have a better sense for these sorts of things than he ever had." She gave his hand a pump.

Rhett slipped his hand from under hers and it instantly felt cold, lacking. He could have so easily turned it over and leached comfort from her, but he had to keep his head on his shoulders when it came to Macy. Uncle Travis was right. Macy could help him—but Rhett had to stay focused on keeping their partnership about working toward what was best for the business.

"So you understand why we have to nix the egg hunt this year?" Rhett asked. "Can you double check the recent bills to see if the ranch has made any deposits to secure vendors? I doubt it, but a quick check can't hurt." His dad had been notorious about scrambling at the last minute to get things done. Rhett tucked the ledger away. "That's potentially thousands of dollars we can immediately save."

Macy held up a hand. "I think recouping as much as we can is the right step. But, Rhett, we can't outright cancel the egg hunt." She tugged a newspaper clipping from her stack of papers and shoved it toward him. "It's already run in the paper."

Of course his dad would set up the announcement while procrastinating on the actual work of pulling together the hunt.

Instead he groaned. The sound made Kodiak's ears twitch. "This is bad."

Macy set down her clipboard. "What if we can run the event without touching your family's money? Or at least, minimally touching it. We can do this. We just have to think it through."

"I don't see how that's possible."

"If we work together, I think we can secure donations and get others to pitch in. I'll look through the bills and see if we can get refunds on the few things he might have secured, and if not refunds maybe we can renegotiate the contract terms." Her eyes lighted with excitement. He could practically see the wheels turning in her head. "If we can do this without too much expense, are you on board?"

"I'm tempted to say yes." Rhett was worried it would be hard to throw an event together so quickly, but his dad had done it all the time. Besides, Rhett knew not to doubt Macy's tenacity. "Though it will be a lot of work in a short amount of time."

"We've faced bigger obstacles together," she said. Macy sent him an excited smile. "I don't doubt what we can accomplish if we both commit to this."

He couldn't say no. Not to that smile. "All right, then. Let's do this."

"Great." She popped up. "In that case, I've got a lot of work to do so I'm going to dive in right away." She reached to grab the clipboard she'd forgotten in her exuberance. "We can do this."

He gave her a thumbs-up.

When she was about to leave, Macy hesitated in the doorway, her back to him. "You know, you don't have to be your father." She slowly turned to face him, her hand braced on the frame. "But you do need to be the best Rhett you can be. You need to live up to the potential God's placed inside you." She moved her hand from the frame so she could hug her clipboard to her chest. "Understood?"

Standing there with her chin held high, her eyes slightly narrowed at him and pure challenge lighting her features… Rhett had never seen anyone more beautiful.

The realization forced all the oxygen from his lungs.

"Mace, I—" His voice cracked.

"I'm going to be here, beside you in this." She pointed at him. "And I'm going to keep challenging you."

That's what he was afraid of.

In the following days, Macy tossed herself into researching how to plan a charity event and began to make a list of all the companies and local residents she could call. She made a second list that she dubbed her pie-in-the-sky list that was made up of actors, famous singers, news anchors at the big stations, radio dee-jays—anyone she believed was worth reaching out to. Even if one or two of them chose to give a monetary donation, it could make a huge difference. Texas was home to plenty of celebrities and many of them were proud to support Texas-based events.

Hey, a person could dream.

It was something she'd learned from Rhett when they were young. Too bad he'd lost his wide-eyed be-lief in chasing after big dreams somewhere along the way. Though his dog-training business had been a bit of a dream chase for him, hadn't it? Maybe there was still a part of the boy she knew somewhere inside the jaded man. Deep, deep inside.

Macy found herself praying while she worked—often more for Rhett than anyone else.

Please help me help him. Give me the right things to say when we interact. I know he's hurting and he prob-ably hasn't talked about it to anyone.

A boy with freckles and a wide grin ducked his head into her office. "Hey there, Miss Howell."

She rose from her desk and smiled at the teenage boy. Gabe had attended Camp Firefly for the past four summers and he volunteered hours at the ranch, muck-ing stalls and helping feed the horses, already. Making him an official intern had been a no-brainer.

The interns were starting today.

Rhett was working with one of his dog-training cli-ents in the far field again, so they had agreed that she would give the kids a quick tour and then hand them off to their appointed mentors to shadow for the day. Macy was happy Rhett had started seeing his clients again and wanted to do whatever she could to encourage him to keep his business alive. It had only been two appointments so far, but she knew he loved training dogs and didn't want him to have to lose Straight Arrow Retrievers.

Initially Macy had challenged Rhett about working with the foster kids, but she had promised herself she would stop forcing Rhett to do things the way his father had. Just because Brock had insisted on training the interns himself, it didn't mean Rhett had to. With that in mind, she had told him she would help run things—help take the load—so it was nice to see he was willing to trust her to do just that.

Macy joined Gabe outside and introduced herself to the seven other interns. She rattled off the speech she'd heard Brock recite multiple times but knew she wasn't doing it justice. Normally Brock spent the first two or three days showing the interns the entire ranch and explaining every part of its workings. He introduced them to every staff member and made sure they knew what to do in an emergency. He got to know them and made sure each one felt valued at the ranch. But with plans for the egg hunt looming over her, each day—each hour— was an imperative for Macy to seek donations and coordinate every aspect of the event. She also had to start devoting time to mapping out the plans for Camp Firefly because summer would be here before they knew it.

So for the first time in the history of Red Dog Ranch, Macy handed the interns over to each of their appointed mentors right after the tour and headed back to her office. She worked on drafting letters to some of the people on her second list—the dream-big list—and emailed them before her nerve waned.

Less than an hour later, Gabe banged open her door. He was panting and his face was tomato red. "There's been an accident. Miss Howell, you've got to come quick!"

Macy sprang from her desk. "What type of accident?"

Gabe was already at the front door, motioning frantically. When he saw she was following he headed out the door and started running for the closest horse enclosure. "This way."

Judson, one of the ranch's field hands who had been assigned to be Gabe's mentor, was crouched over Piper, Rhett's four-year-old niece. Piper was curled in a ball sobbing, her tiny shoulders shaking.

Rhett came tearing across the opposite field, Kodiak at his heels. Rhett's face drained of color as he dropped to his knees beside Piper and lightly brushed her long brown hair from her forehead. "What's wrong, sweetheart?" His chest heaved. No doubt Judson had radioed him and Rhett had sprinted the whole way.

Kodiak whimpered as she pranced around the pair.

"M-m-my aarrrrm," Piper wailed.

It was then that Macy noticed Piper's arm was twisted at the wrong angle. Broken. Macy's stomach threatened to pitch.

And suddenly, as she watched him crouch over Piper, Macy noticed the back of Rhett's neck turn red. "How did this happen?"

"Uncle Rrrrhett. It hu-hurts." Piper's whole body shook. "Huurrrts." Kodiak crawled forward and gave Piper a tentative lick on her cheek.

Macy hadn't noticed Judson take off when they appeared, but he must have headed for the barn. He came back, sprinting in their direction with one of the red emergency totes full of medical supplies that were stowed all over the ranch.

Judson panted. "I called Cassidy. She was in town getting groceries but she's on her way back. She should be here in minutes."

Wordlessly, Rhett took the medical bag and found the sling inside. Since Piper was so small, he knotted the top to shorten it. Then he helped her sit up.

"I'm so sorry, baby girl. This might hurt." He gingerly lifted her broken arm and set it in the sling. She let out a yelp of pain and started to cry harder, her cheeks going red.

Rhett pressed a quick kiss to the top of her head. "You're so brave. That will help your arm not move around too much until the doctor can see it."

She bit her trembling lip and nodded. Despite him living far away for much of her life, Uncle Rhett was her favorite person in the world and it was obvious that she trusted him completely. He'd given her Sheep, the miniature horse, for her birthday and her mom, Cassidy, had often talked about the weekly video chats Piper and Rhett had when he lived far away.

Cassidy's van rounded down the driveway.

Rhett scooped his niece into his arms, avoiding the injured arm.

He turned toward Macy. "Find out what happened and call me."

He gave both Judson and Gabe a significant look. Then he charged toward the van with Piper in his arms.

Seconds later they watched Rhett, Cassidy and Piper head off toward the hospital.

Macy prayed that Piper would be okay and that nothing else was wrong with her, and she prayed for Rhett too. The man was fiercely protective when it came to his family and he was bound to want consequences for whoever had let Piper get hurt.

Thirty minutes later, once Macy had calmed down an upset Gabe and a profusely apologetic Judson, she called Rhett. She'd already texted with Cassidy, but she knew she needed to talk to the boss. "How's Piper?"

"Broken arm and a sprained foot." He sounded tired. "She says the kid put her on one of the big horses bareback. Is that true?"

Macy sagged into the chair at her desk. "Judson went into the barn for a minute. He knows he shouldn't have left Gabe on his own with one of the horses, but we know Gabe well. He mucks the stalls for us all the time." Macy pressed on.

"Piper knows Gabe so she ran out to see him. Gabe said Piper told him she wanted to ride the big horse so he let her sit up there. He turned his back for a second." The teenage boy had been so upset about the little girl getting hurt. He had teared up in Macy's office. "He didn't realize the horse was only green broke. He thought it was one of our calm trail horses. He didn't know, Rhett. He's just a kid himself."

When Rhett didn't say anything, she continued, "Judson was going to teach him how to work the green broke correctly, so he went to get a longer lead line. That's the only reason Gabe was out there alone." She was rambling, but Rhett had to understand that it was an accident, pure and simple. "It could have happened to any of us."

"And if Piper had said she wanted to light the mess hall on fire—" Rhett's words were clipped "—would he have let her do that too?"

Macy dropped an elbow onto her desk and pressed her forehead into her hand. "This wasn't his fault."

"So is it Judson's?"

"It was an accident, Rhett. Accidents happen." She knew it wasn't wise to get into this on the phone, but Macy had always had a hard time biting back her words. Frustration was hard to pack away for later. While Rhett lived by facts, she was fueled by emotions.

"An *accident* took my brother. An *accident* took my dad. I'm done with accidents, Mace."

Ouch. He was right. But facing losses, facing accidents, didn't mean a person should never take a risk again. "Next time—"

"There won't be a next time. Our intern program ends today."

That immediately cooled her thoughts. "You don't mean that."

"I already sent messages to all the teens."

"Rhett, please. Just hear me out," she said. "The intern program doesn't cost the ranch a cent, but it provides free labor. It makes zero sense to cut it when we're trying to save money."

"If a kid other than my niece gets hurt and someone sues us, how's that saving money? Or if an intern got hurt? Managing interns divides the staff's focus. It's really not as mutually beneficial as you might think."

"Rhett—"

"I'll talk to you later, Mace." And he was gone.

Couldn't he understand that even with a mentor nearby things could happen? People got hurt every day. It was called life. Piper was a perfect mix of curious and courageous, which meant she was always taking risks. Rhett wouldn't be able to protect his niece from every bump and bruise in life no matter how hard he tried.

He loved his family fiercely. It was a quality Macy had always found attractive about him, but she found herself wishing he cared about the foster kids too. Maybe it was wrong to put that on him—he wasn't Brock and she didn't want him to be Brock. Really she didn't.

But she was so torn between the family she loved and the children she was dedicated to helping. Macy needed to decide where her loyalties lay. With the man who had once stolen her heart? Or the kids who desperately needed an advocate?

If only the answer could be both.

Chapter Four

Rhett entered the kitchen section of the mess hall where he knew he'd find Cassidy and Piper. It had been a few days since the accident, but he still wanted to make a point of checking on his niece first thing each morning. Guilt clung to his shoulders as he spotted Piper in her cast. If Rhett hadn't been in the far field with all his attention on the dog he was training, he might have prevented her injury.

It confirmed what he had feared all along. He would never be able to run the ranch, the family's charitable foster programs and Straight Arrow Retrievers at the same time. Not well. Not successfully.

Something had to give.

And unless he could find a loophole in the will, it was clear which of the three he would have to let go.

"How's my little soldier holding up?"

Piper rounded one of the wide metal islands in the industrial kitchen. Her hair was back in her normal braided pigtails. She had on jeans, tiny boots and a button-down shirt speckled with pink flowers. "I am *not* a soldier."

The little pout she wore reminded Rhett of Wade so much it made his chest ache. He would do anything to take care of these two ladies—for the brother he had lost. The brother who might still have been around if Rhett hadn't pushed him away.

Rhett cleared his throat.

"Tell him, Mom." She spun toward Cassidy.

Cassidy used the back of her hand to shove light red hair away from her eyes. "It's cowgirl or nothing, Uncle Rhett. You know better."

Rhett dipped his head. "Of course. My mistake. How's our little cowgirl holding up then?"

Piper straightened her spine and held her head higher. "I'm not *that* little anymore."

He bit back his smile. At four years old, Piper barely came above his knees. She took after her mother, petite for her age. Wade had also been the shortest of all the Jarrett siblings. But what Piper lacked in height she made up for in personality tenfold.

Rhett narrowed his eyes, making a show of examining her. "Now that you say it, you do look taller today."

Cassidy hid a grin as she filled a metal pancake dispenser with batter. It looked like a large funnel, but when she pressed the handle it released the perfect amount of batter onto the huge skillet, making it easy to dish out hundreds of pancakes in very little time.

At least, Cassidy made it look easy, but then she had always had a knack for cooking even at a young age. Rhett was sure he would make a mess of everything if he tried to use the contraption. Set him in a pen with five growling dogs? No problem. Ask him to fix break-fast for a crew of thirty workers? Not a chance. Cassidy was the expert here.

Fresh pancake batter sizzled as it cooked. Glass containers full of maple syrup rattled in a pan of boiling water on the nearby stove, permeating the air with their overly sweet scent.

Piper pushed away the sleeve on her right arm, revealing her hot-pink cast. "Look at how many people signed it." She grinned at him as she tapped an inch of blank pink. "I'm saving this spot for Gabe though."

Rhett lightly set his hand on her head. "Gabe isn't going to be back at the ranch, honey."

Her eyebrows went down. "How come?"

Cassidy glanced over her shoulder from her spot near the griddle. "You didn't make him leave because of what happened, did you?" She went back to flipping pancakes, moving the done ones onto a large platter. "Rhett?" she dragged out his name.

The hum of people talking in the mess hall told him that the staff was starting to pile in for breakfast. No time for long explanations. Even if there had been time, he wouldn't have the talk in front of Piper.

Rhett pushed his fingertips against the cool metal of the island. "She got hurt because of him."

And because of me.

Piper tapped on his leg. "He didn't push me."

"I know, but—"

"So it's not his fault." Piper folded her arms and locked onto him with a hard stare. Had she been taking lessons from Macy? All Rhett knew was he was steadily losing to a four-year-old.

"But—"

"Accidents happen." She looked toward Cassidy. "Right, Mom?"

Cassidy directed the kindest, most loving smile at her daughter. "Sometimes an accident can turn out to be the best thing that ever happened to us."

Rhett knew she was talking about becoming pregnant with Piper when she was only eighteen. About the gift that was his niece—a piece of his brother that lived on even though Wade was lost to them. But surely Cassidy hadn't forgotten that Wade had died in an accident of all things.

"Sweetheart." Cassidy motioned toward Piper. "Can you go put the butter on the tables?"

"I can even do it with my cast. It doesn't stop me. Nothing stops me." Piper collected two small plates from the counter and headed into the mess hall. She was used to helping her mom in little ways, especially with the morning meal.

Rhett shoved his hands into his pockets. "She's a lot like her mom."

"Flattery isn't going to get you out of this talk," Cassidy said.

He waited until Piper was long out of earshot before responding, "The fact is most accidents have consequences. Bad ones."

"Don't you think I know that? After what I've been through? Come on, Rhett." Cassidy scooped the last of the pancakes onto the wide platter. "I want Gabe to still have a chance." She passed a platter to Rhett. Her rule had always been every person taking up space in the kitchen had to help. Looked like Rhett would be serving the food at the meal. When she picked up the second platter he reached to take it from her.

She didn't let go right away. "He needed the internship. The boy wants to be a veterinarian and those schools are hard to get into. Scholarships are even harder to come by. He needs to be able to put us on his résumé. If he can show he interned with the animals here, it'll give him a better chance at succeeding. Remember being like that? Like him? Needing a start?"

Of course he remembered. Rhett had been that boy not that long ago.

Chest deflated, he broke eye contact. "I already cancelled the program."

She let go of the platter and folded her arms. "Then uncancel it."

"I can't."

"Being the boss around here you're the one person who can do just that." She sighed, unfurled her arms and dusted her fingers off on her apron. "Everyone deserves a second chance, Rhett. Everyone."

"What if I can't manage the program adequately?"

"Then accept some help." She pinned him with a stern look. "No, I'm not talking about hiring people. Even though you refuse to acknowledge it, you have a huge support system here. So many people willing to help you. But I think you have to learn to be willing to accept help first."

He wasn't really sure he understood what she was getting at and he told her so.

"You know how I said everyone needs a second chance?" Cassidy arched an eyebrow. "Well, that includes forgiveness. Sometimes I think you're holding yourself back for something you think you did wrong. Some sort of penance that maybe you don't even realize you're forcing on yourself. I wish you would forgive yourself for whatever you think you did. You deserve a good life, Rhett. Don't be burdened by something you're forcing yourself to carry, okay?"

Rhett swallowed hard. Cassidy had always been a straight shooter.

"Promise me you'll think about it," she said.

He nodded. "I will."

"But not for too long." She pointed a spatula at him. "You Jarretts can be the worst type of overthinkers."

This time he didn't fight the smile. "I would love to say you were wrong."

"But you know I'm not." Her voice was an odd mix of hope and disappointment all in one. There was more on her mind than their current conversation.

She shooed him toward the door leading out to the mess hall. "Now get breakfast out there before it goes cold."

"Will do, sis."

He knew she was right about people needing second chances. Although, if it was up to her, sweet-spirited Cassidy would give everyone in the world a tenth and eleventh chance. Everyone would have unlimited opportunities to turn their life around for good. But having a sympathetic nature had gotten her into trouble in the past.

He couldn't afford to make the same mistake.

The fact was, Piper's injury rested heavily on his shoulders. The accident wasn't Gabe's fault. No, Rhett was to blame. He had thought he could set aside his responsibilities at the ranch for a few hours a day to continue working with clients. He had been wrong.

Macy finger combed her hair as she rushed up the steps to the mess hall. She shoved through the front doors to discover the dining area empty save for the cloying smell of maple syrup and bacon lingering in the air. She'd missed the staff meal completely but perhaps Cassidy had some leftovers tucked away.

Cassidy stuck her head through the wide serving window that connected the kitchen to the eating area. "If you're looking for Rhett he left down the back stairs a few minutes ago. Said he was making a call. He might still be down there."

"Rhett?"

"Tall, handsome guy." Cassidy held a hand in the air demonstrating how tall he was. "Partial to dogs and cowboy hats. Runs the place," she teased.

"Huh." Macy played along. "You mean the one stubborn as sunbaked cowhide?"

Cassidy winked. "Same guy."

"Not here for him." Macy splayed a hand on her stomach as she entered the kitchen area. "I'm here for food."

"Tough break." Cassidy wiped down one of the metal islands. "I'm fresh out of pancakes."

"That's terrible news." Macy wasn't exaggerating. She had a soft spot for breakfast foods and Cassidy was an excellent cook. Cassidy's pancakes deserved sonnets written about their greatness. "I overslept."

Cassidy stilled. "You?"

"I know." Macy held up a hand in defense. "I was up late working on details for the Easter egg hunt."

"How about this? You come in here and help me with dishes and I'll whip up a batch of chocolate-chip pancakes just for you." Cassidy motioned toward the wash area. "We can talk while we work."

Macy wasted no time rolling up her sleeves and heading to the deep sinks. She fished the scrubber out of the warm water and went to work on the first pan she found. "When I suggested to Rhett that we could plan the egg hunt without using much money, I might have bitten off more than I could chew," Macy confessed. "I've been racking my brain trying to think of businesses we could approach as sponsors and I could ask them, but I know they would be more willing to donate if the pitch was coming from Rhett, you know? Everyone always dealt directly with Brock."

Cassidy carried a few more dirty dishes over to where Macy was stationed and plunked them into the sudsy water. She paused nearby. "So why don't you go and ask him to do just that?"

Cassidy had always been so matter-of-fact about things and Macy appreciated that character trait. Though not a Jarrett by blood, Cassidy was very much a part of their family—more so even than Macy, who had spent her whole life with the Jarretts. Macy's mom and Mrs. Jarrett had been friends since high school, so Macy had been visiting Red Dog Ranch since she was one week old. Where there had been cracks and brokenness in Macy's family, she had seen what she thought was perfection in the Jarretts. They were kind, they loved each other, they spent time together.

Despite everything, she would never be connected to the Jarrett family in the way Cassidy was. Never connected in the way she had always wanted to be. Accepted, but not one of them.

Suds splashed onto Macy's shirt as she forcefully scrubbed a pan. "Rhett has a lot on his plate right now. Besides, I'd love to demonstrate that I can take care of something like this on my own—prove that he can trust me."

"First, refusing help doesn't necessarily mean capable." Cassidy pursed her lips. "Second, Rhett already trusts you completely."

Macy knew Cassidy had a soft spot for Rhett. When the family had finally accepted Wade was gone, Rhett had been the one to track Cassidy down and offer her a place at Red Dog Ranch. Her parents hadn't been supportive of her keeping her baby—they told her doing so would ruin her life. But Rhett had convinced her that she was as good as family to the Jarretts and she and her child would always have a place here. He had been the protective older brother Cassidy had never had.

Macy sighed. "He trusted me at one point in life, but that was a long time ago."

"All right. That's it." Cassidy tapped a finger on the counter. "Out with it, already."

"What—"

"Don't play coy with me," Cassidy said. "It's time you shared what went down between the two of you—because all I know is that one day you two were thick as thieves and then he left the ranch and you two suddenly started avoiding each other. It's boggled my mind for the last three years and I'm never going to get a peep out of Rhett, so you're going to have to be the one to spill."

He didn't want me. I made a fool out of myself.

Macy blew dark strands of hair from her face. "What's there to say? We grew apart."

"Oh, don't feed me that line." Cassidy shook her head. "You won't get out of this that easily." She tossed a dirty dish towel into a laundry basket they kept near the sink. "We're friends, aren't we?"

Macy pulled the plug from the sink, letting the water drain away. "Of course we are."

"Then tell me the truth."

"I want to." Macy trailed her thumb over the scar on her pointer finger. "I just don't think you understand how hard it is."

"Here's what I do understand. If I could turn back the clock to when Wade and I had our last fight—" Cassidy's voice clogged with emotion "—I would have done anything to stop him. To go after him. To get him to come home. *Anything*."

Macy wiped off her hands, making sure they were dry, and then rubbed Cassidy's back. "I know you'd do anything to have Wade back. Wade loved you. I know he did. But what happened between Rhett and me... it's not the same."

Cassidy turned so her hazel gaze connected with Macy's. "You have a chance to make things right between the two of you," she whispered. "A second chance, Macy. Don't squander it. I'd give anything to have that with Wade."

Macy wrapped her arms around her stomach. "Did Rhett ever tell you he offered me a job? He wanted me to leave the ranch with him. Move away. Not together, of course." Macy flushed, hoping Cassidy didn't get the wrong impression. "He offered a high enough salary to cover rent in the area and things like that. An option so I wouldn't be dependent on Red Dog Ranch for a home."

Cassidy popped up so she was seated on the counter. "He never said a word. I'm assuming you said no."

Macy nodded. "I did, but… I went to turn him down in person. Remember I was dating Jim? He broke up with me. Over Rhett. He accused me of being in love with Rhett and not him, and I'm ashamed to admit he was right."

"I honestly don't know why Jim held on for so long. Anyone with eyes knew where your heart was." Cassidy batted her hand. "And we don't need to feel bad for Jim. He's happily married and all that jazz now, so it's all a good ending for him."

"I drove to Rhett's new place right from the breakup and thought about how much I cared about Rhett the whole way there. When he opened the door… I don't know what came over me." Macy wrung her hands and looked away. "I literally clenched my hands in his shirt and yanked him down for a kiss."

Cassidy pumped a fist in the air. "You know it, girl!"

Macy covered her face with her hands. "He froze. He didn't kiss me back."

"He was probably just taken by surprise," Cassidy offered.

Macy swallowed hard. "When I stopped he said 'Why did you do that?' all horrified. He said it a couple times."

"What did you say?"

"Nothing," Macy said. "I turned and ran back to my car."

"Oh, no."

"Oh, yes." Macy shrugged. "He called and left messages for the next few weeks saying he wanted to talk, that—" she put her fingers up to make air quotes "—we needed to discuss what had happened." She lowered her hands. "But I was mortified. I avoided him." After a lifetime of rejection from her father, then the breakup with Jim, which she realized was right but had still hurt, Macy hadn't been able to face Rhett's rejection maturely. If she could turn back the clock she would handle it all differently, but turning back the clock only ever happened in children's bedtime stories. "By the time I decided to swallow my pride five months had come and gone. I called him once, all those months after. He never called me back. And that was it."

Cassidy arched an eyebrow. "You two have talked about this since though, haven't you?"

"It was three years ago." Macy repeated what Rhett had said. No matter how much she wanted to make things right, if Rhett wasn't willing to talk there was nothing she could do about it. "Everything's changed now. It's not worth rehashing."

"Macy." Cassidy hopped off the counter and took her hand. "That man loves you. He always has."

"Yeah." Macy released a long stream of air. "Like a brother."

"You're wrong and I know you don't believe me." Cassidy offered a sad smile. "But I loved one of the Jarrett boys. I know how they think."

Macy needed to steer the conversation away from anything that would make Cassidy think of Wade. "It's later than I thought. Can I take you up on the pancakes another day?"

Cassidy nodded. "You never responded to my text —are you coming to our girls' movie night tomorrow night? Shannon picked out *To Catch a Thief.* Come on, you can't say no to a Cary Grant movie."

"You know me too well," Macy said. "Of course I'll be there."

Cassidy gave her a thumbs-up and then headed toward the back room. She paused when she reached the threshold. "You should talk to him, you know."

"I'm actually going to track down the man in question now." Not that she was going to talk to him about their awkward moment three years ago, but she didn't need to get into a circular argument with Cassidy over it.

Macy checked her watch.

She also had an appointment to keep in town and an idea simmered at the back of her mind. If she could convince Rhett to go along, maybe, just maybe the meeting could be the first step of his softening toward the ranch's mission as far as foster kids were concerned.

Lord, please help me convince him.

"I think he's still downstairs." Cassidy jutted her chin toward the stairwell located along the side of the kitchen which led to the basement area. "I never heard the door open down there. It's heavy and makes a loud sound whenever it closes."

Macy nodded and headed toward the stairs. She knew about the loud door and hadn't heard it slam either. She paused at the top of the steps. When Cassidy was out of sight, Macy tugged out her phone and typed in Straight Arrow Retrievers. Macy had never gone to his website or sought out information about his business because doing so would have been like tearing open stitches for her emotionally. She had avoided all mentions of Rhett in order to protect her heart. If she could pack him away she wouldn't have to hurt.

But he was here now.

She might as well know.

Listing after listing popped up, revealing articles written about the awards that dogs he'd trained had won. One about a dog who now starred on a television show. Another dog he'd trained was being considered for induction into the Master National Hall of Fame—one of the highest honors a hunting dog could obtain.

"Oh, Rhett," she whispered. Her throat felt thick with both pride and sadness. He had accomplished so much in such a short amount of time. And while he had scheduled a few training appointments at the ranch, how much had he truly sacrificed in order to return home and meet the terms of the will so his family could keep the property?

The low timbre of his voice drifted up the stairs. From where she stood, she couldn't make out his words, but she was happy she wouldn't have to go out searching for him.

How many hours had she and Rhett spent as teens, and even into their twenties, hanging out in the mess hall's basement? They had often run to the basement for their breaks during the summer and fall working hours in order to escape the heat and sun outside. Built into the hillside, the large basement area stayed cool even on the hottest day. They used to sit on the pallets, knee brushing knee, and talk about everything.

She pushed cherished memories away. They only

hurt. What was the point of reliving memories when she had no hope of ever making more with her old friend?

Macy tucked her phone into her back pocket, rolled her shoulder and took a deep breath as she headed down the stairs.

Chapter Five

❧

Rhett huddled on a pallet in between a stack of industrial-sized cans of tomato sauce and boxed pasta. He stared at his phone's screen, willing his friend Hank to return the voice mail he had just left. He had discovered he got surprisingly good cell reception in the basement the other day, no doubt because a neighbor rented out land to a company to place a cell tower on his property.

For a second Rhett considered joining Kodiak outside. After he had seen to her breakfast, Rhett had left her basking in the sun by the door that led outside from the basement with a bowl of water nearby. But as peculiar as it sounded, something about the cement walls and low ceiling brought Rhett comfort. Made him remember easier times.

The edges of the long basement were lined with pallets balanced on cinderblocks, a way to keep the non-perishable food stored in a cool area away from the floor. The back end of the basement curved, providing a nook at the end that was great for hiding. Even with all the splendor outdoors, this had always been one of

Rhett's favorite spots on the property. He and Macy had called the back wall home base. If they'd needed to meet or got split up while working or during a game, this was where they'd always found each other later. Their meeting spot.

Something he hadn't thought about in a long time.

Something he probably shouldn't think about.

Still, an image from their talk in his office flashed to mind. Macy with her head held high and a spark of pure stubbornness lighting her face. In that moment, she had taken his breath away and he couldn't get it out of his thoughts. Since then ideas kept pestering him. Why hadn't he come to terms with his feelings for her sooner? That day when she'd kissed him, it had been an unexpected—albeit not unpleasant—shock. Never good about surprises, he had reacted poorly. His mind had started overthinking, making his body freeze...pretty much the worst thing he could have done in the situation.

If he could do it all over again? He would have wrapped his arms around her and he would have kissed her soundly, senselessly. Then he would have begged her to never leave his side.

But he had botched his chance at happiness with Macy. She had called him after the kiss, once. It had been five months after everything had happened, but Rhett had been bitter about her ignoring all his initial calls five months before. He hadn't returned her call, figuring it was her turn to try calling for weeks without an answer. But she had never called again. He always wished he had just swallowed his pride and returned her call.

His life could have been so different if he hadn't been petty in that moment.

A part of him wanted to reinstate their friendship. He missed having her as his closest confidant. But when she had tried to broach the subject he had shot it down, if only to not have to hear her say they should disregard what happened and go back to being friends. The fact was he didn't want only friendship with her and never would. He *couldn't* only be her friend.

But what about the very small chance that she wanted that too?

No. He had to stop that train of thought. Rhett didn't have time for a relationship with Macy or anyone. If he ever entered into a relationship, he would want it to be at a time in his life when he could give his partner the attention she deserved, which was definitely not now.

Not that he wanted one. He was fine alone. Great, even.

He scrubbed his hand down his face.

In another part of the basement they stored extra bed-sheet sets and items staff or guests to the ranch might need. His father had wanted to meet basic needs for any-one staying on their property and never wanted any of the kids to feel embarrassed or ashamed if they didn't have necessities required for overnight stays.

It was something Rhett might not have thought about. Scratch the *might*—he certainly wouldn't have come up with keeping toothbrushes and new stuffed animals on hand. His mind simply didn't work that way. Yet another reminder he had no right attempting to run the foster programs at the ranch. Even if he could right the boat in a financial sense, he would never do Camp Firefly or any of the other programs justice. He lacked so many traits that had been second nature to his dad.

Rhett dropped his head into his hands.

He needed to let go of the grudge he harbored against the foster programs and the kids involved. It wasn't their fault his dad had chosen them over his son. Rhett wanted to let go of his resentment. Truly. But how does someone cut out a piece of their heart that's hurt for thirty years? What would be left if he did let it all go?

Maybe he shouldn't have sent the will to Hank. Maybe the only way to get over his grudge would be to forge ahead, embracing all the foster programs. But they couldn't feasibly keep it up without affecting the long-term security of his family's finances. What a mess. If only he could separate the hurt his father had inflicted from how he felt about the programs.

He stared at the phone again. Should he call Uncle Travis? He closed his eyes. His uncle would tell him to make his dad proud or utter something along those lines. Give Rhett a one-way ticket for a guilt trip he hardly needed, considering he was already good at taking that trip on his own time.

His phone vibrated. Hank.

Rhett answered immediately. "Thanks for calling me back. Were you able to review the files I sent?"

Hank chuckled. "Well, hello to you too, buddy."

"Sorry. It's just—"

"Kidding with you, Rhett. Lighten up."

Rhett used his free hand to rub at a kink on the back of his neck. "Words one rarely hears from a lawyer."

"Oh, now, we're not all bad. You wouldn't be calling me if you thought we were."

"True." Rhett had trained Hank's German short-haired pointer, Riptide, who had gone on to title in the

American Kennel Club's National Hunt Test. After Riptide's training was complete, Hank and Rhett had remained in touch, becoming friends. Being an intellectual property lawyer, Hank had assisted Rhett with trademarking his business.

"I will say—" Hank blew out a long breath "—that's one hefty will."

"I really appreciate you taking the time to look at it for me."

"No problem."

"I haven't had any guidance on it," Rhett confessed. "My family doesn't understand the risks involved." He paused but when Hank didn't jump in Rhett kept speaking. "Tell me you found a loophole in it. There's a way to get out of the part about the extra programs if I need an out, right? I would think the part about serving foster children could be interpreted in different ways." Rhett knew he was rambling but he couldn't help it. Uncle Travis had said the terms of the will were very clear: Red Dog Ranch had to continue being used to serve foster children or Rhett lost the inheritance—meaning his family would lose their home.

The floor above him creaked, making him glance upward. The beams supporting the kitchen and mess hall floors had to hold quite a bit of weight. All the machinery and sometimes hundreds of people. If something broke—how much would it cost to fix any issues? Even replacing pieces of flooring and subfloor here and there added up. The camper cabins all needed work before the camp session, as well. The horse barn had some long-standing issues he needed to address. Maintenance was a constant. More money. More needs.

Rhett's chest felt tight.

"If I need to prove the financial burden or whatever it takes, I can certainly do that."

The fingers on Rhett's free hand had fisted, resting on his knee. He deliberately uncurled each finger. *Relax.*

"Slow down." Hank spoke in a calm tone Rhett had heard him use before when he was in lawyer mode. "I looked over everything and at first glance it seems fairly binding. However, as you know, this isn't my wheelhouse."

Rhett's gaze bored into the gray cement wall opposite him. How had that comforted him minutes ago? Now it reminded him of a cell. Trapped. Cold. Alone. "So you don't think there's a way out for me?"

"Now, I didn't say that."

"Then what are you saying?"

"I'm saying lawyers know lawyers. I have a friend from college—he specializes in estate law," Hank said. "I haven't spoken to him in a few years, but let me reach out to him and see if he's willing to take a look at it for us. I can't promise you anything but I'm certainly willing to try."

"I owe you." Rhett asked about Riptide and Hank promised to call if he heard back from his friend. Rhett shoved his phone into his back pocket and rose. He was too tall to stand straight in the basement so he had to crouch somewhat. It was time to get on with his day. He rounded the corner and came toe-to-toe with Macy. His boots shuffled back a step. Loud and clumsy on the floor.

Macy's dark hair hung over her shoulder, free of its usual ponytail, and Rhett couldn't help but stare. Other than at his father's funeral, lately she had worn it up.

Even under the dim basement lights it had a shine to it, like a raven's wing in the sun. Rhett had the odd desire to tuck her hair behind her ear just to know what it felt like.

Instead, he shoved both hands into his pockets.

When he finally met her gaze her left eye twitched.

Rhett's mind raced back through his talk with Hank. How much of his conversation had she overheard? He swallowed, trying to find words. Why was he having a hard time speaking?

But all she said was, "Found you."

Rhett forced his shoulders to relax. "You always could."

She cocked her head and studied him for the space of a few heartbeats. "Physically, yes."

He scuffed his boot on the floor, a nervous habit. All the long days, all the years spent with Macy, and he had never been flustered around her.

He cleared his throat. "Remember when we used to play hide-and-seek all the time?"

"I do. You never could find me." She crossed her arms over her chest.

He sighed. "I guess you were just too good at hiding."

She shrugged, but he knew her too well to miss the tense set of her shoulders and her inability to maintain eye contact for more than a few seconds. Macy was keeping something from him.

"Maybe you should have looked harder," she said.

They weren't talking about a child's game anymore, were they? Was it foolish to hope she was talking about their kiss? About what might have happened between them? Rhett hedged with, "Next time, I will."

The barest hint of something that looked as if it wanted to be a smile played across her features.

Moving on.

"How long have you been standing there?" Had she pieced together he was enlisting legal help to outsmart his father's will? If she had, Rhett expected her to be furious. But Macy didn't look upset. Maybe a little confused.

Her brows furrowed. "I was hoping I could convince you to drive into town with me."

He rubbed at the back of his neck. She hadn't answered his question. "There are calls I have to make and I need to check the pole barn and do you know we still haven't hired a veterinarian since Lyle retired?"

Tentatively, she touched his forearm. "Those things will all be waiting for you this afternoon. I promise. We could split up those calls. Divide and tackle together."

"I don't know." Had Macy missed him as badly as he'd missed her that first year? How many times had she picked up her phone to call him, finger hovering over his contact? Because he'd done so daily for longer than he would ever admit. He had grieved their friendship.

Grieved what could have been if only he had realized he loved her sooner.

But she had been fine, hadn't she? Happy here with the people and place she had chosen.

She hadn't mourned their friendship. At least, that's what he told himself.

All Rhett knew was after the kiss he'd called her at least twenty times and she had called him once during the three years.

Once.

Letting her in—even for a morning together to do errands—was a risk Rhett wasn't sure he was willing to take. Then again, what could it hurt? It might help if he could get a better sense of her—understand her passion for the foster programs and maybe see them in a light other than what it had done to his relationship with his father.

"Trust me," she said. "Take a leap and trust me on this."

Curiosity made his resolve waver. He crossed his arms. "Persistent much?"

"You know it." Macy tugged keys from her pocket. "We're going into town to secure donations for the egg hunt. When we decided to go forward with the event you agreed we'd do this together, remember?"

"I did, didn't I?" And there went his resolve completely.

She popped a hand onto her hip. "I'm not taking no for an answer."

"Now that right there. That's the Macy I know." He pointed at her. "I know that's true." He rolled his shoulders. "All right, let's head out."

Macy fiddled with the buttons that controlled the radio station.

"How about I do that so you can watch the road?" Rhett's fingers brushed against hers as he reached for the controls. He stopped on a popular country song being played on the local station.

As Macy scanned the road, she could see her scar in her peripheral vision where her hand rested on the steering wheel. Rhett's fingers had just traced against that scar. Did he ever think about the day he saved her from the copperhead?

"I saw this guy in concert last year," Rhett offered. "He sounds this good in person."

The voice on the radio came from Clint Oakfield— one of the biggest touring country-western stars at the moment. His first album had gone platinum and the next two had obtained the same distinction even faster than the first.

"It would be great if we could rope someone like him into donating toward the egg hunt." Rhett's statement was delivered in just a matter-of-fact manner; Macy did a quick double take to be sure he wasn't joking. He wasn't. Who was this guy, dreaming big? He almost reminded her of the boy who had once been her best friend.

"How huge would that be?" Macy whispered.

Rhett's laugh was warm and welcoming. "If anyone could do it, you could."

Macy made a mental note to go to Oakfield's website when she got back to the office and see if there was an option to contact his agent or whoever handled his publicity. People had successfully reached out to celebrities on social media before, as well. What would it hurt to try? If he said no they would be no worse off than they were now, but if he said yes? If Clint Oakfield helped in any way at all…it could be a game changer for Red Dog Ranch and all the foster programs. Even if he donated some signed merchandise that they could raffle off, that would be helpful.

"Speaking of donations." Rhett held the clipboard with the list of businesses Macy had wanted to stop in and talk to. He ran a finger down the first section of the list. "All right, we're six for six on places promising donations. Should we try for seven before heading back?" He caught her eye and the grin he sent her way made her stomach somersault. For the last hour in the car he had been her buddy again, joking, smiling and seemingly excited about the challenge of winning over business owners.

A few of the businesses had promised monetary donations; another two were going to donate candy and small prizes to use in the egg hunt. Yet another promised to rally volunteers to help man the event.

Macy glanced at the clock on the dashboard and her heartbeat ratcheted. Fifteen minutes until she was supposed to meet the Donnelleys at Scoops and Sons for lunch.

And she had yet to inform Rhett about the meeting. Hence the erratic heart.

She snuck a glance at him. Okay, the man's jawline and eyes alone could cause her heart to go out of control, but that wasn't today's reason. Besides, Rhett had already made it clear that he should never be the reason for anything in her life.

The Donnelleys had two adopted children and two foster kids. Often they had more. Mr. Donnelley had grown up in the foster system and had been a teenager when Red Dog Ranch launched many of its programs. They were supporters of the ranch, but more than that, they were friends.

Last night springing a lunch date with the Donnelleys on Rhett had sounded like such a good idea. Now? Not so much. Especially not after they'd stopped by a few local businesses and worked as a team to secure donations.

She and Rhett—a team again.

Macy's mouth felt dry. She needed to tell him. Had to be honest.

Suddenly, Kodiak stood in the back seat and pressed her muzzle into Rhett's ear. Rhett had insisted on bringing her along. Supposedly she didn't do well if she was apart from him for too long, and she had already been outside alone for a chunk of the morning.

Macy couldn't fault Kodiak there.

However, she had the distinct impression that the dog wanted to place herself in between Macy and Rhett as often as she possibly could.

Macy probably should have held her tongue, but she had never been particularly good at doing so. "Ever afraid she might nip you?"

"This brute?" Rhett chuckled and gently nudged Kodiak so she would lie down across the back seat again. "I'd trust her with my life." He held up a hand. "And let's say—theoretically—she did accidentally nip someone. Chessies aren't like other dogs. They're known for their gentle jaws."

"Gentle jaws…on a dog?"

He nodded. "That's why they're perfect birding dogs. They can carry a duck back to you without getting a scratch on it. In fact, a Chessie can be trained to carry an egg in their mouth without breaking it." He jutted his thumb toward the back seat. "Kodiak can."

Macy flipped on the blinker, turning the car in the direction of Scoops and Sons. "You're serious?"

"Of course." His blue eyes lighted with excitement.

"With Cassidy's permission, Kodiak has started to learn how to do a water rescue on Piper. She can take an arm or a part of Piper's clothing in her mouth and tow her back to shore. It's pretty amazing. I mean, we only got to try it twice before Piper got hurt. But Kodiak had trained with a dummy at our old place."

Macy couldn't hide the smile that crept onto her face. Rhett's enthusiasm was palpable.

"Okay, you're right. That is amazing." It was great to see him so animated.

"Of course, all that's on hold now. We can't do it again until Piper's cast is off." He frowned. "But I've been having Kodiak practice with other objects." He unbuckled his seat belt without looking toward the restaurant. "She's stronger than she looks—able to haul a lot while she's swimming."

"About Piper." Macy sucked in a sharp breath as she parked the car in front of the tiny restaurant. "I haven't had a chance to apologize for what happened." She twisted in the seat to face him. "I'm sorry she got hurt and I take full responsibility for what happened."

"Are you trying to convince me to reinstate the interns? Because—"

She touched his wrist. "It was my fault. Mine alone."

"While I appreciate you saying that," he said, shifting the clipboard onto the dashboard and then scrubbing his hand over his face, setting his hat off balance, "I think the fault rests with me. I shouldn't have tried to keep my business going. I should have known continuing to train dogs would only divide my time and attention. I should have been there overseeing the interns. I shoved off that duty—"

"Onto me." Macy pressed her hand against her chest. "And I failed you."

"I doubt you could ever fail me." His voice was so low, so full of emotion, it stirred feelings in Macy's heart she had convinced herself she was doing a good job locking away.

Apparently not.

While Rhett's words threatened to unbind a piece of her heart, she couldn't let that happen. They weren't true. Rhett hadn't wanted her.

He shouldn't say such things.

Her mind suddenly latched onto something else he had said. "Wait. You said you 'shouldn't have tried to keep your business going.' Does that mean—"

"Yes." He tugged his hat off and shoved a hand into his hair. "I have to give up Straight Arrow Retrievers. I don't see any other way around it."

She twisted in her seat, grabbing his arm. "Look at me. You are *not* giving up your business. You care about it too much. It's your passion, Rhett."

"Well, it's not humanly possible to run the ranch, the foster programs, and manage my family and Straight Arrow Retrievers at the same time. Not well. Not successfully. Something has to give and I don't see what else I can cut." He tipped his head back against the headrest.

Her heart went out to him. If only she could convince him to share his burdens. He didn't have to manage everything alone. He wasn't alone at all.

"You have a staff, Rhett. Delegate the ranch duties. We can make this work."

He turned his head in her direction. "You know, you

make me believe it could almost work. That's dangerous, Mace."

She smiled. "I've never been a fan of safe."

Rhett swallowed hard. While they'd been able to make progress for the egg hunt, spending time alone with Macy was messing with his head. Oh, he wanted to keep talking with her. Wanted to keep making her smile and laugh. Wanted to keep hearing her encouragement.

That was the problem.

Friendship with Macy was far too risky.

Macy was determined and hardworking and positive. She was passionate about important things and was willing to fight for what mattered to her. She was beautiful, but then she always had been. He had simply been too bullheaded to allow himself to notice for fear of what it would do to their friendship.

How many things had he lost because of choices made from fear?

But fear—caution—kept a person safe. In the horror movies it was always the brave person who went out to investigate a noise who got the ax first, not the vigilant ones hiding inside. They were smart. They stayed safe. Alive.

Walls and hiding were good things. No one could tell him differently.

Because the truth was Rhett could very easily lose his heart to Macy for good if he wasn't careful. So he would be careful. He had to be. He had too much to juggle, too much riding on his shoulders without additional complications.

Besides, she had rejected him before.

He had to keep reminding himself of that. It was the one thought that could protect him. He stole a glance at her as she used the rearview mirror to fix her hair.

Perhaps the only thing.

He looked through the window, finally taking in where they'd parked: Scoops and Sons, a great diner off the beaten path of town. While out-of-towners more than likely assumed the place was simply an ice cream shop, it was so much more. Scoops was a mom-and-pop eatery that served up some of the best brisket sandwiches and corn cobbler Rhett had ever eaten.

"I like this place." Rhett plucked the clipboard from the dashboard. "But it isn't on the list."

Macy sighed. "Okay, don't be mad."

Never a good way to start.

"Why would I be mad?" In response to his tone, Kodiak sat up in the back seat and let out a low whine.

Macy nervously looked from his dog to him. "I should have said something sooner. We're meeting someone here for lunch. I didn't think it would be a big deal."

Rhett scooted the clipboard back onto the dash. The metal clip caught the sunlight, sending a prism onto the car's ceiling. "That someone being…?"

"Do you remember the Donnelleys?"

Of course he did. Jack Donnelley was a few years older than Rhett and had grown up in the foster system. Jack had been one of the first kids Brock had ever taken under his wing. Rhett's dad had probably spent more time mentoring Jack than he ever had Rhett. Jack had gone on to do well in college, marry a great woman, adopt children from the foster system and continue to foster more. In Brock Jarrett's eyes Jack was as successful as a man could be.

Everything Rhett wasn't.

Rhett narrowed his eyes. He had a hard time believing Macy had forgotten about the animosity between him and Jack. For senior night at Rhett's final football game, Rhett had begged his father to attend. *Just this once, Dad. Please.* Everyone else's parents had come to all the games, but Brock rarely had. *I would, son, but I have to meet with this family...this other kid needs me.* There had always been a million reasons why he couldn't be there—good reasons, ones that made Rhett feel bad about himself when he looked out into the stands, didn't see his dad and tasted disappointment. His dad was tied up with something more important than football.

More important than him.

Rhett shouldn't have been hurt. He was supposed to be old enough to understand that the needs of others were more important than his silly wants and desires. Whatever Rhett was doing was insignificant in his father's eyes. Always had been.

Probably still was.

Rhett rubbed at his jaw.

The last game? Brock had chosen to help Jack Donnelley pack his apartment and move to Red Dog Ranch instead of attending. His dad had missed the awards ceremony. Missed all the nice things Coach had said about Rhett.

Not that it would have mattered.

Rhett's focus snapped back to Macy.

"If you did this to try to convince me to reinstate the intern program," he said, "I already decided to do that." After talking with Cassidy he had realized she was right. He had sent emails to set up meetings to go over new safety protocols with all the staff members who had been appointed as mentors, and after those meetings took place tomorrow he would send emails to all the student interns inviting them back to the ranch.

Macy's eyebrows went up. "You—you did? Why didn't you say something?"

"I tried to tell you earlier, but you cut me off."

She cringed. "I do that a lot, don't I?"

He suppressed a good-natured laugh because he was certain that wouldn't have been appreciated during the type of conversation they were engaged in. But, honestly, Macy had been cutting him off since she had been old enough to learn to speak. It was a part of her personality—overexcited, passionate, always charging ahead. That was… Macy. It was who she was and he would never want her to be anyone different.

He shrugged. "You always have. Usually it's endearing."

Her eyes went wide. She opened her mouth to say something.

But he couldn't go down that road. He shouldn't have admitted that he found anything about her endearing. Life was far too complicated at the moment to let anyone in.

Especially Macy Howell.

Before she could respond, Rhett hooked his fingers over the handle and pushed it open. "Well, let's get on with it then. We don't want to keep them waiting."

She rounded to his side of the car while he was letting Kodiak out.

"You'll still go in and have lunch?" she asked.

Rhett forced a smile. "As long as the Donnelleys are good with eating on the patio where Kodiak is allowed."

"You're sure?" she pressed.

"Listen." Kodiak stopped when he did. "Recently I asked God to help me get over this...this grudge, for lack of a better word, that I've had against the foster programs." He shrugged. "Maybe this is part of it. A step in the right direction."

"Rhett, that's—it's huge."

He jerked his chin toward the restaurant. "Let's go."

Jack and Sophie Donnelley welcomed Rhett and Macy with hugs. Their children, Ashton, Ella, Will and Vicki, were instantly enamored with Kodiak.

"Can we pet her?" Ella's gap-toothed grin reminded him of his nieces.

"Sure." Rhett gestured toward Kodiak. "She loves kids."

After quickly eating, the kids took Kodiak out to a large grassy patch that ran alongside the restaurant. The patio overlooked the area so the four adults were able to keep an eye on them. Sophie had unearthed a tennis ball from somewhere in the recesses of their minivan and Kodiak was living the retriever's dream with four kids willing to play fetch with her.

Jack leaned back in his chair. "I have to tell you, we were worried about what would happen to the ranch after your father passed. You know, I always thought of him as my father figure too."

Rhett worked his jaw back and forth. He forced out a breath. "Yeah, I hear that a lot."

"Oh, I'm sure." Jack's smile was genuine. He had

always been kind, which only made Rhett feel worse about himself for ever having disliked the man. "I haven't seen you in a while, but it feels like we haven't missed a beat. I guess that's because your dad spoke about you all the time."

Rhett caught Macy's eye. "He—he did?"

Jack nodded. "I know he loved all his kids equally, but you held a special place in his heart."

"He was so proud of your dog business," Sophie chimed in.

Rhett's throat felt raw.

Was it all true? Rhett had a hard time wrapping his mind around the idea. When Brock had given him the ultimatum and Rhett had chosen to leave, Brock had been red-faced, yelling. Brock had been the complete opposite of proud. Even after they had patched their relationship back together for Mom's sake, Rhett and his father had forged a tense truce at best.

Not once had Brock looked him in the eye and said he was proud.

Not once had he showed up for a competition that included one of the dogs Rhett had trained.

Rhett let his gaze drift to the field where the kids were playing with Kodiak. His heart twisted. Seeing their joy, their innocence—no, he couldn't harbor a grudge against the foster programs any longer. The kids were blameless in all that had happened to him.

"Ashton's looking forward to his first year at Camp Firefly." Jack rose from his seat to lean on the patio's railing. "We were worried you might end some of the programs your dad had started. New leadership sometimes has different priorities." Jack almost sounded like he was apologizing for judging Rhett incorrectly.

If only he knew how close he had come to striking the truth.

Rhett sighed. The Donnelleys were good people who deserved honesty. "Programs remain the same for now, but we are looking at possibly cutting back." Rhett rushed on, "These things are expensive. Take the egg hunt for example. We've been all over town this morning soliciting donations—and we did well—but it will probably need to be downsized."

Jack turned to face them. "If you still need one, I could probably get you a helicopter for the candy drop, free of charge."

Macy had been reaching for her sweet tea and now her hand froze. "Are you for real?"

Sophie looked as if she might burst with pride. She leaned toward Rhett and Macy. "Jack just got promoted to sergeant in the Aircraft Operations Division. He's one of their pilots now."

Rhett had forgotten Jack was an officer with the Texas Department of Public Safety. He certainly hadn't known the man could fly a helicopter though. "If you're sure, I won't turn down an offer like that."

"It shouldn't be a problem," Jack assured them. "My department encourages us to participate in charity events."

There were hugs when everyone finally decided to part ways. Rhett invited the Donnelleys to stop by the ranch whenever they wanted to, and Sophie promised they would take him up on the offer.

Sophie laughed. "Now that the kids have met Kodiak you know they're going to be begging to see her again."

Chapter Six

Rhett left the office early the next day to check on the interns. Yesterday, after he and Macy had returned home, they had made quick work of the phone calls on his to-do list and had been able to meet with all the staff mentors before dinner, making it possible for the interns to come back today.

Gabe and a few of the others had been assigned to help on the maintenance crew, so Rhett drove one of the four-wheelers out to the fence line where the crew was trimming the long grasses and weeds. Staff had to keep them short so gates between pastures would be easier to use.

Normally he would have walked out to the spot, but at the last minute Rhett had decided to strap a cooler filled with ice-cold water bottles to the back of the four-wheeler. It was only March, but the afternoons got hot.

Rhett found Gabe and the others were working hard under the direction of an aged ranch hand. After confirming with the older man, Rhett had to admit Gabe was a good kid.

Gabe used the back of his wrist to swipe sweat from his brow. "Boss, if you don't mind me asking, how's Piper doing?"

Rhett handed the youth a fresh water bottle. "Nothing fazes that little girl." He pointed at the teenager. "Speaking of, make sure you swing by the mess hall and sign her cast before you leave today."

Gabe saluted him.

"And, Gabe?" Rhett cleared his throat. "I know you have your heart set on becoming a veterinarian." The teenager nodded. "Come see me after you're done here and we can talk about putting you on rotation with everyone who works with the animals so you get a chance to see all sides. I'd be happy to show you what I do for dog training, as well, if that's something you'd be interested in."

Satisfied that the teenager was in good hands, Rhett headed back toward the house. Kodiak happily bounded beside his vehicle the whole way. He left the four-wheeler in its usual place near the pole barn and was about to make his way to the ranch house to see how his mom was doing when he spotted Shannon crouched where they stored the hay bales.

As he entered the barn his boots crunched on gravel, alerting Shannon to his presence. Her head snapped up and her blotchy red cheeks gave her away. Rhett's stomach clenched. She'd been crying, sobbing by the looks of it. Seeing her that way made his heart feel wrung out.

What had he missed?

"Hey." He hastened his steps. "What's wrong?" He sat beside her, his arm instinctively going around her shoulders. Every protective impulse flared inside of him. Were the tears because of her boyfriend, Cord Anders? And if so…was it horrible that Rhett would be happy if they had broken up? Rhett had noticed Shannon changing, shrinking into herself ever since she had started dating the man. If he had his way, he would ban the guy from the ranch. He shoved the thought away. Right now all that mattered was Shannon was upset. He needed to be empathetic no matter the reason for her tears. His sister deserved nothing less.

She dropped her head into her hands and her shoulders shook a few times. "Nothing. I don't know." Her voice pitched higher. "Everything."

Not knowing what to say, he rubbed his hand in a circle against her back.

"I'm so stupid," Shannon breathed out.

"Shh." Rhett pulled her to his side in a hug. "No one talks about my favorite sister like that. Not even my favorite sister."

A watery laugh escaped her lips. "I'm your only sister."

"What's wrong?" he whispered the question again.

She shoved her blond curls away from her face. "I'm losing everything." She looked away, out the barn doors. Her eyes focused on something far in the distance or maybe nothing at all; Rhett couldn't tell.

His gut clenched. He had never seen his sister despairing.

Help me, Lord.

"First there was Wade—" her voice strained over her twin's name "—then Dad." She wiped at another tear. "Now it's Mom."

Rhett's fingers tightened over her shoulder. The Jarretts had experienced their share of losses over the last few years, but they would weather them together. Shannon had to know that. He would always be there for her, no matter what happened.

"Mom's still here," he said. "We still have time with her."

Shannon's head swung back around, her gaze latching onto his as if he could save her from drowning. "Not really, Rhett. You and I both know that. She's not usually *there*. Not anymore. I can't go talk to her. I can't—" Her face crumpled. "I feel like I'm losing myself. I'm so—" A sob broke from her chest. Loud and full of long pent-up pain.

Kodiak pranced nearby, her low, sharp whimpers joining Shannon's tears.

Rhett gathered his sister to his chest. If only there was something he could say to make everything better for her. But he knew words didn't have that type of power. In his life words had always caused far more pain than healing. Only actually being there for a person helped, and if he was being honest, he had failed Shannon in the past on that count. He hadn't been around to support her during the most difficult days at Red Dog Ranch.

He refused to fail her now.

She clung to his arms and shoved her forehead into his collarbone. "Nothing makes me happy. Nothing makes me smile anymore. Everything keeps changing and I hate it, and I hate that I can't handle it."

His sister's words gutted him completely. Rhett wrapped his arms more securely around her. "I'm here," he whispered over and over.

She slammed her palms against him and scooted away. "For how long this time?" Her eyes blazed. "You'd sell it in a heartbeat and leave us again if you could. Walk away and never once look back. Never check on us. Never call. Just like before. The only thing keeping you here is Dad's will. We all know that."

"That's not true." His words came out quietly. He would never walk away from his family again, but he couldn't blame her for making a logical jump based on his past actions. He had left her to bear the burden of their mom's illness and deal with their parents alone after Boone and his family left for seminary. She had been the one the police made a death notice to—alone. How secluded she must have felt, entirely deserted by all her brothers. Rhett could never repay her and now it was evident how much it had taxed her, how much he would forever be indebted to his sister. The knowledge hollowed out his chest.

"You don't care about me. Not really."

"I love you. You know that. I'm sorry for—"

She shot to her feet. "You're trying to get out of the will. I know you are."

"Shannon." Rhett slowly rose to his feet. He put his hands out, the same way he would have approached a scared animal. "When I left? That was an issue between me and Dad. I had a beef with him—no one else." He took a step closer. "You have no idea how sorry I am about the past. I ask your forgiveness for not being here, not supporting you better in all the ways I should have."

"Cord's right." Shannon crossed her arms. "None of you care. Not really."

Cord. Of course.

Rhett's movement stilled.

"Is that where this is all coming from?" he asked, hoping for the truth. Praying he could get through to her about her boyfriend. "That guy is bad news. You've been hurting ever since you got with him. That's not love, Shannon. Love heals people—it doesn't destroy them. I don't think he's right for you."

"He's the only good thing in my life right now." Her voice rose. "And now you're trying to take that away from me too. He warned me this would happen."

"That's absurd." Maybe not his best, most caring word choice. Rhett started again, more kindly. "There are so many people here who love you. If this guy has made you think differently then—"

She let out a derisive laugh. "Cord was right. The whole family is against me. I should have known better than to even bother to try to get you to understand." Shannon turned.

Rhett followed after her. "We're not done."

She sliced him with a glare. "Do you think you're Dad now? Because that's hilarious, Rhett." Her voice was ice. This was not any version of the Shannon he knew. It made a creeping sensation go up his back. "You don't have the right to step into our lives and think you can solve all our problems or be some makeshift patriarch now. If you think that's what we want, well, you're wrong. You could never fill Dad's shoes. Not even close. So don't even try."

"I know that," he said quietly. "I'm not trying to be Dad, but I do want to do the best I can by you. By me. By God. I can't undo the past but I can promise that I will never walk away from you again."

She left and this time he didn't follow her.

While he stared after Shannon's retreating form, Kodiak shoved her nose into Rhett's hand. Shannon was right—Rhett had failed them in the past. All of them, but especially Shannon. He pushed his fingers into Kodiak's coarse fur. Resolve forming.

He had a chance to right the wrongs both he and his father had committed.

For far too long the Jarretts had placed Brock on a pedestal because he was a good man with a big heart. But in a way, their dad had failed them most of all. He had put so many things—admirable things—ahead of his family. From Wade's attention-seeking youth, which had led him down a bad path, arguably resulting in his death, to Rhett's constant struggle with rejection and to Shannon's obvious emotional pain, which had driven her to a man like Cord, it didn't take a genius to see how much Brock's lack of attention had cost their family. Happily married, Boone seemed to be the only one to have escaped a measure of dysfunction, but then again, maybe Boone just hid it better.

Rhett would stay and make the ranch a success. If the lawyer could find a loophole in the will, he would be able to show his family that they—not any program or charity—came first. Rhett would figure out the balance between caring for them and helping people in need, because he was starting to think it was possible to do both. It had to be.

He would prove Shannon wrong on another point too. He would be there when Cord Anders broke her heart. He was willing to weather years of her barbs and pained words if that was what he had to do to prove to her that he was no longer the man who walked away.

Even though the path was well illuminated by a flood lamp hanging near the barns, Macy could have walked the path from her bungalow to the big house with her eyes closed. The door to the Jarretts' house had been open to her since she was a baby and it had become her favorite place when they warmly welcomed her after her mother's sudden death. Macy had only been eighteen and would have been left utterly alone in the world if the Jarretts hadn't ushered her into their fold.

If they hadn't made her a part of their family.

At one time, she had believed she might really become a Jarrett. Until the bottom fell out and she tasted bitter reality about her friendship with Rhett. Friends, only ever friends.

For so many years, their home had been her home… except she hadn't set foot inside since Rhett had been back. It was his domain now and she had not wanted to encroach.

Cassidy had texted Macy twice during the day, reminding her about the planned movie night in the big house. Why had she agreed to go in the first place? Sure, it would be nice to spend time with Shannon, Cassidy and, if she was feeling up to it, Mrs. Jarrett, but there were things she could be handling in the office. More work to get done.

A dog's bark made her jump. With a small yelp, Macy whirled around. When she squinted, she could make out Rhett and Kodiak walking up from the lake.

And was that…she squinted more… Romeo the miniature donkey with them?

Rhett's posture changed the second he caught sight of her, but he relaxed his shoulders a moment later. "Out for a stroll in your pajamas?" he hollered since they were still a ways away, his voice warm.

Macy glanced down, mortified. Her pajama pants were covered with brightly colored T. rexes trying to hug each other but not being able to because of their short arms, and she wore a shirt with big letters that read Surely Not Everybody Was Kung Fu Fighting. Summoning her dignity, Macy trudged through the bluebonnets toward him. At least she wasn't wearing her cow slippers.

"Nice shirt." Rhett handed her Romeo's lead rope. "Where are you headed?"

Macy jerked her thumb to point over her shoulder toward the Jarretts' house. "Girls night. We're watching Cary Grant."

"Ah, yes. Now that you mention it, I seem to recall Cassidy telling me I wasn't allowed in my own living room tonight." His eyes narrowed. "Are those dinosaurs on your pants or are they llamas?"

"No more clothing comments unless you want me to turn this around and make fun of you." She fell into step beside Rhett as they headed in the direction of the nearby barn where Romeo and the miniature horse, Sheep, spent their nights.

Rhett made a show of pretending offense. He glanced down as if taking in his own boots, jeans and button-down. "All right, do your worst. What do you have to say about this?"

Macy stopped and looked at Rhett. The man was all cowboy—broad shouldered, tough muscled, with a shadow of end-of-the-day stubble dusting his chin. She fought the sudden itch to touch his jaw. To run her finger along the planes of his face, back into the hair that curled out from under his hat. His bright blue eyes drew her in and Macy's gaze went to his lips. She sucked in a sharp breath and took a step back.

Even in friendship they had never been forward with each other. Plenty of high fives and backslaps sprinkled with the occasional hugs, but other than the one time he had carried her after the snakebite, there had never been a touch that held meaning beyond "Well done" or "Good to see you."

Well, besides that one kiss.

"I, ah, I can't." Suddenly nervous, she swallowed hard. "You always look, um, really…attractive." Heat flared on her neck and her cheeks.

Attractive. She'd really just said that.

Out loud.

Rhett's laugh was warm. "Attractive, huh? Why do I get the sense you're buttering me up to ask a favor or something? Go on," he joked. "What do you want?"

You. Just you. Even though you're the most stubborn, exasperating man I've ever met. It's always been you. It will only ever be you.

Romeo butted his head into her back, shoving her closer to Rhett. Rhett dropped a hand onto her shoulder, ensuring the small donkey wouldn't be able to push Macy again. However, Rhett kept his hold even after Romeo started munching at a patch of clover.

Macy tipped her head to meet Rhett's eyes. She

licked her lips. "Come on, you have to know by now how handsome you are."

Instead of answering, Rhett cocked his head and studied her.

He was so close and for the first time since returning to the ranch, something about him was different. It felt as if his heart wasn't entirely locked up tonight. She imagined it as a door only slightly ajar, but maybe she could wedge a foot in. Maybe she could make some progress with him. Maybe she could win her friend back.

Kodiak shoved her way in between them. She sat directly on the tips of Rhett's boots and stared up at Macy, her muzzle inches away from Macy's thigh.

Macy groaned. "I get the feeling your dog doesn't like me much."

Rhett's gaze drifted over Macy's features, lingering on her mouth. A shy smile lighted his face, causing the skin around his eyes to crinkle. "She's, ah, jealous."

"Of me?" Macy gripped Romeo's lead line a little harder than necessary. "I can't imagine why."

Rhett's smile widened. "Really?"

A part of Macy wanted to press Rhett to clarify, but a bigger part of her brain screamed a warning. It couldn't be what she hoped. Rhett could never care about her in the same way she cared about him. If he had, their kiss would have gone far differently.

Why did you do that? Why did you do that?

Macy needed to steer the conversation to safer waters for both of their sakes. Rhett was her boss, he had emphatically told her he didn't want to be friends again, and she still wasn't sure if he was on board with saving all the foster programs long-term.

Further talk in this direction would only end with her hurt again.

Macy's thumb instinctively found the scar on her finger.

Rhett sighed, clearly disappointed that she hadn't continued their conversation. But she couldn't go down that road with him. She refused to press him about why Kodiak would be jealous of her. Any chance Rhett and her could have had at a relationship ended three years ago. Besides, Rhett had just started to warm up to her again—to smile and joke with her like the old days. She wouldn't let anything harm the chance to mend their friendship. Not even her desire for answers and closure about *what might have been*.

She had to change the topic and head up to the house. Macy pivoted to face the barn. "Sheep's probably missing Romeo."

Rhett's Adam's apple bobbed. "Right." He scrubbed a hand over his face. "Let's put him to bed then."

With Kodiak on his heels, Rhett fell into step next to Macy. His ever-present shadow made Macy remember something else she had been meaning to discuss with him.

"I looked up Straight Arrow Retrievers," Macy said with all the casualness she could muster. "Why didn't you tell us about all the awards you won? You trained Benny—that dog went to big award shows as a presenter."

Rhett unlatched the barn door and held it open as she led Romeo inside. He took his time catching up. "Would any of it have mattered?" His voice was quiet, almost a whisper.

By the time he came up behind her, Macy had ushered Romeo into his stall. She spun around, finding Rhett closer than she had thought he would be. "Of course it matters. Your accomplishments are worth celebrating. You can't give it up."

"I don't see how I can keep training dogs with everything else I have going on."

"I've watched you out there in the field with them." She poked his chest. "You're happy. Really happy when you're working dogs. I don't want you to lose that."

He pinched the bridge of his nose. "I don't want to talk about this right now. Other things—" his gaze dipped to her mouth "—but not this."

"Then what do you want to talk about?" The second the question passed her lips she wished she hadn't voiced it. She should have said good-night and gone on her way, but his eyes were pleading with her and looking away was near impossible.

He eased the lead line from Macy's grasp, his eyes never leaving hers. "Why didn't you return my calls?"

Unwelcome nerves jangled through her. "You honestly want to have this conversation?" What if they ruined all the headway they had made? Of all the things for him to want to discuss. "Because last time I brought it up you seemed pretty opposed to it."

He stepped back and looped the lead line back on a peg with some other equipment. "I left you so many messages." His back was to her. His shoulders rose on a shaky breath. "For so long you just ignored them—ignored me. I still can't wrap my head around what happened."

"I was embarrassed, Rhett." She threw out her arms. "What did you expect me to do after that?"

Rhett finally turned around. "I wanted you to talk with me." His voice was even. "Friends do that. They talk through things. Do you know how much I missed you the last few years?"

Friends.

And there it was: Confirmation. Friends. Just friends. All he would ever consider her. Why she should have walked away ten minutes ago. Why she had to end this conversation before she was forced to admit to her feelings.

"I wasn't going to take the job," she said, but it sounded lame even to her own ears.

A wrinkle formed between his eyes. "This has nothing to do with the job offer." He took a half step in her direction. "Are you honestly going to keep pretending you don't know what I'm getting at?"

Macy crossed her arms over her chest. "You didn't call me back either. You know, the path goes both ways."

He took off his hat and ran a shaky hand through his hair. "You called once, Macy. Once. *Five* months later."

Kodiak raised her head and whimpered.

Rhett looked at Kodiak, back at Macy, away again. "I shouldn't have raised my voice. I'm sorry, I'm just dealing with a lot here."

"Like what?"

"Shannon hates me." His voice trembled. "She hates me, Mace." He shook his head when she opened her mouth. "And you? Whenever I think…" He backed away. "I'm sorry. I shouldn't have said anything. There's so much on my mind tonight. Forget all this for me."

He was gone before she could say anything else. Between what seemed like flirtation at the beginning of their interaction to the bombshell about Shannon and his obvious hurt, it was hard to wade through what she should think and feel about it all. She was relieved he hadn't pressed talking about their kiss more. Their friendship was just starting to feel comfortable again and a long talk about why he would never think of her romantically would only make her pull away. As much as she wished it was otherwise, they needed to go on as if the kiss had never happened.

She could be his friend again.

Just friends.

It would be enough.

It would have to be enough.

Macy stood in the barn's doorway long after she lost sight of him.

Chapter Seven

When Macy stretched, her spine answered with a series of little popping noises. Sleeping on the floor as a twenty-eight-year-old was a significantly different experience than all the times she had done so at sleepovers as a teenager. Her joints wouldn't thank her.

After her conversation with Rhett, Macy had gone ahead with her planned movie night with the other girls. If only because she'd known Cassidy was bound to show up at her house and drag her, kicking and screaming, to the Jarrett house if Macy had dared to text to cancel. Even still she had been tempted.

Thankfully, Rhett was safely tucked away upstairs when she arrived and stayed that way the rest of the evening while Cassidy, Shannon, Piper and Macy watched movies and consumed a shocking amount of popcorn and chocolate. As usual, Piper was asleep within the first ten minutes of the first movie. Somewhere between watching *To Catch a Thief* and Macy's favorite Cary Grant movie, *Charade*, they all decided to turn the marathon into a sleepover and added *Houseboat* to the lineup.

A wall of windows on one side of the room showed a pink-and-gold wash of sunrise cresting over the hills. Cassidy and Piper were still snoozing together on the large couch, but Shannon's spot in the recliner was empty. Had she gone upstairs to her own room at some point or had she snuck out to meet with Cord? Shannon had been present last night but not engaged.

Rhett and his sister had to have had words yesterday because it wasn't like Rhett to throw around the word *hate*. A sick feeling swam through Macy. She had considered pulling Shannon aside many times throughout the last few weeks, but the time had never felt right. She needed to be a better friend to Shannon in the future.

Keep Shannon safe, Lord. Help her see how much You love her. Help us get through to her. And whatever's going on between her and Rhett—please heal their hurt. She was about to end her plea but then added, *Could You help me with Rhett too? I'm not sure what's going on. I'm not even sure what's happening in my own life anymore.*

Macy had plugged her phone in to charge on the kitchen counter before she had fallen asleep. With all the emails she had sent out recently regarding the foster programs, she liked to check for responses first thing each morning. After getting home from Scoops and Sons, she had sent a message to Clint Oakfield. Was it silly to hope he would respond?

She rose only to spot Mrs. Jarrett peacefully sitting at the head of the dining-room table. The woman looked over at her and smiled serenely. Macy was once again struck by how cruel Alzheimer's was. From the outside, Rhett's mom appeared the same as ever.

It was a shock to see her up and about before her nurse arrived. How long had she been there? Mrs. Jarrett hadn't been well enough to join them last night. But here she was, hands folded over her open Bible, bright and early in the morning, smiling at Macy as if she had been waiting for her. The woman had a way of looking regal, even in her brown robe with her white hair slightly mussed with sleep. Macy crossed into the kitchen, socks padding over the hardwood floor. "Can I get something for you?"

Mrs. Jarrett touched the spot to her right. "Just come and sit with me, dear."

Macy filled two cups with water and brought them to the table. "How are you doing this morning?"

A glass jar on the table held a fragrant bouquet of Texas sage, orange jubilee and gold lantana. Cassidy had told Macy that Rhett picked a new bouquet of flowers at the ranch for his mother every couple of days.

Mrs. Jarrett fanned her fingers over the thin pages of her open Bible. "If you're asking if today is a good day or a bad day for my mind—today I remember. I know myself."

Swallowing hard, Macy glanced toward the staircase and wondered if she should rouse Rhett or Shannon. She knew they would appreciate some time with their mother during a lucid moment. Macy bit her lip. Another part of her wondered if she should broach the topic of Rhett's adoption with Mrs. Jarrett. Every time Macy sat at her desk and looked at the photo of Brock at the opening of Camp Firefly she fought the urge to go into Rhett's office and confess what she knew. Rhett deserved to know the truth about his parentage, but she couldn't break her promise to Brock.

No matter how often she wanted to.

Rhett's mom gazed toward the stairs. "They're both already gone for the day. Rhett left very early. More so than usual. It makes a person wonder why." Mrs. Jarrett trained her focus on Macy. "When will you two give in and get married already?"

Macy choked on the sip of water she had just taken. She covered her mouth.

Unfazed, Rhett's mom continued, "My thickheaded boy may not realize it, but he's loved you his whole life. Still does. I think more now than ever. Some people love each other for a season or while it's convenient, but you two share the growing kind of love—it keeps getting bigger and deeper."

Macy considered acting as if she had no clue what Mrs. Jarrett was talking about, but why? The Jarrett matriarch was lucid, but lately these were rare moments. Macy had always cherished the woman's wisdom and perspective. She wouldn't forsake an opportunity to speak with the lady who had become her second mom.

She filled her lungs with air, let it out. "I'm pretty sure my feelings are no secret, but Rhett never went down that road. I always figured if it was meant to be, it would happen." She shrugged, trying to pretend the admission didn't sting. "So I guess it wasn't meant to be."

"'If it's meant to be'?" Mrs. Jarrett snorted and batted her hand in the air. "What hogwash. Love is work. Hard work. It's late-night tears and fights and forgiving and choosing a person even on their worst days. I've never known such pain as the pain of love. 'Meant to be,'" she grumbled again, as if the words offended her. "Anyone who treats it so carelessly has never truly known it."

Macy's eyes burned. Tears had gathered as Mrs. Jarrett spoke. "When Rhett left the ranch—" Her voice cracked. "He knew me better than anyone and rejected me."

Rhett's mom nodded thoughtfully. "And he will likely hurt you again and you him. That's how living goes." She tapped the table. "That's especially how loving goes."

Macy straightened her spine. "Which is exactly why it would never work for us."

"Sweet child, don't you know?" Mrs. Jarrett covered Macy's hand with both of hers. "God's love is the only one that never lets us down. All others will at some point. We're human, you realize." She cupped her hands around Macy's. "I made mistakes with Brock and the good Lord knows Brock let us down sometimes too. Rhett will do the same and maybe you don't want to hear it, but you will stumble in relationships too—for the rest of your life, my dear. I'm sorry to be the one to tell you these things."

"I know I'm not perfect—"

"*None* of us are." She winked. "But I find that's part of the adventure."

"Do you know he's trying to downsize the foster programs? He would have cut the egg hunt if I hadn't convinced him not to." Macy felt like she was tattling on Rhett. She knew he wouldn't have discussed these things with his mom, but Mrs. Jarrett had been a driving force for establishing Camp Firefly, among other things, and deserved a voice in the matter.

His mom released Macy's hand so she could trace her

finger over a highlighted line in her Bible. "I wonder, does your push to save the things Brock started come from a place of love or do you believe it's your burden, your badge of honor—your pride at stake?" She caressed the highlighted page again. "Right here, 'do all things out of love.' It sounds so easy, but it is the hardest thing that will ever be asked of us because love… love is sometimes the most painful feeling on earth, child. But it's worth it. We have the proof right here." She closed her Bible and tapped the cover. "It's worth every sacrifice, every arrow sent into the soft part of our heart. It's worth it."

As the nurse arrived Macy kissed Mrs. Jarrett on the cheek. "Thank you for your wisdom."

Mrs. Jarrett caught her hand, giving it an extra squeeze before letting go. As Macy left, she blinked away tears. She forced down the emotions talking with Mrs. Jarrett had stirred. But even after Macy had showered, changed and headed into the office, she couldn't shake the oldest Jarrett's words.

Macy and Rhett had hurt each other, but did that mean their entwined story had to end? Macy didn't want it to.

She wished she would have handled last night differently. Been honest. Vulnerable.

If she had been brave and spoken her heart then at least she would know now. She wouldn't be stuck in the Land of Maybe any longer. The truth could have been used to guide her.

Macy finally focused on her phone; an email sparked her interest. She let out a long stream of air. She couldn't wait to tell Rhett about this.

* * *

Rhett brushed his hand over his eyes, hoping no one would be able to notice the lingering hint of tears later on. He hadn't meant to wake up early and visit his father's grave, but here he was.

Rhett knelt in front of the headstone and traced his fingers over his father's name and the small dash in between the date of birth and date of death. The small dash that symbolized his life. It was in the dash that Brock had raised and loved Rhett despite both men's failings. Brock might have dropped the ball in many aspects of fatherhood, but Rhett had never doubted his father's love.

Humid air draped around Rhett's shoulders, causing his shirt to stick to his back. A light breeze rustled flowers placed on nearby grave sites and a colorful pinwheel twirled in the wind, stuck into the ground near a tombstone with birth and death dates painfully close together. If it wasn't for the occasional gusts it would have felt like a summer morning outside instead of the end of March.

"Why me?" Rhett whispered. "Why did you leave the ranch to me? It makes no sense. You had no reason to trust me, to believe in me after—" His voice broke. "After I walked away. I'm so sorry I didn't make it to the hospital in time to say goodbye." He had immediately gotten into his truck and headed for home when Shannon had called him about the accident. But a hundred miles was too far. Too long. His father had passed on fifteen minutes before he parked at the hospital. "I'm sorry, Dad. I'm so sorry I didn't get to say goodbye. Hug you one more time." Tears fell now. *Let them.*

His phone buzzed in his pocket and he tugged it out. It was a text from Jack Donnelley—an image of all of Jack's kids with their arms wrapped around Kodiak as they smiled at the camera. His text said the dog was a perfect mascot for Red Dog Ranch.

Macy had once said the same exact thing.

Rhett turned his phone to silent and tucked it back away.

After a few more minutes Rhett found his way to his truck and eased into the front seat. Why had it taken him so long to visit the grave site?

Last night after talking to Macy, Rhett had gone back to his room, but sleep hadn't come. He had stared up at the ceiling watching the fan blades whip around and thought about all that had gone wrong in his life. If he hadn't frozen that night three years ago with Macy they could have been together now. He might have been home years earlier.

But he couldn't force Macy to talk about their past any more than he could fix Shannon's problems. All night one thought kept pounding through his head— with so much of his life spinning out of control, he needed to focus on the few things he had power over. The biggest being his own heart. Hadn't he asked God to help heal his grudge against the ranch? A piece of that was making peace with his father. Visiting his grave had been the only way Rhett could think to do that.

Without turning his truck on, he gripped the steering wheel and shoved his forehead against it. A sudden throb radiated through his chest, making him gasp for breath. Would life always feel like such a mess? Shannon and the ranch and Mom and Macy. Rhett thought of the Donnelleys—how the ranch had helped Jack when he was younger and how much his kids were looking forward to camp. Rhett's heart twisted. Those kids deserved a place like Camp Firefly. Kids like Gabe deserved a safe space too.

He had asked God to help him release his grudge—coming to terms with his mixed emotions for his father was a piece of moving forward.

Here in the graveyard where thoughts tended to drift toward legacies and how important it was to live with meaning, Rhett finally saw his excuses for what they were—thinly veiled childhood bitterness that he had held on to for so many years. A little boy who wanted his dad to look his way and offer a proud smile, who had wanted to know he came first, if only once. It would never happen, not with Brock gone, and Rhett had to accept that or remain stuck forever.

What was the point of hoarding bad memories, allowing them to take up space in his heart and mind—crowding his life so much that there wasn't room for other things?

Happy, hopeful things.

Rhett was tired of the heavy chains that came with resentment. He didn't want them in his life anymore. Someday, when his body would wind up in a plot not far from his father's, he wanted to know his time had counted. If there was a balance between providing for his family and continuing the events of the ranch, Rhett would find it. He would help heal his family too, if he could.

However, he knew it would be impossible to accomplish any of those things outside of God. Rhett had neglected his relationship with God for far too long. He would never get the last talk or hug with his earthly dad, but he could mend things with God the Father. It was time to go back to church again, time to dust off his Bible and time to open a line of communication through prayer. No matter how strange or strained it might feel, he knew God was there, waiting. Always had been.

Maybe Brock had been too. Rhett would never know because he had squandered the chance to truly reconcile. A mistake he wouldn't make again. Not with God or Shannon or Macy. Not with anyone, if it was up to him. Life was too short, too unpredictable, to hold grudges or allow miscommunications to ruin relationships.

Rhett headed back to the ranch. He had only just parked his vehicle when he caught sight of Macy cutting through the field of bluebonnets toward him. Kodiak trotted at Macy's side, a red ball in her mouth. The two of them looked as if they were racing to put out a fire. The dog was probably miffed at being left behind, but it wouldn't have been respectful to have her in the cemetery and it would have been far too hot to leave her in the vehicle. Rhett exited his truck and strolled to the fence line to meet them.

Macy huffed. "Where have you been? When I saw Kodiak was here but not your truck, I freaked out." Her brows lowered. "And you need to start answering your phone."

Rhett tugged his phone from his pocket. Seven missed calls from Macy. He had turned the vibrate function off after Jack's text had interrupted him. "It was on silent." Her scowl grew and Rhett saw the emotion for what it was—concern. He quickly added, "Sorry if I worried you."

Macy grabbed his wrist. "I *was* worried." She searched his eyes. "Are you okay? It looks like…" She left it there. "Rhett," she whispered. "I know what you said before, but can't we be friends again?"

He covered her hand with his. He instantly found the scar on her pointer finger and couldn't help but trace over it.

Friends.

The word was too small to capture his feelings for Macy.

She knew every rough part of his personality and yet here she was, asking to be friends. Wanting to be a part of his life even though he had hurt her and let her down more times than he could count. She stood toe-to-toe with him even when they disagreed and challenged him constantly, but only because she believed the best of him.

She believed in him. He let that sink in.

Rhett had loved this woman his entire life.

The realization roared through him, shaking him like a powerful storm.

There had never been another woman on the planet in Rhett's eyes. Only Macy. Always Macy. In the past, he had hidden behind their friendship because he had been fearful of losing her if he made a move. Then last night he had come so close to confessing his feelings, but he was glad he hadn't because Rhett was in no position to start a relationship.

Between his father's death, his mother's health and Shannon's anger, Rhett had so much emotional baggage to deal with before he would be ready to be there for a woman.

To be there for Macy.

If she would even want him.

Rhett scuffed his boot into the dirt.

But he could be her friend, couldn't he? They were already acting like friends anyway. "I'd like to be friends again. I'd like that a lot."

The smile that bloomed on Macy's face was the most beautiful thing Rhett had ever seen. "Then tell me what's wrong."

There was no point hiding the truth; he was sure she had already read the evidence on his face. "I visited my dad. His grave site."

"I'm proud of you," she said. "I know how hard that can be." She released his wrist and he wished she hadn't. "About last night…"

Rhett scratched at the spot on his neck where his hat met his hairline. "Can we forget last night? I was a bear." He had snapped at her because he was upset over Shannon and he was frustrated Macy wouldn't discuss what had gone wrong three years ago. Since realizing he would have had to put a relationship on hold anyway while he worked through all the emotional issues he was dealing with, now he was thankful the conversation hadn't gone any further.

She poked him in the ribs. "Bears *can* be cuddly."

"Not all bears." He rubbed the spot she had poked as if she had hurt him.

She blew bangs away from her eyes. "Anyway, your roar has never scared me." Macy plucked the ball from Kodiak's mouth and sent it flying. Kodiak went tearing through the field after it. "I don't think she minds me nearly as much when you're not around."

Rhett braced his arms on the top fence railing. "Stick around and she'll consider you family like we all do." Kodiak sometimes took a while to warm up to certain adults, but once she accepted them they became fully her people.

"Speaking of, Sophie Donnelley texted." Macy came up beside him, her shoulder brushing his arm. "She asked if the kids could stop by and see Kodiak today."

"Of course. I said they were always welcome."

His dog had already returned with the ball and dropped it at Macy's feet. When Macy looked Rhett's way with her eyebrows raised in question he jerked his chin toward the ball. Macy winked and scooped it back up again, lobbing it in the other direction.

Macy squinted and held her hand to her brow to block some of the sunshine. "Kodiak was good with those kids."

"She always is."

"Now, I don't know much about training dogs..." Macy's words were measured. She had obviously been thinking about this and wanting to bring it up for some time. "So I don't know if this is an odd suggestion, but did you ever think of training therapy dogs instead of hunting dogs?" She pitched Kodiak's ball again and pressed a hand to his bicep when he opened his mouth to say something. "Hear me out. How Kodiak was with those kids? I feel like she could be a comfort dog for kids in trauma. She could be the comfort dog for the ranch." Macy spread out her arms, encompassing the whole property.

"Red dog." Rhett smiled, remembering what she had said in the chapel last week and what Jack had texted earlier that day.

Macy wagged her finger at him. "I told you she'd make a good mascot."

Rhett wrapped his hand over hers and tugged her a few inches closer. "I should have believed you."

"You usually come around to my ideas." Macy tapped on his chest. "It just takes some pestering."

"That's because they're good ideas." He stepped back, releasing her. If he had stood there a second longer he might have pulled her closer or said something he shouldn't yet. "Honestly? I'd love to train therapy dogs." Probably more than he enjoyed training hunting dogs. "But I just don't know when I'd have the time, and it takes a different sort of training than I know."

Macy leaned her back against the fence so she was facing him. "What if we got you help?"

Rhett scanned the pasture. "We're trying to save money here."

"Hypothetically, if someone took on more of the ranch's responsibilities?"

"Sure, yes." Rhett laughed at her tenacity. "I'd love that. It's a good dream."

She pushed off the fence. "In the meantime, you should reach out to your clients again and schedule more sessions. I can handle some of your load and I'm thinking we should approach Shannon, give her more responsibility."

Rhett considered the idea. Shannon didn't presently have a position at the ranch. "She seems to be going through some stuff right now."

Macy nodded. "I think having duties, things to occupy her other than Cord, would be a good thing."

"It's a good thought. Let me mull it over some." He

motioned toward the office. "As for now, I have some calls I have to make. Are you heading over?"

"I actually have to run into town." She pointed her thumb in the direction of her car. "But I do want to talk with you about something else. Later, of course. I know you're busy."

Rhett felt his eyebrows rise. He fought the urge to press her to talk now, but if she had wanted to talk over something presently she had had an open opportunity and had chosen not to. He could respect her desire to put off whatever she wanted to say until another time. "How about this evening? I take Kodiak to the lake after supper. Would that work?"

She nodded. "That would be perfect."

"Then later it is." He tipped his hat and Kodiak fell into step beside him. He started thinking about ways he could make their meeting tonight special, a sort of olive branch for the new start to their friendship.

"Hey, Rhett," Macy called after him. He turned to find her a few feet away, her fingers entwined. "If you made a promise to someone, a promise you weren't sure you wanted to keep any longer, what would you do?"

A breeze swept down from the hills, making the bluebonnets bob around them. The field resembled a sea of turbulent waves.

He hooked his fingers on his belt. "Talk with the person who I made the promise to, I guess."

"What if that wasn't an option any longer?" She was clearly talking about his dad. Perhaps his visit to Brock's grave had prompted her questions. Rhett couldn't deny his curiosity was piqued, but after his time at the grave site this morning, Rhett knew he needed to work on trusting. Trust that his dad had had good intentions for handing the ranch to him, trust that God had a hand in all the chaos surrounding Rhett's life. Trust Macy too.

Rhett took a half step in her direction. "The person you made the promise to, were they an upright person?"

Macy had been looking down at her hands but now her focus snapped to him. "One of the best I've ever met."

"Then I'd leave it," Rhett said gently.

"You're sure?" She eyed him. "Absolutely sure?"

Rhett knew she was asking something bigger, something more…but he couldn't figure it out. However, if Brock had told her some secret, Rhett wouldn't press her for it. She would only feel guilt after telling him and he couldn't do that to her.

No matter how much he wanted to.

"I'm sure."

She could keep her old secrets as long as Rhett had the hope of her future.

Chapter Eight

With no time to change or freshen up once Macy got back to Red Dog Ranch, she headed straight to the lakeshore. It was long past the time Cassidy served supper at the mess hall so she knew Rhett would be at the lake by now. Cassidy had texted earlier, asking if Macy had been able to stop for food while she'd been out. Macy had let her know that she was probably going to skip dinner and dive into a pint of mint swirl ice cream waiting back in her small fridge later tonight instead.

Romeo brayed as she passed his enclosure.

"Sorry, buddy, I got nothing. I didn't even get a chance to grab myself food." She reached over the fence and scratched between his ears. He brayed again. "Oh, you impatient little guy, good thing you're so cute. I see you already forgot about the pear chunks I brought you yesterday." Her stomach rumbled.

She left Romeo and continued in the direction of the lake. She hiked up the last hill and paused at the top. Rhett's back was to her as he stood at the end of the long wooden pier with a bundle or some sort of basket by his feet. Kodiak swam after her red ball in the water. A trail of candles burning inside glass jars led the way down the pier to him. The sight caused Macy's pulse to kick up.

Was this…was this a date?

She brushed the thought away. After all, she had been the one to ask him to meet up to talk, not the other way around. Although it was hardly as if Rhett would have set out the candles if he was going to be here alone.

She would not read too much into the gesture.

She would not.

Hopefully, she would believe the statement the more she repeated it to herself.

Kodiak, who had been dropping the ball onto the pier for Rhett to toss out again, swam past the pier to the shore. The dog leapt from the water, gave one great shake and then charged in Macy's direction.

Rhett followed his dog's progress but stayed on the pier. A wide, handsome smile spread across his features as he slipped his hands into his pockets. "See. What did I tell you? She likes you more than me already."

"Hardly," Macy called back with a laugh.

The dog happily head butted Macy's knee and Macy gave her a welcoming pat only to discover that Kodiak felt dry. "How is this dog not wet?" She touched her coarse fur again.

"Double coated," Rhett answered. "Thick under-layer keeps her skin from ever getting wet. The top layer is considered a harsh coat. You know how a duck can go in the water and comes out without being waterlogged?"

Kodiak trailed along beside Macy as she made her

way to the pier. "Don't ducks have some special oil though?"

"Chessies have oil trapped between the two layers of their coat. Works the same way."

Closer to the shore Macy accepted the red ball and threw it out into the lake for Kodiak to go after. Rhett's dog had the endurance of a triathlete.

Rhett came to where the planks connected with the shore and offered his hand. "I have something for you," he said almost shyly.

Macy unsuccessfully fought a wary grin as she slipped her hand into his. "What is all this?"

Rhett led her to the end of the pier. "Cassidy told me you were planning to skip supper tonight. She gave me the candles." He gave a nervous shrug.

Cassidy. Of course. Always trying to set them up. It was too bad the romantic ambiance hadn't been Rhett's idea, but Macy would enjoy it nonetheless.

The pier creaked and swayed with their steps. Macy noticed each jar had been filled a third of the way with sand before a votive was placed inside. Flames flickered as they passed by, giving the pier a dreamlike quality. Fireflies drawn to the lights whizzed around their legs. Croaking frogs, the lake lapping the underside of the boards, their steps and the slight crunch of the tethered canoe against the side of the pier were the only sounds.

Well, besides Kodiak's feverish paddling.

When they reached the end Rhett let go of her hand so he could tug a blanket from the large tote bucket he must have stowed there. He spread the blanket out then looked over at her, turned and looked out at the lake, cleared his throat, scratched the back of his neck.

Was he...goodness, the man was all nerves.

She, of all people, had flustered Rhett Jarrett. Her logical, straight-talking friend couldn't find words. The realization warmed Macy's heart.

"Rhett," she said his name tenderly. "What is all this?"

He cleared his throat again. "Food." He pulled the top off of the tote bucket. "You weren't at the mess hall so I assumed you hadn't eaten. And Cassidy said she didn't think you had and helped me gather some things. I shouldn't just assume that if you're not with us you're not anywhere though, right? You could have been out on a date instead for all I know." He looked right at her, his blue eyes wider than usual. "Were you on a date? Wait." He held up a hand. "Not my business. You don't have to tell me. Unless you want to, that is. If you do, you can."

Macy pressed her hand over his mouth to stop his rambling. Nervous Rhett was by far the most adorable version of Rhett she had ever encountered.

"Cassidy was right. I have not eaten." And at past eight at night she was definitely hungry now. Macy slowly removed her fingers from his lips. Blood thrummed through her veins at a turbulent pace, making her skin feel tingly. "And I wasn't on a date."

She caught the grin he attempted to hide when he ducked back toward the tote to pull out food. "We had a bad start when I came back. I want to start over like two old friends should have." He handed her a small bundle. "Blue-cheese steak wrap."

"My favorite. You remembered?" Macy took a seat on the blanket facing the lake. She unrolled the parchment paper so she could take a bite of the wrap. The bold notes of blue cheese, spinach and freshly grilled steak made her taste buds dance.

"Of course." Rhett produced a glass bowl full of frozen blueberries—a favorite childhood treat. His mom used to sprinkle them over ice cream or hand out bowls of frozen blueberries on hot summer nights while everyone gathered on the back porch to watch the sunset. Next came a thermos and two cups.

"Just Cassidy's sparkling watermelon lemonade."

"*Just* is not the right word." Macy unscrewed the lid and inhaled the sweet scent emanating from the thermos. "She hasn't made this stuff since last summer and I love it. How did you talk her into it?"

Rhett winked. "I have my ways." His bravado fell to sudden nervousness again. "Okay, and these might not be great, but…" He pulled a small tin from the basket.

When he opened the lid, Macy gasped. "S'mores stuffed cookies. You convinced someone to make them? I haven't had these since…" She snagged one from the tin and sank her teeth into it, letting her eyes flutter closed as the perfect balance of chocolate, marshmallow, graham-cracker crumbs and cookie melted on her tongue. "I think it's been at least ten years since I've had one and they're just as good as I remember."

"Oh, good." Rhett rubbed the back of his neck. "Because I made them and I wasn't sure how they would turn out."

Macy's eyes filled with irrational tears. She had to rapid-fire blink to keep them from falling. "You made these? You got the ingredients and mixed them and cooked them…for me?"

His head dipped with acknowledgment. "Your mom's recipe."

"Thank you," she whispered. She wanted to hug him, to kiss him and to cry too. The last time Macy had tasted these cookies her mom had made them. Each time she had unearthed her mom's spiral notebook full of recipes she had started crying, never able to actually make any of the recipes inside. Besides, she wasn't much of a cook or baker to begin with.

Rhett's gesture was an act of love. Plain and simple.

This was the man she had lost her heart to so many years ago.

Rhett hung his legs over the edge of the pier while Macy finished eating. He scuffed his palms along the thighs of his jeans, trying to will them to stop sweating. A lot of good that did.

Macy gently set the tin of cookies down and scooted to sit beside him at the end of the pier. "Tonight… This is…this is so beautiful, Rhett. What you did for me."

I did it because I love you. I'd do this every day if it made you happy. I should have done this a long time ago.

His throat burned with words he had to swallow.

Tonight wasn't the time to declare anything. Tonight was an olive branch, letting her know he was serious about them being friends again.

A candle flickered in the breeze beside him. Cassidy had forced him to bring those along and had even sent a kitchen hand to set it all up. He thought the candles were a bit much for renewing friendship, but he knew better than to argue with Cassidy when her mind was made up.

He braced his hands at an angle so one was behind her, bringing them even closer. Raven strands of her hair danced in the breeze, the long ends traced across his shoulder.

"That day, when I left the ranch…" The words were out before he could consider them.

She scooped her hair to the side and turned toward him so their faces were less than a foot apart. Waning sunlight backlit her and his breath caught for a moment. She was the most beautiful person he had ever seen. She licked her lips, drawing his attention to how much he wanted to kiss her.

He sat up, pulling away from her a bit in the process. She mirrored his posture, leaning forward now so her shoulder bumped his arm.

"You stopped me, on my way out." An image of Macy with tears streaking down her cheeks played in his mind, unbidden. It tore at his heart.

"I was afraid you were going to leave without saying goodbye."

On that day he *had* planned to leave the ranch without saying goodbye to anyone. He had been so angry after his father's ultimatum—stay and stop questioning Brock's methods or leave for good.

He rubbed his hands together slowly. If only it was so easy to dust off mistakes. "You told me I was wrong. You said I had to see my dad's side," he said. "All I heard was you choosing him, choosing this place over me like he'd done so many times."

"When you said it was you or the ranch, I didn't know how to answer," Macy admitted. "I loved your dad as if he was my father. Your family had become mine. I didn't just want to leave everything. My home. When you offered me the job on the spot, it came out of nowhere."

He turned his head her way again. Had to see her eyes. "There was more to it than that. I... I wanted you to pick me. I wanted someone—wanted you—to choose me." For his entire life, his dad had never picked him. Rhett had never felt as if he was first place in anyone's heart. He had wanted to be the top person in Macy's life that day, but he knew it had been wrong to demand she choose him over everything else. He couldn't hold the eye contact—not after that admission—so he gazed out at the lake. "You had been dating that guy."

"Jim." She scooted closer.

"Yeah, him."

She surprised Rhett by laying her head on his shoulder. "I'm tired. Do you mind?"

Rhett fought the urge to turn his nose into her hair and breathe in her scent. "Not at all."

"Jim didn't like you." She adjusted where her head was, nestling even closer. She sighed. "He told me to stop spending so much time with you and I did."

"I noticed." Rhett slipped off his hat and set it beside him. Then he leaned his head to rest it on hers. They had never been like this before, so easy with their physical contact, but it felt right. It made Rhett wonder why he had never put his arm around her or reached out for her before now. "And I didn't like it."

"You were jealous?"

"Practically bursting with it," he said. He swallowed hard. "Then after you showed up and turned down the job..." He omitted the kiss after how the conversation had gone last night. "Then you wouldn't return my calls. It seemed I had successfully run off the one person who had always been in my corner, so I figured I was meant to be alone. Later, when you called—" he heaved a sigh "—I convinced myself you were better off without me."

Macy sat up suddenly and scooted so she was half facing him. She dropped her hand to his knee. "We may be the two stupidest people on the planet."

"I don't follow."

"That kiss? I wanted to be with you, Rhett." She looked away. "I had wanted that for a long time. When things didn't go well... I was horrified, to say the least."

"Mace." He couldn't let her continue to believe he hadn't wanted her. Hadn't imagined that kiss differently a million times over the last three years. "I was surprised. But it was a good surprised," he rushed on. "And I muddled it completely."

"You kept saying, 'Why did you do that?'"

He had only meant to start the conversation.

"It all happened so fast." But it had definitely been the wrong thing to say. However, he had pushed back his feelings for Macy for so long and hadn't allowed himself to entertain the idea that maybe she cared deeply for him, as well.

"When I finally worked up the nerve to call back and you never responded, I assumed it was because you didn't want me. Your messages had just said that we needed to talk so I had no clue if it was a good talk or a bad talk. This whole time I've been telling myself something was missing, something was—" her voice caught "—wrong with me. First my dad, then you." She swiped at her eyes.

Heaviness settled on Rhett's chest and lungs as she spoke. He'd had a hand in causing these insecurities. Aware of them now, he would fight them alongside of her for the rest of their lives in whatever capacity she would allow him to.

"Mace." He caught her face between his hands. "There has never been, nor will there ever be, anything you can do or say that will make me not want you in my life. My pride kept me away—that's on me and only me. You are perfect the way you are and I'd never want you to change. That was a lot of words, but I mean it. You have been my closest friend—my best friend—for most of my life. I'd like to erase everything that happened between us ever since I left and just go back to how we were for so many years."

Macy shrugged from his touch.

"Go back to how we were," she said robotically. "Of course. Friends." Her smile didn't reach her eyes.

"It's getting late. Is it okay if I share the thing I wanted to talk about now?"

His hands dropped away from her. During his spur-of-the-moment conversation he had lost track of the fact that she had been the one who wanted to talk about something. "I bulldozed this whole night, didn't I?"

"I didn't mind. We needed to hash this stuff out."

His hat still off, Rhett ran his hand through his hair. "Please, what was it you wanted to talk about?"

Macy grimaced. "It's business stuff—but I'm really excited."

He grabbed his hat and set it back on his head. "Bring it on."

"Let's clean as we talk." She motioned toward the

basket. Macy started gathering plates and other items and handing them his way to stow in the bucket he had brought. Rhett got up and started gathering the candles.

The sun had finished its dip to the other side of the world and the fields had turned dark. Kodiak lay a few feet away, catching a small nap. If the three of them could have stayed like this then life would have been perfect. Too bad reality knocked hard enough to wake the heaviest dreamer.

They had made their peace, but Rhett still had to make amends with Shannon and chart the best path for the ranch going forward. Running Camp Firefly was a full-time job on its own, and summer was the busiest time with the cattle. On top of that he still had to replace some essential staff members who had left after his father passed. Soon enough Rhett would have to start putting in fourteen-hour workdays just to keep up.

Maybe things would settle down by the time autumn rolled around.

Macy handed him the blanket. "I might have messaged someone about the egg hunt and not told you about it."

He chuckled. The worry in her voice was evident and he wanted to put her at ease.

"So now you have to tell me, huh?"

She rose and grabbed both his hands, giving them one quick pump as she said, "It's Clint Oakfield."

"*The* Clint Oakfield?" Rhett knew he was bound to be gaping but he couldn't help it. The man had recently been inducted into the Grand Ole Opry.

"The one and only. He wants to come to our event and he's bringing all kinds of signed merch to raffle off. He's also made a donation that covers more than half of our expenses. If it's okay with you, of course. He wants to do a few songs and—"

Rhett caught her up in a hug, lifting her clear off the ground. "You're amazing! You know that, right?"

Kodiak bounded to her feet and came over to them, tail wagging, as she picked up on their excitement. When Rhett set Macy down she turned to lavish attention on Kodiak, and he found he was glad for the distraction.

Because without Kodiak's interruption he very well might have kissed Macy and ruined all the steps they had taken toward mending their friendship tonight.

Chapter Nine

The day of the egg hunt had dawned with an over-whelming cloak of muggy air descending onto the ranch. Macy pulled her hair into a ponytail and fanned her face. With all the running around involved for setup and directing others, she was already on her second shirt of the day and was considering changing again or at least freshening up before the candy drop occurred.

She glanced at her watch. There wouldn't be enough time.

Thankfully no one seemed to be letting the unsea-sonably warm, damp weather affect their attitudes, nor had it negatively impacted the turnout. Kids and guard-ians swarmed every inch of Red Dog Ranch. The sight of all of them smiling and enjoying their day filled Ma-cy's heart to the point of bursting.

Every fight, every miscommunication, every late night had been worth it.

The staff and interns had cleared out the largest field in preparation for the candy drop and local businesses had banded together to set up a carnival complete with games, prizes, snacks, horse rides and a petting zoo on the opposite side of the driveway. The little goats included in the petting zoo were the talkative type, filling the air with their bleats. Buses lined the fenced area in the overflow parking section. Clint Oakfield was stationed near the mess hall for photos and signatures, and Jack Donnelley had the helicopter parked near Sheep and Romeo's enclosure. The helicopter was open so kids could go inside, pretend they were flying it and have their pictures taken. A tent nearby served as a place where kids could paint eggs to take home.

Macy decided it was the most successful Easter event the ranch had ever hosted. Wistfully she wished Brock had lived to see this day. He would have been so proud of Rhett, proud of her too.

A sudden stiff wind tore down through the row of hills lining their property, sending some of the promotional signs flying. Macy jogged after them, gathering up the mess.

"Here's another one." A man in a red shirt handed her one she must have missed.

Macy thanked him and stowed the rest inside the Jarrett house, using the diversion as an excuse to also check on Mrs. Jarrett. Rhett's mom observed the event through the floor-to-ceiling, two-story-high windows in the comfort of her living room. For as long as Macy had known the woman, she had been this way—watchful, perceptive and thoughtful. Alzheimer's might have stolen her ability to make new memories or to recall what year she was currently in, but it hadn't taken the truest things about her. Not yet.

"Ah, there's our dear lady." A smile bloomed on Mrs.

Jarrett's face when she spotted Macy. "Looks like a good turnout despite the forecast."

"Everything is going really well," Macy assured her. "Last I heard, it's not supposed to storm until later."

Mrs. Jarrett gestured toward the large bank of windows. "I know we have you to thank for this day. And don't tell me this was Rhett's doing because I know you've worked so hard, dear. I'm so proud of you." She reached out her hand.

Macy grasped it. "You're too kind. You always know how to bless me with the right words."

"Bless you? Oh, child, you're the one who has always been a blessing to this family. Not the other way around, Macy Howell. You are our blessing. I want you to remember that."

You are our blessing.

Could it be true? Macy had never considered herself a blessing to anyone. A burden. Forgettable. Not enough.

Never a blessing.

But Mrs. Jarrett was not one to say anything carelessly.

"Send Brock inside if it gets bad, will you?" Mrs. Jarrett twisted toward the windows again. She drew a blanket around her shoulders. "His joints are probably already barking at him. All this moisture will do that."

Macy urged the nurse on duty to make sure Mrs. Jarrett had extra opportunities to rest today as all the additional people and excitement could make for a rough night for the older woman.

With the knowledge that Mrs. Jarrett was in great hands, Macy headed back outside and surveyed the party from the large wraparound porch. She rested her hand on the walkie-talkie and considered calling Rhett, but she knew he was busy giving tours of the camper cabins to local businessmen who had expressed interest in potentially partnering with Camp Firefly. He was exactly where he needed to be and she wouldn't distract him.

No matter how badly she wanted to.

The weeks leading up to the event had blurred together in a whirl of planning, running errands and scheduling. Rhett had thrown himself into helping and had even called in favors from past dog-training clients, all of which had made a huge difference. Through his connections the price of the food had been covered, among other things. On top of that, the man had spent every weekend working on last-minute maintenance throughout the ranch, but especially devoting extra time and attention toward getting the camper cabins ready for the summer. Time and again she had stopped by on a Saturday to find him knee-deep in manual labor, sleeves rolled up and covered in sweat…handsomer than ever.

It had warmed Macy's heart to see Rhett finally stepping up to help with the foster programs offered at Red Dog Ranch. He went about it in a different way than his father had, but honestly, Rhett had a better mind for the big picture when it came to planning. Macy had come to really appreciate his input and insight. She had come to rely on him.

Not only that but he had started seeing his dog-training clients again. Only a few for now, but it was progress. She had left information about courses for people who wanted to train therapy dogs on his desk and he had promised to sign up for something in the fall.

While she had loved finally being able to work toward a common goal with him, side by side, and while it had been exhilarating and encouraging striving in tandem to make the event a success in such a short amount of time, Macy couldn't help the lingering feeling of disappointment that occasionally tiptoed into her heart.

What had happened to the romantic man she had enjoyed supper with on the pier weeks ago? Perhaps she had misinterpreted everything that evening, but whenever she replayed it—his warm gazes and tender words, his kind gestures like the cookies—she found herself bewildered all over again.

Despite his many mentions of the word *friend*, that night she had wanted him to kiss her. More than she ever had before. But he hadn't. Even after they left the pier, Rhett had insisted on walking her to her bungalow and she was sure he had a reason other than her safety. It wasn't as if she hadn't walked alone on the ranch's property a million other times. But he had strolled beside her all the way to the pebbled path leading to her bungalow, wished her good-night and walked away.

In the following days she had expected him to offer some sort of clarification, but it seemed that Rhett had clammed up again, at least where she was concerned. Oh, he had completely gone all out helping with the egg hunt and had begun intentionally mentoring Gabe, as well. He was talking about hiring some of the interns on for the summer. Rhett had risen to the occasion. Macy had no complaints there.

But it left her wondering…

He felt something for her, something more than friendship. No one could have convinced Macy otherwise, but something was holding him back.

Jack flagged Macy down. "We're going to move up the candy drop. I don't like the looks of that." He pointed to the black clouds piling up in the distance. "Rhett okayed it, but he said to check with you."

Macy radioed to Cassidy. "How are the hams? About done?"

Her walkie-talkie crackled a second later. "We can plate as soon as twenty minutes."

Macy nodded and Jack jogged toward his helicopter. The interns helped direct the crowd to line up near the marked off portions of the large field and Macy followed in their wake. As was tradition, Rhett's uncle Travis took the stage to rattle off instructions.

The helicopter lifted off, beating the air in huge waves. Macy shivered, but the children cheered. Jack circled the field once, allowing the rest of his onboard crew to get into position along the open sides of the large craft. When Travis sounded the bullhorn the helicopter crew began dropping candy out of the helicopter until the field was colorful with it.

Although raindrops weren't falling at the ranch yet, the sky just beyond their property had turned pitch-black with rain. A storm would rip through Red Dog Ranch within minutes. As Jack's helicopter left the area kids were allowed to converge on the field to fill their bags. Macy wanted to urge everyone to go quickly, but the kids hardly needed to be told.

Macy ran toward Romeo and Sheep's enclosure. "I know neither of you appreciate getting rained on." She attached lead lines to both of their halters and walked them toward the barn. Halfway there, Romeo pinned his ears back and started braying. He planted his hoofs.

"Come on, you goof." Macy tried to coax him with a promise of a treat later. "Let's get you inside and everything will be fine." But the tiny donkey balked.

Rhett appeared beside her, his brow creased with worry. "This storm is bearing down quicker than they predicted." His head swiveled in the direction of the approaching storm. "It looks like a wall of clouds. I can't say I've ever seen anything like it."

Macy tossed the lead lines over her shoulder to free up her hands. She grabbed both animals' halters and used the leverage of all her weight to lean in the opposite direction. "We just need to get people inside."

Rhett pushed Romeo's rear end, getting the donkey moving again. "I'll send everyone to the mess hall."

"You deal with the people and I'll get everything else stowed away," she called after him as he headed to the stage.

Kodiak took off after Rhett, but suddenly stopped and looked back at Macy. She whimpered low in her throat.

Rhett glanced back. "Stay with Macy."

Kodiak charged to join her as Macy fumbled with the lock on the barn.

Rain began to ping off the roofs, the dirt. One second it was sprinkling and before she could open the barn door it was pouring down. Cold water trickled down her spine and her legs.

As she secured Sheep and Romeo in their stalls she heard Rhett on the loudspeakers directing people toward the mess hall. A heartbeat later, a loud crash of thunder had Romeo bucking in his stall. Macy hoped someone had seen to the group of horses that were being used for rides.

Kodiak pressed close to Macy's legs.

"You can stay in here, girl." Macy ran her fingers over the dog's coarse fur. "You'll be safe and dry and don't need to worry about me." Macy made for the door and Kodiak matched her step for step.

"I said stay." Macy made her voice commanding.

Kodiak barked and followed Macy as she plucked one of the shared heavy-duty raincoats from a peg on the wall and made her way outside.

Macy looked down at the dog beside her. "You're just as stubborn as your master, aren't you?"

Kodiak met her eyes and barked again. Her last command from Rhett would be followed to the letter, no matter what Macy told the dog.

Macy tugged the hood of her coat up. "Well, come on then. We've got work to do."

"It's warm inside. And smell that?" Rhett sniffed the air for the benefit of the scared, young kids filing past him. "Nobody makes ham like our cook, Miss Cassidy. And if I were you, I'd snag an extra one of her cheddar-cheese rolls. Believe me." Rhett held the mess hall's front door open until the last person had entered.

Due to the storm, many people had opted to get on the road instead of stay for the meal the ranch always hosted as a fund-raiser afterward. Rhett couldn't blame them for heading out. He prayed they all made it to their destinations safely. It looked as if it was going to be one wicked storm.

He secured the door then shook rain off of his hat. Outside the sky was as dark as midnight despite it only being four in the afternoon. Bright veins of lightning spliced through the black. They lighted up the grounds below the hills for a heartbeat. Rhett frantically scanned the area through the windows along the front porch of the mess hall, looking for any families that might still be out there, but the main fields where they'd held the event were deserted.

The rumble that followed the lightning was immediate and powerful. Inside the mess hall younger kids screamed and ducked their heads under tables.

Rhett lingered in the entryway with his hat still clutched in his hands, waiting for Macy and Kodiak. He wasn't even going to deny that fact. He was fully aware that Macy was smart and capable and did not need him fretting over her because of a thunderstorm.

Yet here he was.

He wouldn't be able to relax until he saw her safe inside.

Rain pelted the building hard. It was as if someone was heaving bucket after bucket of water against their windows. The south pasture near the lake would flood. It always did during bad storms. Thankfully, rain of this magnitude was a rarity. And they had moved the cattle to a different field to get them away from the event, so that wouldn't be an issue.

Wind bent smaller trees sideways. There would be plenty of shingles to fix tomorrow.

Rhett paced the small area and worked his hat around

and around in his hands a few times before he remembered his cell phone. Because of dog training, he was in the habit of keeping the contraption on silent. What if Macy had tried to call? What if she needed him? She had warned him to turn the thing on occasionally.

He tugged his phone from his pocket and his heart leapt when he saw one missed call and a voice mail. He thumbed the screen to unlock it. One missed call from Hank, his lawyer friend, who had started booking training sessions for Riptide again. Hank had already told him that the will was as ironclad as they had originally believed, but Rhett didn't care any longer.

Uncle Travis popped his head into the entryway hallway. "You're needed."

Rhett stopped pacing. "Have you seen Macy or Shannon?" His sister was usually actively involved during events, but he hadn't seen her all day. Hopefully she was in the house with their mom.

His uncle gave Rhett a thoughtful look. "I saw Macy on my way in. She said she was going to gather as much of the setup stuff as she could before the worst of the storm rolled in. Good thing too. Stuff from the games would have ended up all over the ranch with this wind."

Rhett headed toward the door. "She shouldn't be out there alone. I should be helping her."

His uncle snagged his arm. When Rhett looked back to argue, Travis jerked his head toward the speaker system set up at the front of the mess hall. "This shindig always starts with a word from the owner and a prayer. It's tradition."

"But—"

"Macy is a grown woman who knows what she can

handle. You're the owner. These people are your responsibility. You are needed here." Uncle Travis ushered Rhett away from the doorway. "I'll try to get in touch with Shannon if that would ease your mind."

Rhett nodded and tucked his phone away, but he glanced through the front windows one last time. Macy was out there and so was Kodiak. *Keep them safe, Lord. Please watch over them.*

When Rhett stepped into the dining area, a hush fell over the crowd. He dipped his head as he walked. Rhett made eye contact with a few of the children on his way to the front of the room. One little boy flashed him a thumbs-up so Rhett returned the gesture and added a wink for good measure.

The aroma of freshly baked rolls and chocolate cake along with ham and caramelized pineapple drifted through the room. Rhett's mouth watered. Cassidy and her crew of volunteers had spent all day in the kitchen working on the feast. He couldn't wait to taste everything.

The speaker system was used primarily during the summer months for making announcements or telling the campers to simmer down on occasion. They hadn't used it recently and Rhett absently hoped it was still functioning. Rhett picked up the microphone and tapped it twice. It worked just fine.

"Good afternoon and thank you for braving the storm for this event," Rhett started. He hadn't planned anything to say. In truth, he had forgotten about the little spiel his dad had always given. Brock's talk had lasted a few minutes, a sermon of sorts. Often it included the salvation message.

Rhett let his focus slowly trip across everyone in the room. So many kids and all of them either waiting for a permanent home or waiting for their homes to become a safe place for them once again. Seeing so many of them in front of him, it tore at his heart. After visiting with them all day and seeing their hopeful faces, now Rhett knew that he wanted to help them to continue to be the legacy of Red Dog Ranch.

No matter what, he would choose these kids. This life. This place.

The legacy not only his dad had secured for him, but God too.

He would figure out a way to keep all the programs, turn a profit at the ranch and still train dogs on the side. With Travis, Macy, Cassidy, Shannon and many others—there were plenty of them to divide the work between. Together they would make it a success.

For the first time in what felt like years, Rhett finally understood his dad's passion and drive and he wanted to lay down all his past hurts to honor all his dad had built.

Rhett blinked against the sudden rush of emotions. "I know many of you must have wondered what would happen to Red Dog Ranch after my father passed." He found Uncle Travis in the room and for a heartbeat he pictured Brock there too, beaming and happy. Though this wasn't for his dad any longer; it was for Rhett. "A wise man once asked me if I knew the heart of God when it came to this place and I'm ashamed to admit I brushed his challenge off. But God has this funny way of not letting us forget something like that."

A loud rumble of thunder shook the building and the lights browned out for a few seconds. People in the crowd murmured worriedly. He needed to keep this short and sweet.

Rhett began to walk between the tables as he spoke. "How do we know the heart of God?"

"The Bible!" a little girl called out.

Rhett pointed her way. "Great answer. The Bible shows us God's heart. And what are we celebrating today?"

"Easter!" This time a chorus of kids joined in.

"That's right, Easter. The greatest showing of God's heart for this world. Our heavenly Father loves us so much that He wanted to make a way for us to never be parted from Him. He loves us enough to sacrifice His son so that we can have a relationship with Him." Rhett headed back to the front of the room. "So back to my friend's question—do I know the heart of God in this matter? Yes, well, yes I do. The heart of God, the answer to every question concerning what I should do—what each of us should do in our lives—is love. In any situation we have to ask ourselves, 'What is the loving thing to do?' Then we have our answer."

Cassidy stood near the pass-through, ready to hand out the food. Rhett caught her wiping a tear away.

"My father left behind a legacy of love and I mean to continue it."

The dining hall erupted with cheers and applause. A man seated nearby got to his feet and threw his arms around Rhett in an awkward hug. Clearly Macy hadn't been the only person worried about how Rhett would run Red Dog Ranch.

"How about we say a prayer and then dig in to this food?" Rhett smiled at the crowd. "It smells amazing."

But before Rhett could bow his head Jack Donnelley slammed open the side door so loudly it caused people at nearby tables to jump out of their seats. Jack rushed toward Rhett with the intensity of a bomb-sniffing dog on patrol.

Jack reached Rhett, phone in hand. "My dispatch center just called. Tornado warning. It's touched down less than a mile away. It could be on us in minutes, maybe less." Jack's police training showed as he calmly delivered the information. "We need to get people to safety."

Hands shaking, Rhett got back on the microphone. "Change of plans. We're under a tornado warning. I need everyone to proceed in a single-file line down to the basement."

A few people yelled and more started to cry, but everyone got to their feet quickly and headed toward one of the sets of stairs. Thankfully, there were plenty of adults to help guide the children. Jack, Uncle Travis and Rhett each manned the top of one of the three entrances to the basement, directing people to go down and as far back as they could.

Rhett sent Macy a text:

Tornado. Get inside.

He almost typed I love you but wasn't that something that should be said first instead of texted? He loved Macy. The last few weeks had cemented that truth and thinking of her outside in the storm… All the road-blocks he had imagined between them suddenly felt insignificant. He had made peace with his father and let go of his pain and had done all he could to care for his mother. Besides, if he waited to act on his feelings until everything in his life was perfect the time would never come.

Fear had made excuses easy to believe, but he refused to chart his steps by fear any longer. Next time he saw her he would tell her how he felt. She might reject him, but he would deal with it if she did.

But a text stole some of the power away from declaring love. Then again, what if he never got the chance to tell her? What if...

He refused to think like that.

Cassidy had immediately whisked Piper to the basement and Rhett could hear her instructing people to get on their knees and cover their necks.

Keep people safe, Lord. Please protect all these people.

Maybe the tornado would miss the ranch. Maybe it would change course.

The building started to rattle under an onslaught of wind. Rhett instructed people to head down the steps a little quicker. They were almost done. Almost everyone now.

With his phone in his hand, Rhett willed Macy to call him. To tell him she was fine, tucked away somewhere safe. But he couldn't think only of her either. Other people depended on him. Rhett pulled up the number for the phone his mother's on-duty nurse carried and hit Call.

He didn't even let her greet him. "A tornado's touched down. It's close. Get to the lower interior bathroom. Put Mom in the tub. Grab pillows, blankets—anything to protect yourselves. Stay in there until one of us comes to get you guys."

"Understood." The nurse hung up.

Rhett's mind raced. His ears popped, more painfully than on any flight he had ever been on. The deep sink he was standing near gurgled and then the drain made one long, desperate suctioning sound. Rhett hurtled down the steps to join the others in the basement.

While Northern Texas experienced a fair amount of tornados, they were far less common in the hill country. And with Red Dog Ranch so far away from any of the local towns, he had never even heard a siren before and it wasn't as if they had their own alert system.

Tornados happened, but in thirty years Rhett had never seen one, never been in one.

The deafening howl outside told him that was about to change.

Chapter Ten

Even though she was wearing a heavy coat the rain started to pelt Macy so hard it physically hurt to be outside anymore. And it was cold. Horribly, painfully cold now.

The rain suddenly switched to falling sideways. Dime-sized hail clanged on a nearby roof, coming closer, peppering the ground.

Macy's teeth rattled and her legs trembled as she made her way through a patch of mud. She would catch a cold from this adventure; there was zero doubt in her mind about that. She should have headed inside ten minutes ago—should have gone in with everyone else instead of trying to be useful.

Macy turned to head toward the barn. It was a smelly place to ride out the weather, but it was near and would provide adequate shelter from the wind and wetness. A pole barn full of machinery and the Jarretts' ranch house were also within proximity, but both were farther than the solid oak barn where Romeo, Sheep and the other horses were kept.

When hail was part of the equation, Macy would choose close over comfort.

However, she couldn't make out the barn any longer. Darkness disoriented her. It was as if her eyes were closed. Macy pivoted a full 360 degrees, scanning the area, squinting, but it was no use. She couldn't even tell if she was facing in the correct direction any longer.

Dread pooled like a cooling ball of lead in the pit of her stomach. Weighty. Impossible to escape.

Kodiak rubbed against her leg and Macy steadied herself with a hand on the dog's shoulder. Kodiak's body shuddered under her fingers. Macy winced as her ears suddenly popped with an excruciating and sudden change in pressure.

Then she heard it.

A roar.

The sound of a train engine but louder. It vibrated through her whole body, her bones.

Tornado.

The wall of rain clouds had hidden a tornado.

An angry churning funnel headed directly toward the barn Macy had wanted to seek shelter in only moments ago. If the tornado stayed its course the horse barn would take a direct hit. The rest of the horses were in the pasture so they had the ability to get out of the way, but Sheep and Romeo were inside the building. And there was no time to set them loose; she wouldn't be able to make it. Macy's heart slammed into the back of her throat and sickness washed over her. If something happened to them, she had put them in there. She would be at fault.

But she couldn't think about that right now. Macy had to get to safety.

Go. Move. Get out of here.

A tiny piece of debris slammed into Macy's arm and she cried out as if she had been shot. Warmth seeped over the area. Hot and burning. Blood.

Macy grabbed for Kodiak's collar and yanked her toward the ranch house. "Run! We have to run."

She took off toward the house, knowing Rhett's faithful dog would stick close. She could do this. She could protect them. She could beat this storm.

Faster. Go. Faster.

Her legs burned. She slipped in deep mud and fell onto all fours. Her hands suctioned into the mire. Kodiak shoved her head under Macy's chest as if the dog was trying to lift her up. Macy scrambled forward on all fours, trying to get purchase.

Winds ripped a long swatch of fencing up out of the ground with a sickening crunch and tossed it in a tangled heap only yards away. A huge old tree snapped and took flight.

Wood from the horse barn began to splinter. The barn walls buckled and heaved behind her. Macy looked back to see the roof fly off and go up into the sky as if it weighed nothing. Gone.

Gathering additional debris, the funnel grew darker, larger. Its furious howl filled her ears until it was all she could hear, all she could think about.

She found her feet again and started for the ranch house. If she ran fast enough, she could still make it. She could skid inside and go under the huge, heavy table in their formal dining room. The room had no windows and sat almost in the center of the home, next to their interior bathroom where hopefully Rhett's mom was by now.

Macy was close enough. She would make it. Everything would be okay. It had to be. God hadn't brought them this far just to—

Kodiak's high-pitched yelp brought Macy up short. She whirled around to see Rhett's dog on the ground ten feet behind her with a large sheet of metal pinning her back half to the ground. Kodiak's front paws dug forward in an effort to pull herself out, but it was no use. Kodiak collapsed, her yellow eyes seeking out Macy.

If Macy kept moving she could make it to shelter in time, but she would have to leave Rhett's dog behind.

Not going to happen.

Macy plunged back toward the storm. Stiff winds sent rocks and other debris hurtling around her. Something scraped the side of her face. She pressed on. She dropped to her knees beside Kodiak. "It's okay, girl." Macy wrapped her fingers around the edge of the sheet of roofing. "I won't leave you."

She heaved the piece of metal with all her might. It was heavy and awkward. Her back spasmed, her biceps felt as if they were being shredded and her legs shook. Under normal circumstances Macy couldn't have budged the thing with only her strength. Macy grunted, putting all her weight into it, and was able to lift the debris enough for Kodiak to army crawl out of the opening.

Another loud, nauseating groan and the pole barn shattered like a child's art project constructed out of toothpicks. Large sections crashed onto the ground around them. That building was full of machinery—heavy metal and steel machinery that the tornado would toss around like confetti. Macy threw her body over Kodiak and braced her arms over her own neck and head.

They would never make it to the house now.

Get to the lowest point.

It was the only thing she could remember about tornados. Since all the structures that could protect them were too far away, they had to get over the hill to the lower area near Canoe Landing. Doing so might take them out of the path entirely. Macy hoisted Kodiak to her paws.

"Please be able to stand."

Kodiak had to be sixty to seventy pounds so there was little chance that Macy could carry her too far. The dog limped but kept up with her. They rushed down the hill, skidding and sliding their way down. Macy's arm and cheek stung like fire.

The lake was full of junk the tornado had tossed around and the shores were littered, as well. Macy grabbed a large piece of wood that must have been torn from the horse barn and wedged it up so they could get into the ditch under it. At least the board would deflect smaller debris. She reached back and hauled Kodiak to the lowest point, this ditch that fed into the lake, just as the winds increased and the funnel twitched toward them. Macy wiggled into the small space so she was lying across Rhett's dog, then she pulled the wood up over them and prayed.

Kodiak burrowed her muzzle into Macy's neck so her nose was beside Macy's ear. The noise of the dog's steady breathing mixed with the sounds of destruction above them. Macy braced her arms tighter over their heads and slammed her eyes shut as if that would help.

"I'm here, sweet girl," Macy whispered.

Was this it? After everything, was this how her life ended?

Facing the possibility of death, Macy's mind raced back through twenty-eight years of life. Her father leaving, her mother's death, being all alone at only eighteen. The last ten years living with the Jarretts and her friendship with Rhett. The work she had done at the ranch and the lives she had come into contact with because of Brock's mission. Late nights spent giggling with Shannon and Cassidy. Quiet moments with Mrs. Jarrett.

Her evening on the pier with Rhett.

Macy had never felt truly loved and accepted in her life. She had always believed there was something defective about her. Some reason why no one wanted to commit. Why no one stayed.

But…it had always been a lie, hadn't it?

You're the one who has always been a blessing to this family. Not the other way around, Macy Howell. You are our blessing.

The Jarretts had welcomed and loved her as is. Shannon and Cassidy had become sisters to her. Macy had a place to belong—people who would miss her and mourn for her if this was her end. They hadn't loved her for all the late nights she'd spent in the office or the weekends she'd pitched in with the animals or the programs she had helped launch. It hadn't mattered what she had done or accomplished.

They had just loved…her.

Macy had always been enough, just as she was.

Tears stung her eyes; they leaked onto Kodiak's fur.

She had treated God the same way, hadn't she? Always trying to do enough and accomplish more so she would feel as if she deserved His love.

What an absurd way to live. She had no more power or ability to earn God's love than she had to stop this tornado. The might of the terrible tornado paled in comparison to an almighty God—and He loved her. He had sent His son to die for her.

"Forgive me," she whispered. "I love You. Thank You for loving me. If…if this is when I meet You, I'm ready. Just please take care of all these people. I love them so much. Take care of Rhett."

She prayed the mess hall would be untouched.

Something large slammed into the side of the building and the lights flickered. Someone in the basement wailed uncontrollably.

Seconds after Rhett's boots hit the basement's concrete floor the whole building plunged into darkness. Kids screamed and the soothing voices of many adults followed. Not wanting to step on anyone, Rhett fumbled around. His hand glanced against the doorknob on the door that led to the walk out where trucks made deliveries. It was a sturdy door, but in the end it was only wood.

Not good.

A tornado could wrench that door open and suck people out. He was suddenly very thankful for his dad's foresight in insisting on an unconventional basement being built at the ranch, but the first thing Rhett would do was make this entrance more secure.

If he made it out.

Rhett braced his back against the door as if that might help and then he groped for the lock, found it and slipped it into the locked position. The small bolt probably wouldn't help much, but Rhett was willing to take every measure he had at his disposal to protect all the people gathered at his ranch.

His ranch.

Not his dad's. Not Brock's mission or dreams.

Rhett's.

All the glass windows upstairs shattered. It sounded like a series of rapid bombs going off in a war zone. The building started violently shaking and the door behind him vibrated like a jackhammer.

The tornado was passing over them.

Please, Lord, please. I don't care what happens to me but protect these people. Protect Macy and Kodiak and the rest of my family.

Metal rattled and crashed in the kitchen above them. If there was a person screaming a foot away from him, Rhett wouldn't have been able to tell. He could only hear the storm—there was only the tornado and it was all encompassing.

The walls of the building creaked and popped, moaning under the storm's violent onslaught. Something boomed against the door. It sounded like someone was smacking it with a huge metal chain. The bottom corner peeled back with such sudden force Rhett gasped. Wind lashed in. Just as quickly, tiny debris shoved through the crack in the door frame—nails and wood and a mess of other items—until the small opening was plugged.

Then there was nothing. No wind, no pounding. Rhett could hear his heartbeat reverberating in his ears.

"Is it…" a tentative voice said nearby. "Do we think it's over?"

"Gabe?" Rhett reached toward the voice.

Gabe grabbed his arm. "It's me, Mr. Jarrett."

Rhett yanked the teenage boy into a bear hug. "We're safe. I think it's over." He lifted his head away from Gabe's. "Jack? You nearby?"

Jack's face became illuminated by his phone. "It's dissipated." Jack turned toward the expanse that was the long dark basement. "It looks like the tornado is done but everyone needs to stay put. I know it's uncomfortable in here and not fun to stay with the lights out, but this is the safest place."

Gabe shuffled his feet. "But I thought you said it was all done?"

Jack inclined his head. He fiddled with something on his phone that kept it illuminated. "It is, but the aftermath can be just as dangerous as the storm itself. Downed power lines and sharp objects everywhere. It's not safe to send everyone out yet." He typed into his phone. "EMS is on the way." He turned toward Rhett. "I'm heading out to assess. You're welcome to join me."

Rhett had pulled out his phone but couldn't get a signal. "My phone's not working." There was no message from Macy. No calls from his mom or Shannon.

Jack held up his phone. "Department phone. I'm connected to a different system. Normal cell infrastructures will be bogged down for the next few hours." Jack stepped toward the door. "Are you coming or staying?"

Rhett looked back into the darkness that held all the people who had come to the ranch expecting a fun day. He had a duty to take care of them, but he also needed to check on his mom and he needed to find Macy, Kodiak and Shannon. In the rush Rhett hadn't been able to touch base with Uncle Travis to see if he had made contact with Shannon.

"Found it," broke in a voice and then a flashlight came on. Cassidy held it, with Piper beside her. "Go, Rhett. We'll take care of everyone here."

Clint Oakfield appeared nearby. "She's right." He sent Cassidy a tentative grin. "We'll take it from here. For as long as you need." He clasped Rhett's shoulder. "You go do what you need to do."

Rhett and Jack shouldered the door open and light spilled in. Clint stacked a few milk crates together to form a makeshift bench for him and Cassidy, then as Rhett and Jack left they heard the country entertainer sing the first few notes of "Amazing Grace" while a chorus of voices joined in.

Emotion clogged Rhett's throat as he stepped clear of the mess hall and surveyed the terrible destruction across the ranch below him. The sky was still menacing, gloomy with a thick fog spreading into the lower sections of his land, but he could see plenty clear enough to know that Red Dog Ranch would never be the same again.

There was a mess of splinters where once there was a row of ten camper cabins. Hunks of steel hung from the trees they passed while other trees were shaved down to only gnarly bent trunks. One of their largest tractors lay on its side in what used to be the horse pasture. Where had that thing been parked beforehand? Nowhere near where it rested now. A bus had been tossed into the office building and cars that had been parked along the driveway were totaled—on their roof or sides, all windows blown out, frames twisted into odd angles.

"It's pretty messed up, huh?" Gabe's voice made Rhett whirl around.

"What are you doing here? You should be back in the basement."

Gabe crossed his arms over his chest. "You'll need help finding Miss Macy. I want to help. Besides, Cassidy said I could go with you."

Rhett considered arguing with the teenager but Jack broke in. "Stick close. Don't wander anywhere without either me or Rhett. Understood?"

"Understood." Gabe nodded. "I'll be like a shadow."

Rhett, Gabe and Jack picked their way carefully down the hill, stepping over tree limbs and other materials Rhett couldn't make sense of at the moment.

Seeing his ranch ripped to pieces made Rhett's eyes burn. Both of the barns were completely gone. He had no idea how his animals had fared. Did he still have cattle? Horses? The mess hall was still standing but a portion of the roof was gone. The Jarrett family home looked like it had managed to stay together.

Thank You, God.

Rhett began to move a little faster.

Jack kept pace with him. "I'm so sorry."

Rhett swallowed around the lump in his throat. Once, twice, three times before he could speak. "I, ah, for a long time I really didn't like this place." Hot shame poured through his chest but he pressed on. "My father…"

Jack stopped and set a hand on Rhett's shoulder, pulling Rhett to a stop. "He loved you, but he never said it. His heart was divided between his family and the ranch. I know."

Rhett nodded. "But I love this place." He gazed out over the absolute destruction in front of him. "I love— but I realized it all too late. Why am I always one step behind?"

A theme in his life. Too late to say goodbye to his father. Too late to stop Wade from taking off and ultimately getting killed.

Would he always be one step behind in his life? Doomed to not realize or appreciate all he had been blessed with? He truly was as bullheaded as people said. Why hadn't he been grateful about his inheritance? Sprung to action immediately to help kids. *Kids.* How had he missed every clue Macy no doubt dropped about her feelings earlier in their relationship?

Jack's even voice broke through his thoughts. "It's never too late. As long as you've got breath, don't let anyone—even your own stubborn self—tell you it's too late." Jack jutted his chin toward the ranch house. "You guys go check on your mom first. I'm going to head down the main road and do my best to clear a path so the emergency vehicles can get as close as possible."

"Should we come help you?" Rhett felt torn. He wanted to do the right thing, but fear for his loved ones was eating at him.

Jack held up his hand. "You worry about your family. I'll deal with this. A crew will be here to help in no time. We'll do all we can to search for survivors and secure your area. From the looks of it, Red Dog Ranch took the brunt of this storm."

"Thank you, Jack." Rhett owed the man so much

more than a thank-you. He owed him an apology too. "I've never been much of a friend to you and I wish—"

Jack shook his head. "No more worries, man. Seriously. Just take care of this place. It means a lot to me."

"Me too," Rhett said and meant it.

Rhett hadn't yet made it to the steps leading up to the porch when the front door pounded open and Shannon jogged out.

"Rhett!" She was down the steps in seconds and launched herself at him. Breath whooshed out of his lungs as he tried to keep his feet and catch her at the same time.

"I'm so sorry." Her body shook with tears. Her blond curls were wild. "If something had happened to you..." She dug her fingers into his shoulders. "If you had... I've been so cruel these past few weeks. We fought and—" her voice broke "—I've been—"

"Hey," he said tenderly and set her back so he could see his sister's face. "I love you, kid. I'm glad you're safe."

Her face twisted and she started crying harder. "I l-love you t-too. I'm sorry for—"

"Shh." He leaned forward, pressing a kiss to her forehead. "All that's forgiven and forgotten. I should have been there for you more than I've been in the past. I will be. That's a promise."

She swiped at her eyes.

"Mom?" Rhett asked.

"She's scared and confused and keeps asking about Dad, but she's fine. The nurse too. We rode it out in the bathroom," Shannon said. Her eyes went wide. "The family room though—the wall of windows is gone and there's a small tree in there. But other than that the house looks okay. Out here?" She groaned.

"Macy and Kodiak?"

Shannon's focus snapped back to him and she shook her head. "Macy wasn't with you?" Her brow scrunched. "I just assumed. They're both always with you."

"They weren't with me." The words hurt.

He should have made Macy come inside. He should have never nodded along when she said she was going to clean up the event. He had unknowingly sent Kodiak into the heart of a storm. If something had happened to either of them because of things, because of material, replaceable stuff...

Jaw involuntarily clenching, Rhett fisted his hands. "I have to find her."

God, let them be alive. Let them be all right. Help me find them.

Chapter Eleven

Macy couldn't tell how much time had passed since the storm had ended, but it had stopped just as suddenly as it had begun. One second the gusts were trying to tear the sheet of wood off of them and the next all was still. Quiet.

She tried to bend to reach the phone tucked into the back pocket of her jeans, but her arms were pinned in front of her body and she couldn't make out the watch on her wrist even though it was inches from her face.

Was it night already? Was anyone looking for them?

A few birds tittered and somewhere nearby a group of cattle bellowed back and forth to one another. Each sound filled Macy with an almost irrational amount of joy because both noises spoke of hope to her. She had witnessed the horse barn and the pole barn being annihilated, but maybe, just maybe, that was the total loss to the ranch. Maybe all of the cattle and horses were fine. Maybe even now Sheep and Romeo were grazing in one of the pastures as if nothing was wrong.

She squeezed her eyes shut. She couldn't think about

the little horse and donkey. Couldn't let her mind go there. As long as she was under the board and couldn't see the totality of destruction, she had hope. She needed to cling to it.

However, no matter how hard she tried to be positive, it was almost impossible to chase all her unconstructive thoughts away.

What if no one came to free them because no one else had survived? What if she and Kodiak had lived through the tornado's assault only to be trapped under rubble, unable to get free? What if they survived the tornado but died because they were trapped in the aftermath?

Macy's heartbeat hammered in her neck and her temples. Her head pounded. A few tears escaped from her closely shuttered eyes.

Stop.

Thoughts along those lines would help no one. Least of all her.

Stay calm. Keep a clear head. Just keep breathing.

Macy could wiggle her toes, her feet. It was dark and muggy, but she could breathe. The only thing she couldn't do was lift the piece of wood from off of her and Kodiak. While originally the door-sized plank hadn't been very heavy, debris had obviously piled up on top of them to the point that Macy wasn't strong enough to push the covering up enough for them to shimmy out.

Maybe if she rested a bit?

God, I know You see us. I know You care. Please, be with me and Kodiak. Help us feel like we're not completely alone.

Her whole body ached and her muscles burned. Rain and mud had soaked her clothes, and her hair was completely waterlogged. A tremor worked its way through her body. Something substantial and sharp pressed against her left ankle. Kodiak let out a low whimper right before her warm tongue traced up the side of Macy's face, ending at her ear.

What would she have done without Rhett's dog along for comfort and company? Macy would be far more panicked without the warm fluff of Kodiak beside her.

"We made it." Macy nuzzled the dog. "Now we just have to get out of here."

As if her words had stirred the dog to action, Kodiak started wiggling. In an effort to get up, the dog's paw came up and scratched down Macy's arm.

"Ouch. Settle down," Macy commanded her. "You did so well. Just a little longer."

But Kodiak tried to switch positions again. She let out a series of whines and then barked. Macy hushed her, but Rhett's dog continued barking loudly. Her hot breath made the already cramped space feel tight and damp. Macy was about to tell the dog to zip it again when a noise above them caused her to still. Items were being moved. Things were shifting off of their board.

Someone was up there.

"Macy!" Rhett yelled and the desperation in his voice made Macy's heart twist. "Mace, are you there? Dear Lord, please let her be okay. Let me find her. Let her be here."

Macy tried to say something, but her voice was so raw there was no way he heard her. She cleared her throat, trying again. "I'm here. Help! We're under here."

"Thank You, God." Rhett sounded close to tears. "You can breathe? You're all right?"

"I think so."

"Don't move. Let us lift the worst of this away." More stuff shifted above them. "I'm here, Mace. I won't leave until I leave with you in my arms. You have my word."

Kodiak barked frantically again.

Macy grew antsy. Now that she knew rescue was close she felt like she wanted to crawl out of her skin. She didn't want to wait. Couldn't wait. She was too closed in. She wanted to shove the board off of them and never see this ditch again. But she knew Rhett was right. She had no idea what kind of mess was piled above them. There could be live wires for all she knew. There could be a car precariously balanced over them.

I won't leave until I leave with you in my arms.

After what seemed like an eternity but was probably more along the line of minutes, light broke over Macy's face as the board was finally lifted away. Macy spotted Gabe first and while she was happy to see that the teenager was okay, she wanted to find Rhett's bright blues. She groaned, blinking hard, and took a shuddering breath.

Rhett was at her side in a heartbeat. "You have no idea. I thought—I feared—" He placed a hand on the small of her back as he assisted her with sitting up. "I've never been happier to see someone in my whole life."

Her lungs ached. Macy coughed a few times. "I heard you praying."

Rhett smiled gently. "I do that now."

Macy turned to say something more but Kodiak chose that moment to lurch toward Rhett so she could cover every inch of his face and neck with happy dog kisses. She whined and then licked, whined and then licked. Her whole body trembling.

Rhett's laugh was pure joy. A tear slipped down his cheek as he kissed the top of Kodiak's head. "Good girl. You are such a good girl, Kodiak. You heard my whistle, didn't you? You barked so well. That's how we found you."

Kodiak inched closer to Rhett and then let out one sharp yelp. Rhett's eyes went wide.

Macy sucked in another shuddering breath. "She's hurt. It's one of her back legs, I think."

Rhett's eyes found hers.

"Rubble fell on her. She was pinned."

Rhett's blue gaze raked over Macy's face, her body. "You're hurt too." He lightly touched her face. "You're covered in blood."

"I'm okay." Macy smiled despite the situation. "I love you, Rhett Jarrett. I don't want another second to go by without saying that. I've loved you—"

Rhett's mouth was on hers before she could finish. He kissed her lightly, tenderly, as if he was afraid anything more would break her. But Macy needed more. She fisted her hands into his shirt and yanked him closer. Rhett's hat slid off his head as they deepened their kiss. Macy had almost died today, but this kiss? This kiss was life and air and love and acceptance—everything she'd ever wanted. She was caked in mud, blood and sweat. She was soaked through but none of it mattered.

Macy let go of Rhett's shirt so she could wrap her arms around his neck. She loved this man. She wanted to stay in his arms forever.

The sound of someone *loudly* clearing their throat finally broke them apart.

Gabe smirked at them. "I'm sorry to interrupt y'all but…" He shrugged and held Rhett's hat out to them.

Rhett accepted his hat but kept his other arm firmly around Macy's back, supporting her. He shoved his hat onto his head and then slipped his hand under her knees. With Macy snug in his arms he got to his feet. He looked over at Gabe, who was still smiling wickedly at them. "Think you're strong enough to carry Kodiak back to the house?"

Gabe rolled his eyes. "Mr. Jarrett, I don't 'think'— I *know*."

Macy rested her hand on Rhett's chest to get his attention. "I can walk."

Rhett's arms tightened. "I'm not letting you go." He looked back at Gabe. "She tolerates a fireman's carry well. Do you know what that is? Over the shoulders?"

Gabe dropped to his knees and helped Kodiak get positioned around his neck.

"Lift with your knees," Rhett instructed.

Kodiak's brow wrinkled and she looked over at Rhett and Macy as if she wanted to ask them if they were really going to allow this kid to do this to her, but Gabe rose with minimal wobbling and headed up the hill in the direction of the house.

When they were alone Macy studied Rhett's face. She wanted to scrub away the worried crease in his brow. He noticed she was staring and cocked an eyebrow.

"You found me," she said. She wrapped an arm more securely around his neck.

"I was so scared," he confessed in a small voice.

"It was like our old hide-and-seek days."

His arms tightened. "I would have never stopped looking for you. I would have turned over every piece of rubble, searched in every place until I had you in my arms."

She tried to make light of it all, cheer him up. "Well, you won this round."

"Kodiak helped." Rhett took the hill slower. His gaze swept over Macy again. "I'm worried about this blood. Tell me what hurts."

"I'm alive, Rhett." Her laugh had a raw edge to it. Tiredness will do that. "What does it matter?"

Rhett stopped at the top of the hill and set her down on a wooden stool that must have been blown there from one of the barns.

He cupped her face in both his hands. "It matters because I love you. Everything about you matters to me. Every single thing." The muscle in his jaw popped. "When I thought... When I didn't know... When I couldn't find you..." He pressed his forehead to hers and took a long, slow breath. "I was such a fool not to say something sooner. Not to *do* something. I thought I had time. I thought we had time." He eased back again and brushed the hair out of her face that had fallen from her ponytail. "I love you so much, Macy. I'll spend the rest of my life trying to show you how much."

"Rhett." Her voice was barely a whisper. She was entirely overcome by the strength of his words.

"Now tell me what's hurt," he said.

He picked her back up and she told him about the projectile hitting her arm and the scratch on her face. "Other than that I think I'm just really sore."

Rhett had to step over wreckage all the way back to the house. Tears freely flowed down Macy's cheeks. Red Dog Ranch was completely destroyed. Finally unable emotionally to face the destruction any longer, Macy buried her face in Rhett's neck.

"It's all gone," she whispered. "Everything's gone."

She felt the muscles in his arms flex.

"Everything that matters made it," he murmured against her hair.

In the days after the tornado Rhett spent most of his time managing the cleanup effort. He kept a running list of things that needed to be replaced and repaired. The handwritten list currently covered ten pages, front and back. And it kept growing.

Jack Donnelley examined the two-story-tall, boarded-up wall of the family room. "New windows coming this weekend?"

Rhett finished his tea and set the mug in the sink. "Yes, thankfully. It's a cave in here without them."

Jack crossed his arms. "Have you decided what to do about the rest of the property? All the cabins?"

Rhett pinched the bridge of his nose. "Honestly? I have no idea."

"Take it one day at a time," Jack said. "And no matter what you decide, my family and I will be here to support you."

"Even if I did away with Camp Firefly?" Rhett didn't know why he had tossed the question out there. Jack had come to know God because of Camp Firefly. The program meant the world to him. Of course he would want Rhett to reinstate it. But the cabins had been leveled and he'd been told it could take months for the insurance money to come through. So unless someone dropped a bundle of money and a crew of hundreds of workers on their doorstep, the ranch wouldn't be ready to host visitors for a long time.

Summer was only six weeks away.

"Like I said." Jack pulled on the gloves he wore to sift through rubble. The man had been stopping by in his off-hours to volunteer. "Whatever you decide, we care about your family, Rhett. You Jarretts might as well be cousins as far as I'm concerned. I want whatever is best for you guys and only you can make that decision."

Rhett thanked Jack before he headed outside, and not for the first time Rhett regretted how he had treated the man in the past. Jack had proved to be an invaluable help and an even better friend. Because of the man's position with the Texas Department of Public Safety he was able to schedule relief workers, and since Red Dog Ranch had been the hardest hit out of anywhere, many of the volunteers were being diverted to them. Jack had been instrumental in coordinating transportation, food and lodging on the day of the tornado for all the remaining guests who had attended the fund-raising supper. He had also opened his house to Shannon and Rhett's mom for the time being. Rhett had chosen to stay in his family's house while the work was being done.

Lives had been lost in the tornado, but none of the casualties had occurred at Red Dog Ranch. It was something Rhett found himself thanking God for multiple times a day. The morning after the storm they had held an impromptu church service in the small chapel near the mess hall, which had made it through the tornado completely unscathed. Rhett and the staff had sung worship songs together and had prayed and thanked God for His protection.

Rhett's property was mostly totaled, seven of his

horses were missing, and at least an eighth of his cattle had perished, but Macy's arm wound and a ranch hand with a broken leg had been the worst of their injuries. Much to Piper's dismay no one had been able to locate Sheep and Romeo, which Rhett knew Macy felt terrible about, but they hadn't found their bodies yet either so Rhett kept reminding both of them that there was hope.

When Rhett finally decided to go into the office and assess the damages there, Kodiak tried to limp beside him, but the full cast on her back leg slowed her down considerably. Rhett sighed. He felt sorry for her. She couldn't go in the water, couldn't play fetch, couldn't do any of the things that she loved.

"Ah, ah, you." Rhett picked his dog up and carried her back to the front porch of the family home. "I know it eats you up, but you have to stay off that leg. Don't look at me with those sad eyes. Doctor's orders." He set her gently on the large dog bed he had hauled out there for her minutes ago.

Kodiak harrumphed loudly but she laid her head down.

"Stay," Rhett commanded her. She had undergone surgery the night of the tornado and had had her back leg casted. Rhett had spent the night with her at the emergency vet clinic and hadn't slept a wink.

He still felt drained but he wasn't sure if it was from not enough sleep or all the stress. More than likely it was a hefty mix of the two.

Rhett had worked fourteen-to sixteen-hour days since the storm and during that time he had put off going to the office. He had told himself it was because there were plenty of other physical needs to attend to. Why should he spend time in the books when there were things to fix and repair? The office had been unreachable for the first forty-eight hours due to the fact that the tornado had seen fit to redecorate the building by dropping a bus on the front half of it. Rhett hadn't been allowed in there until someone from the city had approved the structure.

They had done so yesterday morning but Rhett had found other tasks to keep him busy.

In truth, he had avoided it because it had been his father's domain and Rhett had faced so many losses and setbacks, he wasn't sure he could handle seeing the rest of his father's possessions destroyed.

But it was time.

The bus had smashed into Macy's section of the office so Rhett approached the back door, which led directly into his study. It was the door Macy had admonished him for sneaking out through that first night. Rhett sucked in a deep breath and then eased the door open. He was instantly hit with a strong musty scent. His dad's books were scattered all over the room. The large desk was still in its place and for some reason that was enough to coax Rhett the rest of the way into the space. There was plenty of water damage from a large gap in the wall near the roof. Most of his dad's papers were shot.

Rhett's throat burned as he assessed the area.

Each smashed book, every scattered page and broken picture frame felt like another piece of his dad being taken away. He hadn't mourned his father properly when he passed, but Rhett let the full impact of his death rest on him now as he stood in his father's demolished office.

His dad was gone. The thought hollowed him out just as much as the first time he had thought those words.

Brock had been gone for more than a month, but knowing and accepting were two very different processes. Rhett would rebuild, but he would make it his own. The traces that had made it feel as if Brock was simply gone on an errand and would return later—all of that was gone.

On the other side of the room the painting his mom had created of a herd of longhorns hung half off the wall, and there was another gaping hole in the wood paneling behind it. His mom had given the painting to his father as a Valentine's day gift and Brock had cherished the thing. When Rhett still called Red Dog Ranch home not a week had elapsed without Brock gesturing at the painting and saying something like, "Look at that picture, my boy. That right there, it holds the secret to the most important thing in my life." Rhett had always assumed his dad meant his wife. Marriage.

Rhett made his way across the room to adjust the painting but the hook was gone. In fact… He lifted the painting away and balanced it on a chair to keep it away from the water. There was something behind the painting. What looked like a small fireproof chamber was built into the wall, perfectly concealed behind the painting. He pulled on the small handle and the door swung open to reveal a shoebox tucked inside. Rhett drew the box out.

Heart pounding, he carried it to the desk and sat down. He opened the lid and the contents made his fingers shake as he tried to make sense of what was inside. A little stuffed red dog that was somehow familiar even though Rhett couldn't remember ever seeing it before. And paperwork. An adoption certificate with his name and the names Brock and Leah Jarrett. His parents.

But it didn't make sense.

Rhett dug into the box again and found pictures. A baby in a blue onesie sleeping next to the red stuffed dog. A baby laughing while he clutched the little red stuffed animal. He carefully flipped each one over and, sure enough, someone had written the dates on the backs. The pictures were of him. There were more papers in the box but Rhett didn't know if he could handle what he might find. He braced an elbow on either side of the box, pressed a hand to each of his temples and stared at the contents. Spots flashed in his vision. He felt like a fish that had just been torn from the water and was left gasping for air.

Brock and Leah weren't his biological parents.

Rhett's head pounded.

The back door to his office creaked on its hinges.

"Rhett!" Macy burst in. "We found them! Sheep and Romeo. They were at the old Tennison Pond."

Rhett never took his eyes off the certificate of adoption. "That's great. Real great." He spoke with no voice inflection.

"Are you all right?" She stopped a few feet away.

Rhett ran trembling fingers over his jaw. "I'm not sure."

Macy stepped closer. She scanned the desk and breathed, "Brock wanted to tell you. He loved you, Rhett."

Rhett's head snapped up. "Did you know?"

Macy held up her hands. "Let me explain."

"For how long?" He ground out the words.

Her gaze darted away from his. She licked her lips. "It's been less than two years."

"*Two years?*" Rhett shot to his feet. He jabbed at the

adoption certificate. *His* adoption certificate. "You've known for two years that I was adopted and you kept it from me? How could you do that to me?"

She flinched and took a step back. "I had to, Rhett. Please."

Rhett fought the rash urge to hurtle the shoebox across the room. Did everyone know? Was it some joke, some great prank they thought they could play with his life? He was thirty years old and just finding out the truth.

They had lied to him. His whole life. It had all been a lie.

He wasn't a Jarrett.

Macy's shoe crunched on some of the wreckage in the office and the sound brought Rhett swiftly back into his surroundings.

Rhett released a rattling breath. "I'd like you to leave."

"Hear me out."

"Right now." He worked his jaw back and forth. "Please, just leave me alone."

"Rhett."

"I don't want to talk to you about this. Not now."

He needed some time. Needed to process. Needed to be alone.

He braced his hands on the desk and sank back into his chair. He suddenly felt very tired and very drained and Rhett didn't think he could have kept standing if he had wanted to.

He focused on the chamber in the wall that had hidden Brock's secret.

Rhett heard the door open again. Heard slow footsteps. Then nothing.

She was gone and he told himself it was for the best.

Chapter Twelve

"**A**ll right." Sophie Donnelley dried off the last cup, set it in a cupboard then pivoted to face Macy. She leaned against the counter. "We've left you to your own devices long enough. It's time to spill."

Macy hugged her middle as she considered how best to dodge the conversation Sophie clearly wanted to have. "I don't know what you're talking about."

Not true.

I'd like you to leave.

I don't want to talk to you about this.

Rhett's words flew through her mind like they had a hundred times since she left Red Dog Ranch. Guilt had draped itself around Macy, weighing her down. She had held a piece of truth about Rhett's life and had kept it from him.

In thirty-six hours Rhett hadn't called her. Hadn't texted.

She wouldn't blame him if he never forgave her.

That day she had sat in her bungalow for an hour before deciding the only way to give Rhett the space he needed would be to actually leave the property. Red Dog Ranch had been her home for the last ten years and before that it had been her second home. All her friends were tied to the ranch in some way. Most of them lived on the property.

After packing a bag, initially she hadn't known where to go. She could have rented a hotel room in town, but she'd ended up absently driving around for a while. Intermittently switching between praying, turning up her music, pulling over to cry, praying some more. Without really meaning to she had finally ended up pulling into the Donnelleys' driveway.

Macy had almost left but Jack had happened to arrive home at the same time, and he had let her know that Shannon and Mrs. Jarrett had moved back to their property a few hours earlier because the windows had been installed and the power was back on. Then he'd told Macy he and Sophie wouldn't hear of her going anywhere else as he'd ushered her inside.

"Nice try." Sophie draped the dish towel over her shoulder. She eyed Macy the same way Macy had seen her stare down her children when they needed a talking to. "Spill whatever it was that brought you to our door in tears yesterday with your belongings. Let's start there."

She couldn't evade the Donnelleys' questions forever. Talking was inevitable. Besides, Macy had never been one to hold in her words.

Except about Rhett's origins.

Except for the *one time* she most definitely should have talked.

Macy gestured toward the table. "We should sit first."

"Jack and the kids are zonked out already so we can

talk all night if you need to." Sophie joined her there a few minutes later with two cups of sweet tea in hand. Macy told Sophie about when Rhett left the ranch and their first kiss. Then she shared about how she and Rhett had been treating each other like boyfriend and girlfriend ever since the storm.

"I've loved him for so long and we've been through so much but…but I kept something really important from Rhett. Something he deserved to know." Macy decided that Sophie didn't need to hear every detail of the secret she'd kept from Rhett for her to understand and give advice. Besides, Rhett had only just learned he was adopted and now it was his right to tell or not tell people as he chose.

There had been a time when Macy had almost asked Uncle Travis if he knew the truth, but she hadn't been able to think of a way to broach the subject without revealing what she knew. If Travis did know, he had never said anything.

When Macy finished telling her story, her chest felt empty, completely hollowed out. It had taken more than an hour and two refills of sweet tea to explain everything.

Sophie tapped a finger on the table. "When he asked you to leave—"

"*Told* me to leave."

Sophie arched an eyebrow. "He told you, like a command?"

"I'm not sure, actually." Macy shoved a hand through her hair. Her eyes hurt. She hadn't slept much last night. "It happened so fast."

And her guilt might have been adding to the story.

Sophie's head tilted in thought. She pursed her lips then asked, "Did he say he wanted you gone forever?"

Rhett hadn't needed to say forever because Macy had seen it in the way he wouldn't make eye contact, in his broken posture. Trust was hard fought and easily broken in Rhett Jarrett's world.

"He won't want to see me again. Not after this," Macy said. "Last time it took three years before we spoke. With what I kept from him this time around?" Macy hugged her middle again. Maybe she could keep her heart from feeling as if it was slinking away to some cave to hide. Probably not. "This is far worse. This could be forever."

"You only feel like that in the moment. But it sounds like last time around you two didn't talk for three years for no other reason than you were both too stubborn and scared to return each other's calls. How about try being vulnerable this time around and reaching out—with the understanding, of course, that he may need some time to process and that's okay? Rhett taking time is not a rejection. You understand that, right?"

But Sophie didn't know what Macy had kept from Rhett. Macy had stumbled upon Rhett's adoption paperwork when Brock was having the fireproof chamber installed. She had begged Brock to tell Rhett, but Brock had insisted she promise not to tell him. Supposedly he had made a promise to Rhett's birth mother that Rhett would never know he was adopted.

Later Macy had wondered more about the circumstances of Rhett's birth. Why would a mother not want her child to know about his origins? She had approached Brock about it twice more within the first month of finding out, asking him to tell Rhett, but Brock had said he could never tell. He convinced Macy that Rhett would feel betrayed and could leave the family for good if he discovered the truth. With as divided as Rhett and Brock had been after Wade's death, Macy had hardly wanted a hand in driving them even further apart so against her better judgment she had agreed.

Sophie's voice broke through her thoughts. "Did Rhett actually say 'I don't want to see you again'?"

"He didn't have to." Macy's eyes burned. She needed to go to sleep. Needed to stop talking. "I really messed everything up, didn't I?"

"I wouldn't be so sure. Honestly, I feel like you're making some leaps based on assumptions." Sophie's lips tipped up encouragingly. "I know we haven't spoken much about it specifically, but you're a woman of faith, right?"

"I believe in God, yes." Macy uncurled her arms so she could trace a notch in the table. Her other hand moved to cup the cool glass of tea. "Actually, when I was stuck in the tornado I had this moment of revelation. You see, my entire life I've felt like I didn't measure up—not to my family, my friends or to God—but during that storm I realized that God's always loved me and I didn't have to do anything to earn His love."

"That's a wonderful knowledge to have, isn't it? There's a Bible verse we've been going over in the women's study group I'm a part of." Sophie thumbed through a stack of papers on the table that was full of kids' artwork. "I thought I had my notes here somewhere." She pushed the papers away. "I can't find the study sheet but the gist of it was that God never forsakes those who trust Him. The Bible mentions that truth many times. It's almost as if God knew we would need to hear it over and over before we believed it." Sophie smiled across the table. "God has not left you, He has not forsaken you and He will see you through this. Hang on to that."

Macy sighed. "God might be willing to ride this bumpy train with me, but what if Rhett's not?"

"I wouldn't lose faith in Rhett if I were you," Sophie said. "Give him time to absorb whatever it is he just learned about. Right now, be there for him in ways you can."

Macy's sharp laugh held no humor. "I don't think he wants me to be there for him at all."

"Nothing is stopping you from praying for him." Sophie winked. "And you're resourceful so I'm sure you'll think of other ways too." They cleared the table and both headed for bed but Sophie caught Macy's arm before she could turn toward the guest room. "Can I pray for you?"

"Of course." Macy took the other woman's hand. They bowed their heads and both ended up praying for Rhett and the ranch and each other.

"And thank You for never forsaking us. Never leaving. Thank You for loving us just as we are." Sophie squeezed Macy's hands. "Amen."

However, even after Macy was tucked away in the guest room for the night she was restless. It wasn't even late yet but the kids had an early bedtime and Jack had stumbled to his bedroom after tucking the kids in, saying he was running on empty. Macy put on her pajamas and got into bed but turned the light back on a few minutes later. What if Rhett or Shannon had sent an email? She dug through her things for her phone and her laptop.

She had a missed call but it was from Gabe the intern, not one of the Jarretts. "So, I know things aren't great right now," Gabe said in the message. "But I have an idea to help the ranch get back on its feet. Do you still have Clint Oakfield's number? Call me, okay?"

It wasn't late yet, but her throat was sore from talking with Sophie so she decided to call Gabe back in the morning. Gabe's call and her talk with Sophie worked together to shove Macy's brain into hyperdrive. Sophie was right; she didn't have to be at the ranch to help and support them. And she didn't need Rhett's approval to help. God had placed Red Dog Ranch in her life and she would fight to rebuild it however she could.

Macy opened her laptop and did a quick internet search for crowdfunding sites. She let her cursor hover over the top site for only a heartbeat before she clicked it. *Do it. Do it before you can think better of it.* It took her fifteen minutes to set up a page asking for donations; most of that time was spent typing out a passionate and heartfelt plea in which she detailed the storm's destruction, as well as all the amazing programs the ranch offered free of charge to foster families. She mentioned Rhett's desire to train therapy dogs, as well. She prayed her love for her favorite place shined through. When it was done she pressed for the page to go live before she could convince herself not to. With two clicks she linked the donation page to two of her social media accounts and then slammed her laptop closed.

Macy flipped off the lights and curled back into bed.

Had she just made another colossal mistake? Would her actions serve to drive Rhett further away? No, she'd done what she knew was right, what God would want her to do, and she could live with that.

Macy loved Rhett. No matter what happened, she always would.

But if the past few weeks had taught Macy anything, it was that she couldn't build her life on one person or one place or even one mission. She could only build her life on God and what God would have her do.

And that would be enough.

Rhett—

I'm writing this because Macy keeps insisting you deserve to know and you deserve answers. I suppose if this is in your hands then you moved your mom's painting and I'm sure you have a heap of questions. Why would your mom and I keep something like this from you? Why did we work so hard to ensure you wouldn't discover the truth? You have every right to be upset and angry. I don't blame you for either. I do hope you can find it within you to forgive an old fool.

You and me have been at odds ever since we lost Wade, and I don't know how to put that to right. I think if I would have told you the truth about your adoption I might have lost you too, and I couldn't have borne that.

Years ago your mother and I were volunteering at a youth group when we met your birth mom. She was scared and alone and she knew she couldn't keep you, but she loved you with such a protective love. I want you to know that, Rhett—you have never lived a day when you weren't fiercely loved by your birth mother, by me and your mom and by God. She had grown up in the system and it had failed her. A family had adopted her, but they'd always made her feel secondhand and more as live-in help than a branch in their tree.

She dreamed bigger for you. You've always reminded me of her in that way. When we told her we wanted to adopt you, that you were an answer to our prayers, she made us promise to treat you as our flesh and blood. We would have anyway, but the promise was important to her, and your mom and I are people of our word.

Perhaps I should own up to a more selfish reason too. From the first day you were in my arms you were my child, Rhett. I never saw you as anything but a Jarrett. I was a sentimental fool who wanted it to always stay that way. When you chose to leave us I told myself that you would have left sooner had you known, so then I guarded the secret even more doggedly.

For that I'm sorry.

Now you know our secret, but I can't go any further. We promised your biological mother if you ever did discover you were adopted, we would still protect her identity. She gave you the red stuffed dog you loved so well. You carried that thing everywhere your first few years.

If you haven't figured it out by now, your mom and I walked away from the life we had once we adopted you. We used Grandpa Jarrett's oil money to purchase this ranch. I didn't know a thing about cattle! But I did know I wanted to help kids. You opened my heart up to this life—to all of life. Every choice after that was made because of our great love for you. You filled our hearts and our lives with so much joy it overflowed. We wanted to give that joy to others, so we created a safe place for foster children to enjoy—a place that could feel like a second home.

Red Dog Ranch has been and always will be a symbol of our love for you. You made us parents. You made us a family. We are forever grateful for the gift of you. I'm so proud of you and the man you have become, son.

With all the love in my heart,
Dad

Each time Rhett reread the letter he felt something different. At first it was anger and betrayal but that faded into shades of acceptance tipped with disappointment.

Was it possible to track down his birth mother?

Did he want to?

Rhett hardly knew.

Folding the paper back up, Rhett tucked it into the pocket on his shirt where it would be close to his heart. He rested his hands on the edge of his belt as he looked out the newly installed floor-to-ceiling windows of the family room. Moonlight rippled over the large lake that sprawled behind the Jarrett family home. They had dredged the last of the debris from the lake yesterday morning and Rhett found he was glad he had moved that task up the prioritized list. The lake was a special place for him.

Red Dog Ranch has been and always will be a symbol of our love for you.

A lump formed in the back of Rhett's throat. He

rubbed a fist over his collarbone to try to dispel the feeling, but it lingered. Maybe it always would.

He had been so bitter over this place, so wrong.

His phone vibrated in his back pocket and as he fished it out he wildly hoped it was Macy. Rhett owed her an apology. He was still upset about her keeping such a huge secret from him, but he shouldn't have pushed her away.

When he asked her to go, he had meant he needed a few hours to himself. When Shannon told him Macy had left the ranch, Rhett had figured she had wanted some space too and he had respected that by not bothering her with calls. But when her car hadn't appeared today, Rhett had started to worry. Had his words driven her away?

Rhett didn't know where she was staying. The few times he had worked up the nerve to call her today, her phone had been off and her voice mail was oddly full.

He would find her at some point and he would ask her to come home. He couldn't run the place without her. He wanted her around, near him.

He glanced at his phone screen: Boone.

Boone blinked at him over the face-to-face connection program on their phones. Rhett had talked with most of his family about being adopted, but he hadn't been able to catch his brother yet.

"How's the ranch doing?"

"It's a mess." If only he was exaggerating.

"The pictures you sent of the damage turned my stomach. We wish we were there to help," Boone said. "Oh, and before I forget, I'm supposed to tell you June and Hailey say hi."

Rhett's brother Boone had met his wife, June, in high school. They had always joked about their names rhyming and had teased that they would pick their kids' names to rhyme, as well. When Hailey was born there was speculation about what her name would be... Thankfully they went against the rhyming scheme.

Rhett's watch showed that it was after eleven in Maine where Boone and his family lived. He chuckled softly. "I'm sure they're both long asleep by now so tell them hi in the morning for me."

"We keep late hours in seminary." Boone's yawn followed quickly.

Rhett glanced over at his mom asleep in her recliner and Kodiak snoozing near his mom's feet. "There's something I need to tell you." Rhett plunged right in and told Boone about discovering the shoebox in their dad's office and explained what he had found inside.

Boone was quiet when Rhett paused, but finally he let out a low whistle. "Wow. That's a lot to deal with all at once. How are you holding up?"

"Boone." Something had been bothering Rhett since he had learned about being adopted and he had to get it off his chest. "You're technically the oldest Jarrett. Dad's will names you as the heir in the event that something happens to me or if I'm unable to serve as director." Rhett heard Boone make a disgruntled noise on the other end of the line so he rushed on. "This inheritance... I know you said you don't want to run the ranch, but if that ever changes, if you ever want to take this from me—"

But it wasn't Boone who answered Rhett first. It was their mom.

"Why, that's the daftest thing I've ever heard you say." His mom pounded her hand on her armrest. Evidently she hadn't been sleeping all that deeply after all.

Kodiak's head swung up. She sleepily blinked in Rhett's general direction.

Rhett turned up the volume on his phone. "Mom's on with us."

Their mom curled her finger, a silent command for Rhett to draw closer. He obeyed. He crossed over to her and knelt at her feet.

She cupped his cheek in her weatherworn hand. "You are my firstborn son. It doesn't matter that someone else bore you—you were my first child, my first little love." She ran her thumb in a light caress over his skin. "God knew you were the brother Boone, Wade and Shannon needed. And He knew you were the son who would first make me a mother. No secret, no hurt can make any of those things untrue."

Rhett swallowed hard.

"This family has loved you and prayed for you and cheered for you since before you were even born. You are ours, child. Ours," his mom continued more firmly. "And you always will be."

Boone's face lighted up Rhett's phone screen. "I'm one hundred percent going with Mom on this one."

"Smart boy." Their mom beamed at both of them.

The front door opened and Shannon tiptoed in. She started when she spotted them in the family room. "Way to scare a girl silly! You guys are still awake?"

"Join us." Rhett motioned for her to come over. "We're on with Boone."

"Aww, Boone! My favorite middle brother." Shannon shrugged off her purse and skidded across the wood floor to sit beside Rhett. She tossed an arm over his shoulder and reached to hold her mom's hand in her other. Rhett eased back so he was sitting on his ankles. He kept the phone so Boone could see all three of them.

Rhett took a deep breath. "Since I have most of the family here I'd like to ask for some advice." They were missing Cassidy, but she and Piper had their own house on the property and they would be asleep by now.

Mom's brow bunched together. Her gaze darted around the room as if she was searching for a lost item. "Where are Brock and Wade? Do we need to wake them?"

Boone's focus went to Rhett and Shannon. "I, ah, I think this is plenty of us for an opinion."

Rhett had worried that the family gathering might confuse his mother. He needed to be more careful with how he phrased things.

"As everyone here knows, the ranch suffered heavy damages. Besides our barns, Camp Firefly—mainly the cabins—was the hardest hit part of our land." Although that didn't mean a whole lot. The tornado had carved a path from one end of his property line to the other. As if the storm had wanted to wage a war on Rhett specifically. Much of the ranch looked like it had been walloped with a meat tenderizer. "Now we need to decide what we're going to do."

Shannon's fingers tightened on his shoulder. "Wait. You're not planning to rebuild?"

Rhett looked away from them and worked his jaw a few times. "We don't have enough money. Insurance only helps to a point and even if they end up helping more, it won't be quickly enough to host camp." He spoke slowly, evenly delivering the information so everyone understood what they were facing. "At the least, I think we need to consider cancelling this summer."

"We can't." Shannon sat up a little more, letting go of their mom's hand in the process.

"If God wants our mission to continue, He will find a way." Their mom rested her hands in her lap. "You'll see."

Rhett rubbed his jaw. "Everyone made it through the storm safe. I think we should be grateful with that huge blessing from God and not expect a bunch more."

"Do you think there's a cap to how much love God can shower on us?" Their mom laughed gently. "Do you think He ever says, 'Oh, that's enough, I'll stop showing them my love'?" Mom leaned forward and whispered, "God delights in loving us. Don't forget that."

Shannon bit her lip and sought Rhett's eyes. "What about the family holdings?"

"That money is for the family to live off of." Rhett sliced his hand through the air. His heart had changed toward the foster programs, but he was still firm in his belief that the business account shouldn't mix with the family's personal money. "That's the legacy I want to leave to my nieces."

Boone spoke up first. "Legacy isn't money—you know that, right?"

"Boone's right." Shannon's fingers drew across his back as she leaned away from him. "The Jarrett family legacy is this ranch and what this ranch stands for."

Rhett knew that. He did. But he also knew that he had some tough business decisions ahead of him.

"Your nieces don't need you to worry about leaving them with a nest egg." Boone straightened in his chair. Rhett had to bite back a smile because he could tell Boone was about to launch into what they called his pastor mode. Boone had always been the bookish one in the family.

"The Bible talks a lot about treasures in heaven," Boone said. "Meaning we should be doing things that please God instead of amassing things here on earth." His hand came into view. "Now, I don't think that means that we don't take care of our family or make sound business choices. But I do think when we use the word *legacy*, as Christians it should only ever be in the realm of a legacy for the Kingdom. What are we devoting our time and energy and resources on earth to? Things that matter in eternity or not?"

"You do know you're not a minister yet, right?" Shannon teased.

They laughed and the conversation turned to catching up, but Rhett was unable to keep his mind from wandering. It wasn't the first time he had considered how people would remember him after he was gone someday. As morbid as it sounded, it was something that had crossed his mind often since his father had passed away.

How did Rhett want to be remembered?

As a man who took care of his family or someone who ran a successful business? Why couldn't he be both? But as the voices of his family—the family God had chosen for him—drifted over him, Rhett knew his answer was neither of those things. It didn't have to be one or the other.

Rhett would choose God.

He would trust God with the ranch and with his family.

He would hand it over. All of it.

Chapter Thirteen

"Rhett!" Shannon pounded on his bedroom door. "Rhett Jarrett, you need to get out of bed this instant and come downstairs."

Rhett groaned and sat up slowly. After they had hung up with Boone last night Rhett had headed outside to pray and clear his head. He had ended up staying up until past two in the morning and was not yet ready to handle any amount of his sister's exuberance.

Although it was nice to catch a glimpse of the old Shannon again. She was still dating Cord, and Rhett was praying about how he should deal with their relationship. Rhett knew for sure that Cord was no good for his sister, but his sister was an adult and he couldn't force her to break up with someone either.

He glanced at his clock and discovered to his embarrassment that his family had let him sleep until noon.

"Open up now, Rhett. I mean it." She kept knocking. "Or I'll barge in and pour water over your head like when we were kids."

"I'm up," he muttered. He raked his hand down his

face then rose. "And if I remember correctly, you got in trouble for that."

"Worth it," she called through the door.

Rhett grinned and crossed the room. Good thing it was only his sister because he usually wouldn't wander out of his room in his old sweatpants and undershirt. He pulled open the door and had to shield his eyes against the sunlight streaming into the hallway through the wide glass panels in the window seat. "So where's the fire?"

Shannon latched onto his wrist and tugged him over the threshold. "The place is swimming with reporters. They're all asking for you. I tried to hold them off but they keep showing up."

Reporters?

That didn't make any sense.

Rhett caught the ridge of trim around his door so she couldn't tug him forward anymore. "Slow down. What are you talking about?"

"Downstairs." She trained both of her pointer fingers downward. "Some from the papers and a couple from the internet. There are even ones out there with camera crews and they all want to see your pretty mug." She let go of him and pursed her lips. "Oh, you need to change. Maybe shower too?" She pulled a face. "No, that will take too long." She put her fingertips on his chest and gave him a push back toward his room. "Go make yourself presentable."

"Call me slow, but I'm not following any of this." Rhett crossed his arms. "Why would reporters have any interest in talking to me?"

Shannon gave a long suffering huff and tapped on

her phone. She pulled open a webpage and shoved the phone in his face. "This is why."

Rhett jerked his head back and snatched the phone from her so he could hold it at an angle where he could see the screen. A picture of Sheep and Romeo was splashed across the top of the page.

Fund-raiser by Macy Howell: Red Dog Ranch

The bar showing donations was already past its goal and a small flag in the corner announced that it was a trending fund-raiser. The page went on to talk about all the lives the ranch had touched and changed, Macy's included.

This place is home not just to the generous family that runs it free of charge to participants, but it becomes home to every foster child who steps onto the ranch. It's the only taste of home some kids ever know. When I was a lost child it became my home too.

She went on to explain all the free programs offered at Red Dog Ranch, followed that with detailing the destruction wrought by the tornado and ended with a call to action.

I've known the ranch's amazing owner, Rhett Jarrett, all my life and he's the one who taught me long ago to dream big, impossible dreams, so I've placed the amount we need to raise high. There are only weeks left until camp starts. Will you dream big with us?

Rhett's throat burned with emotion. "I need to find her."

"What you need to do—" Shannon grabbed his shoulders, turned him slightly and guided him all the way into his room "—is change and deal with all these people waiting in our dining room."

"You're right." Rhett crossed to his closet and pulled a fresh shirt off a hanger. "But when I'm done with them, I'm going to figure out where she went."

"Macy?" Shannon cocked her head. "Oh, she's over at the Donnelleys'."

Rhett's mouth was probably wide open. "Jack told you but not me?"

"No." She batted the suggestion away. "It took me all of ten seconds of thought to realize that Macy literally had nowhere to go but the Donnelleys' unless she went to one of the hotels. I guessed." Shannon shrugged. "I went there a few hours after she left and sure enough, there she was."

Jack hadn't said a word. Not that Rhett had told his new friend that he was trying to find Macy, but it was curious that her staying at their house hadn't come up. Then again, Rhett hadn't confided in Jack about what had happened between the two of them. Additionally, Macy very well may have asked the Donnelleys not to tell anyone she was staying there and the Donnelleys would have honored her request.

Just like his parents had honored his birth mom's request.

Still, Shannon had figured out Macy's whereabouts when he hadn't put two and two together. "I can't believe I didn't figure that out."

Shannon didn't even attempt to hide her eye roll. "Seriously, Rhett, where else would she have gone?"

Nowhere.

The thought gutted him.

Red Dog Ranch was her home—her world. And he had unintentionally shoved her out in the cold.

"I need to apologize to her."

Shannon's answering laugh was quick and sharp. "Oh, you need to do a lot more than that."

He scrubbed his hand down his face. "I never told her to leave the ranch. It was a miscommunication."

"And then some," Shannon said.

"Point made." He held his hands out.

"My advice?" She sauntered into the hallway. "A lot of groveling, some pleading and definitely kneeling down when you beg that woman to marry you, okay?"

Rhett swallowed a few times and then nodded. "I will."

"Get her back, Rhett. She's family."

He smiled at his sister and then he shut the door so he could get ready.

The afternoon flew by in a blur of interviews and phone calls. Not only had Macy's online fund-raiser gone viral, but Clint Oakfield had penned a blog entry about his experience at the ranch when the tornado hit and he had shared it everywhere he had an online presence. He expressed how he cared about the vision of Red Dog Ranch and he implored his fans to stand behind the rebuilding efforts. People in the comment section were offering to donate supplies or put together teams of free labor. Clint ended his post with a promise to host a benefit concert with all proceeds going to support the ranch's foster programs. He pledged to partner with Rhett and the ranch for as long as they would let him.

Once the first interview aired they had to forward the office line to the house phone and Shannon was flooded with incoming calls.

"How does Macy handle this all day? I can't answer these fast enough." Shannon set the phone down to re-fill her water. "Everyone wants our address so they can send checks. People are planning workdays and want-ing to coordinate the best way to help. Our voice-mail box has already reached capacity!"

Cars started showing up in the driveway full of peo-ple who wanted to hand Rhett a check or drop off con-struction materials. There were crews lined up to begin rebuilding the cabins starting next week.

Rhett had never said thank-you so many times in his life. It was overwhelming.

God delights in loving us. Don't forget that.

He should have known better than to doubt his mom's wisdom. God's love had no cap, no end. Rhett felt like he was flooded in blessings, but instead of wondering like usual when it all would end or if there would be a trade-off, he was simply thankful.

Uncle Travis had reminded Rhett about the Bible verse that said to whom much is given, much is re-quired. At the time Travis had been talking about Brock's will. But Rhett had been given an inheritance far greater than three thousand acres of gorgeous Texas Hill Country. God had given Rhett an inheritance of love—the deep and abiding, never-giving-up type of love that no man could ever hope to deserve. He had been given much and he would spend the rest of his life making sure every person who stepped onto his property got to experience the same love too.

And he needed to start with Macy.

Macy had spent most of the day staring at her computer screen in shocked awe as she witnessed the donation amount grow. She hadn't expected it to catch fire overnight quite like it had. Of course it was a good thing—Red Dog Ranch would have an opportunity to rebuild faster and return more quickly to being a safe haven for hurting kids.

Macy slammed her laptop closed and slung her purse over her shoulder. It was time to go to the ranch. She wasn't going to sit around waiting for three years like last time.

Macy burst out the Donnelleys' front door and charged directly into a solid chest. Hands took hold of her arms, steadying her. Rhett's handsome face—his strong jaw and shocking blue eyes—came into view and her heart squeezed. She loved this man.

She needed a little space so she would be able to say the things she had planned to.

Macy shrugged out of his hold. "Jack's not home."

Rhett eyed her. "I'm here for you."

Trying not to let his words derail her, Macy gripped on to her purse strap as if it was a lifeline. "I'm going to take an educated guess and assume you know what I've done?"

Rhett took off his hat and worked it around in his hands. His hair stuck up in the odd, adorable way it always did. "If you mean I need to thank you for single-handedly saving the ranch, then yes, I know about that. And I'm forever indebted to you for doing so." He looked down at his hat. "I wouldn't have acted that swiftly or even thought to take that measure." He peeked at her with a tentative smile on his face. "You sure know how to take on the world and win. I'm glad I have you in my corner…that is, if you still want to be."

It took every ounce of her restraint not to close the gap between them. "I should have told you about being adopted. I should have told you when I first found the paperwork. I'm so sorry, Rhett. You have no idea how sorry I am."

"Why didn't you tell me?"

She wove her fingers together. "I looked up to Brock so much. I think I had him on a bit of a pedestal. He was there for me when I had no parents." She shrugged. "A part of me felt like I owed him for letting me live here and giving me a job and basically giving me a family too. Selfishly I didn't want to jeopardize that." She rushed on, "And you and I weren't speaking, and when you came here we avoided each other so I convinced myself it wasn't my secret to tell—that you wouldn't have wanted to hear it from me anyway."

He nodded his understanding.

Macy sucked in a breath. "And I didn't want to drive you further away from your family either. Brock was really afraid of that happening." She took a half step closer. "I should have said something when you got back to the ranch."

His eyes searched hers.

"But I held on to this idea that I had to honor Brock by keeping the secret. As if it was even more important since he was gone. That probably sounds stupid, but I feel so much loyalty to him and I'm sorry. I'm so sorry and I don't know how I can even ask you to forgive me for keeping something so huge from you, but I am. Is this something we can get through?"

He reached toward her, slipped a piece of hair behind her ear. He left his hand there to cup her face as he said, "I'm pretty sure we can get through anything as long as we're together."

Macy pressed her cheek into his hand. "I thought about telling you so many times and I came close but—"

"But you're a woman of your word—one of the many things I love about you—so you kept a promise to a man who was like a father to you." Rhett's voice was full of tenderness. "I see only someone doing something admirable. You have nothing to apologize for." He splayed his other hand over his heart. "I'm sorry I told you to leave."

"You had every right."

The muscles along his jaw stretched taut. "I only wanted an hour to collect my thoughts. I never thought you would take it as me asking you to leave the ranch. Please." He rested his forehead against hers. "Don't ever leave again."

"Never," she whispered.

He stepped back, set his hat on and thumbed toward his truck. "I brought someone else who wanted to see you." He whistled and Kodiak's head popped through the window. Her tail wagging was evident from where Macy stood.

Macy couldn't help but smile at seeing Kodiak. "How's she doing?"

"Good, but she misses you." Rhett stepped into her line of vision again.

"Wait. Rhett." Macy grabbed his arm. "I forgot to tell you. There's this organization in California that specializes in training therapy dogs and they caught wind of our fund-raiser. They reached out to me with an offer for you. They want to fly you out there for a week or two this fall so you can learn their methods and connect with their trainers. I think it would be amazing."

Rhett's mouth opened, closed, opened again. "I feel like this is the right moment to say I finally understand the phrase 'my cup runneth over.'"

Macy held out her hand. "Should we head home?"

"Well, we actually need to talk about that." Rhett took her hand. "See, I don't want you back as the assistant."

Macy's heart plummeted. Had she heard him wrong? "But, Rhett, I—"

"I want to hire you as my codirector," Rhett said. "Equal decision-making power."

"Codirector of the ranch," said Macy, trying out the title. "Are you kidding?"

"I've never been more sure of anything in my life. I can't run the ranch without you. But more than that." He took a step forward and held out his other hand so they were facing one another again. "I need you in my life. I want you beside me in all things."

She slipped her hand into his. "Rhett."

He glanced at her lips and then met her eyes. "I can't promise a perfect life or even an easy one, but I can promise to love you every day for the rest of my life."

"I never wanted perfect." She brought their joined hands up between them. Macy looked into his eyes and knew she wanted to wake up to the sight of him every morning. "I only ever wanted you."

He let go of her hands only to slip his fingers into her hair. "I love you, Macy."

Macy tipped her face up. "I love you too."

Last time his kiss had been slow and gentle, but this kiss was sure and full of tomorrows. This kiss proclaimed love and promises. He angled his head to deepen their kiss at the same time she tiptoed her fingers to the hair at the nape of his neck. When they finally came up for air they both just grinned at each other.

His expression instantly sobered. "Macy, I don't have a ring. I thought of a speech on the way over but I'm so nervous it's fled. Will you—"

"Of course I'll marry you." Heart full, Macy laughed and tugged him close for another kiss. It was a quick peck that left her wanting ten more. She moved in for another but then stopped. "I interrupted you again, didn't I? And in the middle of… I'm sorry, Rhett, I couldn't help it. I've been waiting to be able to give you my answer for years."

"A few more kisses and we'll call it even." He winked.

"I like your terms." She playfully jabbed him in the ribs.

They climbed into his truck but Macy only scooted so far as the middle seat of the bench so Kodiak could stay sprawled with her cast in the passenger seat. Kodiak laid her head on Macy's thigh and let out a long, contented sigh. When Rhett got in, Macy looped her arm through his. He pressed another kiss to her temple and pointed the truck in the direction of Red Dog Ranch.

Toward home.

* * * * *

Award-winning author **Mindy Obenhaus** lives on a ranch in Texas with her husband, two sassy pups, and countless cattle and deer. She's passionate about touching readers with biblical truths in an entertaining, and sometimes adventurous, manner. When she's not writing, you'll usually find her in the kitchen, spending time with family or roaming the ranch. She'd love to connect with you via her website, mindyobenhaus.com.

Books by Mindy Obenhaus

Love Inspired

Hope Crossing

The Cowgirl's Redemption
A Christmas Bargain

Bliss, Texas

A Father's Promise
A Brother's Promise
A Future to Fight For
Their Yuletide Healing

Rocky Mountain Heroes

Their Ranch Reunion
The Deputy's Holiday Family
Her Colorado Cowboy
Reunited in the Rockies
Her Rocky Mountain Hope

Visit the Author Profile page at LoveInspired.com for more titles.

THEIR RANCH REUNION

Mindy Obenhaus

Forget the former things; do not dwell on the past. See, I am doing a new thing! Now it springs up; do you not perceive it? I am making a way in the wilderness and streams in the wasteland.

—*Isaiah* 43:18–19

For Your glory, Lord.

Acknowledgments

A big thank-you to Captain Glen Vincent, Village
Fire Department, for your twenty-nine years of service
as a firefighter and for your willingness to share your
knowledge.

Thanks to Wendy Jilek at Colorado Kitchen and
Bath Design, Montrose, Colorado, for your input on
the kitchen-design process.

Much appreciation to Catrina at ServPro of Montrose
and Telluride.

And I couldn't have done any of this without the love
and support of my incredible husband. Thank you for
being my rock.

Chapter One

If she had to look at one more spreadsheet, she'd go batty.

Overdue for a break, Carly Wagner pushed away from her laptop at the oak kitchen table, poured another cup of tea and wandered into the parlor of her Victorian home. The late morning sun filtered through the windows, bathing the somewhat formal though still cozy room in warmth. Taking a sip of her Cream Earl Grey, she glimpsed the photo of her great-grandmother on the mantel and smiled. Granger House was more than just her home. The bed-and-breakfast was a way of life.

She let go a sigh. If only she didn't have to keep taking in these bookkeeping jobs to help build up her savings. But if she hoped to send her daughter, Megan, to college one day...

She was just about to sit in the powder-blue accent chair when something outside caught her attention. Easing toward the side window, she noticed a vehicle in the driveway next door. She fingered the lace curtain aside and peered through the antique glass pane.

That truck did not belong there.

Her neighbor, Olivia Monroe, Livie to everyone who knew her, had been dead for six months. Since then, no one had set foot in that house without Carly's knowledge. Until now.

Narrowing her gaze on the ginormous black F-350, curiosity mingled with concern. After all, Livie's house now belonged to her. Well, maybe not completely, but Lord willing, it would, just as soon as she convinced Livie's grandson, Andrew, to sell her his half. That is, once she finally mustered the courage to call her old high school boyfriend. Then she would finally be able to act on her dream of expanding Granger House Inn and kiss bookkeeping goodbye.

Allowing the curtain to fall back into place, she paced from the wooden floor to the large Persian rug in the center of the room and back again. What should she do? She hated to bother the police. Not that they had much to do in a quiet town like Ouray, Colorado. Then again, if it was nothing, she'd look like the nosy neighbor who worried over everything.

No, she needed to do a little investigation before calling the cops.

She headed back into the kitchen, depositing her cup on the butcher-block island before grabbing her trusty Louisville Slugger on her way out the back door. The cool air sent a shiver down her spine. At least, that's what she told herself. Realistically, it was rather mild for the second day of March. Perhaps the sun would help rid them of what remained of their most recent snowfall.

Making herself as small as possible, she crept across the drive and around the back of Livie's folk Victorian.

Banging echoed from inside. Or was it her own heart slamming against her rib cage?

With Livie's house key clenched in her sweaty palm, Carly drew in a bolstering breath and continued a few more feet. She soundlessly eased the metal storm door open just enough to insert her key into the lock of the old wooden door. Then, thanks to the ongoing hammering sound, she slipped inside undetected.

The seventies-era kitchen, complete with avocado-green appliances and gold countertops, looked the same as it had every other time she'd been there in recent weeks. Pathetic. She still couldn't understand why Livie would do such a horrendous thing to this charming house. Carly could hardly wait to get rid of that ugly old stuff and replace it with a look that was truer to the home's original character.

Bang. Bang. Bang.

Carly jumped, sending her renovation ideas flying out the window. At least until she took care of whoever was in the parlor.

Raising the bat, she tiptoed into the short hallway, past the closet, until she could see who was making that racket.

She peered around the corner, nearly coming unglued when she spotted the male figure crouched beside the wall on the other side of the kitchen, using a hammer and a crowbar to remove the original trim moldings.

She slammed the tip of the bat onto the worn wooden floor with a crash. "*What* are you doing to my house?"

The man jumped. Jerking his head in her direction, he hustled to his feet until he towered over her.

Carly gasped. *What is he doing here?*

Eyes wide, she simply gaped. The perpetrator wasn't just any man. Instead, Andrew Stephens, Livie's grandson, stood before her, looking none too pleased.

Heat started in her belly, quickly rising to her cheeks. Though it had been nearly twenty years since they'd dated and she'd seen him a few times since, her mind failed to recall that the boy she once knew so well was now a man. A very tall, muscular man with thick, dark brown hair, penetrating brown eyes and a stubble beard that gave him a slightly dangerous, albeit very appealing, look.

His surprise morphed into irritation. "Your house?"

She struggled for composure, jutting her chin in the air while trying to ignore the scent of raw masculinity. "You heard me." Aware she wasn't acknowledging the complete truth, her courage suddenly waned. "Well, half of it anyway."

Andrew eyed her bat. "I'm not sure where you're getting your information, Carly, but this house belongs to me." Shifting his tools from one hand to the other, he moved closer. "And I have a copy of my grandmother's will that proves it."

Oh, so he thought he could intimidate her, did he? Not to mention call her a liar?

She laid one hand over the other atop the bat. "That's odd. Because I received a letter from Livie's lawyer, along with a copy of her will, and it stated that the house passes equally to both you and me." And while her plan was to offer to buy out his half, this probably wasn't the best time to bring that up.

He cocked his head, his expression softening a notch. "Are you okay? You haven't hit your head or something, have you?"

She sucked in a breath, indignation twisting her gut. Wasn't it enough that he'd broken her young heart? Now he thought she was crazy. Well, she'd show him.

Resting the bat on her shoulder, she whirled and started for the back door.

"Where are you going?"

"I'll be *right* back." She stormed out the door and marched over to her house, kicking at a dwindling pile of snow along the way. Did he really think she was going to let him plead ignorance when she had proof? That house was half hers and she refused to be bullied.

Once inside Granger House, Carly went straight to her bedroom, opened the small safe she kept tucked in the corner and pulled out the large manila envelope. Let Andrew argue with this.

Leaving her bat in her kitchen for fear she might actually be tempted to use it, she again made her way next door, irritation nipping at her heels. She would not let Andrew stand between her and her dream.

When she entered this time, he was in the kitchen, arms crossed, leaning against the peninsula that separated the eating space from the food-prep space, looking better than an ex-boyfriend should.

She removed the papers from the envelope and handed them to him. "Page three, last paragraph."

She watched as he read, noting the lines carved deeply into his brow. So serious. Intense. And while he had never been the carefree type, it appeared the big city might have robbed him of whatever joy remained.

When he glanced her way, she quickly lowered her gaze. Just because she hadn't seen him in forever didn't give her the right to stare. No matter how intriguing the sight.

"I don't get it." He flipped back to the front page. "This will was drawn up only a year and a half ago." He looked at her now. "The one I have is at least five years old. Meaning this—" he wiggled the papers— "supersedes that."

Carly rested her backside against the wood veneer table, her fingers gripping the edge. "So, are you saying you *didn't* receive a letter from your grandmother's lawyer?"

He shook his head. "Not that I'm aware of."

This was her chance to make her move. Before she chickened out. "I'm sorry to hear that. However—" she shoved away from the table "—we can take care of this quite easily." She lifted her chin. "I'd like to buy out your half. I've been looking for a way to expand my bed-and-breakfast, and this house is the perfect solution. Besides, you're never in Ouray—"

"I love this house. Always have. You know that."

While she knew that Andrew the boy had loved the house, she could count the times Andrew the man had set foot in Ouray since moving to Denver right after graduation. A move that was supposed to be the beginning of their future together. Instead, it had torn them apart.

Refusing to let the painful memories get the best of her, she crossed her arms over her chest. "Until today, when was the last time you were in this house?"

"After my grandmother's funeral."

"And the time before that?" She awaited a response. After a long moment, he shoved the papers back at her. "This house has been in my family for four generations. And I'm not about to let that change anytime soon. Even for you."

Andrew hadn't been this bowled over since Crawford Construction, one of Denver's largest commercial builders, offered to buy out his company, Pinnacle Construction. Even then, he hadn't been totally unaware. He'd heard rumors. But this revelation about his grandmother's house took him completely by surprise.

There was no way he was going to sell Carly half of the house that rightfully belonged to him. There had to be some mistake. He hadn't even been notified of the change to Grandma's will.

Watching out the kitchen window as Carly made her way back to Granger House, her blond curls bouncing with each determined step, he could think of only two explanations. His grandmother was crazy, or Carly had somehow coerced her into changing her will, giving his high school sweetheart half of the house that had been promised to him from the time he was a boy.

He continued his scrutiny, chuckling at the memory of Carly holding that baseball bat. Coming into the house, not knowing who was inside, took a lot of guts. Apparently the shy girl he'd once known no longer existed. Then again, that was a long time ago. She'd since become a wife, a mother, a widow... Not to mention one of the most beautiful women he'd ever seen.

Shaking off the unwanted observation, he waited for her to disappear inside her house before digging the keys out of his jeans pocket and heading out the door. He had to get to the bottom of this and fast. For months, he'd been looking forward to updating this old home to use as a rental property. Now, as he awaited the closing on his next business venture, he had eight weeks to do just that.

He climbed into his truck and fired up the diesel engine, daring a glance toward Granger House. With its sea foam green paint, intricate millwork and expansive front porch, the historic Victorian home looked much the way it would have when it was first built nearly one hundred twenty years ago. Today's guests must feel as though they're stepping back in time.

His gaze drifted to the swing at the far end of the porch. Back when he and Carly were dating, they spent many an evening there, holding hands, talking about their plans for the future. Plans he once thought would include her.

But that was then. This was now.

He threw the truck into gear and set off for his grandmother's lawyer's office, only to discover the man was out of town for the week. Frustration burrowed deeper. He didn't know what to do. Perhaps his father would have some insight.

Andrew's shoulders slumped. Seeing his father meant a trip to the ranch. Something he hadn't planned to do just yet.

If he wanted answers, though, it was his only option.

He maneuvered his truck onto Main Street, past the rows of colorful historic buildings, to continue north of town, beyond the walls of red sandstone, on to the open range. A few minutes later, he passed under the arched metal sign that read Abundant Blessings Ranch. Why his parents had named the place that, he'd never understand. Their lives were far from blessed, working their fingers to the bone with little to nothing to show for it.

He'd never live like that again.

Bumping up the gravel drive, he eyed the snow-capped mountains that stretched across the far edge of the property, beyond the river where they used to fish and swim.

A couple of horses watched him from the corral as he passed the stable. Red with white trim, it was the newest building on Stephens' land. Apparently the trail rides his father and oldest brother Noah offered during the summer months had been successful. That, in addition to the riding lessons Noah taught, had likely funded the structure.

The old barn, however, was another story. Closer to the house, the rustic wooden outbuilding had seen better days. The roof sagged, the pens on the outside were missing most of their slats and the ancient shingles were in sore need of replacing. Better yet, someone should just bulldoze the thing and start fresh.

A task he could easily take care of once they were well into spring. But he'd be back in Denver by then, the proud owner of Magnum Custom Home Builders.

He pulled alongside his father's beat-up dually, killed the engine and stepped outside to survey the single-story ranch house.

Though the sun was warm, a chill sifted through him. He wouldn't have believed it possible, but the place looked even worse than it had six months ago when he was here for his grandmother's funeral. The cedar siding was the darkest he'd ever seen it. The house, along with the large wooden deck that swept across one side, could use a good power-washing. Not that Dad, Noah or his younger brother, Jude, had the time. Before the cancer took its toll, the house had always been Mama's domain. And with five sons eager to please her, she was never at a loss for help.

The back door opened then, and Clint Stephens stepped outside, clad in his usual Wrangler jeans and chambray work shirt. "I thought I heard an engine out here." Smiling, his father started toward the three short steps separating him from Andrew, the heels of his well-worn cowboy boots thudding against the wood.

"How's it going, Dad?"

"It goes." His father cocked his graying head and peered down at him. "You no longer feel the need to tell your old man when you're coming back to Ouray?"

Andrew pushed the mounting guilt aside. "Maybe I wanted to surprise you." Hands shoved in his pockets, he perched his own booted foot on the bottom step. "I was planning to do some work on Grandma's house, but it seems she changed her will. You wouldn't happen to know anything about that, would you?"

"I do. I'm kinda surprised you don't, though."

"Why?"

"Didn't you get a copy of the new one?"

"No, sir."

"Hmm…" His father rubbed the gray stubble lining his jaw. "Guess we'd better have a talk, then." He turned back toward the house. "I just put on a fresh pot of coffee. Care to join me?"

After toeing out of their boots in the mudroom, they continued into the family room. Though the mottled brown carpet Andrew remembered from his childhood had been replaced with wood laminate flooring, the room still looked much the same with its oversize furniture and wood-burning stove.

He eyed the large Oriental rug in the middle of the room. Mama had been so tickled when he'd given it to her the Christmas after the new flooring had been put in. Said the rich colors made her simple house feel more grand.

While his father moved into the kitchen that was more like an extension of the family room, or vice versa, Andrew stood frozen, held captive by the wall of framed photos at the end of the room. Baby pictures of him and his brothers. Graduation photos. Milestones and achievements. There had never been a prouder mama than Mona Stephens.

Guilt nearly strangled him. He hadn't even had the respect to be here when she died.

"You still take it black?"

Turning, Andrew cleared his throat before addressing his father. "Just like you taught me."

The corners of Dad's mouth twitched. "There's some roast beef in the fridge." He motioned with a nod. "Help yourself if you're hungry."

Considering Andrew hadn't eaten anything since he pulled out of Denver well before sunup…

He spread mayonnaise on a slice of white bread, recalling his last visit before his mother's death. Despite chemo treatments, she still had his favorite foods waiting for him. From homemade apple pie to beef stroganoff, the most incredible aromas filled the house.

He glanced around the dated L-shaped kitchen. This old ranch house would never again smell so good.

"If you didn't get a copy of the new will, how'd you

find out about the change?" Dad eased into one of the high-backed chairs at the old wooden table near the wall.

"Carly paid me an unexpected visit." He picked up his sandwich and joined the old man. "So, what gives? Grandma promised her house to me. I have a copy of her will that proves it. Why'd she make the change?"

Dad set his stained mug inscribed with #1 Dad atop the table. "Carly meant a lot to Livie. She was a friend, a caretaker and the granddaughter she never had."

"Okay, but Carly isn't family."

"Not by blood. But like I said, Livie thought of her as family. They were very good friends, you know."

"No. I didn't know." Andrew took a bite. Sounded like Carly went to great lengths to worm her way into his grandmother's life, all to expand her bed-and-breakfast.

"After Carly lost her husband, she and Livie grew even closer. Your grandmother understood what Carly was going through."

Something Carly probably used to her advantage.

"No one can understand the pain of a young widow better than someone who was also a young widow." Dad lifted his cup and took another sip of coffee. "That aside, your grandmother had her concerns that you might sell the place." His gaze settled on Andrew. "Making Carly half owner might have been her way of ensuring that the house remained with someone she loved."

"But I've always wanted that house. That's why Grandma left it to me in the first place." That and the fact that none of his brothers were interested. "I would never consider selling."

"You were in Denver, hardly ever came home."

Guilt wedged deeper. Even if he'd found the time

to come back, he wasn't sure he could face the judgmental looks he was bound to receive from his brothers. As though he'd betrayed them for not getting here before Mama died.

"What are you planning to do with the house, anyway, son?"

His appetite waning, Andrew wrapped his suddenly cold fingers around the hot cup his father had given him. "Open up the bottom floor, add an extra bath, update the kitchen... I was hoping to have it ready by the high season to use as a rental."

"Sounds like quite an undertaking."

Andrew shrugged, still suspicious of the relationship between his grandmother and Carly. "You know, Carly mentioned something about wanting to expand Granger House Inn. You don't suppose she shared those plans with Grandma in hopes of getting her hands on that house, do you? I mean, it is right next door."

His father's brow furrowed. "It's possible she made mention of it. But Carly's not the scheming type. You know that."

Did he?

"Apparently she's pretty determined," Andrew said, "because she offered to buy my half of Grandma's house."

Lips pursed, Dad nodded in a matter-of-fact manner. "You gonna take her up on it?"

"No." Andrew shoved his sandwich aside. "What was Grandma thinking?"

Dad chuckled, lifting his cup. "Doesn't really matter, son. You and Carly are just going to have to find a way to work it out."

Chapter Two

"Yes, we do have an opening for Easter weekend." Sitting at her kitchen table that afternoon, Carly settled the phone between her ear and shoulder, grateful for the distraction. Her mind had been reeling ever since her encounter with Andrew.

She brought up the reservations page on her laptop. "The Hayden Room is available. It has a queen-size bed, a private bathroom and a spectacular view of Hayden Mountain."

"Oh, yes. I think I saw that one on your website." Excitement laced the female caller's tone. "It's beautiful."

Carly couldn't help smiling. Actually, all of their guest rooms were on the website. Something that had garnered Granger House many a booking. The problem she most often encountered, though, was when a group of people or a family required more space or multiple rooms she didn't have available. That was exactly where Livie's house would benefit her. Not only could she book the three rooms there individually but also market the entire house to those larger parties. Whatever the case, the addition of Livie's house would virtually double her income.

"I guarantee you won't be disappointed." She took hold of the phone. "Would you like to reserve it?"

"Yes, please. For Friday and Saturday night."

Ah, yes. There was nothing Carly loved more than a fully booked weekend. Especially this time of year when things tended to be a little sparse. Looked like she'd better get her breakfast menus planned. Though it was still a few weeks away, Easter weekend was extra special. There'd be ham to prepare, biscuits, scones...

She took the caller's information, hanging up as the kitchen timer went off.

Standing, she grabbed a pot holder and moved to the commercial-style range to retrieve a large baking sheet from the oven. Within seconds, her kitchen was filled with the aromas of cinnamon and vanilla.

She crossed the wide expanse of original hardwood and deposited the pan on the island. Until learning she'd inherited half of Livie's house, Carly had been saving to remodel the kitchen at Granger House. While the room was large, it had one of the worst layouts ever, with the stove by itself at one end of the room and the refrigerator clear over on the other. Not to mention the lack of counter space. But since she'd be using that money to buy out Andrew's half of Livie's house, she'd just have to live with it a while longer.

Too bad Andrew had to be so difficult. Okay, so the house had been in his family for generations. She'd give him that. But unless he was planning to move back to Ouray, what possible use could he have for it? The place would just sit there empty.

Nope, no matter how she looked at it, there was no way this co-owning thing was going to work, and she couldn't help wondering why Livie had set things up that way. Unless...

She picked up her spatula to remove the cookies, then stopped. Oh, say it wasn't so. Livie had never tried to play matchmaker for Andrew and her while she was alive. Why would she do it in death?

No, no. Carly refused to believe it.

Still shaking her head, she shoveled the cookies from the baking sheet to the cooling rack. Regardless of Livie's intentions, no matter what they might have been, Carly would simply have to figure out how to convince Andrew to sell her his half. She would not let him rob her of another dream. Not when this one was so close.

Back when she first took over Granger House from her parents seven years ago, she had grand ideas and had expressed an interest in expanding when the house on the opposite side of them came on the market. Her late husband, Dennis, had never been fond of the idea, though, so she'd tucked those dreams away. After his death two years later, she was too busy caring for Megan and simply trying to keep up to even think about anything other than what was absolutely necessary. But as Megan got older, Carly would occasionally revisit her daydreams. Still, with the other house no longer available, that's all they were.

Until Livie's death. Suddenly it was as though God had granted the desires of her heart in a way she never would have imagined. After all, just like Granger House, Livie's house was only a block off Main Street, affording guests easy access to just about everything in town. And the fact that a narrow drive was all that separated the two houses made it the perfect candidate for her expansion.

At least until Andrew showed up, thinking he was going to claim his inheritance.

She let go a sigh. How was she, a simple small-town girl who'd spent her entire life in Ouray, going to convince some bigwig businessman like Andrew? It wasn't as if their romantic history would score her any brownie points.

Her gaze drifted to the cookies. And plying him with food wasn't likely to do the job, either.

Lord, show me what I should do. Because right now, it looks as though Andrew and I are at an impasse.

The back door opened then, bringing a surge of cool air as nine-year-old Megan bounded inside.

"Mmm…cookies." Her daughter dropped her backpack on the wooden floor.

"You're just in time. They're fresh out of the oven."

Without bothering to take off her coat, Megan rushed over and grabbed one. "Yay, snickerdoodles!" She took a big bite.

Carly snagged her own cookie, pleased that her daughter appreciated her culinary skills. And running a bed-and-breakfast, she was almost always cooking something. If not directly for her guests, then she was trying out new recipes. Something her friends benefited from, making it a win-win for Carly. They gave her feedback and she didn't have to worry about her waistline. Well, not as much, anyway.

"How was school?"

With the cinnamon-coated treat sticking out of her mouth, Megan shrugged out of her coat. "Good." She dropped the puffy thing on a hook near the door before plopping into one of the Windsor-style chairs at the table to finish her snack. "Who's at Ms. Livie's house?"

Carly glanced out the window to see Andrew's big black truck once again in the driveway. With all the noise that thing made, she was surprised she hadn't heard him pull in.

Why was he back, anyway? After watching him leave this morning, she'd hoped he'd decided to stay away until they reached an agreement.

"That would be her grandson, Andrew." She grabbed a glass from the cupboard and continued on to the refrigerator for the milk.

"Do I know him?" Megan's blue eyes followed Carly as she moved toward her daughter.

She set the glass, along with another cookie, in front of her. "He's the one who played cards with you, me and Livie a couple of years ago."

"When Ms. Livie's daughter died, right?"

"That's him." She ruffled Megan's straighter-than-straight strawberry blond hair, a trait she definitely didn't inherit from her mother. But after decades of fighting her natural curls, Carly had finally learned to embrace them. "You have a good memory."

"Why is he at Ms. Livie's house now, though?" Megan picked up the second cookie. "I thought she gave it to you."

Carly cringed. She'd had no business mentioning that to Megan until the estate had been settled. Yet in her excitement over the news all those months back, she'd blurted it out without thinking.

"She gave me half of it. And she gave Andrew the other half."

"Which half is yours?"

Carly puffed out a laugh. She could only imagine what was going through her daughter's nine-year-old mind. As if Carly and Andrew could just slap a piece of tape down the middle.

"Unfortunately, it's not quite that simple." And if she couldn't get Andrew to sell her his half, she'd be stuck taking in people's accounting books until Megan graduated college.

Megan stood, dusting the crumbs from her hands. "Can I go over there?"

"I don't think that's a very good idea right now." If ever. At least, not with Andrew there. Mr. Serious likely wouldn't tolerate kids.

Still, she couldn't help wondering what he was up to. Not after catching him removing baseboards this morning. Baseboards he'd better plan on putting back, because she wasn't about to stand by and let him strip the home of its character.

"On second thought, maybe we should go over there and say hi." And if their presence happened to remind him that she was keeping tabs on him, so be it.

Megan paused at the island, looking very serious. "We should take him some cookies."

Hand perched on her hip as she watched her daughter, Carly wasn't sure how she felt about the suggestion. However, it was Livie who'd always said you caught more flies with honey than with vinegar. And right about now, there was one big fly Carly was interested in catching.

"I think that's a terrific idea."

"Well, that's just great."
Andrew dropped his phone on the counter in his

grandmother's kitchen. He'd been calling his attorney's cell all afternoon. When he finally decided to try the office, he learned that the man was in court and wouldn't be available until tomorrow.

He blew out a frustrated breath. This was not how he'd envisioned this day playing out.

Pushing away from the cabinet, he paced the ugly gold-and-brown vinyl floor while he waited for a pot of coffee to brew. He knew it was a long shot, but perhaps Ned could find a way to get Grandma's will overturned and the original reinstated. Then all of his problems would be solved.

You and Carly are just going to have to find a way to work it out.

Hmph. Dad always did look at things simplistically. The only thing simple about the dispute between him and Carly was the fact that they both wanted this house.

As the coffeemaker spewed out its last efforts, Andrew grabbed a mug from the cupboard. If it hadn't been for Carly, he could have had at least one wall taken down by now. Enough to give him an idea of how the house was going to look with an open concept. Instead, he was left with a whole lot of nothing to do.

Leaning against the counter, he took a sip. He'd loved his grandmother dearly, but leaving her house to both him and Carly had to be the craziest idea she'd had since she went white-water rafting down the Uncompahgre River at the age of eighty-three. Except for sharing a game of cards after his mother's funeral, he and Carly had barely spoken in seventeen years. Not since the day she turned down his marriage proposal and walked out of his life forever.

Relegating the unwanted memories to the darkest corner of his mind, he scanned the sorry-looking kitchen. While he wasn't about to give up on getting his grandmother's old will reinstated, he could still be proactive, just in case things didn't work out the way he hoped. Near as he could tell, there were only two ways out of this predicament. And since selling his half to Carly was out of the question, that left him with only one option— he'd have to buy out Carly's half of the house. Something that chafed him more than he cared to admit.

Aside from paying for something that was rightfully his to begin with, he'd have to come up with an offer better than hers. Sweeten the deal, so to speak, making it too good to refuse. Much like the company who'd just bought him out. And left him with a tidy chunk of change. Carly would be able to do whatever she liked with Granger House and leave this house—and him—alone.

"Hello, hello." As though he'd willed her to appear, Carly pushed open the back door, knocking as she came.

Try as he might, he couldn't ignore the fact that she was still one of the most gorgeous women he'd ever seen. The kind that could take your breath away with her natural beauty.

Her blond curls brushed across her shoulders as she held the door, allowing a young girl to enter first.

Her daughter had grown quite a bit since the last time he'd seen her. What was her name? Maggie? No, Megan.

"Hi." The girl smiled up at him with blue eyes reminiscent of her mother's and waved. In her other hand she held a small plate covered with plastic wrap. "We brought you cookies." She handed them to him.

So these were Carly's weapons of choice. Children and food. Ranked right up there with little old ladies.

His conscience mentally kicked his backside. Dad was right. Carly wasn't the type to try to steal his grandmother's house. However, that didn't mean he was simply going to hand it over.

While Megan wandered off as though she lived there, he set the plate on the counter and helped himself to a cookie. "Snickerdoodles. How did you know I was in need of a snack?" He took a bite.

The feisty blonde watched him suspiciously. "What brings you back here?"

He chased the first homemade treat he'd had in a long time with a swig of coffee. "I'm—"

"Uh-oh." Megan's voice echoed from the next room. "Somebody made a mess."

After a moment, Carly tore her gaze away from him and started into the front room.

Andrew set his cup on the counter and followed.

Rounding the corner into the home's only living space, he saw Megan pointing at the small stack of baseboards he'd begun to remove this morning. Before his plans were rerouted by Carly.

"I was doing a little work."

Carly lifted a brow. "I'm not sure what kind of work it was, but you need to put those back."

Irritation sparked. Who was she to start giving him orders?

"Whose is this?" Now on the other side of the room, Megan rocked back and forth in his grandmother's glider, pointing to the duffel he'd left by the front door. He wouldn't go so far as to call the kid nosy, but she was definitely curious. Not to mention observant.

"That would be mine." He turned to find Carly watching him.

Both brows were up in the air this time. "Planning to stay a while?"

This was ridiculous. He should not be interrogated in his own house. "As a matter of fact, I am. For several weeks. Which reminds me—" he crossed his arms over chest "—I think we need to set up a time to talk." Glancing at Megan, he lowered his voice. "Privately."

Mirroring his stance, Carly said, "I was thinking the same thing."

"At least we're in agreement about something."

"I'm going upstairs." A sigh accompanied Megan's announcement, quickly followed by the clomping of boots on the wooden steps.

Andrew knew just how she felt.

With Megan gone, Carly addressed him. "I'm curious. Before you learned that you were not the sole owner of this house, what were your intentions for it? I mean, were you planning to move in?"

"Temporarily, yes. I'm going to update the place and use it for rental income."

Seemingly confused, she said, "Where will you be?"

"Denver, of course."

Lines appeared on her forehead. "Let me get this straight." She perched both hands on her hips. "You don't want me to use Livie's house for my bed-and-breakfast, yet you want to turn it into rental property?"

"In a nutshell, yes."

"Why not just rent your half to me?"

It wasn't that he didn't like Carly. He wasn't purposely trying to thwart her plans. But this house was supposed to be his and his alone.

He dared a step closer. "Because, should I come back to Ouray, I want to be able to stay here. *Without* having to share it with someone else."

She shook her head. "So you'd rather pay me half of the rent money you get? That makes no sense."

"Pay you? Why would I—?"

"Mommy?" Megan hopped down the stairs, one loud thud at a time.

Carly seemed to compose herself before shifting her attention to her daughter. "What is it, sweetie?"

The girl tugged on Carly's sleeve, urging her closer, then cupped a hand over her mother's ear. "We should invite him for dinner." For all her implied secrecy, Megan had failed to lower her voice.

A look that could only be described as sheer horror flitted across Carly's face. Her eyes widened. "Oh, I'm sure Andrew already has plans for—"

"Nope. No plans at all." Fully aware of her discomfort, he simply shook his head, awaiting her response.

Clearing her throat, Carly straightened, looking none too happy. "In that case, would you care to join us for dinner?" She practically ground out the words.

He couldn't help smiling. "Sure. Why not?"

Watching them leave a short time later, he knew good and well that Carly was no more excited about having him for dinner than he was about sharing his grandmother's house. But as Grandma was fond of saying, it is what it is.

Who knew? Maybe they'd have an opportunity to talk. And if all went well, by the time this evening was over, Grandma's house would belong to him and him alone.

Chapter Three

Carly removed the meat loaf from the oven and put in the apple pie she'd tossed together at the last minute. Throw in some mashed potatoes and green beans and it was comfort food all the way. She'd need all the comfort she could get if she hoped to make it through an evening with the man who had once been able to read her every thought.

Using a pot holder, she picked up the pan of meat and headed for the island. *Nope. No plans at all.* She all but flung the pan on the counter, sending spatters of tomato sauce across the butcher-block top.

She grabbed a rag and wiped up the mess, knowing good and well that Andrew was simply trying to get her goat. And enjoying every minute of it, no doubt. Just like he did back in high school. Only she was no longer the timid girl who was afraid to stand up for herself.

After throwing the rag into the sink, she returned to the stove to check the potatoes. Fork in hand, she lifted the lid on the large pot.

It irked her that Andrew was planning to use Livie's house as a rental. Why wouldn't he just let— Wait a minute.

Steam billowed in front of her.

She was half owner. That meant she had a say in what went on next door. He couldn't use it as a rental without her permission.

Smiling, she poked at the vegetables. Yep, they were done.

She replaced the lid and carried the pot to the sink. This whole dispute would be over if Andrew would simply agree to sell. Unfortunately, for as eager as she was to discuss purchasing his half of the house so she could move forward with her expansion plans, she wasn't at liberty to talk business with Megan in the room. Which meant this whole evening was a waste of time.

That is, unless her idea of plying Andrew with food actually worked.

Holding the lid slightly off-center so as not to lose any of the potatoes, she drained the water from the pot. Maybe he'd be in such a state of gastronomic euphoria by the end of this evening that it would be impossible for him to say no when she again extended her offer.

Dream on, girl.

"Can I help?" Megan emerged from the adjoining family room at the back of the house, directly off the kitchen. Carly's parents had built the addition when she was young as a private space for the family. Now Carly appreciated it more than ever, because it allowed her to keep an eye on her daughter while she worked in the kitchen.

"Of course you can. Care to set the table?"

"Okay."

Carly opened the cupboard to grab the plates.

"Not those plates, Mommy."

"What?" She glanced down at her daughter.

"We need the guest plates." Meaning the china she used for the bed-and-breakfast. And this time of year, guests were predominantly limited to weekends.

"Sweetie, we don't use those for regular meals."

"This isn't a regular meal. Mr. Andrew is company, so we need to eat in the dining room with the pretty dishes."

Oh, to be a child again, when everything was so simple.

Lord, help me make it through tonight.

"Okay. Let me get them for you."

They moved around the corner into the dining room, and Carly retrieved the dishes from atop her grandmother's antique sideboard. Meat loaf on china. That'd be a first.

Leaving Megan in charge of the table, Carly returned to the kitchen to mash the potatoes. She pulled the butter and cream from the large stainless steel refrigerator.

"Which side do the forks go on?"

Closing the refrigerator door, Carly grinned, recalling how she used to help her mother and wondering if Megan would one day take over Granger House Inn. If so, she'd be the third generation to run the B and B. Not that she was in any hurry for her daughter to grow up. Carly was already lamenting Megan's occasional usage of Mom instead of Mommy.

"On the left."

A knock on the back door nearly had Carly dropping the dairy products she still held.

Megan must have heard it, too, because she raced past Carly and threw open the door.

Carly deposited the butter and cream on the counter and hurried behind her daughter. "Young lady, what have I told you about looking to see who it is before you open the door?" Not that there was much to worry about in Ouray. Still, a mother could never be too cautious in this day and age.

"Sorry."

"Evening, ladies." A smiling Andrew stepped inside, looking far too appealing. His hair was damp, and he smelled freshly showered.

Closing the door behind him, Carly eyed her flour-speckled jeans. Clearly he'd done more primping than she had. An observation that had her as curious as it did bothered.

"Welcome to our home." Megan swept her arm through the air in a flourish.

"Thank you for inviting me." He stooped to her daughter's level. "This is for you." He handed her a small brown paper gift bag with white tissue sticking out the top.

Megan's eyes were wide. "For me?"

"Yep. And this one—" straightening, he turned his attention to Carly "—is for your mother."

Carly's heart tripped as she accepted the package. A hostess gift had been unexpected, but the fact that he'd thought of both of them had her reevaluating their guest. At least momentarily.

"Th-thank you."

"Can I open it?" Megan looked as if she was about to explode with anticipation.

"Of course. What are you waiting for?" Andrew

looked like a kid himself as he watched Megan pull out the tissue, followed by a small rectangular box. "My own cards!"

"Did my grandmother ever teach you how to play Hearts?"

"I don't think so." Megan eyed him seriously.

"Looks like I'll have to carry on the tradition, then. Perhaps we can play a game after dinner."

"Okay." Megan excitedly removed the plastic wrapping. "I can practice shuffling now, though, can't I?"

"You sure can." Andrew looked at Carly again. "You can open yours, too."

Her stomach did a little flip-flop as she removed the tissue and pulled out a small box from Mouse's Chocolates. "Ooo…"

"I hope you like truffles."

She lifted a shoulder. "No, not really."

His smile evaporated and, for just a moment, she felt bad for messing with him. Then again, after the way he'd coerced her into this dinner invitation, why should she care?

"Oh, I'm sorry. I thought most women—"

"I love them."

The corners of his mouth slowly lifted as he wagged a finger her way. "You had me going for a second."

Looking up, she sent him a mischievous grin. "Good."

She moved back toward the island, glad she had potatoes to keep her busy for a few minutes. Was it her imagination or did Andrew's brown eyes seem a touch lighter tonight? Like coffee with a splash of cream. Maybe it was the blue-gray mix in his flannel shirt.

Whatever the case, it might be best if Megan kept him occupied for a while.

When they sat down to dinner a short time later, Andrew surveyed the table. "This is quite the spread." His gaze settled on Carly. "I wasn't expecting you to go to all this trouble."

Again, her insides betrayed her, quivering at his praise. "No trouble."

"Yeah. My mommy cooks like this *all* the time."

Suspecting her daughter was attempting a little matchmaking, Carly added, "Not all the time. And we rarely eat in the dining room."

He glanced about. "That's a shame. This is a nice room."

"Oh, it gets plenty of use with the bed-and-breakfast." She eyed her daughter across the table. "Shall we pray?"

After dinner, Andrew followed through with his promise and taught Megan Livie's favorite card game while Carly cleaned up the kitchen. Not only was she surprised by his patience with Megan and the gentle way he encouraged her, she greatly appreciated it. While Dennis had been a good father, he always seemed to have more time for his work than he did for his family. A fact that had Carly practicing the art of overcompensation long before his death.

With the dishes done, Carly joined them in the dining room.

She smoothed a hand across her daughter's back. "I hate to put the kibosh on your fun, but tomorrow is a school day."

"But I'm beating him. Please, can we finish this game?"

As much as Carly wanted to resist, to tell Megan it was time for Andrew to leave, she didn't have the heart. "Go ahead."

Fifteen minutes later, with her first win under her belt and promises of a rematch, a happy Megan scurried off to get ready for bed.

Andrew pushed his chair in as he stood. "Think we could talk for a minute?"

"Um…" Carly's body tensed. While she had planned to reissue her offer to purchase his half of Livie's house, she wasn't sure she had the energy tonight. Then again, maybe he'd had a change of heart and was willing to accept her offer. "Okay. Let's go out front."

He followed her through the living room, past the carved wooden staircase and Victorian-era parlor chairs. "You've got a bright kid there. She's a fast learner."

Carly tugged open the heavy oak and leaded glass door. "I've always thought so."

Outside, the chilly evening air had her drawing her bulky beige cardigan around her. Moving to the porch swing, she sat down and stared out over the street. Once upon a time, she used to dream of finding someone who would sit with her and hold her hand while they talked about their day, the way her parents always had. Like she and Andrew used to do. And Dennis was too busy to do.

Now she knew better than to dream.

To her surprise, though, Andrew joined her on the swing. Close enough that she could feel the warmth emanating from his body.

"This has been a full day," he said.

If she thought her mind was muddled before he sat down... "Yes, it has." And she could hardly wait for it to be over.

He stretched his arm across the back of the swing, his long legs setting them into motion as he surveyed the neighborhood without saying a word.

For a split second, she wondered what he would do if she were to lean into him and rest her head on his shoulder. Would he wrap his arm around her and hold her close, the way he used to? Or would he push her away?

Feeling the cold seep into her bones, she pushed to her feet. "What was it you wanted to talk about?"

He hesitated a moment before joining her. Took in a deep breath. "I'm willing to pay you the full value of the house for your half."

Her jaw dropped. "Do you have any idea how much property values have risen around here?"

He shrugged. "I can afford it."

His words sparked a fire in her belly. He hadn't changed a bit. With Andrew, everything was about money. Making it, having it... Just like her late husband had been.

Well, he'd sorely underestimated her.

"I don't care if you offer me a million dollars. There are some things that just can't be bought. Including me."

Refusing to listen to another word, she stormed into the house and slammed the door behind her.

By noon the next day, Andrew was at his wit's end. Carly's adamant refusal last night, coupled with his former admin assistant's acknowledgment that a certi-

fied letter from Ouray had indeed come for him a few
months back and was left on his desk, had him more
confused than ever.

Tucked in a corner booth at Granny's Kitchen, a local
diner he remembered as The Miner's Cafe, he listened
to the din of the early lunch crowd and pondered what
remained of his burger and fries. One would think he'd
be used to Carly's rejection by now. At least last night's
dismissal hadn't stung as much as when she'd refused
to marry him.

He sighed, dipped a french fry into some ketchup and
popped it in his mouth. Seventeen years later, he still
wasn't sure what had gone wrong. But last night revealed
something he hadn't expected. Despite everything, Carly
still held a very special place in his heart. Simply being
near her stirred up what-ifs and could-have-beens.

Rather absurd, if you asked him. They didn't even
know each other anymore. Besides, he was headed back
to Denver just as soon as he finished Grandma's house.
And he knew all too well how Carly felt about the big
city.

His phone vibrated in his pocket. He wiped his hands
and slid out the device, happy to see his attorney's name
on the screen.

He pressed the phone against his ear. "Hey, Ned."

"Judging from all the missed calls I have from you,
I'm guessing you're eager to talk to me."

"Yes." He straightened in the wooden bench. "I was
beginning to think you were avoiding me."

Ned laughed. "Sorry, buddy. I didn't think you'd be
in need of my services so soon. Don't tell me you're
bored with Ouray already."

Surprisingly, Ouray had been anything but boring this time around.

"No, but I do have a problem." He pushed his plate aside and proceeded to explain the change to his grandmother's will. "Is there any way I can get this will revoked and the original reinstated?" He reached for another fry, awaiting his lawyer's response.

"Was your grandmother of sound mind? Did she have dementia or anything?"

"Not that I'm aware of." Though given her decision to split the ownership of the house, he was beginning to wonder. If it had been one of his brothers, he could understand it. But Carly wasn't family.

"Then it's highly unlikely you'd be able to get it overturned."

Andrew wadded his napkin, tossed it on the highgloss wooden tabletop and raked a hand through his hair. He'd anticipated as much. Still...

"Can I get you anything else?" Beside him, the waitress smiled down at him.

"One minute, Ned." He eyed the unquestionably pregnant blonde. "I'm good, thank you."

She slid him his check. "My name is Celeste if you need anything else. Otherwise, you can pay at the register on your way out."

"Good deal. Thank you." He again set the phone to his ear. "Sorry about that." He grabbed the ticket as he slipped out of the booth. "So, what are my options?"

"You could—"

The town's emergency siren shrieked to life just then, making it impossible for Andrew to hear anything. "Hold on again, Ned." He stepped up to the register and paid his tab as the high-pitched wail of fire trucks added to the discord.

When the madness finally settled, he stepped outside and resumed his call. "Okay, let's try this again." The cool midday air had him zipping up his jacket.

"And here I thought Ouray was just a sleepy little town."

Andrew looked up and down the historic Main Street. "Apparently not today."

Ned chuckled. "As far as options, you could offer to buy out the other person's half."

Crossing the street, Andrew let go a sigh. "Already did."

"And?"

"She slammed the door in my face." A quick glance heavenward had him noticing the plumes of thick, black smoke billowing into the air a few blocks away. Pretty significant fire, if you asked him. And fairly close to his grandmother's house.

A wave of unease rolled through him. "Uh, Ned, I'm gonna have to call you back."

He shoved the phone in his pocket, quickening his pace until he reached the corner. When he did, he peered to his right.

Dread pulsed through his veins as every nerve ending went on high alert. The fire trucks were in front of his grandmother's house.

He broke into a run. One block. Adrenaline urged him forward. Two blocks.

"Oh, no." Heart sinking, he came to a halt.

Across the street, smoke rolled from the back of Granger House Inn. Flames danced from the kitchen's side window, lapping at the sea foam paint, threatening the historic dentil moldings and clapboard siding.

One of the firemen barked orders, orchestrating the chaos, while others flanked the corner of the house, their hoses aimed inside.

But where was Carly?

"Andrew!"

He jerked his head in the direction of his brother Jude's voice.

A police officer for the city of Ouray, his younger brother vehemently motioned him across the street.

Andrew hurried toward him.

"We need you to move your truck out of Grandma's drive."

"Sure thing." He tugged the keys from his pocket and threw himself into the vehicle, the smell of smoke nearly choking him.

As he backed into the street, he spotted Carly's SUV in front of her house. Where was she? Was she safe? Could she have been trapped inside? Oh, God. Please, no.

He quickly parked on the next block before rushing back.

People had gathered on the opposite side of the street, watching the horror unfold.

He scanned the faces, looking for Carly. She had to be here somewhere.

He again eyed the flames, feeling helpless. Sweat beaded his brow as panic surged through his body. *God, she has to be all right.*

Spotting Jude in the middle of the street, Andrew jogged toward him. "Where's Carly?"

"In the ambulance."

Ambulance?

He ran past the cluster of onlookers to the emergency vehicle parked a few houses down.

Drawing closer, he finally saw her, standing near the rear bumper, attempting to pull off the oxygen mask while the female EMT fought to keep it over her face.

Andrew had never been so glad to see someone.

He slowed his pace as Carly ultimately ripped the mask from her face. "I don't need this." She coughed. "That's my house." More coughing. "I need to—"

Andrew stepped in front of her then. "You *need* to let the firemen do their job. And you *need* to get some good air into your lungs." He pulled the mask from her hand, noting the resignation in her blue eyes as she looked up at him, her bottom lip quivering. "At least for a little bit."

The fact that she didn't resist when he slipped the respirator over her head still surprised him. But when he reached for her hand, she quickly yanked it away.

He groaned. Stupid move. Who was he to try to comfort her?

Only then did he notice the way she cradled her hand, holding it against her torso. The redness. She'd been burned.

"I think we'd better get you into the ambulance."

She shook her head. "I want to see what's happening." The words were muffled through the plastic mask.

Andrew eyed the male and female EMTs. "Can she sit here while you look her over?" He gestured to the rear bumper.

They nodded.

He looked at Carly. "You promise to let them do what they need to do?"

A cough-filled moment ticked by before she finally agreed.

The female EMT checked Carly's vital signs as the man went to work on her hand. All the while, Carly's tearful gaze remained riveted on Granger House.

Andrew could only imagine the flurry of emotions threatening to swallow her at any moment. The uncertainty, the grief… He wished he could make it all go away.

He sat down beside her as the man wrapped her hand in gauze. "What happened there?" Andrew pointed to the injury.

"I had gone to the bank." She coughed. "When I got back—" looking up, she blinked repeatedly "—I opened the back door and the…flames were everywhere."

His eyes momentarily drifted closed. Thank God she was okay.

Unable to stop himself, he slipped an arm around her shoulders and pulled her close. Despite wearing a jacket, her whole body shook.

Returning his attention to the house, he saw that the smoke had started to turn white, a sign that the fire was almost out. However, there was no telling what kind of damage it had left in its wake. Granger House was more than Carly's home. It was her livelihood. Without it—

As if she'd read his thoughts, Carly lifted her head, her eyes swimming with tears. "What am I going to do?"

Chapter Four

How could this have happened?

Carly stood beside the towering conifer in front of Livie's house a couple of hours later, her arms wrapped tightly around her middle. Staring at Granger House, she felt as though she were fighting to keep herself together. In only a short time, the fire had ravaged her majestic old home, leaving it scarred and disheveled.

At the back of the house, where the kitchen was located, soot trailed up the once beautiful sea foam green siding, leaving it blackened and ugly. Windows were missing and, as she strained to look inside, all she could see was black.

She breathed in deeply through her nose, trying to quell the nausea that refused to go away. If only they would let her go inside. Perhaps she'd find out things weren't as bad as they seemed.

The loud rumble of the fire engine filled her ears as firemen traipsed back and forth, returning hoses to their trucks. Carly eyed her gauze-wrapped hand. At least it didn't sting anymore. The smell of smoke would be forever seared into her memory, though. Not to mention the heat of those flames.

Tilting her head toward the cloud-dotted sky, she blinked back tears. Save for a few years, she'd spent her entire life at Granger House. It was more than her home…it was family. An integral part of her heritage. Now she could only pray that the whole thing wasn't a loss. Even insurance couldn't replace that.

But what if it was a total loss? What would she do then?

"Can I get you anything? Are you warm enough?" The feel of Andrew's hand against the small of her back was a comfort she hadn't known in a long time. From the moment he appeared on the scene, Andrew had yet to leave her side. For once, she was grateful for his take-charge attitude. His presence was an unlikely calm in the midst of her storm.

"No, thank y—"

"Oh, my!"

Carly turned to see Rose Daniels, a family friend and owner of The Alps motel. Hand pressed against her chest, the white-haired woman studied the carnage. Beside her, Hillary Ward-Thompson, a former resident who'd recently returned, appeared every bit as aghast.

Carly knew exactly how they felt.

The dismay in Rose's blue eyes morphed into compassion as she shifted her attention to Carly, her arms held wide. "I came as soon as I heard." She hugged Carly with a strength that belied her eighty years. "You poor dear. Are you all right?"

She nodded against the older woman's shoulder, tears

threatening again, but she refused to give in. She needed to stay strong.

After a long moment, Rose released her into Hillary's waiting embrace.

"I hate that this happened to you." Hillary stepped back, looking the epitome of chic with her perfectly styled short blond hair and silky tunic. Then again, Carly wouldn't expect anything less from the former globe-trotting exec.

"How can we help, dear?" Rose shoved her wrinkled hands into the pockets of her aqua Windbreaker. "Just tell us what you need."

"Besides food, that is," Hillary was quick to add. "Celeste has already talked to Blakely and Taryn. They're planning to bring you dinner." Her daughter, Celeste Purcell, owned Granny's Kitchen.

Carly hated that she'd added to their already hectic lives. "They don't have to—"

"Nonsense, darling." Hillary waved a hand through the air. "That's what people do in Ouray. You know that."

All too well. She'd been on the receiving end when Dennis died. Since then, she was usually the one to spearhead donations. A role she was much more comfortable with.

"There's also a room for you at The Alps should you and Megan need a place to stay," said Rose.

Carly felt her knees go weak. In the chaos, she'd forgotten all about Megan. What kind of mother did that? How would her daughter react? Would she be scared? Sad?

Andrew moved behind her then. Placed his warm, strong hands on her shoulders. "Thank you, Rose, but that won't be necessary. Carly and Megan can stay in my grandmother's house if need be."

Hillary's gaze zeroed in on Andrew. "Do I know you?"

Andrew shook his head. "I don't believe so." He extended his hand. "Andrew Stephens."

The woman Carly suspected to be somewhere around sixty cautiously accepted the offer. "Hillary Ward-Thompson." She let go, still scrutinizing Andrew. "You wouldn't be related to Clint Stephens, by any chance?"

"Yes, ma'am. He's my father."

Hillary's espresso eyes widened for a split second. "You favor him a great deal."

"So I've been told." Seemingly distracted, Andrew shot a glance toward the house before peering down at Carly. "It looks like the chief might be ready to talk with you."

"We won't keep you, dear." Rose's smile was a sad one as she moved forward for another hug. "I'll touch base with you later. Until then—" she let go "—you're in my prayers." Turning to leave, she patted Andrew on the arm. "I'm glad you're here."

"Thanks, Rose. So am I."

Carly was glad, too. Without him, she'd be curled up in a corner somewhere, bawling like a baby, clueless about what to do or where to turn. But why was *he* glad?

As the two women continued down the sidewalk, Ouray's fire chief, Mike Christianson, approached. "Good to see you again, Andrew." The two men briefly shook hands.

"You, too, Mike. I just wish it were under better circumstances."

Carly swallowed hard as her former schoolmate turned his attention to her. Now married with three kids, Mike was a good guy. She knew he wouldn't sugarcoat anything. Though the harsh reality was what she feared the most.

His features softened as his weary green eyes met hers. "The good news is that the fire never made it to the second floor."

Her shoulders relaxed. That meant her guest rooms were okay. But what about her and Megan's rooms on the first floor? The kitchen, parlor and family room?

"Most of the damage was confined to the kitchen and family room."

"How bad?" She absently rubbed her arms.

He hesitated, his gaze momentarily falling to the ground before bouncing back to hers. "I'm afraid you're not going to be able to stay here for a while, let alone host any guests. Kitchen is a complete loss."

So far, Carly had managed to keep her nausea in check. Right about now, though, she was quickly losing that battle. She didn't know which was worse—not being able to stay at Granger House or not hosting any guests. No guests meant no income, but to have her home taken from her...

Where was that oxygen mask?

As though sensing she needed help, Andrew slipped his arm around her while he addressed Mike. "Do you know what caused the fire?"

Mike nodded, his lips pressed into a thin line. "As most often happens, it was a cooking fire."

Confused, Carly shook her head. "Cooking? But I wasn't— Oh, no." She felt her eyes widen. Stumbled backward, but Andrew held her tight. Her hand flew to her mouth, horror flooding her veins. "The chicken." The earth swirled beneath her. Sweat gathered on her upper lip. "I forgot." She looked at Mike without really seeing him. "And I went to the bank."

A churning vortex of emotions whirled inside her. A feeling she'd experienced only one other time in her life. The night she learned that Dennis had died. And just like that time, this was all her fault, and poor Megan would be the one paying the price for Carly's mistake.

Andrew recognized the self-reproach that settled over Carly the moment she learned the cause of the fire. He was all too familiar with the hefty weight of guilt. He'd carried it for the last two years, since the day he'd given work a higher priority than his dying mother. When he'd finally made it to her bedside, it was too late. He never got to say goodbye or tell her how much he loved her.

He shook off the shame as the fire trucks pulled away. He had to do everything he could to help Carly. He could never turn his back on her. Especially now.

Still standing in his grandmother's front yard, he eyed his watch. School would be letting out soon. And if Megan came walking up here, unaware of what had happened, Carly would blame herself even more.

He wasn't about to let that happen. "What do you say we go meet Megan?"

Carly's deep breath sent a shudder through her. "I guess that would be best. Give me an opportunity to prepare her before she sees the house."

As they walked in the direction of the school, the

extent of Carly's nervousness became clearer. The constant *zip, zip, zip* sound as she fiddled with the zipper on her jacket was enough to drive anyone crazy.

Still a block away from the school, he touched a hand to her elbow to stop her. "Anything you care to discuss?"

Her blue eyes were swimming with unshed tears as she peered up at him, her bottom lip quivering. "What am I going to say to her? I mean, what if she hates me?"

Seeing her pain made him long to pull her into his arms. "Hates you? Why would Megan hate you?"

"Because the fire was my fault." She crossed her arms over her chest and held on tightly. "Because of me, my daughter won't be able to sleep in her own bed tonight. Won't be able—"

"Now hold on a minute." Using their height difference to his advantage, he glared down at her. "It's not like you meant to start that fire. Being absentminded one time does not make you a bad mom." Softening his tone, he reached for her good hand. "Instead of focusing on the bad, play up the good. She's nine years old. Kids that age love sleepovers, don't they? Tell her she gets to have an extended sleepover at my grandmother's."

Lifting only her eyes, she sent him a skeptical look. "That's the only good thing you could come up with?"

It did sound kind of lame. "Well, I haven't seen the extent of the damage yet, but it sounds like you might be getting a new kitchen, too."

"Like Megan's going to be impressed with that." She started walking again, shoving her hands into her pockets. "I'm just going to have to trust God to give me the words."

When they met Megan at the school, she was her typical exuberant self. Obviously no one had mentioned anything to her about the fire. In a town as small as Ouray, that was unusual. Good, but unusual nonetheless.

The kid walked between them, her purple backpack bouncing with each step. "Did you make cookies today?"

He glanced at Carly to find her looking at him, her expression teetering somewhere between nervous and petrified. Did she really believe her daughter would hate her?

Hoping to reassure her, he offered a slight smile and nodded, as if to say, *You can do this.*

She nodded back. "No, sweetie. There was a little problem at home today." Stopping, she looked into her daughter's eyes. "A big problem, actually. There was a fire. In the kitchen."

Confusion marred Megan's freckled face.

"The fire chief said we're going to have to stay somewhere else for a while."

Megan looked up at her mother through sad eyes. "Where?"

"At Livie's."

The girl turned to Andrew then. "But where will you stay?"

"At the ranch."

Her eyes went wide. "You have a ranch?"

"No. It's my dad's."

"Oh." Her gaze drifted away, then quickly shot back to him. "Can I see it sometime?"

He couldn't help laughing. Whoever said kids were resilient was right. "Sure."

Several minutes later, with gray clouds moving in from the west, hinting at snow, the three of them stood at the back of his grandmother's drive, staring at Granger House. The charred back door stood slightly ajar, windows in both the kitchen and family room were gone, and soot marked the window frames where the flames and smoke had attempted to reach the second floor.

Carly rested her hands upon Megan's small shoulders. The girl's blue eyes were wide, swimming with a mixture of disbelief and fear, her bottom lip showing the slightest hint of a tremor.

Poor kid. The fire hadn't just robbed her of her home. It had robbed her of her security, as well. He had to find a way to make her feel safe again. To protect both her and her mother from any more pain. And standing here staring at the ruins of their beloved home wasn't going to do that.

He rubbed his hands together. "It's getting chilly out." He stepped between the two females and Granger House. "I'll tell you what. Why don't you two go on inside my grandmother's house and make yourselves at home while I survey things at your place?"

Both sent him an incredulous look.

"The fire chief said it was fine. I'll just see what kind of damage we're talking about."

"I want to go with you." Carly looked at him very matter-of-factly. "I'm going to have to see it eventually. Might as well get it over with so I know what I'm up against."

"Okay." He still didn't think it was a good idea, but… "What about Megan?"

"I want to go, too."

Carly smoothed a hand over her daughter's strawberry blond hair. "Are you sure, sweetie?"

The girl nodded, not looking at all sure of anything.

"All right, then." Still skeptical, he went to his truck to retrieve some flashlights from the toolbox in the bed. With the electricity out, it was likely to be pretty dark in there. "We'll go through the front door. Perhaps you'll each want to gather up a few things."

"Such as?" Carly watched him as he pulled out the flashlights.

"Whatever you can think of. Clothes. Toiletries." Assuming they hadn't been consumed in the fire. "Things you use day to day." He closed the lid on the large metal box. "Okay, let's go before it gets dark."

The trio climbed the wooden steps onto the front porch.

As soon as Andrew pushed the antique door open, they were met with the strong odor of smoke.

"Eww…" Megan held her nose. "It stinks."

Carly put an arm around her. "I know, sweetie."

Inside, the parlor looked unscathed for the most part, save for the slight tinge of soot on the walls. He turned on his flashlight and aimed the beam around the room for a better look.

"Don't worry." He glanced at Megan now. "They have people who can take care of that and make everything smell like new."

"Really?"

Killing the light, he gave her his full attention. "Have I ever steered you wrong?"

That earned him a smile.

They moved collectively into the dining room, where

all the antique furniture appeared to be intact. But as they neared the door to the kitchen—

"Can I check my bedroom?" Megan's room sat off one end of the dining room, while Carly's was on the opposite end.

Carly glanced his way. "Would you mind going with her while I grab some things from my room?"

The fact that she trusted him with her daughter meant a lot. "Not at all."

Megan turned on her own flashlight and slowly moved into her room.

Andrew followed, relieved to see that, like the parlor and dining room, the mostly purple bedroom remained intact, though perhaps a little damp from all the water the firemen had used.

"Go ahead and take some clothes. I know they're probably wet or smell like smoke, but we can toss them in the wash."

While she opened drawers and pulled out items, all of which seemed to be purple or pink, with one random blue piece, he tugged the case from her pillow to hold the clothes.

"Oh, no."

He stopped what he was doing. "What is it?"

Head hung low, the girl frowned. "My cards. I left them in the family room."

If cards were her greatest loss, he'd count himself blessed. Still, they were important to her. "No worries. I'll pick you up a new deck tomorrow."

Her gaze shot to his. "Really?"

"Cross my heart—" he fingered an X across his chest "—and hope to die."

She threw her arms around his waist. "You're the best, Andrew."

The gesture stunned him. Or maybe it was the intense emotions her hug evoked in him. He'd never had much interaction with kids. But this one was definitely special.

A few minutes later, when he and Megan returned to the dining room with a pillowcase full of clothes and shoes, he dared what he hoped was a stealthy peek into the kitchen. And while it was too dark to see everything, what little he did glimpse didn't look good. Or even salvageable.

"Ah, good. You got some clothes." He jumped at the sound of Carly's voice. Turning, he saw her standing beside the table, holding a large tote bag.

"We did, so it looks like we're ready to go." He did not want to allow Carly in the kitchen. At least, not now. Maybe tomorrow, after the shock had a chance to wear off.

"Not yet." Carly set her bag atop the dining room table. "I'd like to see the kitchen."

"Let's do that tomorrow. It's getting dark outside anyway, so you won't be able to see much."

Leaving her bag behind, she took several determined steps toward him and stopped. "I want to see it. Now."

Chapter Five

Talking tough was one thing. Putting words into action was another. And try as she might, Carly couldn't persuade her feet to move across the wooden floorboards of her dining room. Still, she had to do this, had to see her kitchen, because not knowing left far too much to the imagination.

She drew in a bolstering breath, the sickening smell of smoke turning her stomach. At least her great-grandmother's dining room set and sideboard had been spared, as had the antique pieces in the parlor and her bedroom. Her gaze traveled to the opening that separated the dining room from the kitchen. Based on the charred swinging door, she doubted things on the other side of the wall had fared so well.

"You're sure you want to do this?" The uncertainty in Andrew's voice only solidified her determination.

"Yes." She eyed her daughter. "Megan, you stay with Andrew."

Willing one foot in front of the other, she eased toward the kitchen door, her mouth dry. Her heart thudded against her chest as though it were looking for escape.

The closer she drew to the kitchen, the more bleak things became. She reached out a steadying hand, only to have her fingers brush across the scorched casing that surrounded the door. Trim that was original to the house, now burned and blackened. And she had yet to see the worst of it.

Two more steps and she rounded into the kitchen. She clicked on the flashlight Andrew had given her.

Her heart, which had been beating wildly only seconds ago, skidded to a stop. The space was almost unrecognizable. Soot-covered paint peeled away from the walls, dangling in pathetic strips. Floors and countertops were littered with water-soaked ash and all kinds of matter she couldn't begin to identify or explain. She always kept a clean kitchen, so how could—?

Looking up, she realized the ceiling was gone. Over a hundred years of drywall, plaster and who knew what else now strewn across the room, exposing the still-intact floor joists of the bedroom above.

How could she have been so careless? This would take forever to fix. Where would she even begin?

The once dark stained cabinets that Carly had painted white shortly after taking over the house were blistered and burned. The butcher-block island top, salvaged from the original kitchen, had met a similar fate.

Noting her commercial range at the far end of the room, she tiptoed across the wet floor, tears welling as she ran her hand over the soot-covered stainless steel. It had been only two months since she'd paid it off.

"Mommy?"

She blinked hard and fast. She couldn't let Megan see her like this.

Turning, she saw her daughter standing in the doorway, lip quivering, holding up a blackened, half-melted blob of blue-and-white fur.

A sob caught in Carly's throat. Boo Bunny, Megan's favorite stuffed animal. The one her father had given her, the one she still slept with every night.

As the cry threatened to escape, Carly pressed a hand to her mouth and quickly turned away. She'd failed her daughter not once but twice, throwing her life into a tailspin from which she might never recover.

"Megan," said Andrew, "why don't we go outside and get some fresh air?"

Out of the corner of her eye, Carly saw Andrew escort her daughter from the room. She appreciated his intervention, as well as everything else he'd done for her today. Without his steadfast presence and guidance, she would be an even bigger mess.

After pulling herself together and taking a quick perusal of the partially burned-out family room, she joined Andrew and Megan on the front porch. The two were sitting in the swing, and Carly was pretty sure she overheard something about another game of cards. If it made her baby happy, she was all for it.

"Ready?" Andrew stood and handed Carly her tote.

"Yes."

"I'm hungry." Megan hopped out of the swing.

Peering at the sky, Carly was surprised to see that the sun had already dipped below the town's western slope. Though it wasn't dark yet, Ouray lay bathed in shadows. And her daughter had yet to have her after-school snack. Carly shook her head, disgusted. Add that to her list of failures.

A black, late-model SUV pulled alongside the curb just then, coming to a stop behind Carly's vehicle.

"Cassidy!" Megan bounded down the stairs as Celeste Purcell and her two daughters, Cassidy and Emma, got out.

Carly glanced back at Andrew, then tugged her tote over her shoulder and followed.

The three girls hugged and were practically giddy by the time she reached Celeste.

Her very pregnant friend met her with a sad smile. "Oh, Carly." They hugged best they could with Celeste's swollen belly between them. Then, with a final squeeze, Celeste stepped back, her brown eyes focused on Carly. "How bad is it?"

"Pretty bad." She drew in a shaky breath, still clueless about how to move forward. "At least the major damage was confined to the kitchen and family room."

Celeste pointed to Carly's tote bag. "Mom and Rose said you're going to stay next door."

"Yes, at Livie's house." She poked a thumb toward the home. "Andrew said— Oh, wait." She twisted to find Andrew standing behind her. "Celeste, this is Andrew Stephens. Andrew, Celeste Purcell."

"You were in the diner today." Celeste smiled.

He rocked back on his heels, Megan's pillowcase full of clothes at his feet. "I was. Good food, by the way."

"Speaking of food…" Celeste started toward the back of her vehicle, moving past the chattering trio of girls, to open the hatch.

The girls' giggles warmed Carly's heart. Perhaps her daughter would be okay after all.

Celeste tugged at a large box. "I brought you some enchiladas, chips and salsa for dinner and a pan of Granny's cinnamon rolls for breakfast." She started to lift the box, but Andrew intercepted her.

"Let me get that." He took hold of the cardboard container. "Smells fantastic."

Carly reached to close the hatch. "You didn't have to do all that, Celeste."

"Sweetie, if the roles were reversed, I know you'd be doing the same thing for me."

The crunch of gravel under tires drew their attention to the street.

The approaching Jeep eased to a stop in front of Livie's house. Blakely Lockridge, Rose's granddaughter, and Taryn Coble, Celeste's sister-in-law, soon emerged.

"Sorry we're late." Taryn tossed the driver's door closed behind her before falling in alongside Blakely. "I had to feed the baby."

"How is the little guy?" Carly eyed the new mother.

Taryn blushed. "He's just perfect."

"You won't be saying that once he starts walking." Blakely had a toddler herself, as well as an almost-teen. And Carly was pretty sure she'd heard recent mention of another one on the way. Her strawberry blonde friend addressed her now. "How are you holding up?"

"I'm still standing." Though given the opportunity, she was certain she could collapse at any moment.

"And we thank God for that," said Blakely.

"Mommy—" Megan tugged on Carly's jacket "—I'm hungry. Can the girls and I have a treat?"

Carly looked down at her daughter, her heart twisting. Other than what Celeste had brought, she had no food. Nothing to give her daughter, no—

"Oh, I almost forgot. There are some cookies in the box, too," said Celeste. "Help yourselves."

As Andrew pulled a plastic container from the box and handed it to Megan, Taryn said, "Blakes, that sounds like our cue to unload."

"Unload?" Carly watched the two women as they returned to Taryn's Jeep.

"We thought you might be in need of a few groceries." To emphasize her point, Blakely lifted two brown paper bags from the backseat.

Andrew nudged Carly with his elbow and nodded toward Livie's. "Would you mind catching the door?"

Celeste and her girls said goodbye as the rest of them made their way inside. In no time, every horizontal surface in Livie's kitchen, countertop and tabletop, was covered with bags and boxes. And the aroma of those enchiladas wafting from the oven had Carly's stomach growling.

Blakely emptied butter, eggs, fruits and vegetables from one bag and put them in the fridge. "We'll let everyone know where to find you, because there will be plenty more food."

"Oh, and Dad said to tell you he'll be by first thing tomorrow morning." Taryn folded an empty bag. Her father was Carly's insurance agent. "He was stuck in Grand Junction today. Otherwise he'd be here now. However, he's already contacted a restoration company out of Montrose, and they should be here anytime."

The outpouring of support had Carly feeling overwhelmed. She was blessed to have such wonderful friends. Yet as they continued to work, small arms worked their way around her waist, and she gazed down into her daughter's troubled blue eyes. Carly couldn't help worrying. While Megan had been able to laugh with the girls, reality had again taken center stage. Now it was up to Carly to make things better. And she'd do whatever it took to make that happen.

Andrew had forgotten how generous the people of Ouray could be. When cancer claimed his mother two years ago, the donations of food were almost more than his brothers and dad could eat. A scenario that had played out again when his grandmother died last fall.

He eyed the goodie-covered counter in his grandmother's kitchen, recalling that summer his dad had gotten pneumonia. Andrew was only fifteen at the time, his brother Noah, eighteen. That was the worst summer ever as the two of them worked the ranch without their father. Thanks to the town's generosity, though, their family never went hungry.

Now, seeing Carly the beneficiary of their goodwill warmed his jaded heart. He couldn't think of anyone more deserving. The outpouring of support also reminded him of how different Ouray was from the big city. Everyone banding together for the common good.

While Carly put Megan to bed, Andrew called his father and brought him up to speed, telling him about the fire and letting him know that he'd be staying at the ranch. Then he went to work, trying to clean up the kitchen and put away as many things as he could. Whatever would help Carly.

People had been stopping by all evening, dropping off casseroles, baked goods and groceries. Some had even gone so far as to bring clothes and toiletries—those things people used every day but didn't give much thought to until they didn't have them.

Glancing around the outdated room, he could hear the sound of a generator coming from next door. Per the insurance company, the restoration team had arrived from Montrose shortly after Blakely and Taryn had left. So when more people arrived with food, he took the opportunity to slip over to Granger House. The crew had immediately gone to work assessing the extent of the damage, not only from the fire but from smoke, soot and water, as well. They'd also begun the water removal process to prevent further damage and boarded up the back door and broken windows. This was only the beginning, though. Getting rid of all traces of smoke and soot would likely take weeks.

He shoved two more boxes of cereal into the already overstuffed pantry. Had it really been only yesterday that he left Denver? Closing the door, he shook his head. So much had transpired since then. Just thinking what lay ahead for Carly had his brain spinning. Though he doubted she had a clue.

Instead, her sole focus was her daughter, and rightfully so. But come tomorrow, she was going to be bombarded with a lot of things that would need to be addressed right away. And with Carly teetering on the brink of collapse, he couldn't help feeling that he should step in and help guide her through the aftermath. After all, he was a contractor, and she was…the woman he'd once planned to marry.

He closed the pantry door and leaned against it. They'd dated the last two years of high school and had their future planned out. Or so he'd thought. He went off to college in Denver, and she followed the next year. Then he left school in favor of the construction job he'd taken over the summer. The money was good, meaning they could marry sooner and start on a solid foundation, instead of struggling the way his parents had.

But between his work schedule and her classes, they rarely saw each other. Before he knew it, she was ready to go back to Ouray. Hoping she'd stay, he proposed. But she wasn't interested in building a life in Denver. And he had no interest in coming back to Ouray. His dreams were far too big for this small town.

Movement had him turning to see Carly coming into the kitchen. She looked like the walking dead. Only much prettier, of course.

She stopped abruptly, her weary gaze skimming the kitchen. "Where did everything go?"

"Pantry, cupboard—" he pointed "—pretty much anyplace it would fit." He paused, suddenly second-guessing the decision. Who was he to organize someone else's kitchen? A woman's, no less. He was just a single guy whose refrigerator had more empty space than actual food. Besides, Carly probably had her own way of organizing. "You're welcome to move things wherever you like, though."

"No. I'm sure they're just fine where they are." Her tired blue eyes found his. "Thank you for doing that for me." Her praise did strange things to his psyche.

"Megan go to sleep okay?"

"Surprisingly. I was afraid we might have a problem without Boo Bunny, but she barely lamented not having it. At least, not once I told her I'd let her pick out a new stuffed animal at the toy store."

"I take it Boo Bunny was the blue-and-white blob she found at the house."

"Yes. Her father gave it to her."

"No wonder she was so attached." After a silent moment, he said, "They're still hard at work next door, so don't be surprised if you hear noises."

"How can they do that? I mean, there's no electricity."

Smiling, he eased toward her, wanting to prepare her for tomorrow. "That's what generators are for."

"Oh, yeah." She covered a yawn with her gauzed hand. "I forgot about that."

She was beyond exhausted.

Whatever he'd planned to talk to her about could wait until morning. Right now she needed sleep.

Moving into the living room, he picked up his duffel. "I should go so you can get some rest."

She didn't argue but followed him outside. "I figure one of two things will happen. Either I'll be asleep as soon as my head hits the pillow, or my mind will be so busy thinking about things that I won't get any sleep at all."

"Well, for your sake, I hope it's the first one." He looked up at the full moon high in the sky, illuminating the snow on the surrounding mountaintops.

The hum of the generator next door filtered through the cool air.

"What a difference twenty-four hours can make, huh?" There was a hint of hoarseness in Carly's voice.

Curious, he faced the woman who was now beside him.

"Last night at this time, I was slamming the door on you."

"Oh, that." He adjusted the duffel in his hand. "Well, this hasn't been what I would call an average day."

"No. Me, either." She rubbed her arms. "I appreciate everything you did for us today, Andrew."

"I didn't do much."

She peered up at him. "You were there for me. I needed that." With two steps toward him, she pushed up on her toes and hugged him around the neck. "Thank you." Her words were a whisper on his ear, soft and warm. And he felt his world shift.

Releasing him, she turned for the door. "Good night."

Still stunned, he managed to eke out "Night" before she disappeared into the house.

Climbing into his truck a few minutes later, he shoved the key in the ignition and waited for his breathing to even out. Carly stirred something inside him that he hadn't felt…well, since they were a couple.

That was not good. Because despite today's events, there was still the issue of his grandmother's house. And that was a battle he intended to win. Even with this little hiccup.

Shifting his truck into gear, he headed in the direction of the ranch. He had only eight weeks before he was needed back in Denver. After that, he didn't know when he'd be able to break away to work on Grandma's house. Which meant he had to settle the question of ownership quickly. Something Carly wasn't likely to discuss until Granger House was up and running again. Meaning he'd have to see to it that the repairs didn't take any longer than necessary. And that left him with only one option.

He'd have to do the work himself.

Chapter Six

The air was crisp the next morning as Carly walked a seemingly rejuvenated Megan to school. After much reassurance that Granger House would not forever smell like smoke, her daughter was quick to offer up suggestions for both the kitchen and the family room. Starting with turquoise cabinets and a purple sofa.

Now, sitting at Livie's kitchen table, Carly couldn't help but chuckle. While those were indeed beautiful colors, they weren't exactly appropriate for a historic home such as Granger House.

Nursing her fourth cup of tea, she stared out the window at the large blue spruce that swallowed up much of the backyard. She'd spent half the night second-guessing her refusal of Andrew's offer to pay her full price for her half of this house. That would pay for Megan's college and then some.

But it would also mean giving up her dream. Something her brain was too muddled to think about right now. At this point, her mind couldn't fully process anything.

Regardless, her daughter's attitude this morning had apparently rubbed off on her. She was ready to roll up her sleeves and get busy on the repairs. Because the sooner that happened, the sooner she'd be back in business.

Her phone vibrated, sending it dancing across the table's wood veneer.

Picking it up, she saw her mother's number on the screen. She'd called her parents last night, after Andrew left, to tell them about the fire. So why was Mom calling now? Carly hoped she hadn't added to her mother's worry. After all, with Carly's father recovering from back surgery, the woman had enough on her plate.

"Hi, Mom." She pressed the device against her ear and took another sip of the English breakfast tea Blakely had so graciously brought her.

"Morning. I just wanted to check in and see how you were doing. Please tell me you were able to get some sleep. You sounded absolutely exhausted last night."

"I was." Too many crazy thoughts running through her head for any real sleep, though.

"You're still at Livie's, I take it."

"At the moment. I'm waiting for Phil so we can go over the insurance stuff."

"Oh, I so wish I could be there to help walk you through this mess."

"I'll be fine, Mom. Dad's health is far more important than holding my hand. Besides, I've got Phil and Andrew to help me."

"Be sure to tell Andrew we said thanks for letting you and Megan stay at Livie's."

"What do you mean thank him? I am part owner, you know."

"Okay, then tell him I appreciate all the support he's given you. Not every man would be willing to do that. Especially one you have a history with."

"Point taken." She still didn't know what she would have done without him and was grateful she didn't have to find out. "Just so you'll know, I did thank him for his help."

"That's my girl."

The doorbell rang.

"I need to let you go, Mom." She stood and started toward the front door.

"Call me later?"

"I will."

"Love you."

She paused at the front door. "Love you, too." Ending the call, she shoved the phone in the back pocket of her jeans and tugged open the solid oak door. "Hi, Phil."

"Good morning." He wiped his feet on the mat before stepping inside. "Sounds like the restoration guys are hard at work next door."

She nodded, pushing the door closed. "I'm pretty sure they were here all night. Either that or they left late and were back at it by the time I took Megan to school."

"That's good. The sooner we jump on this, the better off you'll be."

"Amen to that." She pushed up the sleeves of her sweater, grateful her folks took care of the asbestos back in the eighties. Otherwise she'd have to wait weeks on abatement alone. "I am ready to put this behind me ASAP."

"In that case, shall we head next door?"

"Oh. Okay."

"You sound disappointed."

"No. I guess I just thought we'd have to go over my policy or something."

Feet shoulder width apart, the silver-haired man thumped his tablet against his thigh. "I've already done that. The damage and contents are covered, minus your deductible, of course."

"How much will that be?"

"Two percent of whatever the total is. I won't know for sure until I've assessed the damage."

Nodding, she mentally crunched some numbers. Looked like she'd have to tap into the money she'd planned to use to purchase the other half of Livie's house. Money that had originally been set aside for a kitchen reno. Talk about irony.

"You also have business interruption. That covers whatever profits would have been earned during the restoration process."

"Yes, I remember Dad insisting I put that in there."

Phil lifted a brow. "Aren't you glad he did?"

"Definitely." She again reached for the door. "I guess we'd best head on over to my house, then."

Outside, the restoration company's generator echoed throughout the neighborhood. The sun had risen higher in the sky, chasing away the early morning chill. As she approached Granger House, though, a dark cloud settled over her. Things had looked pretty bleak when she surveyed the damage last night. Now, in the light of day, they'd likely appear worse. She wasn't sure she could go through that again.

Do you want Granger House up and running or not?

She didn't have to think twice.

Drawing from the steely reserve that had served her in the past, she pushed through the front door. After a brief discussion with the restoration crew, she and Phil stood in her burned-out kitchen. With no heat and blowers going since last night to dry things out, the place was freezing. For now, at least, the blowers had been turned off.

A high-powered floodlight connected to a generator illuminated things as Phil moved about the room, taking measurements and making notes on his tablet. "I don't suppose you have an inventory of your belongings, do you?"

"Only the antiques." She rubbed her arms. "Why? Is that bad?"

"No." He sent her a reassuring smile. "It just means you'll have a little homework to do."

"Such as…?"

"You'll need to walk through each of these spaces mentally and write down everything that was in them. Everything from appliances to salt shakers. Storage containers, pots, pans, utensils…anything that was lost."

"I can do that."

"By the way, did you have any reservations on the books?"

Reservations? "How could I have forgotten something so important? I have bookings for this coming weekend and just about every weekend after that."

"I'm afraid you'll need to contact those people."

She blew out a frustrated breath. "I've got their information on my—" She gasped. Her laptop?

She hurried to the heavily charred table that now rested on two legs. "Where did it—?" Lowering her gaze, she spotted the half-open computer lying on the floor. Her heart sank as she lifted the partially melted, soot-covered device. The business she'd worked so hard to build was crumbling before her very eyes.

Feeling a hand on her shoulder, she looked into Phil's warm gaze.

"Do you have remote backup?"

Obviously she hadn't had enough tea. Or sleep. "Yes." Dennis had been a computer guru, so the concept of remote backup had been engrained in her.

Thank You, God.

"Good. We'll cover a new laptop." He took hold of the one she still held in her hand and set it aside. "In the meantime, I have one you can borrow. I'll bring it by later today." Turning, he continued. "The restoration company will clean everything in the house, from carpets to draperies to anything else that was affected by the smoke or water."

"That's good to know."

"Did you have a contractor in mind?"

"For what?"

"To do the work on your kitchen. Looks like you'll be getting a new one."

"Oh." While she supposed that was good news, she never realized there would be so many things to consider. "No. I—"

"Hello?" Andrew stepped into the kitchen. "I thought I might find you here." He continued toward them. "Phil. How's it going?" The two men shook hands.

"Good. How 'bout yourself?"

"Not too shabby." Wearing a lined denim jacket over

a beige Henley, he rested his hands on his hips. "You two been going over everything?"

"Actually, I was just asking Carly about contractors."

"I guess I showed up at the right time, then." He smiled at Carly. "Since you and Megan will be staying at my grandmother's, that leaves me with nothing to do. So—" he shrugged "—I'd be happy to offer my services."

"Uh…" Working with Andrew? That would mean seeing him every day.

"I'd be able to start right away."

Phil's gaze darted between Carly and Andrew before settling on Carly. "A good contractor who can start immediately? That's pretty rare."

Probably. But still…

She crossed her arms over her chest. "What do you think it'll take? Two, three weeks?"

"More like five or six," said Andrew.

"Weeks?" Granger House couldn't be closed for that long. And she definitely wasn't willing to spend that much time with Andrew. She glanced at Phil, hoping he'd concur that five weeks was far too long.

"Sounds about right to me."

She felt her body sag. If that were the case, waiting for another contractor would only mean the project would take even longer. And she didn't want Granger House out of commission any longer than necessary.

But working with Andrew?

Seemed as though she didn't have a choice.

Squaring her shoulders, she looked him in the eye. "Have at it, then. The sooner things get started, the better off we'll both be." Because seeing Andrew, day in and day out, was the last thing she wanted to do.

* * *

Sunday afternoon, Andrew stood in the shell of Carly's kitchen, the space illuminated by portable floodlights he'd hooked up to a generator, awaiting her thoughts on her new kitchen layout. With the help of his younger brothers, Matt and Jude, along with Carly and even Megan, they'd gutted the space, removing everything from cupboards to appliances, debris, you name it. They salvaged what they could and tossed the rest into the Dumpster he'd had brought in.

On Friday, he went to the city to see about permits. To his surprise, they said he'd be able to pick them up Monday afternoon. Something that never would have happened in Denver. He grabbed his travel mug from atop his toolbox and took a swig of coffee. He was proud of Carly, the way she'd pulled herself up by her bootstraps and dug in to get the job done. Not everyone would have been able to bounce back so quickly. Then again, most people didn't have a kid like Megan to spur them on. She'd definitely kept things lively during the demo, chattering almost nonstop about school, her friends and how the fire had practically made her a celebrity.

Shaking his head, he chuckled. Megan was a great kid. In some ways much like her mother, while in others quite different. Like her outgoing personality. Growing up, Carly had definitely leaned more toward the timid side. Something she'd obviously grown out of.

He was glad he was able to help them. Even if his motives weren't as pure as they should have been. Working on Carly's place also gave him an excuse not to be at the ranch. It wasn't that he didn't love his father.

On the contrary, he rather enjoyed spending time with him. The old man was always up for a good conversation. But the ranch was so…depressing. Sometimes he felt as though the place just sucked the life right out of him. Like it had his mother.

Shaking off the morbid thought, he turned off the noisy blowers the restoration company had kept going almost from the moment they arrived, then glanced at his watch before strolling into the dining room. Where was Carly?

He'd told her that, since they were starting from scratch, she was free to do just about anything she wanted in terms of layout. Instead of sharing her thoughts, though, she'd paced the wooden floor virtually the entire weekend, tapping a finger to her pretty lips as she hemmed and hawed.

Well, now he needed some decisions so he could get the ball rolling first thing tomorrow.

Just when he was about to head next door to check on her, she strolled through the front door, looking much cuter than most of his clients.

"Sorry I'm late." Her blond curls bounced around her shoulders. "Someone called wanting to make reservations for this summer."

With Granger House Inn's landline out, she'd been able to get calls forwarded to her mobile phone.

Hands tucked in the pockets of her fleece jacket, she shrugged. "It felt good to *book* a reservation instead of canceling." Reluctantly she'd contacted all of her upcoming clients, letting them know about the fire and offering them a discount on a future stay. Even though her insurance policy had coverage for business interruption, he knew she was worried about Granger House Inn's reputation and felt the incentive might help smooth things over.

"Well, then, I guess we'd better get going on things. Can't have a bed-and-breakfast without a kitchen." Besides, the faster he finished Carly's house, the faster he could move on to his grandmother's. Though he still might not complete it before heading back to Denver.

Of course, that was assuming he and Carly could come to an agreement. But that was a discussion for another day.

"Where's Megan?" he tossed over his shoulder on his way into the kitchen.

"At a friend's."

Once inside the space that had been stripped to the studs, some of which were damaged by the fire and would have to be replaced, he clapped his hands together and rubbed them vigorously. "Okay, so what are we doing?"

Carly opened her mouth as though she were ready to share her vision, then snapped it shut, her shoulders drooping. "I don't know."

He tamped down his rising frustration. "Carly, you spend a lot of time in this room and do a *lot* of cooking. Haven't you ever dreamed of having more counter space or better lighting? More storage?"

"Yes. At one time, I was even saving to have the kitchen remodeled. Then I got the news from the lawyer about your grandmother's house and my plans changed." She met his gaze. "Still, I never had any really cohesive plans."

"But it's a starting place." He took a step closer.

"Tell me what some of your thoughts were. Some of the things you were wanting."

"That's just it. My thoughts are too jumbled together right now for me even to begin to sort them out. It's like somebody just dumped a five-thousand-piece puzzle in front of me and told me to put the thing together without ever looking at the box cover. The only things I know for sure are that I want a kitchen that is efficient and looks like it belongs here. Nothing ultracontemporary or trendy." Suddenly a bit more animated, she started to pace. "I want classic. And white. Something nice and bright."

Efficient and classic. Now they were getting somewhere. "Hmm… Megan's going to be one disappointed little girl."

Carly turned to look at him.

"She's pretty stoked about the turquoise, you know?"

That earned him a laugh. And hopefully lightened her mood.

"Now let's talk layout," he continued. "Where would you like to put the sink?"

Her brow puckered in confusion. "Right where it's always been. I mean, you can't just move a sink."

He couldn't help smiling. "Yes, believe it not, you can. Especially in a situation like this, when you're starting from scratch. All we have to do is move the plumbing."

"You can do that?"

"With the help of a licensed plumber, yes." He crossed the room, his work boots thudding against the floorboards. "What would you think about putting it here, under the window?" He stood in front of the currently boarded-up opening. "That way, instead of look-ing at a blank wall while you're doing dishes, you can look outside."

Her nose scrunched. "That would be better. But then, what would I put where the sink used to be?"

Good grief. Had she never watched HGTV?

He moved back to where she stood. "Are you famil-iar with the kitchen work triangle?"

"Sort of, yes. Sink, stove, fridge, right?"

"Exactly. So rather than having your stove way over on the other side of the room—which was an obvious afterthought—what if we put it where the sink used to be?"

Her blue eyes scanned the room. "What would you think about using some vintage and reclaimed pieces? Cabinets, perhaps?"

He kept his groan to himself. The search for those items could take forever, leaving him no time to work on his own planned renovations. Watching Carly wander the kitchen, though, her thoughts finally taking flight, he couldn't help being drawn in. The sparkle in her eyes made it impossible. Instead, he found himself wanting to make her dreams come true. Even if she wasn't sure what those dreams were.

"What would you think about adding a pantry? And a bigger island? One people could sit at."

Her expression unreadable, she simply blinked. "That would be amazing. But how?"

"Carly, this is a *big* space." He stretched his arms wide. "Don't confine yourself to the way things used to be. You said you wanted to expand the B and B. Here's your starting point." Considering he still had no plans to budge on Grandma's house, he probably should have phrased that differently. But the faster she moved, the faster he could get back to working on his own project.

"We can do this, Carly. Together." He took a step closer. "So what do you say? Shall we take a chance on something new and fresh?"

Chapter Seven

Thanks to the wonderful people at the local internet provider, Carly no longer had to tote Phil's laptop to the local coffee shop for access. Instead, she could remain at Livie's and surf the web to her heart's content. And ever since her meeting with Andrew last night, she'd done just that. However, her heart was anything but content. On the contrary, the countless hours spent staring at the computer screen, looking at Victorian-era kitchens, trying to decide what she wanted, had only confused her more. Sure, she'd seen a lot of things that looked great, but how would they work for her?

Having Andrew breathing down her neck wasn't helping any, either. She knew she needed to make a decision, but a kitchen was a long-term commitment. One she had no intention of rushing into, regardless of how hard he pushed. A well-thought-out kitchen took a lot of careful planning. After all, it wasn't simply a room. It was an extension of her. And if past experience was any indication, it's where she'd be spending most of her time. So she was determined to get it right.

If only she were able to envision what the finished product would look like. The images she'd seen online gave her some clue, but she had yet to find a kitchen the size of hers. And that only added to her frustration.

In the meantime, Andrew was awaiting her decision. "Cabinets alone can take up to six weeks to come in," he'd said.

Did he think she was purposely dragging her feet? That she wasn't eager to get back into her house?

Pushing away from Livie's kitchen table, she went to the counter and poured herself another cup of tea. *God, I could really use a heaping helping of clarity here.*

A knock sounded at the door.

Cup in hand, she made her way to the front door and tugged it open to find a smiling Andrew. As if she needed any more pressure.

"What are you doing?" He followed her back into the kitchen.

Tucking her irritation aside, she pointed to the laptop. "Same thing I've been doing for two days."

"Any progress?"

She set her mug on the table and glared at him. "No. And I'd appreciate it if you would stop bugging me about it. When I make a decision—"

"Get your coat. We're going to get you some help."

Her gaze narrowed on him. "What? You're taking me to a shrink?"

"No. I'm taking you someplace where they will help you visualize your new kitchen."

He was taking her. Did he think she was incapable of making a decision on her own? Not that she didn't appreciate all of his hard work and persistence. Without his take-charge attitude, her kitchen would still be in shambles.

Still, she'd learned the hard way that the only one she could truly count on was herself. She was the one who had to live with her choice, not Andrew. Besides, all of this togetherness was getting a bit unnerving.

What are you afraid of? Andrew is nothing more than an old friend.

Yeah, a really cute old friend.

You wanted to know what your new kitchen was going to look like.

She huffed out a breath. "Okay, let's go."

Forty-five minutes later, he pulled his truck up to a kitchen design showroom in Montrose.

Inside, there were kitchen vignettes, all in different styles. Some were sleek and contemporary, while others were rustic. Still others leaned more toward the classic look.

"Welcome to Kitchen and Bath Showcase." A petite saleswoman Carly guessed to be not much older than her thirty-six years approached, her high-heeled pumps tap, tap, tapping against the gleaming tile floor. "I'm Marianne."

"Hi, Marianne." Andrew extended his hand. "Andrew Stephens. We spoke earlier this morning."

"Yes." Her gaze moved to Carly. "Andrew tells me you're having some problems visualizing your new kitchen."

"I'm a bit overwhelmed, yes."

"That's entirely understandable. And exactly why we're here." Marianne gestured toward the kitchen displays to their left. "Let's take a stroll over here." She led them into the maze of sample kitchens. "I understand you have a Victorian home."

"That's correct. So I don't want anything contemporary."

"Oh, no. A Victorian demands something timeless."

Timeless? That would work.

Marianne led them past a vignette with knotty wood cabinets, black countertops and a rustic wood floor. "Are you thinking stained or painted cabinetry?"

"Painted. I want light and airy."

"Something like this?" Marianne motioned to an all-white kitchen with a dark wood floor that warmed the whole space.

"Wow." Carly stepped onto the hardwood. Smoothed a hand across the beautiful island topped with Carrara marble. The cupboards were simple. Classic. And she liked the white subway tile backsplash.

"Marianne, did you receive the pictures and dimensions that I emailed you?" Andrew was beside Carly now.

"I did, and I already have them plugged into my computer. Once we settle on a few things, we can get to work."

"What do you think, Carly?"

She tried to ignore the feel of his hand against the small of her back and concentrated on the kitchen. "It's exactly what I want. But I still can't envision the layout."

"Come with me." Marianne motioned for them to follow.

On the opposite end of the showroom, Carly and Andrew settled in on one side of a long desk while Marianne pecked away at her computer on the other side until she'd pulled up a screen with the outline of Carly's kitchen. Everything from windows to doors was marked out.

"What I was thinking—" Andrew pointed at the large monitor "—was that we put the sink under the window on this wall, the stove over here—" he pointed again "—and then in this corner, a nice walk-in pantry."

"Were you wanting an island?" Marianne addressed Carly.

"Definitely. Granger House is also a bed-and-breakfast, so I need lots of counter space for prep work."

"I was thinking a large one about here." Andrew circled his finger in the open space across from the sink. "Perhaps with some seating."

"I have an idea." Marianne moved her mouse to direct the cursor on the computer screen. "Where does this door lead?"

"To the dining room," said Carly.

"If we put the sink on that wall under the window, your guests will be able to see the dirty dishes."

Carly leaned in closer. "You're right. I hadn't thought about that." Not exactly something she wanted her guests to see.

"So what if, instead of putting the sink here—" the woman made a few clicks on her mouse "—we leave that as a long counter you can use as a staging area?"

Carly straightened. "That would be amazing. But what about—?"

"The sink?" Marianne smiled. "You've definitely got enough room for an oversize island." She drew that out on the screen. "You could have seating on the far side. Over here, across from the stove, you could have your sink and dishwasher, and you'd still have plenty of countertop between the two for prepping food, rolling out dough, whatever."

Carly was getting more excited by the minute. But never had she been more thrilled than when Marianne typed everything into her computer and showed her an image of her new kitchen. No more guesswork or wondering. She could see everything for herself.

"That's amazing. I never would have thought I could have something like that. I won't know what to do with all that storage."

"Believe me, you'll figure it out." Marianne pushed away from her desk. "Let's go look at some door samples and colors."

On the drive back to Ouray, Carly felt as though the weight of the world had been lifted off her shoulders. "I'm so glad you took me there, Andrew. Thank you."

"You're welcome." Hands on the steering wheel, he stared straight ahead.

Watching him, Carly realized he'd been the answer to her prayer. This trip had given her the clarity she'd asked God for this morning. She pressed against the leather seat of his truck, wondering again where she would be without him. He'd been her rock this past week, supporting her, guiding her through all the chaos. Something she never would have expected. Even from her husband.

Suddenly sullen, she turned away and looked out the window at the mountains that loomed in the distance. By their fifth wedding anniversary, Dennis had lost interest in their marriage. In her. Even with Megan in the picture, his work at a local internet technology firm took a higher priority than family. Customers demanded his time and got it. Leaving little to nothing for her and Megan.

Never again would she take second place in someone's life. If she ever fell in love again—which she had no intention of doing—she'd take first place or nothing at all.

Andrew awoke Tuesday morning, ready to get to work on Carly's kitchen. He was glad he'd taken her to the design showroom. He understood that some people had trouble visualizing things. And when talking about something as expensive as a kitchen, you wanted to get it right. But thanks to Marianne, Carly now knew exactly how her new kitchen was going to look.

He'd need to stop by the hardware store before he could get started, though. At first he thought that would require another trip to Montrose. Then his brother Noah reminded him there was now one in Ouray.

Armed with electrical wire and boxes, he exited the store, feeling more invigorated than he had in a long time. Probably because he'd spent far more time in the boardroom than on the job site this past year.

The cool morning air swirled around him as he eyed the snow-covered peaks that enveloped the town and the rows of historic buildings up and down Main Street. For the most part, Ouray looked the same as it always had. Growing up, he'd felt as though Ouray held him back. There was a lot he wanted to achieve. But the tiny town had so little to offer that he couldn't wait to break free. Yet something about the town now felt…different. Less constricting.

Shrugging off the weird vibe, he loaded the supplies into his truck and headed for Granger House.

Aided by the floodlights, he spent the rest of his morning swapping out the damaged studs and marking off the layout of the new kitchen. Since Marianne had flagged their cabinet order as expedited, he hoped they'd be able to shave some time off the six-week turn-around. Before cabinets, though, the kitchen's original hardwoods would need to be sanded, stained and sealed. Something that would prevent anyone from working in the kitchen for as much as a week while things dried.

However, there was plenty to do before then.

With the studs in place, he began drilling holes for the new wiring. He sure hoped Carly showed up soon. He was starving. But also grateful that she'd volunteered to feed him. Otherwise he'd have to make a run somewhere to grab something, and that would only take more time.

Since he'd turned off the blowers, he was able to hear when the front door opened.

"Get it while it's hot." Carly entered the kitchen carrying a brown paper bag in one hand and a thermos in the other.

He stopped what he was doing and set his drill on the floor. "You don't have to tell me twice."

"Good." Looking particularly pretty in a soft purple sweater that brought out her eyes, she set the items atop his makeshift worktable that consisted of two sawhorses and a sheet of plywood. "I've got grilled cheese on rye and some homemade tomato soup."

"Perfect." Especially since the house was still without heat.

She pulled two foil-wrapped sandwiches from the bag. "I didn't know how hungry you'd be, so I made you a second if you want it."

His stomach chose that moment to rumble.

Carly grinned, reaching for the old-fashioned thermos she must have found hidden away at his grandmother's. "It's in the bag whenever you're ready." She removed the lid, which functioned as a cup, and poured in the hot, steaming liquid. "Here you go."

"Thanks." His fingers brushed hers as he took hold of the cup. Their gazes collided, triggering the strangest sensation. Something akin to an electrical jolt. And judging by the way Carly quickly pulled away, her cheeks pink, he guessed she'd felt it, too.

He took a bite of his sandwich, chalking the whole thing up to static electricity.

Looking at everything in the room except him, she picked up her sandwich, peeled back the foil and took a dainty bite.

"I'll be starting on the electrical shortly," he said between bites. "If everything goes according to plan, drywall should be going up by the end of the week." He was rambling when he needed to shut up and eat.

"What about windows?" Setting her sandwich on the work table, she pointed to the boarded-over spaces where the windows and the back door once were.

"Thanks for the reminder. I was going to ask if you wanted to stick with the same size windows or, in the case of the one over here—" he moved to where he'd once suggested they put the sink "—would you like to go with something bigger?"

"Wouldn't bigger look out of place with the rest of the house?"

"Yes. So rather than go bigger with the actual window, we would simply add another window or even a third, like they did in other parts of the house."

"But what about the inside? The casings and such?"

"Not to worry. I spoke to Jude about it when we were doing the demo, and he said he could easily duplicate what's there now so everything would be seamless." When not on duty, his policeman brother was an extremely talented woodworker.

Carly didn't respond. Merely roamed the space, one arm crossed over her midsection, her other elbow resting on it as she tapped a finger to her lips. A stance that meant she was thinking about something. And usually spelled trouble for him. Was it the window she was thinking about or something more?

"I don't know about having the sink on the island. I mean, it's always been over here." She gestured to the wall behind her.

"Facing a blank wall." Sandwich in hand, he stepped closer. "Now you'll be able to see your entire kitchen when you're at the sink. Not to mention into the family room. You'll be able to see Megan."

"True. But I'm not sure how I feel about having the refrigerator at the far end of that counter. I'm used to having it closer to the dining room."

"It's not that much farther. And remember, you've got a bigger island now." Wadding up the foil from his first sandwich, he moved beside her. "It's a little late to start second-guessing things, Carly. The cabinets are already on order."

"Yes, but better to make changes now than later."

Why did she have to make any changes at all? "I thought you liked the new design." She was so excited when she saw the mock-up on the computer.

"I do. But it's so…different." She started pacing again. "What if I don't like it?"

"Look, I know you're afraid of change, but believe me, change can be good."

She whirled toward him then. And if looks could kill… "I am *not* afraid of change. But we're talking about a lot of money here, and I want to make sure I get things right."

"Whoa, easy." Holding his hands up, he took a step back. Why was she suddenly so defensive? "I'm not trying to cause any trouble."

His ringtone sounded from his jeans pocket.

He tugged out the phone and looked at the screen. His attorney. "Excuse me." He turned away. "Hey, Ned."

"I've got the latest numbers for Magnum Custom Home Builders."

Just what he'd been waiting for. "And?"

"Looks good. Matter of fact, real good."

"Gross profit?"

"Seven figures."

"Impressive." He glanced behind him to find Carly still wandering. "What kind of debt are we looking at?"

Ned rattled off the numbers.

"Not bad. Any property for future development?"

"Yes, though I don't have the details."

This time when he turned, he found Carly glaring at him. "Hey, I need to go, Ned. I'll touch base with you later." He ended the call and drank the last of his soup before approaching Carly. "Now, where were we?"

Arms crossed over her chest, nostrils flared, she said, "Everything is about money with you, isn't it?"

"What are you talking about? I'm purchasing a new business."

"Even back in high school, you were consumed with money."

"Yeah, so I could help my parents. You know better than anyone how they struggled to make ends meet."

"So you say."

He wasn't sure what had gotten under her skin, but she sure seemed eager to push his buttons.

He took a step closer until they were toe to toe. "Noah and I worked ourselves to death. Yet it wasn't enough. So forgive me if I refuse to struggle like my parents did." He turned away then, trying to ignore the pain and regret welling inside him.

"Funny, I never heard your parents complain. And why would they? I mean, five sons, a thriving ranch... Sounds to me like your folks had a pretty good life."

He jerked back around. "Then why did my mother die so young?"

Chapter Eight

Gray skies and freezing temperatures were the perfect match for Carly's mood. Standing outside Ouray's one and only school, she burrowed her hands deeper into the pockets of her coat, trying to get warm while she waited for Megan. More than three hours after she stormed out on Andrew, she still felt like a heel. She'd foolishly lashed out at him after he accused her of being afraid of change. He had no idea that those words would haunt her to her grave. That those same words were the reason she lost her husband.

She huffed out a breath and watched as it hung in the air. Somehow she had to make things right. Because the anguish on Andrew's face when he mentioned his mother still gnawed at her. She'd wanted to hurt him the way he'd hurt her. Apparently she'd succeeded. Now she was wrestling with herself, trying to come up with some way to make up for being so callous.

"It's f-f-freezing," said Megan several minutes later on their walk home.

"I told you it was going to get cold. But no...you refused to listen to your old mother and chose to wear your spring jacket."

Megan giggled. "Come on, Mom. You're not old."

Did the kid know how to get on her good side or what? "Well in that case—" she wrapped an arm around her daughter "—I've got some hot cocoa for you when we get home."

"What are you waiting for, then?" Megan took off running. "Come on."

When they reached Livie's house, Andrew was loading his truck. After a quick glance their way, he turned and stalked up the front steps and into Carly's house, shoulders slumped, looking every bit as miserable as he had when she left him.

She patted Megan on the shoulder. "You go on in. I'll be there shortly."

"What about the cocoa?"

"It's in the pan on the stove."

Megan's eyes widened. "Mom, you didn't—"

"No, I didn't leave the stove on. Pour some into a mug and then heat it in the microwave for a minute and a half."

"One, three, zero?"

"You got it."

Her daughter darted toward the house.

"There are some cookies on the counter, too."

A smiling Megan shot her a thumbs-up as she pushed through the door.

Carly tugged at the crocheted scarf around her neck and started next door as Andrew emerged from Granger House, carrying his toolbox. "How's it going?"

He shrugged. "Wiring's done."

"Sounds like progress." She shuffled her feet, waiting for him to respond, but he didn't. So much for small talk.

What do you expect after the way you went after him?

She moved to the far side of the truck where he stood, arms resting on the side of the pickup bed. "Look, I'm sorry for what I said earlier. I had no right to attack you like that."

He looked at her now, pain still evident in his dark eyes. "So, why did you?"

She swallowed hard. She couldn't tell him about Dennis. That she was the reason he was dead. Hands shoved in her pockets, she toed at the gravel in the drive. "Stress, I guess."

He nodded. "I can understand that."

He could?

"I know I can't take back what I said, but I'd like to make a peace offering in the form of dinner."

He lifted his head to stare at the darkening clouds. "I'm not really in the mood—"

"I brought you some hot cocoa, Andrew."

They turned to see Megan moving ever so slowly toward them, now wearing her winter coat, a steaming mug cradled in her mitten-covered hands.

He whisked past Carly to her daughter and took hold of the cup. "I was just thinking how nice it would be to have a hot cup of cocoa. How did you know?"

Megan's smile grew bigger by the second. "I don't know. I just did."

He took a sip. "Mmm…this is really good."

"My mommy makes the best cocoa. She says it's a secret recipe."

Carly felt herself blushing when he glanced at her.

"I was just asking Andrew if he'd like to join us for dinner." She knew she was playing dirty, basically suggesting her daughter help coerce him, but she couldn't help herself.

True to form, Megan bounced up and down, hands clasped together. "Oh, please say yes. I want to play cards again."

Carly had been grateful, if not a little surprised, when Andrew presented Megan with a new deck the day after the fire. Megan had told her he said he would, yet Carly still doubted. The gesture had taught her that, among other things, Andrew was a man of his word.

He looked at Carly for a moment as though weighing his options. Or trying to come up with a way out. Finally he met Megan's gaze. "What time should I be here?"

Carly was glad he accepted her invitation. However, when he showed up at Livie's shortly after six, as opposed to the six thirty she'd suggested, she could have kicked herself for allowing Megan to go to a friend's. Because if she knew her daughter, she'd be home precisely at six thirty and not a minute before. Leaving Carly alone with Andrew until then.

"Make yourself at home," she tossed over her shoulder on her way back through Livie's parlor after answering the door. Her steps slowed as she approached the kitchen, though. This *was* his home. Half of it, anyway. Seemed her thoughts of a buyout and renovations had taken a backseat since the fire. Still, that didn't mean she was ready to give up on her dream.

Standing at the avocado-green stove, her back to him, she could feel him watching her. Normally being alone with him wouldn't have been a big deal. They'd actually been getting along quite well. But after putting her foot in it this afternoon…

"So, you're buying another business?" She turned.

He stood at the end of the peninsula, making an otherwise bland brown flannel shirt look incredible. "Yes. A custom home builder."

She retrieved three plates and three bowls from the cupboard, feeling like an even bigger jerk for tearing into him. "I imagine you're grateful to have some time off, then." She breezed past him on her way to the table. "You know what they say about all work and no pla—"

One of the so-called unbreakable plates slipped from her hand then, crashing to the floor and shattering into a million tiny pieces.

Gasping, she slowly set the remaining dishes onto the table and stared at the shards splayed across the gold-and-brown vinyl floor, all around her socked feet.

"Don't move." Andrew was beside her in a flash. "Are you okay? You're not cut, are you?"

She shook her head, still shocked. That plate had virtually exploded. "I don't think so."

"Good." He studied the mess. "Let's try to keep it that way."

She sent him a curious glance. "What do you have in mind?"

"Only one thing I can think of." With that, he scooped her into his arms and started into the living room, the pieces of glass grinding beneath his work boots.

"Really? This is your only solution?" Resting one

hand against his chest, she could feel his muscles. "You couldn't have simply swept up the stuff around me?"

His grin was a mischievous one. "Why would I do that when this is so much more fun?"

"Fun for you, maybe. For me, it's just—" *Torture* was the only word that came to mind. Being in Andrew's arms felt so…good.

"Just what?" In the parlor, he had yet to put her down. "I—I…"

His playful smile morphed into something different. More intense. His gaze probed hers, questioning. As if…

Her gaze drifted to his lips, though she quickly jerked them back to his eyes. The corners of his mouth tilted upward as if he knew what she was thinking.

The front door burst open. "It's snowing!"

They turned to see a stunned Megan.

Andrew quickly set Carly's feet on the hardwood floor.

Carly smoothed a hand over her sweater. Lost in Andrew's embrace, she'd forgotten all about the time.

A quick glance at Andrew revealed how red his face was. And if the heat in her own cheeks was any indication, she was just as crimson.

Megan's eyes narrowed for a second before she crossed her arms. "Were you guys kissing?"

"No," said Andrew.

"Of course not," Carly added.

Without further discussion, Andrew promptly returned to the kitchen and went to work sweeping up the broken glass, allowing Carly to get dinner on the table. And, fortunately, Megan let the subject drop. Likely because she was more interested in the card game Andrew had promised her after dinner.

"Come on, Mom. You need to play, too." Megan dutifully wiped off the freshly cleared table.

"But what about the dishes?" Carly turned on the water at the sink.

"Don't worry." Sitting in his chair, Andrew shuffled a deck of cards. "They'll still be there when we're done." His grin had her narrowing her gaze.

"Great." She turned off the water, and returned to her seat. "You'll be able to help me, then." Or maybe not. That would only keep him here longer, and they'd had enough togetherness today.

"Megan—" he watched Carly as she tossed the dishrag into the sink "—would you mind grabbing a couple of spoons?"

"What for?"

"I'm going to teach you a new game."

Her daughter's nose wrinkled. "With spoons?"

"I remember that game." Carly had played it many times with Andrew's family. "There are only three of us, though."

He leaned closer. "Figured we'd start her off slow."

Recalling the oft raucous times they used to have at the ranch, she said, "Good idea."

Andrew dealt the cards and explained the rules to her eager daughter. The first person to get four of a kind and grab a spoon was the winner.

Things were rather timid the first couple of rounds. Then it was a free-for-all until Megan and Andrew were fighting over the same spoon. Carly watched with amusement as her daughter stood beside him, wrestling the utensil from his hand.

"No…" He threw his head back. "It's mine, I tell ya. I was first."

Megan giggled, tugging with all her might. "Uh-uh."

Finally he relinquished the trophy, as Carly knew he would. What she hadn't counted on, though, was his laughter. Carefree and unrestrained, like when they were kids.

Making her laugh, too.

Gasping for air, he looked at her, his smile pensive. "Do you know how long it's been since I've done that?"

She wasn't sure if he was talking about the game or the laughter. Nonetheless, she said, "It's often the simple things that bring us the greatest pleasure."

"In that case, this is the greatest pleasure I've had in a long time."

She believed him. And that made her very sad.

Three days after Andrew had literally swept Carly off her feet, the aroma of her tropical shampoo still lingered in his mind.

And that was not a good thing. He was still thankful Megan had walked in when she did. Otherwise, he might have done something foolish, like kiss Carly. And that would have been a mistake. A relationship between them would never work. He was Denver, she was Ouray, and that's the way they would always be.

Yet as he pulled up to his grandmother's house Friday morning, he couldn't stop thinking about that game of Spoons and the pleasure it had brought him. It had been a long time since he'd done something just for fun.

Work consumed most of his time. Then he'd go home to an empty house and collapse into bed. But now he found himself wondering—what if he had someone to go home to? A family. How different might his life look then?

Not that it mattered. He was a confirmed bachelor. One who needed to pull himself together, gather his thoughts and concentrate on today's mission. He was taking Carly and Megan, who was out of school for a teacher in-service day, on another trip to Montrose. This time they'd be looking at appliances, lighting, carpeting for the family room and such. Unlike yesterday, when they'd gone to choose the marble slabs for her countertops, nothing was needed immediately, but knowing how overwhelming the process could be, he thought it would be a good idea to get Carly started now.

A fresh dusting of snow covered the ground as he stepped out of his truck into the chilly midmorning air. Though with the sun coming out, it was likely to be gone by afternoon. Just as it had vanished earlier in the week.

It still surprised him that Megan wanted to go with them. Then again, after walking in on him and Carly the other night, she might have thought they needed a chaperone.

He continued up the walk and knocked on the door.

Megan opened it a few seconds later, already wearing her coat. "Hi."

"Hi, yourself. Looks like you're ready to go." Movement had his gaze shifting past her to her mother.

"We sure are." Wearing her puffy white jacket, Carly joined them.

"Okay, let's get on down the road, then."

They piled into his truck and pulled out of the drive.

He'd just turned onto Main Street when his phone rang through the truck's speakers and the name Dad appeared on the dashboard's touch screen caller ID.

He pressed the button on his steering wheel. "What's up, Dad?"

"You still in Ouray?" His father's deep voice boomed through the cab of the vehicle.

"Yes, sir."

"Carly and Megan with you?"

He glanced at Carly in the passenger seat and smiled. "Yes."

"Hi, Mr. Clint," yelled Megan from the backseat.

The familiarity surprised Andrew. Between Grandma and church, he supposed their families had always been intertwined.

"Morning, darlin'. Tell Andrew he needs to bring you and your mama by the ranch on your way to Montrose. I got somethin' I want to show you."

Andrew struggled to come up with what that something might be. His father was gone when he left that morning, and they hadn't spoken. But recalling how eager Megan was to visit the ranch...

"Okay, Dad. We're on our way."

"Abundant Blessings Ranch." Megan read the sign as they pulled onto the property. "This is where you grew up?"

Unfortunately. "I did."

She scooted to the driver's side of the truck and pressed her hands against the glass. "Cool. You have horses."

"Well, my brother and my dad do, anyway."

Megan's head poked between the two front seats. "Where's your mom?"

The question took him by surprise. Somehow he managed to keep it together, though. "She died."

"Oh, yeah." She lowered her head. "I forgot." When she looked up again, she said, "My daddy died."

He was taken aback by her candor. Not a hint of sorrow or regret. Then again, she was young when her father passed away. Not old enough to have regrets.

"Looks like the barn could use a fresh coat of paint." Leave it to Carly to take the subtle approach.

He glanced her way. "Or a demolition crew."

Dad emerged from the barn as Andrew pulled his truck up to the house.

Megan was the first to open her door and hop down onto the gravel. "Hi, Mr. Clint." She waved.

His father coughed as he approached. "Young lady, I think you've grown six inches since the last time I saw you." Which most likely would have been at church.

The kid grinned, straightening to her full height. All four-foot-whatever inches of her.

Carly stepped forward to hug the old man. "How are you, Clint?"

"Not too bad." Releasing her, he smiled, his dark gaze sparkling as it met each one of theirs. "Come with me. I've got something to show you."

Andrew couldn't help wondering what his father was up to. Whatever it was seemed to have the old man pretty stoked.

The trio followed him into the rundown barn.

The smell of hay, earth and manure filled Andrew's

nostrils as he eyed the old gray rafters overhead. The place looked a little better from the inside, but not by much. The roof was still shot.

Dad led them to one of the stalls, the wooden gate creaking when he opened it.

Megan gasped when she saw the two brand-new foals. "They're so *cute*."

"Easy, sweetie. We don't want to scare them." Carly kept her voice low and slipped an arm around her daughter's shoulders. "But they are adorable."

Andrew had to agree. The twins were chestnut colored, and each had a white blaze that stretched from the tops of their heads to their noses. It had been a long time since he'd seen a newborn anything.

"Where's their mother?" asked Carly.

Andrew suspected the answer but waited for his father to respond.

The old man coughed, his expression grim. "She had a tough time with the delivery."

Carly eyed him now, understanding lighting her baby blues. "So they're orphans?"

Dad nodded.

Andrew stepped closer and reached a hand into the pen to pet the soft fur of the first foal. "Remember when you and I used to help feed the calves way back when?" He looked at Carly now.

"How could I forget?" She moved beside him to pet the other foal. "They were so sweet, so little."

Megan looked perplexed. "Did you used to work here, Mommy?"

"No. But I used to hang out here a lot."

"How come?" Megan tilted her head, looking very serious.

Pink crept into Carly's cheeks. "I just liked being here."

"Your mama and Andrew used to be very good friends," said Dad.

Andrew caught his father's smirk before the old man went into another coughing fit. The sound was eerily familiar, reminding him of that summer Dad battled pneumonia. And how protective his mother had been from then on whenever he caught something as simple as a cold.

Urging Megan to pet the foal in his stead, Andrew moved toward his father. "Have you been to see a doctor about that cough?"

"I don't need no doctor. It's just a little chest cold." He leaned against the stall and changed the subject. "You know, these foals are going to require a lot of care and feedings. Unfortunately, time is one of those things I don't have a lot of."

"I can help, Clint," said Carly. "Matter of fact, I'd be happy to."

"Me, too." Megan bounced beside her mother.

Andrew wasn't sure how he felt about them spending time at the ranch. It reminded him too much of when he and Carly were dating. Ironically, some of his best memories were of their experiences together at the ranch.

"I thought I heard voices in here."

They all turned to greet his older brother, Noah. After years on the rodeo circuit, he now lived at the ranch and helped his father with the cattle, though his main focus was on the horses, as well as the trail rides and riding lessons they offered in the summer. Which made Andrew wonder…

"How come you've got the foals in here? I'd think you'd want them down at the stable."

"I asked him the same thing." Noah glared at the old man.

"And I told you, I want them close to the house." When Dad looked Andrew's way, his eyes shimmered. "They were Chessie's babies."

Mama's horse. The one Dad had given her. Now Andrew understood.

While Dad went over the details of feeding the foals with Carly and Megan, Andrew took Noah aside. "How long has he been coughing like that?"

"A couple days, I guess."

Andrew mentally kicked himself for not paying closer attention. Just because he didn't like being at the ranch didn't give him an excuse to ignore his father. From now on, he'd have to keep a closer watch.

Chapter Nine

Carly breathed in the scents of the ranch as she made her way into the barn late Monday morning, armed with two feeding bottles. While some people might think the barnyard smells offensive, she found them rather comforting. Until Andrew brought her and Megan here on Friday, she'd never realized how much she missed the place.

During her high school years when she and Andrew dated, there were days when she spent more time at Abundant Blessings Ranch than she did at her own house. It was here that she'd learned how to fish and milk a cow, shimmy under a barbed wire fence without getting cut. And she was thrilled that her daughter would now get a chance to experience at least some of what the ranch had to offer. Abundant blessings indeed.

Too bad Andrew didn't feel that way about his own family home. She still didn't understand why he thought the place so abhorrent. Did he really believe the ranch had caused his mother's early death?

The babies were standing when she made it to their

stall. One even tried to whinny, though it sounded more like a series of happy grunts.

"You guys know I've got food, don't you?" She swung open the gate and stepped inside the hay-covered space.

Immediately both foals nudged her hands with their velvety noses, eager to eat.

"Hold on a second." She positioned herself between them and lowered the bottles, one on each side of her.

Elsa and Anna—she still couldn't believe Clint had let Megan pick the babies' names—wasted no time latching on, behaving as though they hadn't eaten all day. In fact, this was their sixth feeding since midnight.

Noah and Andrew had taken turns, insisting their father sleep. The man's cough had grown increasingly disconcerting, and they'd also heard him wheezing. So, despite his father's objections, Andrew had taken him to the doctor.

She looked from one chestnut foal to the other. "You two need to slow down or you'll get a tummy ache."

While the twins continued to eat, she leaned against the wooden wall and contemplated all the crazy twists and turns her life had taken recently. Inheriting Livie's had meant she was one step closer to her dream coming true. But between Andrew's refusal to sell and the fire at Granger House, she'd once again been forced to relegate her dream to a back burner. Even if she could talk Andrew into selling, would she still be able to afford to buy him out?

After finally making it to the one-stop home improvement center late Friday, her eyes were opened to just how much everything was going to cost. Even little things like cup pulls and knobs for the kitchen cabinets, a sink, and pendant lights for over the island were more than she'd expected. Sure, she had good insurance, but that money would only go so far.

She let go a sigh, wondering why all of this was happening now. Was she not supposed to expand the bed-and-breakfast? Did God want her to keep taking in bookkeeping?

The thought made her cringe.

About the time Elsa and Anna finished draining their bottles, she heard the sound of gravel crunching under tires outside. That, coupled with the sound of a diesel engine, told her it was Andrew and his father.

She exited the stall, pausing to make sure the old latch was securely in place. "You girls take a nap. I'll be back later."

When she departed the barn, both father and son were getting out of the truck.

She shielded her eyes from the sun as Andrew tossed his door closed.

"So, what'd the doctor say?" Noah hollered as he jogged from the stable, his concern evident. He must have seen them drive up.

Andrew waited until they were all at the back of the truck. "He's got pneumonia. And he's been sentenced to bed rest."

"Oh." Her gaze drifted to the older man making his way up the steps, looking none too happy.

Noah shook his head. "He's not going to like that."

"Sputtered about it all the way home," said Andrew.

"Probably would have been better if they'd just put him in the hospital. I mean, what are we going to do?"

Noah glanced from his brother to his father. "Hog-tie him?"

Andrew followed his brother's gaze. "I think we might have to hire someone to look after him. Besides, he wouldn't listen to us, anyway."

"That's silly." Tucking the two empty bottles under her arm, Carly brushed a windswept hair away from her face. "Why not just let me take care of him?"

Both brothers sent her the strangest look.

"At least during the day. I'm here helping with the foals anyway. And with Granger House out of commission, it's not like I have a whole lot to do."

She turned her attention solely to Andrew. "Besides, I want to help. Your family has always been so good to me, this is the least I can do."

"Are you sure you can handle him?" Noah's dark brow lifted. "He can be pretty stubborn, you know."

"I'm not worried." She watched the older man shuffle into the house. "Clint and I get along fine. He's a good man."

The brothers looked at each other as though sharing a silent conversation before turning back to her.

"Thank you, Carly," said Noah.

"If he gets to be too much, though," said Andrew, "you just let us know."

She smiled. "I will. But I doubt that'll be necessary." She took two steps toward the house, paused and turned back around. "Come on. I'll fix you guys some lunch."

After a quick meal of canned soup and roast beef sandwiches, Andrew headed back to town to work on Granger House, and Noah returned to his work in the stables. Clint settled into his recliner and willingly agreed to the breathing treatment the doctor had ordered. He fell asleep shortly thereafter, so she took the opportunity to sneak out and feed the foals.

When she returned, Clint was still sleeping, so since Andrew had offered to pick up Megan from school and bring her to the ranch, Carly pushed up her sleeves, ready to give the ranch house some much-needed TLC. The Stephens men weren't necessarily messy, but there was something to be said for a good, thorough cleaning. Especially in the kitchen.

She cleared the off-white Formica countertops of clutter before scrubbing them down with bleach, along with the sink and stove. Next she cleaned out the refrigerator, wiped it down, then grabbed a package of chicken from the freezer. All the while, she'd periodically poke her head around the corner to check on Clint, pleased to see he was still asleep. Rest was exactly what he needed to get better.

While the meat thawed in the microwave, she searched the cupboards, trying to figure out what she could make the guys for dinner. Their pantry didn't have a whole lot of variety. Canned soup and veggies, some tomato sauce, pasta... A casserole, perhaps.

Inspired, she put the chicken on to boil. No sooner had she set the lid atop the pot when the sound of Clint's raspy breathing drew her into the adjoining family room. He was awake now, his forest-green recliner upright, and he was looking a bit pale.

"How are you feeling?" She knelt beside his chair, resting a hand on his forearm.

"I know my boys asked you to stay here. But there's no need to fuss over me, young lady. I've been taking care of myself for a long time."

She bit back a laugh. While Clint Stephens might indeed be capable of taking care of himself, his wife, Mona, was the kind of woman who went above and beyond when it came to her men. Tough when she had to be, but not afraid to spoil them, either. Something Carly had always admired.

"I understand. I'm pretty good at taking care of myself, too. But everyone needs a little help now and then. If it hadn't been for Andrew and other folks around town, I never would have made it through these last couple of weeks." She patted his arm. "Now, what can I get you?"

He clasped his hands over his trim belly. "I reckon I could use a cup of coffee."

She was thinking more along the lines of juice or tea.

"I like it black. And strong." A man's man through and through.

"Coming right up." She pushed to her feet. "And just for the record, Andrew and Noah did not ask me to stay with you. I volunteered."

The older man seemed a little more amicable after that. He turned on the television situated in the corner of the room and watched some police show while she assembled the chicken spaghetti casserole. She put the pan in the oven and washed her hands before going to check on him again.

His chair was empty.

"Clint?" Her gaze darted around the room. She checked the hall to see if perhaps he'd gone to the restroom. Then she heard sounds coming from the mudroom.

She entered to find the man wearing his coat and hat and heading out the door.

Suddenly grateful for being a little on the small side, she darted around him to block the opening. "Just where do you think you're going?"

"I have a ranch to tend to."

"Not under my watch, you don't." She held her ground. Even when he closed what little distance there was between them, to tower over her. Though she had no doubt he could push right past her if he really wanted to. She could only hope that—

"Young lady, I suggest you get out of my way." Determined dark eyes bored into hers.

But she had no intention of letting Andrew and Noah down. One way or another, she would win this battle.

Clouds gathered over the mountains to the west as Andrew's pickup bumped over the cattle guard at the entrance to Abundant Blessings. He couldn't remember ever being this eager to get to the ranch. Not that it was the ranch spurring him on. Instead, he was worried about his father.

Why had it taken him so long to notice Dad's cough? If he hadn't been there, would Noah have picked up on it? He didn't want to cast stones at his brother, but what if Andrew hadn't been in town? Suppose Dad had gotten sick and Noah hadn't realized it until it was too late?

What if his father had been at the end and Andrew didn't get a chance to say goodbye?

Truth be told, that was the part that had bothered him all afternoon. What if something happened to his father and he wasn't there? What if he never got to say goodbye?

He drew in a deep breath, refusing to let that scenario play out again.

Then there was Carly. He and Noah had practically dumped the old man on her. It wasn't her responsibility to take care of him. No, either he or Noah should have stayed with their father until they could hire someone.

"I hope Mommy hasn't fed the foals yet." Megan's words as she squirmed in the passenger seat pulled him out of his thoughts. She was every bit as impatient as he was to get to the ranch, albeit for different reasons.

"Are you kidding?" He glanced her way. "You saw how much they ate this weekend. Even if she did feed them, they'll be ready to go again in no time."

She giggled. "Yeah, they were *really* hungry."

Since both Noah's and Dad's trucks were parked close to the house, he pulled up to the far end of the deck. He shifted into Park, his gaze suddenly drawn to the entrance to the mudroom. Why was Carly standing in the open doorway? And why was her stance so rigid, her arms crossed?

Beyond her, he glimpsed his father. Cowboy hat atop his head, he glared down at Carly, looking fit to be tied.

Andrew's heart twisted. How could he have been so naive? He should have known better than to leave her alone with the old man. Clint Stephens was as stubborn as they came. No one except his wife had ever tangled with him and come out a winner. And from the looks of things, Dad had every intention of winning the battle of wills brewing between him and Carly.

Andrew exited the truck and grabbed Megan, tucking her behind him as they climbed the three steps onto the deck.

"Clint Stephens, you get back in that recliner right now or I'll have Noah and Andrew here so fast it'll make your head spin." Apparently neither Carly nor his father had noticed them.

A bone-chilling breeze kicked up as he moved beside the house, lifting the collar on his jacket. Looking down at Megan, he touched a finger to his lips.

Eyes wide, she nodded, seemingly understanding his silent request.

Peering around the corner, he continued to watch. A part of him was ready to rush to Carly's side and give his father a piece of his mind. But the other, more rational part told him to stay put and let her handle things. Because despite his father's intimidation tactics, she was doing a good job of holding her own. Much like his mother had done.

The thought made him smile.

His father continued to stare Carly down, but she wasn't budging. Dad started coughing then, his body convulsing. The cold air must have gotten to him.

Showing no mercy, Carly said, "You might think you're ready to go out there, but your body is telling you otherwise."

The old man continued to cough.

She stood her ground, though. "You gonna be stubborn and ignore it? Or are you man enough to listen to what your body is trying to tell you?"

Andrew had to smother his laugh. She had his dad's number, all right.

His father removed his hat and turned around.

"Okay, then." Carly's posture eased. "Let's get you settled." She stepped away from the door, closing it behind her. She'd obviously won the battle of wills. Just like his mama.

He breathed a sigh of relief, another thought niggling his brain. He'd underestimated Carly. Not to mention his father. It irked him to no end to think that his father had tried to bully her.

He glanced back at Megan. "Your mama's one tough cookie, you know that?"

The kid grinned. "Can we go see the foals now?"

"Sure."

The foals attempted to nicker as he and Megan made their way into the barn. He pushed the door closed, glad that the dilapidated structure still blocked the wind.

While Megan petted and talked baby talk to Elsa and Anna, he tried to wrap his brain around the wayward thoughts that were suddenly bombarding him. Until now, he'd always thought of Carly as the girl he once loved. But seeing the tough yet tender way she dealt with his father had him realizing she'd become an amazing woman.

"I thought I saw you two sneaking in here." Noah closed the door, armed with two bottles. "Megan, you think those babies are hungry again?"

She nodded, her smile morphing into a giggle as one of the foals nuzzled her neck.

Grinning, Noah handed her one of the bottles. "Looks like we'd better hurry before they decide to make a snack out of you."

"Have you been in the house yet?" Leaning against the side of the stall, Noah offered the second bottle to Elsa.

Andrew shook his head. "No. Though we did witness an interesting exchange between Carly and the old man."

His brother's eyes narrowed. "How so?"

Andrew explained what had transpired.

"Maybe Carly isn't the right person to watch Dad, after all."

"Are you kidding? She's perfect," said Andrew. "I mean, when was the last time you were able to get the old man to back down?"

"Good point."

"Besides, Carly volunteered. It's not like we coerced her or anything."

"True."

"I talked to Jude. He's working a double shift today but should be in tonight."

"That's good. I'm going to need him to help me with the cattle." Noah smirked. "That is, unless you'd like to help me."

Andrew held his hands up. "Don't look at me. I've got plenty to do at Granger House."

"Excuses, excuses." His big brother dragged the toe of his well-worn boot through the dirt. "I called Matt."

Their middle brother and Dad had always had a volatile relationship, but even more so after Mom passed away. She was the glue that had kept things together. Without her... "How did that go?"

Noah shrugged. "You know Matt. He doesn't say much. Just that things are busy at the Sheriff's department, but he might stop by." They shared a knowing look, neither believing that Matt would actually show.

"What about Daniel?" Their baby brother was the

adventurer of the family and currently white-water rafting in South America. "You need me to contact him?"

"Nah, I'll email him tonight, let him know what's going on. It's not like he can do anything anyway." Noah pushed off from the wall. "Mind taking over for me? I need to run back up to the stable."

The two traded places.

"Guess I'll see you at supper," said Noah on his way to the door.

"Who's cooking? You or me?"

One side of his brother's mouth lifted. "Neither. I checked in with Carly earlier. Said she's got us covered."

When the foals finished eating, Andrew and Megan made their way to the house. Stepping inside, he was overcome with the most incredible aromas. Food the likes of which this house hadn't known since his mother's passing.

Moving from the mudroom into the main part of the house, he was taken aback. His father was in his recliner with a plastic mask over his mouth, looking very pale.

Beside him, Carly turned off the machine that provided the breathing treatments. "Feel better now?"

Dad nodded and removed the mask, his hesitant gaze drifting to Carly's. "Thank you."

Andrew almost fell over. If he hadn't heard it for himself, he never would have believed it. Carly had definitely won the old man over.

And Andrew couldn't say he blamed him.

Chapter Ten

By midday Tuesday, Carly had cleaned just about everything she could clean at the ranch house. She fixed herself another cup of tea, scooped up the mug and leaned against the pristine counter, watching Clint sleep in his recliner. His continued wheezing was cause for concern. She'd hoped there would be some sign of improvement, yet things were, perhaps, even a little worse. Then again, it had been only twenty-four hours. She prayed he might turn a corner tomorrow. In the meantime, she'd do her best to keep him comfortable, well rested and nourished.

The timer she'd set on her phone vibrated in her back pocket since she didn't want to risk waking him.

She set her cup on the counter and turned off the timer before retrieving two large baking sheets of oatmeal raisin cookies from the oven. Chocolate chip had been her first choice, but since there were no chocolate chips to be found at the ranch house... Maybe she'd pick some up for tomorrow.

Spatula in hand, she transferred the cookies to the cooling racks she'd laid out on the long wooden table.

It felt good to cook for other people again. That's one of the things she missed the most about Granger House Inn being out of commission.

She was off the hook for tonight's dinner, though. Rose Daniels had gotten wind of Clint's illness and called Carly earlier, wanting to know how the townspeople could help.

Carly had thanked her and then, as tactfully as she could, went on to express her concerns about Clint's health and potentially exposing him or any visitors to unwanted germs. To which Rose replied, "You're right, dear. I'll just let everyone know that the Stephens have got you to cook for them, so no meals are needed." And then the woman promptly volunteered to bring them some pulled pork for tonight.

Setting the empty baking pans in the sink, Carly chuckled. She could only hope to have a heart as big as Rose Daniels's.

After washing the baking sheets and moving the cooled cookies to a storage container, she glanced around the room. Surely there was something productive she could do. She wasn't one simply to sit and twiddle her thumbs. Maybe she should start bringing her laptop so she could knock out some bookkeeping while Clint was asleep.

Cup in hand, she wandered down the hallway to see if she'd missed anything. She'd washed Clint's sheets as well as dusted and vacuumed his room but had vowed not to enter any of the brothers' rooms. Noah had moved back in after leaving the rodeo circuit a few years back; Jude still spent much of his time here, helping his father with cattle; and Daniel kept his room for the rare occasion he wasn't traveling. Which he was currently doing, so Andrew was occupying the space.

Continuing to drift, she entered the small room that had been Mona's crafting space. Spools of colorful ribbon still hung from dowels attached to the wall, while decorative papers and fabric had been tossed into baskets and boxes and pushed against the walls, as though someone had cleaned up the space without really knowing where things went.

On the far side of the room, a long countertop stretched the length of the wall with shoe boxes and a stack of books piled in one corner. Moving across the worn beige carpet, she realized that they were scrapbooks. She set her cup down and lifted the cover on the top one. The first page was blank, as were the second and third pages. They all were.

Perplexed, she closed the scrapbook, set it aside and reached for the next one. Also empty. Three, four and five, too. Hmph.

Picking up her tea, she took another sip. Maybe they were just extras.

As she lowered the cup, her gaze fell to the boxes beside the scrapbooks. Just regular old shoe bo—

What was that?

She leaned in for a closer look at the one on top. There was a handwritten *N* in one corner.

Returning her mug to the counter, she tugged the box toward her, casting a glance over her shoulder to make sure no one was coming. She had no business doing this. These could be Mona's most cherished possessions. Yet something compelled her to look.

With the first box in front of her, she glimpsed the

corners of the second box, finally spotting an *A*. Nudging it aside, she moved on to the third box. Sure enough, there was an *M* on one of its corners.

She grabbed the box with the *A*, set it atop the one already in front of her and lifted the lid to discover dozens of photos. A smile played on her lips at the sight of a baby Andrew staring up at her. All that dark hair. Simply adorable.

Picking up the photo, she turned it over. It was labeled Andrew—4 months old.

As she continued to look through the box, she saw that some photos had been grouped together. Each bundle was tied with ribbon and had a slip of paper tucked on the top, describing what the photos were about. Labels such as Andrew—Ranch Photos, Andrew—Scouts... In addition, every picture had extensive notes written on the back.

She returned Andrew's photos to the appropriate box before checking the other four. Each was organized in the exact same manner, and there was a separate box for each of Mona's five boys.

Carly could only imagine the time this must have taken. Talk about a labor of love. But that was so like Mona.

She glanced at the empty scrapbooks. Five scrapbooks, five boxes. Had Mona intended to put together a scrapbook for each of her sons?

Except her plans never came to fruition. Carly leaned against the counter. Could she pick up where Mona left off?

She quickly put everything away, tucking it all back the way she had found it, and returned to the family room with a renewed sense of purpose.

Later, after Clint woke up and had accepted another breathing treatment, she brought him some cookies, settled on the overstuffed loveseat next to him and told him what she had found.

"That's all she did during those last months." Clint leaned back in his recliner. "All she could do, really. She always liked to give the boys something sentimental at Christmas. Those scrapbooks were supposed to be their gift that year." His voice cracked. "The cancer got her before she could make them, though."

Carly battled her own emotions, covering by retreating to the kitchen to get him some more juice.

When she returned, she set the glass on the table beside him before taking her seat again. "What would you think about me completing the scrapbooks in Mona's stead?"

"No." He shook his head. "It wouldn't be the same."

"I'm afraid I'd have to disagree." She stood and started toward the hallway.

"Where are you going?"

"You'll see." Determined to overcome his objection, she grabbed Andrew's box and brought it to his father. Opening it up, she said, "Just look at how orderly and detailed Mona left everything. As though she were hoping someone would pick up where she left off."

Tears filled the older man's dark eyes as he fingered his wife's handwritten notes. "She did all this?" He sniffed and continued to dig through the box.

After examining the contents, he looked over at Carly. "You might be right." He placed the lid back on the box and handed it to her. "It would be a shame to let all of my wife's hard work go to waste." He smiled then, his cheeks wet with tears. "I believe she would be very appreciative if you completed this project that was so near to her heart."

"I would be honored to do it, Clint."

He dabbed his eyes with a napkin before reclining again. "I know I haven't been the easiest patient, but I thank you for taking care of me, Carly."

She smiled, grateful that they'd managed to come to an understanding yesterday.

"And for giving Andrew a reason to hang around a while, though I'm sorry it had to be at your expense."

She blinked away the tears that threatened. "Believe it or not, Clint, your sons still need you. Which is precisely why you need to get well."

Things were looking up by Wednesday afternoon. At least in Andrew's mind. His father was doing better, Carly's new windows and door had been installed, and Marianne had called from the design studio to say that the cabinets would be shipped sooner than expected.

Now, as he made his way to the ranch with Megan, his mind was reeling. Since the timeline had been bumped up, he needed decisions from Carly. Namely appliances. They'd looked at tons of them this past weekend, but aside from the special-order commercial range, Carly was still mulling things over. The time had arrived to make those purchases.

Walking into the ranch house, he was again greeted with the smells of home. An aromatic dinner and a hint of something sweet. He could get used to coming home to Carly. A beautiful woman, great company, fantastic cook…

While Megan went on inside, he paused in the mudroom, confused by the train of thought his mind had taken. After all, he'd soon be headed back to Denver to embark on the next phase of his life. And Carly would never leave the life she'd built for her and her daughter.

He gave himself a stern shake before meeting her in the kitchen. "Good news. Your cabinets are arriving early." He followed her from the stove to the refrigerator. "So we need to get your appliances on order ASAP."

Carly poured a short glass of milk and put three snickerdoodles on a plate. "Sorry, but I can't think about the kitchen right now." She crossed to the table and set both in front of Megan and her homework. The woman was like a well-oiled machine.

She faced him now. Worry puckered her brow as she shoved the sleeves of her black sweater to her elbows. "Your father's fever is up."

"What?" The old man seemed to be doing so well this morning. How could things change so quickly?

"I've already contacted the doctor. Trent's going to drop by on his way home, possibly give him a shot of antibiotics." She heaved a sigh. "If that doesn't work, he's going to the hospital."

Andrew's heart skidded to a halt. "But… I thought he was doing better." He eyed his dad in the recliner, thanking God that he was in Ouray and not Denver. Though if he were, he'd have come immediately. He'd learned that lesson the hard way. Still, what if he lost his dad? What would he do? They were getting on so well.

No, he wouldn't let anything happen. He couldn't.

He watched as Carly went to his father, touched a hand to his cheek, then returned to the kitchen with his empty glass.

"Why isn't he in bed?" Andrew practically barked out the words as Carly returned to the kitchen.

Carly's blue eyes narrowed. "Because he refused. If he's more comfortable in his chair, then let him be in his chair." She glanced at the empty glass in her hand. "I need to get him some more juice."

"I'll get it." Andrew took the cup from her and headed to the fridge for some apple juice. His hands were shaking as he tipped the carton. He bumped the glass, spilling the juice all over the linoleum floor.

He let out a frustrated growl.

Next thing he knew, Carly was at his side. She laid a hand on his arm and smiled up at him, as if understanding more than just his frustration over the juice. "I've got this." Taking hold of the glass, she turned to her daughter. "Megan, why don't you take Andrew out to feed the foals? I think he could use some fresh air."

He hated to leave. Still, he knew Carly was right. He'd thought things were on the upswing. Now he needed to come to terms with this latest turn of events. Apparently Carly knew him better than he thought. Not that that was anything new.

While he and Megan fed the foals, he raked a hand through his hair and stared at the holes in the ancient roof. Dad was only sixty-five. Too young to die. He should have been enjoying retirement, not spending all his time worrying about this stupid ranch.

God, why is this happening? First Mama then Grandma... Are You ready to take Dad, too?

Lowering his gaze, he shook his head from side to side. Who was he to be questioning God?

Nobody, that's who. He had no power. He didn't

cause the sun to rise and set. He didn't tell the rain and snow to fall from their storehouses.

No, he was a mere man. One who often failed to recognize that he wasn't in charge. That he didn't always get his way. Life was always changing. And not always according to his plan, amplifying the conviction that his job was simply to have faith. Even when he didn't understand.

When the doctor arrived a short time later, Andrew, Megan and Noah joined everyone inside. The doctor gave Dad a shot of antibiotics, along with instructions for Carly to call tomorrow with an update on his progress.

Andrew walked him out. "Thank you for coming out, Dr. Lockridge."

"No thanks necessary. I pass right by here on my way home." He reached for the door of his truck. "And call me Trent."

Andrew nodded. "Thanks, Trent."

Between the doctor's visit and a dinner of homemade chicken noodle soup, Andrew's mood was much improved. Then again, that was the kind of meal that was therapeutic on so many different levels. Throw in a few snickerdoodles and he happily agreed to take care of the dishes while Carly gave his father another breathing treatment.

The fact that she'd stayed so late said a lot about her concern for his father. It was a school night, after all, and Megan would need to get to bed soon.

When Andrew and Noah finally convinced her that they'd take turns monitoring their father, Carly donned her coat, telling Megan to go say good-night to the foals.

The cold night air fell around them as Andrew

walked her to her SUV. He eyed the starry sky. "They're saying we might be in for a snowstorm."

"Not surprising. It is only March, you know." Stopping beside the vehicle, she shoved her hands in the pockets of her fleece jacket and looked up at him. "How are you doing?"

"Better, thanks to you."

"I didn't do so much. It's Trent who saved the day."

He couldn't argue that. Just knowing he was willing to stop by after hours meant a lot. Thanks to him, Dad was resting comfortably and, Lord willing, the shot would have him feeling better tomorrow.

He dragged his fingers through his hair. "I sure hope so."

As he lowered his hand, she took hold of it. "I know you're scared."

His eyes searched hers, a weight settling in the pit of his stomach. She knew him too well. But did she have any idea just how scared he was? Did she understand why? Did she know that he'd ignored Noah's repeated pleas for him to come and allowed himself to become so busy that he wasn't even there when his mother died?

Then, as if reading his thoughts, she dropped his hand and wrapped her arms around his neck. "You're a good man, Andrew. And a good son." She kissed his cheek before letting go. "Megan, come on, sweetie. Time to go."

A flurry of emotions swirled through him as he watched her drive away. He was grateful God had brought her back into his life. Because with Carly around, he suddenly didn't feel so alone.

Chapter Eleven

Talk about a dilemma.

Carly awoke the next morning, eager to get to the ranch to check on Clint. Yet not quite as eager to see Andrew. Why on earth had she hugged him last night? That made twice in recent weeks she'd allowed herself to get caught up in her emotions. This time she'd even kissed him. On the cheek, but still... When he'd had the opportunity to kiss her that night at Livie's after she'd dropped the plate, he hadn't taken the chance.

To make matters worse, when she did arrive at the ranch shortly after dropping Megan off at school, he'd barely said goodbye before he was out the door. As if he couldn't bear to face her.

Fine by her. She was feeling a little sheepish herself. Obviously Andrew's only interest in her was as a friend, client and caretaker for his father. As it should be. So why did it bother her so much?

At least she could take heart in the fact that Clint was doing better. She'd prayed all night that he would show some sign of improvement by this morning, and from what she could tell, he was. He had more color and seemed to be more alert. Best of all, his fever was down.

Now it was up to her to make sure it stayed that way. Forward progress was good. Going backward wasn't. She couldn't let her guard down with either Clint or Andrew.

As for Clint, she'd have to monitor his temperature, bump up the number of breathing treatments, and make sure he got the fluids and rest he needed. Whatever it took to keep him out of the hospital.

"It's downright freezing out there today." Eyeing Clint, she added two more split logs to the wood-burning stove that kept the common areas of the house nice and toasty. "And from the looks of those clouds—" she nodded toward the picture window "—we might be in for a little snow, too."

"Glad I don't have to worry about going out there, then." Clint burrowed deeper into his recliner, adjusting the blanket over his legs. A hint, perhaps, that he still had a long road to recovery.

"No, you do not." She closed the glass doors on the stove, smiling, then slipped her hands into the back pockets of her jeans as she straightened. "The only thing you have to worry about is getting well. So you just relax and take it easy."

She retrieved the remote from the arm of the couch and punched in the numbers for Clint's favorite channel. The one that played all the old Westerns.

Seeing the cowboy-hat-clad hero that appeared on the screen, she couldn't help noticing how similar his attire was to Clint's when he was working the ranch. Then it dawned on her. These were the shows Clint would have watched as a kid growing up in Ouray. No wonder he'd wanted to become a rancher. She could only imagine the childhood dreams he'd fulfilled since he and Mona bought the land that was Abundant Blessings Ranch all those years ago. They'd been partners in every sense of the word. Something Carly admired.

Her parents had been the same way about Granger House Inn. So when they passed it on to her, she'd envisioned Dennis and her fulfilling the same role. But his interest in the B and B was limited to income. Everything else seemed to fall on her.

Not much of a partnership.

Now, as she finished cleaning up the kitchen from breakfast, Clint was asleep, so she took the opportunity to head into Mona's craft room to start working on the scrapbooks. Every time she so much as thought about them, she got excited.

Talk about an awesome responsibility. Thankfully, Mona had all of the details written out. Even so far as to state how the pictures were to be arranged.

Standing at the long counter with the first blank scrapbook open, she took a deep breath and lifted the lid on Noah's box of photos. Such a cute baby. Though, truthfully, the Stephens boys all kind of looked the same. Dark hair, dark eyes…until you got to Daniel. Blond, blue-eyed…a complete departure from the rest of them. That boy definitely favored his mama.

Once she had removed all of the photos from the box, she noticed the colorful papers and cutouts used for scrapbooking tucked in the bottom. She picked up a small envelope and found that it was unsealed. More instructions, perhaps?

She pulled out the note card adorned with Colorado columbines, opened it and read.

My dearest Noah…

Carly covered her mouth with her hand, a lump forming in her throat. Mona had even written them letters… when she knew she was dying.

The first time I held you in my arms, I knew I was created to be a mother. You were my sunshine on cloudy days, always quick with a smile. But that smile faded when Jaycee died—

Carly blinked away tears. Noah had lost his wife when she developed an infection after miscarrying their first child. And a grieving Noah returned to the rodeo circuit, as though daring God to take him, too.

Closing the card, she tucked it back into its envelope. It wasn't hers to read. Though she was more determined than ever to complete this task.

Lord, thank You for allowing me to find these boxes. Please guide me and help me bring Mona's vision to life for her boys—

Uh-oh. Voices echoed from the main part of the house. Andrew. Noah.

Drat. She must have lost track of time. Was it lunchtime already?

She scrambled to put everything back into the box, praying neither of the brothers would find her and spoil this magnificent surprise.

Shoving the box alongside the others, she hurried

down the hall, pausing to take a deep breath before rounding into the family room. Sure was a lot of commotion going on. Didn't they realize they were going to wake Clint?

When she continued into the family room, she saw Noah adding more wood to the already more-than-sufficient stack along one wall and Andrew hauling in multiple bags of groceries. Surely this wasn't the end of the world.

"Looks like you guys are preparing for the worst." She crossed to the kitchen, where Andrew had begun unloading everything from pantry staples to milk, eggs, meats and cheeses. "It's just a little snow."

They looked at each other before Noah addressed her. Something that was really starting to bug her. If they had something to say— "Storm's moving in quicker than expected."

Andrew pulled two boxes of cereal from one bag. "And a Pacific disturbance is giving it lots of fuel."

Okay, even she knew that wasn't good. After all, she'd lived her entire life in Ouray.

Arms empty, Noah moved toward her. "We're under a blizzard warning from this evening until tomorrow or the next day."

"I had no idea." She should have paid closer attention to the weather this morning. Because if this came to fruition, keeping both Clint and the foals safe would be a challenge. Particularly if the electricity went out. She just hoped the guys were up to the challenge. "I guess I'd better plan to leave early today so I can pick up Megan. We'll have to hunker down at Livie's."

"Actually…" Andrew came alongside her then. So

close she could feel the warmth radiating from his body. Though that was nothing compared to the warmth she saw in his coffee-colored eyes. "I'd feel better if the two of you stayed here."

Did he really think her that helpless? Or did he simply want her here to take care of Clint? Well, he was a big boy and *she'd* been taking care of herself and Megan for a long time, so she didn't need—

"I need to know that you and Megan are safe." He caressed her cheek with the back of his hand, rendering her virtually speechless.

There wasn't a thing she could do except swallow the lump in her throat, look up at him and manage to say, "Okay."

By the time Carly served up a hearty dinner of beef stew and homemade bread, the wind had really kicked up and snow had begun to fall, right along with the temperature. Now, as Andrew burrowed deeper under the quilt his grandmother had made, the winds howled, rattling the bedroom windows.

Staring at the blue numbers on the alarm clock, he was surprised that the electricity had stayed on past midnight. Typically they would have been plunged into darkness by now. At least until someone fired up the generator.

He breathed a sigh of relief that Carly and Megan were here, safely down the hall in Jude's room. Since his policeman brother was needed in town, he'd opted to stay at Matt's. Even if he hadn't, though, Andrew would have gladly given up his room—well, Daniel's room—and slept on the couch. Whatever it took to make sure that Carly and Megan were comfortable and taken care of.

A loud crack sounded from outside, sending Andrew bolting from his bed. More cracking, followed by a crash.

Confused, he lifted the blinds on the window and looked outside, but the snow was coming down too heavy to see anything else.

A million scenarios ran through his mind as he rushed from the room.

Noah was already in the mudroom, coat in hand.

"What was that?" Andrew asked his brother.

"I have no idea, but I intend to find out."

Andrew grabbed his own coat, put that over the Henley and sweatpants he'd worn to bed and shoved his feet into his boots, the actions reminding him of when they were kids. Always wanting to keep up with his big brother. "I'm coming with you."

Outside, the snow was coming down sideways, propelled by the force of the wind. Even with the floodlights, it was nearly impossible to see.

Noah looked left, then right. "We'd better check the barn." He had to yell to be heard over the wind.

Andrew followed him through the snow. "What's that noise?" There was something else besides the wind. Something...alive.

Noah stopped in front of him. Turned his head. "I hear it, too."

Andrew squinted, trying hard to see past all of the white.

Suddenly his eyes widened. "The barn!" Or rather, what was left of it.

"The foals!" Noah darted ahead.

Andrew was on his heels. Drawing closer, he could see that the entire section where the foals were had caved in. But they were still alive. That was the sound he heard.

Together, he and his big brother examined the collapse, trying to determine where the horses were and how to get to them.

"I'll be right back." Andrew sprinted to his truck for some flashlights. Once he returned, it didn't take long to find the animals. Unfortunately, they were wedged between the wall that still stood and a large amount of debris. And they were too spooked to come out on their own.

Noah ducked under the wreckage in an effort to reach them.

"Andrew!"

He turned at the sound of Carly's voice. "What are you doing out here? Get back—"

She put one booted foot in front of the other, her eyes widening. "The foals? Are they—?"

"No." Noah emerged from the rubble then. "But they're trapped."

"Where?" Beside Andrew now, she stooped to look.

Both men shone their flashlights, the snow pelting their faces.

"That timber—" Noah motioned with his light "—is holding things up." Lowering the beam, he looked at Carly. "It's also preventing me from getting to them. I can't get past it. I'm too big."

"I'm not."

Andrew recognized the expression of determination on her pretty face.

He looked at his brother, his heart constricting. With this kind of wind, it was only a matter of time before that timber went down, too. And when it did, the foals would likely be crushed. So the thought of sending Carly in there didn't settle well.

Noah stared at him as if waiting for Andrew's approval.

Carly clutched his arm. "We can't let them die."

He knew that. Didn't mean he had to like it, though.

He met her gaze now. "You'd better be careful. Things could topple at any second."

"I will." A hint of trepidation puckered her brow. "I promise."

Andrew and Noah kept their flashlights aimed on the foals, providing as much light as possible for Carly as she made her way into the barn.

Andrew's heart wrenched, his breath hanging in his throat. *God, please keep her safe—*

Before his prayer was finished, she had shimmied under the timber, all the while talking to the foals. Coaxing them. How she managed to keep a soothing tone to her voice amid this chaos was beyond him.

One horse tentatively moved toward her, then the other.

"Come on, babies." Beside him, his brother cheered them on, though not loudly enough to scare them.

A few seconds later, Carly managed to slip behind the foals and urge them to safety.

"Better get ready to grab one." Noah positioned himself in front of the opening.

Elsa came out first, and Noah scooped her into his arms.

Andrew moved into place and duplicated his brother's move with Anna.

Suddenly, a loud crack ripped through the air.

"Carly!"

The timber had given way.

She was just about out when boards and shingles began raining down on her. She covered her head with her hands and arms. Then she went down.

He started to put the horse down, but she saw him.

"No!" Lying on her stomach, she struggled to break free. "I'm okay." A grimace belied her words. She grunted. "I'm just stuck."

He couldn't bear the thought of leaving her.

"Andrew?"

Over the raging wind, he looked at her again.

Her blue eyes pleaded with him. "Go!"

Noah nudged his arm. "Let's get them to the stable."

The stable? Carrying a hundred-pound weight? That would take forever. But with no bridle or rope to lead them, he held the foal tight and made his way to the stable as quickly as possible, willing God to propel his every step.

Once the horses were settled into a stall, he left Noah to take care of them and rushed back out into the blinding snow.

He ran as fast as he could. His lungs were burning, his face numb despite the sweat that beaded his brow, but it didn't matter. Carly was all he cared about.

Anger burned in his gut. Dad had no business keeping those animals in that decrepit barn. Even after Noah had suggested they move them for the duration of the storm, the old man insisted they remain near the house. Now Carly might have to pay for his foolishness with her life.

Approaching the barn, he skidded to a halt. Through almost whiteout conditions, he saw his father pulling Carly from the rubble.

Somehow she managed to stand, but she was limping. Andrew rushed to help.

"I'm fine," she said. "My ankle was caught, that's all. Just get me inside."

Megan met them at the door, her blue eyes wider than he'd ever seen. "Mommy? Are you okay?"

"I'm fine, baby." She hugged her daughter.

"What about the foals?" Megan fretted. "Are they okay?"

"Yes, they are." Andrew dusted the snow from his hair. "They're in the stable with Noah."

"That's a good girl you've got there, Carly." His father patted Megan on the back. "Stayed put, just like I asked her to."

Andrew felt his nostrils flare. "The foals should have been kept in the stable to begin with. It's safer, more secure…"

His father's gaze momentarily narrowed before he began to cough.

"Andrew, I need you to stoke the fire for me, please." Carly's expression told him she was none too happy with him for calling his father out. He didn't care, though. It needed to be said. He'd seen enough pain and suffering here at the ranch to know that there was no room for poor choices.

He dutifully tended the fire while Carly helped the old man to his chair.

"I think it would be wise to do another breathing treatment." She reached for the nebulizer.

"Oh, if I have to," the old man wheezed.

"Yes, you have to. But what do you say I reward you with some hot cocoa when you're done?"

Hands clasped in his lap, the old man gave a weak smile. "I'd say things are looking up. Care to join me, Megan?"

"For cocoa? Oh, yeah."

With his father settled, Carly headed into the kitchen.

Andrew followed, noting there was still a slight hitch in her step. Her ankle had to be killing her. She shouldn't even be on her feet. "You're sure you're okay?"

She pulled the milk from the fridge. "I'm fine. I just needed a little help getting out from under all that weight." At the stove, she poured the milk into a pan. Added some sugar, cocoa and cinnamon.

He came up behind her, laying a hand against the small of her back. "You know, if it hadn't been for you, those foals would have been crushed."

She continued to whisk the mixture as though trying to ignore him. "I'm just glad they listened to me."

He tucked her damp curls behind her ear. "You're their mama. They know your voice."

She peered up at him now, her tremulous smile warming him from the inside out.

What would he have done if something had happened to her? Because if there was one thing tonight had shown him for sure, it was that his feelings for Carly had moved far beyond friendship.

Chapter Twelve

Carly opened her eyes several hours later and stared into the predawn darkness of Andrew's brother's bedroom. Beside her, Megan's even breathing confirmed that she was still sound asleep. No wonder, with all the excitement they'd had last night. Or rather, earlier this morning.

Unfortunately, excitement was becoming all too familiar to Carly. The last two weeks of her life had hovered somewhere between a nightmare and a dream. First the fire, then planning the perfect kitchen, caring for Clint and spending time with Andrew. Time that had involved a plethora of emotions, everything from fear to bliss. Andrew made her feel things she hadn't felt in forever. Things she'd vowed never to feel again.

So, as she eased out from under the covers now, careful not to disturb her daughter, she couldn't help wondering what might be in store for her today.

The freezing-cold air sent a shiver down her spine as she tugged her bulky cable-knit sweater over the base layer she'd slept in. The electricity must have finally fallen prey to the storm. Fortunately, when she'd picked up Megan from school yesterday, they'd had time to stop by Livie's to grab some toiletries and extra clothing.

Stepping into her jeans, she was pleased to discover that the ankle caught in the collapse no longer bothered her. Curious, she put all of her weight onto it.

No pain at all.

When the barn came crashing down on her, she'd feared the worst. Instead, God had protected her and the foals.

She eased into the chair beside the door, sending up a prayer of thanks as she shoved her feet into a pair of fuzzy socks. She also lifted up her concerns for Clint, praying that being out in the wind and freezing temps last night hadn't set back his recovery. The man needed to be healthy again so he could return to doing the things he loved so much. Such as tending this ranch.

With that in mind, it appeared her mission for today was clear. To see to it that the Stephens men and Megan were taken care of. This blessed assignment had filled that void left by the B and B, giving her purpose once again. One far better than bookkeeping.

Emerging from the bedroom, she softly closed the door behind her so as not to wake Megan and padded silently down the hall.

The faintest hint of light appeared through the picture window in the family room while flames danced behind the glass doors of the wood-burning stove, as though someone had recently stoked the fire. And the aroma of fresh-brewed coffee filled the air.

"Good morning." The sound of Andrew's voice sent her heart aflutter.

Rubbing her arms, she turned to see his silhouette approaching from the kitchen. "Morning."

"Noah went out to fire up the generator." Andrew stopped in front of her now, coffee mug in hand, the soft glow from the fire illuminating his amazing eyes. "So we should have some lights soon."

"Lights are good." But she was more interested in heat. She moved closer to the stove. At least it was warmer out here than in the bedroom.

Then she noticed Clint's empty recliner. She prayed that he was warm enough in his room and that he was sleeping well.

Turning, Andrew went back to the kitchen. "How's the foot?" He opened one cupboard, then another, though it was difficult to make out what he was doing.

"Believe it or not, it doesn't hurt at all."

"Really?" He continued whatever it was he was doing. "That's good." A minute later he returned to her side with a second mug. "One English breakfast tea."

"Thank you." She took hold of the cup with both hands, savoring the warmth from both the tea and the gesture. She liked the way Andrew anticipated her needs. And that he'd wanted her and Megan to ride out the storm here at the ranch.

"You have no idea how terrified I was when that barn came down on you." His expression took on a more simmering mood. His eyes narrowed, his nostrils flared. "This stupid ranch is nothing but a source of trouble." His gaze bore into her. "I don't know what I'd do if I lost you again."

Carly froze.

Lost? To lose, one must have possession in the first place. Did he have her? Or her heart, anyway?

Uncomfortable with the intensity of his stare, she took a sip, peering out the picture window at a sea of white. "Looks like things are improving out there." The ferocious winds of last night had died down, though they still had the capability to send snow drifting across the open range, hindered only by the mountains that stood in the distance.

"Thankfully." His agitation seemingly waning, he retreated to the overstuffed sofa and motioned for her to join him. "Did you sleep okay?"

After an indecisive moment, she eased onto the comfy cushions. "Like a rock. How about you?"

"Ditto." He reached his arm around her then, as though it were the most natural thing in the world, caressing her no doubt reckless curls with his fingers. The gesture, as opposed to the cold this time, sent a wave of chill bumps skittering down her arm. "Because I knew you and Megan were safe."

Her heart raced with anticipation. A thousand what-ifs played across her mind. Were these the actions of an old flame turned friend? Or did Andrew truly feel something more for her?

Movement caught her eye before she could assess things further. Megan shuffled toward them in her fleece pajamas, her strawberry blond hair in full bed-head mode.

"Good morning, sunshine." Andrew inched over, allowing her to sit between them.

Her daughter gave a sleepy smile as she snuggled between them.

"Sleep well?" Carly laid her head against her daughter's.

These were the moments she cherished. The quiet times with just her and Megan.

Except it wasn't just them. Andrew was there, too. And in that moment, it was as if they were a family. Her, Megan and Andrew.

Her heart rate accelerated again. Did she dare to dream? Dare to consider a future that consisted of something besides just her and her daughter?

With Andrew it would be so easy.

But she wasn't cut out for marriage. Or rather, marriage wasn't cut out for her.

No, there would be no fairy-tale endings for her. She gave up on dreams when Dennis lost interest in her as his wife. He no longer wanted her. When he died, they were simply two people existing in the same house. Definitely not the kind of marriage she'd envisioned.

She wasn't about to travel down that road again. A road littered with broken promises and shattered dreams. Besides, Andrew was going back to Denver in a few weeks, anyway. So the sooner she got back to town, back to Livie's house, back into the B and B, and back to her old life, the better off she'd be.

The lights in the kitchen came on then. The timing couldn't have been better.

She pushed to her feet. "Breakfast will be ready soon." And, Lord willing, she and Megan would be on their way back to town shortly thereafter.

* * *

Thanks to a gas stove, they'd just finished a breakfast of pancakes and bacon when Jude called from town to let them know that the power was out all over Ouray proper. Information that suited Andrew just fine. Because the more reasons he had to keep Carly and Megan at the ranch, the better. And since his grandmother's house had neither a working fireplace nor a generator, there wasn't any room for Carly to argue.

While she gave his father a breathing treatment, Andrew took Megan to the stables to feed the foals. Now that the wind had died down, things weren't too bad outside.

"Whose snowmobile?" Megan pointed to the machine Noah had parked outside the stable. Evidently his brother had been too lazy to walk this morning.

"That would be Noah's."

"Oh." She frowned, adjusting her shimmery purple stocking cap.

"What's wrong?"

"I was just thinking how fun it would be for you, me and Mommy to go for a ride."

"I see." He couldn't say he blamed her. Being cooped up inside was never fun. Especially when you were a kid. And there were no other kids around.

He reached for the door to the stable. "You know, we have two more back at the house."

"Really?" She stepped inside, her entire face lighting up. "Could you take us for a ride? Oh, please, please, please." She clapped her purple mittens together.

The sight made him chuckle. Come to think of it, he

hadn't been snowmobiling in forever. Odd, since it was something he'd always enjoyed.

Surrounded by the smell of hay and horses, he looked down at Megan. How could he turn down such a cute plea?

"It's okay with me. But it's almost lunchtime, so we'd better wait until after that. And only if your mama agrees."

"Yay!" She threw her fists into the air like Rocky Balboa and danced around.

"But first we need to feed Elsa and Anna."

While Megan gave the rapidly growing foals their bottles, he found Noah adding fresh hay to the stalls and put a bug in his ear about her request. He knew good and well that Carly wouldn't leave his father unless someone was there to look after him.

By the time they arrived back at the house, Carly was at the stove, working on grilled ham-and-cheese sandwiches and tomato soup.

In her eagerness, Megan practically stumbled right out of her boots trying to get to her. "Mommy, Andrew said he would take us for a snowmobile ride. Please, please, can we go?"

Carly flipped another sandwich. "We're about to have lunch."

"No, *after* lunch."

Turning ever so slightly, her mother narrowed her pretty blue eyes on him while addressing her daughter. "Sweetie, we'll need to go home soon."

He didn't get it. Carly had seemed fine when she woke up this morning. But ever since breakfast, she'd been more…standoffish. And he didn't have the slightest clue why.

"Not as long as the electricity is out." He grabbed a carrot stick from the bowl on the counter and bit off the end. "You two will freeze."

She pursed her lips, returning her attention to Megan. "Okay, you can go for a short ride after lunch."

"What about you?" Megan cocked her head, her bottom lip slightly pooched out. "I want you to go, too."

"I have to take care of Mr. Clint."

"I can do that." Noah's timing couldn't have been better. "You go on and have fun with Andrew and Megan."

Now that all of her objections had been overcome…

Andrew lifted a brow. "What do you say, Carly? You used to enjoy snowmobiling when we were kids."

She removed one sandwich and added more butter to the pan before answering. "I suppose a short ride wouldn't hurt."

He wasn't sure what she considered short, but he planned to make the best of it.

When lunch was over and the kitchen was clean, Andrew and Megan went outside while Carly settled Dad in for a nap. Andrew needed to make sure the largest of the machines, one all three of them could ride on, was gassed up and ready to go.

"This is going to be so much fun." Megan watched his every move.

He sure hoped so. The whole notion of a snowmobile ride didn't seem all that appealing to Carly. Something he found rather strange considering she used to plow circles around him when they were younger. A fact she never let him forget.

After returning the gas can to the shed beside the house, he fired up the machine. Revving the engine, he looked at Megan. "Shall we take 'er for a test run?"

No having to ask her twice. She hurried off of the deck and hopped on behind him.

He handed her a helmet. "Safety first."

She tugged it on, and he helped her fasten it before taking a spin around the house.

When they returned, Carly was waiting on the deck, helmet tucked under her arm as she pulled on her gloves. "Are you purposely trying to wake your father?"

He glanced back at Megan, who was wearing the same uh-oh expression he was. "Did we really wake him?"

"No. But with all that racket, you could have." She slipped her helmet on, then climbed aboard, wedging her daughter between her and Andrew. "Drive someplace *away* from the house, please."

He eased on the thumb throttle until they were a good ways from the house before picking up speed. Snow was flying as they bounded over the frozen pasture, headed toward the river. Behind him, Megan wasn't the only one laughing. Obviously Carly had changed her tune. Or rather, the ride had changed it.

When they reached the river, he killed the engine. They all climbed off the machine and removed their helmets.

"That was so much fun." Megan's smile was rivaled only by her mother's.

"Yeah, it was." He smoothed a hand over his hair, his gaze drifting to Carly. "It's been a long time since I've done that."

"Me, too." Leaving her helmet on the machine, Carly shoved her hands into the pockets of her puffy jacket. "I think the last time I did it was with you." She surveyed the river and the mountains just beyond. "And I believe we ended up right about here."

"Can I go exploring?" Megan squinted up at her mother.

"Yes. But stay away from the river."

"Okay." The kid took off down the bank, past the large cottonwood tree he and his brothers used to swing on.

He eyed Carly. "Shall we follow her?"

She smiled then. "Please."

As they walked, his mind flooded with memories. Most of which included Carly. "I guess we used to come down here a lot back in high school."

She watched her daughter scoop up a mound of snow, shape it into a ball and throw it at a tree. "We sure did. I've always loved it out here."

"Really? Why?"

She sent him a frustrated look. "Andrew, you have got to stop being so negative about this place and focus on all the good things the ranch has to offer." She swept an arm through the air. "Do you not see this? It's so peaceful here. It's easy to understand why your parents loved this ranch so much. They had their own little refuge from the world."

He glanced around. Too many struggles for him to see it that way.

He turned back to her. Through her eyes, though, everything looked better.

"I guess we did do a lot of walking along this path."

Of course, it wasn't so much about where they were as it was just being with her. He focused on the river. "I was always comfortable sharing things with you. Like I could tell you anything and you'd understand."

Whap!

"Hey!" He twisted to see Megan grinning at him.

"Gotcha." She pointed to the spot where her snowball had struck him in the arm.

"Oh, so that's how you want to play." He scooped up a wad of snow and packed it into a ball before taking aim at Megan.

"Missed me—"

His second shot was a direct hit.

Next thing he knew, it was every man for himself. Except he was the only man, and Carly and Megan had joined forces against him.

As the snowballs continued to fly, he charged Carly, tackling her into a snowdrift.

Both winded, they stared at one another as their breaths hovered in the chilly air. Holding her in his arms, their faces so close…

"You know, we didn't always just talk while we were out here," he whispered.

For a moment, her eyes searched his, as though they were lost in time. Then the redness in her cheeks deepened. She rolled to her side, and he helped her to her feet.

"We'd better get back to the house," she said, dusting the snow from her pants. "I don't want to leave your father for too long."

Reluctantly he fired up the snowmobile. Him and his big mouth.

When they arrived at the house, his brother Jude was pulling up.

Still wearing his police uniform, he got out of his truck and met them on the deck. "Looks like you guys were out having some fun."

"It was awesome," said Megan.

Jude turned his attention to Carly. "You'll be glad to know that the electricity's back on in town."

"That's excellent news." Smiling, she glanced at her daughter first, then at Andrew. "I'll just check on your father and we'll be on our way."

So much for trying to keep her at the ranch. Now he needed to figure out why she was suddenly so eager to leave.

Chapter Thirteen

Carly was glad to be back home, or at least to Livie's house, instead of under the same roof as Andrew. But by noon Saturday, she couldn't help feeling that the ranch was where she needed to be. Though it had nothing to do with Andrew and everything to do with Clint.

Okay, perhaps a small part of it had to do with Andrew.

She transferred a batch of peanut butter cookies from baking sheet to cooling rack, the sweet aroma beckoning her to sample just one. Maybe two. Or ten.

Resisting, she set the empty baking pan aside and blew out an annoyed breath. In her eagerness to get away from Andrew and the crazy notions his presence seemed to evoke, she'd practically abandoned his father. Sure, Noah and Andrew knew how to give him breathing treatments and would see to it that he took his medicine, but would they monitor him as closely as she did? Would they remember to take his temperature? And what if Andrew needed to work on her kitchen to make up for the time lost to the storm? Without her there to look after Clint, he wouldn't be able to leave.

Megan shuffled into the kitchen from the parlor, eyeing the cookies. "Ooo, can I have one?"

"Help yourself." The more Megan ate, the fewer there were to tempt her.

Her daughter grabbed a treat before dropping into one of the faux leather swivel chairs at the table. She swung her leg back and forth. "I'm bored."

She wasn't the only one.

Grabbing a cookie for herself, Carly rounded the peninsula to join Megan at the table. "What would you like to do?"

Megan broke off a piece of cookie. "Can we go to the ranch? I'm worried about Elsa and Anna."

"You don't think Andrew and Noah can take care of them?"

"Yeah, but it's not the same."

Just like having the brothers care for Clint wasn't the same. "You're right. It's not."

She bit into her cookie, the peanutty taste sending her taste buds into a frenzy. Hard to believe it hadn't even been a week since Clint's pneumonia was diagnosed. Meaning he was far from being out of the woods.

You said you would take care of him.

And even argued against them bringing in someone else to do so. Yet she'd bailed, all because things got a little too cozy with Andrew. If that didn't sound like a coward, Carly wasn't sure what did.

She polished off her cookie and stood, dusting the crumbs from her hands. "Okay, let's go."

Under a crisp blue sky, they headed north on Main Street in her SUV. Seemed the warmer temperatures had brought out all of Ouray today. The sidewalks were bustling with people. With the storm past, everyone was eager to be out and about and, no doubt, ready for spring. Herself included.

Continuing outside of town, Carly found herself second-guessing her impromptu decision. Maybe she should have called first. After all, she'd left them high and dry. What if the Stephens men were upset with her?

Butterflies took wing in her midsection as she pulled into the ranch. This was such a bad idea.

No, leaving so abruptly yesterday was.

Bumping up the long drive, she tightened her grip on the steering wheel. Too late to turn back now.

They had barely come to a stop when Megan grabbed the container of cookies Carly had made, hopped out of the vehicle and started up the deck. Oh, no. Megan was used to following Andrew into the house. What if she walked in without knocking?

Carly shoved her door open and planted her booted feet on the wet gravel. "Megan!"

Her daughter stopped immediately. Looked at her.

She sucked in a calming breath. "Wait for me, please."

A few moments later, the two of them knocked.

When Andrew swung the door open, his expression was somewhere between surprise and relief. Though his smile told her he was glad to see them.

"How's Clint?" She stepped into the mudroom, breathing a little easier.

"Not too good, I'm afraid."

Her breathing all but stopped. This was her fault. If she hadn't run out on them…

"He's refusing his breathing treatments." Exasperation creased Andrew's forehead. "Won't even let me take his temperature."

"That's not good." And the fact that she could hear the older man wheezing before she was halfway to the family room escalated her concern.

Pushing up the sleeves of her light blue Henley, she knelt beside Clint's recliner. "What's this I hear about you not taking your breathing treatments?" She hated the annoyance in her voice, especially since it was directed more at her than him.

He looked at her with a mischievous grin. "I was just thinking I might oughta do one."

Okay, now she was annoyed with him. Had he been refusing them on purpose?

She pushed to her feet, dug her fists into her hips. "Clint, do you want to get well or not?"

He brought his chair to an upright position. "Now, don't go gettin' yourself all worked up. I said I'd do one."

"Mmm-hmm. And what if I hadn't shown up?"

Despite looking somewhat pale, there was a glint in his eye as he glared at her. "Guess we'll never know."

Guilt kept her quiet and had her stepping aside to ready the nebulizer.

"You need to take your medicine, Mr. Clint, so you can come to the stables and see Elsa and Anna." Her daughter looked very serious as she addressed the older man. "They're getting bigger every day."

"That's 'cause they've got you takin' care of them," he said.

"Speaking of Elsa and Anna—" Andrew smiled down at Megan "—would you like to go see them?"

"Uh-huh." Her head bobbed like crazy with excitement. Then again, those horses were her main reason for wanting to come out here.

"Where's Noah?" Deciding she'd better take Clint's temp before the breathing treatment, Carly retrieved the thermometer from the side table.

"Checking horses and cattle." Andrew was already on his way into the mudroom with a happy Megan. Carly genuinely appreciated his attentiveness to her daughter. Something Megan had rarely received from her father.

Alone with Clint, Carly pulled the beeping thermometer from his mouth. 98.8. Not too bad. "You were being stubborn again, weren't you?"

"I love my sons dearly, but they don't have your bedside manner."

His words pricked her heart. He wasn't just counting on her. He trusted her.

She shoved the thermometer back into its case, finding it tough to look him in the eye. "I'm sorry for deserting you."

Grabbing the nebulizer mask, she tugged on the elastic band.

Before she could slip it over his head, he reached a hand up to stop her. "Carly, I'd like to ask you a favor."

Lowering her hands, she said, "What's that?"

"I'd like you to help me keep Andrew in Ouray."

Confusion narrowed her gaze. "Keep him in Ouray? For how long?"

"Forever."

Her heart tripped and stuttered. Andrew in Ouray? Forever? What would that mean for her? For them? Staying away from him was challenging enough as it was.

"But Andrew's built a life in Denver," she said. "He's about to close on a new business. Besides, you give me too much credit. What could I possibly do to make Andrew want to stay in Ouray?"

"All Denver has done is steal his joy. When he first got here, his eyes had lost their spark. But now...he looks better than ever. And you're partly to thank for that." He wagged a finger in her direction. "You, my dear, have far more influence over my son than you think."

Carly begged to differ. If anyone had influence, it was Andrew. Every time she saw him, she felt like a teenager again. He was her first kiss. Her first love.

But he'd chosen work over her. Just like Dennis had done.

"Mind if I think on it for a bit?"

Lips pursed, he sent her a frustrated look. "Don't take too long. We haven't got much time."

Standing again, she slipped the mask over Clint's face. For his sake, she might drop a few hints to Andrew if the opportunity presented itself. For her heart's sake, though, she couldn't help hoping they'd fall on a deaf ear. If Andrew stayed, he'd fight even harder to keep his grandmother's house. Leaving her dreams of expanding the B and B in the dust.

By Tuesday, Dad was doing noticeably better. His color was back, there hadn't been any fever spikes since the weekend, and the coughing and wheezing had subsided considerably. All because of Carly and the care she'd been giving him.

Andrew was envious. He wished he could spend as much time with her as his father had. Because if there was one thing he'd learned since returning to Ouray, it was that life was better with Carly around.

Lately, though, they barely crossed paths. Only when he brought Megan to the ranch after school. Even then, Carly didn't seem to have time to stop and talk like before. Instead, she'd get dinner on the table and she and Megan would be on their way.

Sometimes he couldn't help wondering if she was purposely avoiding him. Ever since the blizzard, things had been different, though he didn't have a clue why.

He wound his truck past the red sandstone formations north of Ouray. In the last few days he'd made great strides in bringing Carly's old home back to life. The mitigation team had completed their work over the weekend, allowing him to get started on the floors.

He frowned. Now that the refinishing process was complete, he'd need to allow a couple of days for the floors to dry. This would be the perfect time for him to get some work done on his grandmother's house. But with Carly and Megan living there, that was out of the question.

Hands on the steering wheel, he eyed the open rangeland with its rapidly dwindling snowpack. He and Carly hadn't even discussed Grandma's place since the fire. But now that things were winding down at Granger House, leaving him only a couple of weeks before the closing on Magnum Homes, he'd need to find a way to bring it up. As a businessman, he could appreciate Carly wanting to expand the B and B. But as the great-grandson of the man who built the house in question, he refused to let it leave the family. Something Carly should understand better than anyone.

Turning in to the ranch with Megan, he hoped that

maybe tonight he could convince Carly to stay for dinner. Or that he could at least carve out a little time to talk with her before she left.

"Are you looking forward to seeing your grandparents?" Carly's in-laws had invited Megan to come and visit during spring break next week.

"Uh-huh." She craned her neck, trying to see the corral as they continued past the stable. No doubt looking for the foals. "My cousin, Mia, is going to be there. We always have fun. Who's here?" She pointed to the unfamiliar white SUV parked beside his father's dually.

"I don't know," he said.

He eased the pickup to a stop, surveying the dingy ranch house in front of him and the partially collapsed barn in his rearview mirror. There never had been any shortage of work around this place, but he'd never seen things look this bad, either. He supposed he could help. If he had the time. Which he didn't. At least, not now.

Grabbing his thermos, he exited the truck. He could hardly wait to see what kind of food Carly had waiting for them today. He really did enjoy walking into the house and being greeted with the aromas of fresh baked sweets and dinner in progress.

When he and Megan entered the mudroom, they were met with the sound of laughter. And a voice he didn't recognize.

He sniffed the air. Carly had been baking, all right, but where was the savory smell of tonight's meal?

Disappointment wove through him, even though he knew it was wrong. It wasn't like Carly was their maid. She was taking care of his father out of the goodness of her heart, and he had no right to expect anything more.

Yet he did want more. He liked coming home to her. Liked sharing the events of his day with her.

He supposed he'd better get used to it, though. Because once he went back to Denver, he'd have no one.

Inside the family room, Dad sat upright in his recliner, while Carly was on the couch beside the blond-haired woman who'd stopped by Granger House right after the fire. What was her name? Hillary something.

Dad was the first to see them. "There they are." He held his arms out. "How's my favorite nine-year-old?"

Megan giggled, dropped her backpack and gave the old man a hug.

"How was school?" Dad had become quite enamored with Megan over the past week or so. The kid had a way of bringing out the best in his old man.

"I got a hundred on my math test."

"Excellent."

"News like that deserves a brownie." Carly stood, eyeing Megan first, then Andrew, before continuing into the kitchen. "You remember Ms. Hillary, don't you?"

Megan waved. "Hi." Seemingly shy, she remained beside his father.

"Good to see you again, Hillary." Andrew nodded in her direction.

The woman studied him a moment. "Yes. We met the day of the fire, correct?"

"Yes, ma'am."

"Hillary and I were in school together," said Dad.

"Though I was much younger than your father," she was quick to add.

"Three years isn't that much difference." The old man frowned.

Carly returned with a plate of brownies in one hand and a stack of napkins in the other. She offered a treat to Megan first, along with a napkin, then continued around the room. "Hillary brought dinner for you guys."

You guys? As in just him, Dad and Noah?

"Pot roast, smashed potatoes..." Hillary waved a hand. "Celeste does so much cooking anyway, we're never going to know when that nesting urge hits her."

Carly set the plate on the side table at the end of the couch. "If she's anything like me, she'll be cleaning everything in sight a couple days before going into labor."

Hillary touched a long fingernail to her lips. "Yes, I seem to recall that when I was close to delivering Celeste, too."

"Hillary Ward. A grandmother." His father's smile held a definite air of mischief. "I always thought world domination woulda been more your style."

"That's Hillary Ward-Thompson." The woman pushed to her feet. "And no, darling, not *world*. I prefer corporate domination."

"So how come you're back in Ouray?" Dad looked up at her, one graying brow lifted in amusement.

She tugged on the hem of her crisp white blouse. "According to my doctor, I put too much of my heart into my job and it couldn't keep up. So, considering I have two granddaughters now and another grandchild on the way, I decided there were better ways to spend my time than jet-setting across the globe."

"Woman, you're too young to retire."

"Who said anything about retiring?" Hillary glared at his father. "I'm merely redirecting my focus."

Andrew caught Carly smiling at the pair. Not that

he could blame her. Watching the interaction between Hillary and his father was more entertaining than most television shows.

His phone rang in his pocket. He pulled it out to see his attorney's name on the screen. "Excuse me, please." He made his way down the hall to his bedroom. "What's up, Ned?"

"Hey, good news. I just got word that the closing date for Magnum has been moved up."

"Moved up?" A few weeks ago, that would have been great news. But now… "To when?"

"Two weeks from today."

"Two weeks?" He raked a hand through his hair. Granger House would barely be done by then. What about his grandmother's house? That had been his sole purpose in coming back to Ouray in the first place.

"I think the sister is afraid her brother will change his mind."

Change his mind? But they had an agreement.

"That time frame isn't going to be a problem, is it?"

He stared out the window, eyeing the mountains just past the river. "Sorry. My father's been ill. And I've been busy with a project." Not the one he'd initially intended, but one he was coming to wish would never end. "I'll be there, though. Go ahead and email me the details."

A lead weight formed in his stomach as he ended the call. Why did they have to move the closing up? Usually it was the other way around. And for once, he would have preferred it that way. Because for the first time in his life, he actually wanted to be in Ouray.

Chapter Fourteen

Carly wanted to keep her baby here at home.

Watching Megan pack, she tried to douse the ache in her heart with another cup of tea, all the while keeping one eye glued to the window, waiting for the Wagners' arrival. Sure, Megan had gone to visit Dennis's parents before, but never without her. Like it or not, though, her daughter was growing up. And it was important that she maintain a relationship with her father's parents.

Still, the kid didn't have to act so excited about leaving.

If only Carly could go with her. But between the repairs at Granger House, helping with the foals and looking in on Clint, there was no way she could break away.

She huffed out a breath. Sometimes being a grown-up was such a pain. She'd much rather throw herself on the floor and kick and scream until Megan agreed to stay.

"There they are!" Megan practically squealed. She rushed to the bed and tugged her new Hello Kitty suitcase onto the floor. The *thwamp, thwamp, thwamp* of the wheels as she rolled it across the wooden planks was like a hammer to Carly's heart.

Willing herself to remain calm, she joined her daughter in the parlor as Megan threw open the door.

"Mia's here, too." Both Megan's fists went into the air and she jumped in circles. "Yay!"

Carly peered out the window with the sudden suspicion that having Megan visit was more Mia's idea than her grandparents'. She didn't doubt that the Wagners loved her daughter, but she often got the feeling that Megan was more of an afterthought because she didn't live in Grand Junction like their other grandchildren. Something they'd tried to change for years when Dennis was alive. His parents had played a big role in Dennis's push to move there.

Shaking away the less than pleasant thoughts, Carly set her mug on a coaster atop a side table and moved on to the door.

Mia had rushed ahead of her grandparents, and she and Megan were already hugging on the porch.

Carly pushed the storm door open.

Beverly Wagner waved and gave a half smile as she meandered up the walk. Of course, she never actually looked at Carly. She was too busy scrutinizing Livie's house. Granted, it hadn't been modernized and wasn't in pristine condition, but it was still charming and comfortable. Not to mention convenient. And far better than a hotel room.

Behind Beverly, her husband, Chuck, made eye contact and grinned. "Hello, Carly." He always was the more laid back of the two, able to see the good in everything. Including her.

After a round of hugs and a report on details of the fire, Carly took them next door to Granger House to show them the progress on her new kitchen.

Passing through the front door, she said, "I'm still amazed that they managed to get rid of the smoke smell."

Megan pinched her nose. "It was *disgusting*."

Chuck smiled and ruffled his granddaughter's hair. "From what I hear, those restoration teams are pretty good."

"And here's your proof." Carly gestured to the sitting area in the parlor. "Not a trace of soot or smoke." Everything there looked virtually the same way it had before. She drew in a relieved breath. "We were blessed that the fire was contained to the kitchen and family room."

"Yes, you were." Chuck came alongside her, wrapping an arm around her shoulders. "And we're thankful that neither you nor Megan was hurt."

Beverly hugged Megan, a genuine smile lighting her typically sober face. "Yes, we are."

Tears pricked the backs of Carly's eyes. Blinking, she led them into the dining room where, again, everything had been restored. The ceiling and walls were soot-free and the antique furniture cleaned. Even the molding around the door, the one that had been charred, looked the way it used to. "I still can't believe this room was untouched by either the fire or the water."

At the opening to the kitchen, she paused. "But this is where we took the worst hit." Excitement bubbled inside as she tugged the protective plastic sheeting to one side, allowing Mia and the Wagners to see in.

"They just installed the cabinets yesterday." She led them into the space. In addition to the cabinets, the freshly painted drywall made everything look so fresh and new, despite the wires that still peeked out of holes where light fixtures, switches and outlets would go. "Andrew covered the floors with this paper so they wouldn't get scratched. But they're a beautiful dark walnut color. Andrew said—"

"Who's Andrew?" Beverly's judgmental gaze narrowed and shifted to Carly.

"My contractor."

"Her *boy*friend." Megan giggled with her cousin, grinning like a goofball, batting her eyelashes.

Perhaps telling her goodbye might be easier than she first thought. "Megan… Andrew and I are friends, but he is *not* my boyfriend."

Megan fisted her hands on her hips, drew her eyebrows downward. "Well, he should be." She looked up at her grandparents. "He's really nice. And he has a ranch."

Carly cringed. While she appreciated Megan's fondness for Andrew, this kind of talk was putting her in a very awkward position.

She turned to her in-laws and forced a smile. "His father has a ranch. Andrew lives in Denver. He's visiting his father." She then glared at Megan, albeit ever so subtly.

Though Beverly didn't say anything, Carly couldn't help noticing the look of disapproval on her face. The silent commentary the woman no doubt had regarding Carly being seen with another man.

By the time they pulled away ten minutes later, Carly wasn't sure if she wanted to cheer or cry. In the end, crying won out. Four whole days without her baby. How would she survive?

The best thing she could do now was redirect her attention. Find something else to concentrate on besides her daughter's absence.

Considering she'd focused on few things besides her daughter in the last nine years, that was going to be tough. The only person she could think of who needed her attention now was Clint. And even he didn't really need her anymore. Still, she'd agreed to take care of him and that's just what she'd do.

And in the evenings, after tending to what little bookkeeping she had, she might even make some headway on Mona's scrapbooks. With Clint's approval, she'd brought all of the boxes back to Livie's earlier this week.

She gathered her things to head to the ranch, yet before she could make it out the door, another round of tears had her reaching for a box of tissues. The doorbell interrupted her pity party, though.

Dabbing her eyes, she drew in two deep breaths and opened the door to find Andrew standing on her front porch.

He opened the storm door. "You miss her already, don't you?"

All she could do was nod as tears streamed down her cheeks once again. Talk about a poor excuse for a grown-up.

Moving inside, Andrew enveloped her in his strong embrace. The smell of fresh air and coffee wrapped around her as he stroked her back, her hair.

She savored his strength. And boy, did he feel good.

"How about this?" He set her away from him.

Still lost in the fog of his embrace, she struggled to focus.

"Tell me one thing that you've been dying to do but couldn't do with Megan."

She hadn't done anything without considering Megan in…ever. She shrugged, forcing her brain to think. "I don't know. Go see a movie at the theater." She looked up at Andrew. "One of *my* choosing."

He stood there staring at her as though she'd lost her mind. Then… "Get your jacket. We're going to the movies."

Carly watched him, recalling the look in her mother-in-law's eye when they discussed Andrew. Going to the movies with him would be almost like a…a date.

And what would be wrong with that?

Clint. "Wait, wait, wait… What about your father? What if he needs help?"

"Sorry, I forgot to tell you. Daniel's back home."

"When did he get in?"

"Last night. Noah and I have filled him in on everything, and since he's eager to spend some time with the old man…" He held out his hand. "This day is all about you."

Andrew couldn't bear to see Carly so sad. When he arrived at his grandmother's house early this afternoon, his intention had been to discuss their joint ownership and what to do with the place. But after seeing the heart-wrenching look on her face, he couldn't bear to broach the topic. All he wanted now was to see Carly smile.

"So, what would you like to see?" Standing in front of the movie theater in Montrose, the bright midday sun shining down on them, he watched Carly as she stared at the marquee. Considering there were only three shows to choose from, it shouldn't take her long to decide. Not like the multiplexes in Denver that showed twenty-plus movies all at the same time.

"Well, they are showing that new romantic comedy with Matthew McConaughey. But I hate to do that to you."

"Do what to me?"

"Make you sit through a rom-com."

"Are you kidding?" He stepped in front of her now. "I happen to be a big Matthew McConaughey fan." Though he would have preferred a nice horror flick. Something good and scary that would have Carly reaching for him.

"No, you're not."

He slapped a hand to his chest and stumbled backward. "Madam, it wounds me that you would question my sincerity."

She looked at him with pretty, tear-free blue eyes. "Okay, fine. Mr. McConaughey it is, then."

They purchased their tickets then headed straight for the snack bar. After all, neither of them had eaten lunch, and the aroma of popcorn was too powerful to resist.

"Would you like butter on that?" The freckle-faced girl on the other side of the counter eyed him first, then Carly.

"Definitely," said Carly. "Oh, and a box of Junior Mints, too, please."

Andrew wrinkled his nose. "You still dump those things in the popcorn like you used to?"

"Of course. How else are you going to get that whole sweet and salty experience?"

Andrew caught the girl's attention. "Make that two popcorns, please."

Carly elbowed him in the ribs. "You didn't used to complain."

"Because back then I had enough money for only one popcorn." Grinning, he reached for his wallet. "Now I can afford my own."

The sun had drifted into the western sky when they left the theater a couple of hours later.

"Okay, I'll admit it," he said as they strolled across the parking lot. "That was a pretty good movie."

"What do you mean, admit? I thought you were a big McConaughey fan?"

He stopped beside the truck. "I am. But not *every* movie can be great."

She laughed, shaking her head. "You're such a goof."

"Perhaps." Leaning toward her, he rested one hand against the truck, effectively trapping her. "But am I a cute goof?"

Her gaze lifted to his. "Maybe."

His eyes drifted to her lips, lingering there for one excruciating moment as he contemplated kissing her. "What's something else having Megan around stops you from doing?"

After a moment, her smile turned mischievous. "Eating dessert first."

While it wasn't exactly the answer he was hoping for, he couldn't help laughing. He straightened and opened her door. "What have you got in mind? Ice cream, cake, pie…? Or maybe something more decadent like a crème brûlée?"

She let go a soft gasp. "I *love* crème brûlée."

That dreamy look on her face was all the encouragement he needed. "One crème brûlée coming up."

He drove them to one of Montrose's finer dining establishments.

"Andrew, I'm not dressed for a place like this."

He looked at her skinny jeans, riding-style boots and long gray shirt. "What are you talking about? You look great."

Since it was still early, they were seated right away, and in a cozy booth, no less. Something that wouldn't have happened in another hour or two. Not on a Saturday evening.

He promptly ordered two crème brûlées, then leaned back against the tufted leather cushion.

"Thank you." Across the table, Carly rested her chin on her hand and stared at him. "I wasn't sure I was going to make it through this day and—" she smiled "—you've turned it into something wonderful."

"You deserve it." He sent her a wink.

Blushing, she unfolded her white linen napkin and placed it in her lap, all the while taking in the river rock fireplace and the rustic wood beams. "So, tell me about your life in Denver. I haven't heard you talk about it much."

"Probably because there's not much to talk about."

Her gaze jerked to his so fast he was surprised she didn't get whiplash. "Oh, come on, Andrew. You owned one of the most successful commercial construction companies in Denver. I'm sure your life is anything but boring."

He lifted a brow. "How do you know Pinnacle Construction was successful?"

"Because your father told me."

"Oh." A minor ding to his pride. He was kind of hoping she'd Googled him or something. Not that there'd be much to find.

The waitress approached. "Two crème brûlées." She set Carly's in front of her before serving his. "Can I get you anything else?"

"Not right now," he said.

Carly was the first to crack through the caramelized sugar, coming up with a spoonful of custard.

"Cheers." She lifted her spoon into the air, then shoved it into her mouth. Her eyes closed as she savored the dessert.

"Any good?"

"Best I've ever tasted."

"Good." He cracked the hardened shell on his brûlée, knowing he needed to answer her question, to tell her something about himself. But what? "Life in Denver isn't much different than living anywhere else. There's work, church..." He took a bite. "Mmm..."

"What do you do when you're not at work?" Watching him, she scooped another spoonful.

Unfortunately, there wasn't much to his life outside work. He'd rather stay at the office than go home to an empty house. Not that he'd tell her that. "The usual stuff. Watch TV, go to the gym." Man, did he lead a pathetic life or what?

At least here he had his dad or one of his brothers to keep him company. He glanced across the table. Though, given the choice, he'd rather spend his time with Carly and Megan. With them, even normal, everyday stuff was more fun.

He managed to change the subject by bringing up an old classmate, and by the time they finished their dessert, he'd caught up on just about everyone in Ouray, both old and new. And as the lights dimmed, he asked the waitress to bring menus again so they could order dinner.

After their food arrived, he knew it was time for him to share one more thing with her. He could only pray it wouldn't ruin the whole night.

"My lawyer called this week." He cut into his prime rib. "Seems they've moved up the closing date on my new business."

"I guess you're looking forward to it, huh?" Was it his imagination or was there a hint of disappointment in her tone? "Home builder, right?"

"Yes. Custom homes." He stabbed another piece of meat. "I learned about it just before I closed on my old company. The owner passed away unexpectedly and neither of his kids was interested in the business. Seemed like the perfect opportunity." Of course, that was before he came to Ouray. "Don't worry, though. I'll have your kitchen completed and you'll be moved back into Granger House before I leave."

To his relief, she smiled. "I know you will."

"I just hope Dad's back on his feet by then."

"You worry about him, don't you?" She cocked her head, poking at her seafood pasta with her fork.

"It's no secret that I was so wrapped up in my work, I didn't make it back home before my mother died. I don't want to make that mistake again."

Reaching across the table, she laid her hand atop his. "Your mother knew that you loved her, Andrew."

"I know. But I never got to say goodbye. And that will always haunt me." He wanted to kick himself as soon as the words left his mouth. *You're trying to make her smile, not depress her.*

Fortunately, the conversation was on the upswing by the time the waitress delivered their check. It was well after dark when they arrived back in Ouray. He walked Carly to the door of his grandmother's house and escorted her inside.

"Thank you for a wonderful time." Her smile, different from any he'd seen all day, and exactly what he'd set out to achieve, did strange things to his insides. "I can't remember the last time I had so much fun."

"Like I said earlier, you deserve it." Unable to stop himself, he caressed her cheek. "You give so much of yourself to others. But surely we didn't cover everything. So if there's something else you'd like to do before Megan comes home—"

"As a matter of fact, there is." She chewed her bottom lip.

"And what might that be?"

"This." Before he realized what was happening, she pushed up on her toes and kissed him. A kiss that nearly knocked him off his feet.

She started to pull away, but he wrapped his arms around her waist and pulled her closer. Her fingers threaded through the back of his hair as their lips met again. He could stay this way forever.

Because, whether he planned to or not, he had fallen in love with Carly all over again.

Chapter Fifteen

It had been a long time since someone had made Carly feel as special as Andrew had yesterday. He'd catered to her every whim and, at the same time, made her feel like a woman instead of just a mom, caretaker or friend. He'd awakened something in her she'd thought she'd never feel again. Something she was too afraid to name. Because acknowledging it left her open for disappointment. Heartbreak. And yet she'd kissed him.

What *had* she been thinking?

Now here she sat, wedged in a church pew between Andrew and Clint. Every time Andrew shifted the slightest bit, she caught a whiff of fresh air and masculinity that reminded her of that kiss.

As if she needed any reminder. She'd had a hard time thinking about anything else since it happened. Even now, her heart thundered at the memory. Here in church, of all places.

Straightening, she eyed the wooden cross over the pulpit, trying hard to focus on Pastor Dan's sermon. A message based on Isaiah 43. She smoothed a hand over the pages of her open Bible.

"Sometimes we get so bogged down in the past that we forget to open our eyes to the future God has for us," the pastor said.

The future? Something she found very frightening. While her past might not be all that pretty, the future was unknown, and uncertainty was always scary. Especially when it involved the heart. Her gaze momentarily darted to Andrew.

If the future was so frightening, why did she keep thinking about that kiss and contemplating all sorts of what-ifs? Hadn't Andrew told her that he would be going back to Denver once her kitchen was done? That he was about to sign off on another business?

God, I know that anything You have for me is better than I could possibly want for myself. Help me not cling to what I want and be open to Your will.

In the meantime, she would immerse herself in Mona's scrapbooks and do whatever it took to stay away from Andrew.

After the service, the Stephens men congregated on the sidewalk outside the church, beside the towering white fir. Everyone except Matt, that is, who was on call with the sheriff's department.

While Carly wanted simply to whisk right past them, it would be rude for her not to say hello to Daniel, the youngest of the Stephens boys. This was the first she'd seen him since he'd returned from his latest adventure.

She eased beside him. "How was Peru?"

"Awesome." With his medium-length blond hair, blue eyes and sparkling smile, he looked like a young Brad

Pitt. "Rafting the Cotahuasi River never gets old. You should try it sometime."

She practically burst out laughing. "Daniel, I haven't even rafted the Uncompahgre since I was a teenager. And that's in my own backyard."

He chuckled. "Why don't you join us for lunch and I'll show you some photos?"

Lunch? No. She had scrapbooks waiting for her. "I'm sorry. I can't—"

"'Course she's joining us." Clint rolled up the sleeves of his blue plaid button-down shirt.

Her gaze narrowed. "I'm surprised you're even here. You know, you still haven't been cleared by the doctor." Though, looking at him now, one would have a hard time believing he'd been sick. His color was back to normal, he was clean-shaven and, with his salt-and-pepper hair neatly combed, he looked quite handsome.

Lord willing, the doctor would give him the all-clear at his checkup tomorrow. The poor man had given up just about everything he loved to do these past couple of weeks, so she hoped he'd be allowed to return to most, if not all, of his normal activities around the ranch.

"It's only church. It's not like I'm out herdin' cattle." One corner of his mouth lifted then. "But if you're that worried, you'd best come on to the house and help these boys keep an eye on me."

She shook her head. "Don't think I don't know what you're up to, Clint." And even though she really would have loved to join them, the thought of spending another day with Andrew was what worried her most.

"You don't even have to cook," added Noah.

"That's right." The gleam in Andrew's brown eyes

sent goose bumps down her spine. "We've got everything taken care of."

"Come on, Carly." Daniel nudged her with his elbow. "It'll be fun."

That's what she was afraid of.

She studied the conifers scattered around the vacant lot across the road, backdropped by Hayden Mountain. Perhaps it wouldn't hurt to go for a little bit. She could look at Daniel's pictures, have some lunch, then tell them she had a prior commitment and needed to leave. They didn't have to know it was the scrapbooks.

"You guys sure drive a hard bargain."

After a quick stop by Livie's to change clothes, she drove to the ranch. She could do this. Having everyone around would naturally deflect her attention away from Andrew.

When she entered the ranch house, her stomach growled at the mixture of smells. She was delighted to learn that they'd prepared elk burgers, homemade french fries, coleslaw and brownies. And they wouldn't let her set foot in the kitchen except to eat. These guys really did have a way of making a woman feel like a queen. Mona would have been proud.

After the meal, while Jude and Andrew cleaned up the kitchen and Clint settled in his recliner, Carly sat at the table with Daniel, poring over the photos on his tablet.

"That looks pretty intense," she said as he turned off the device.

"Most extreme white water in Peru."

"And you think I should try it?" She bumped him with her shoulder. "I think you need your head examined." Laughing, she looked up and saw Andrew leaning against the counter. Evidently they were done with the kitchen.

"Well, guys, I hate to cut this short." She stood and stretched. "But I have some things I need to take care of in town."

Each of them gave her a quick hug, except Andrew, who insisted on walking her out.

"I didn't know you needed to leave so soon," he said as they emerged onto the deck. "I was hoping we could go for a walk."

"I really—"

"Just a short one." His crooked smile made him look like the Andrew she remembered from high school. The one who had been able to talk her into just about anything.

Say no. No, no, no... "Okay."

He started toward the pasture. "Can you believe we're closing in on your completed kitchen?"

"Finally." She tilted her face heavenward, allowing the sun to warm her face. "It feels like it's taking *forever.*" Though it also left her with a lot of mixed emotions. Once her kitchen was done, Andrew would be gone.

"You know what the preacher said this morning about not dwelling on the past?" Andrew took hold of her hand.

"Yes." Ignoring that annoying voice in her head, she entwined her fingers with his.

"Do you ever do that? Dwell on the past."

"More often than I care to admit."

"Me, too." He continued across the winter-weary

landscape, looking straight ahead. "But then the verse he referenced went on to say that God was doing something new. And that 'Do you not perceive it?' part almost felt a smack upside my head. Like, 'Don't you get it, buddy? I'm working here.'"

She puffed out a laugh, eyeing the cattle in the distance.

"I'm not sure, Carly, but I think God is doing something new in my life."

"Like what?" She peered up at him, squinting against the sun's glare.

"I don't know." He drew to a stop beside the river, taking in the rushing water before looking at her. "Maybe it's this new business venture. But selling my company—something I never imagined I would do—coming back here and reconnecting with my family." He squeezed her hand and smiled. "Reconnecting with you."

Her heart pounded.

"And this ranch." He let go of her hand and bent to pick up a small rock. "Remember after the blizzard, when we came out here on the snowmobile?"

"Yes."

Tossing the pebble in his hand, he said, "You challenged me to start looking at the good things the ranch had to offer."

"I remember that." She picked up her own stone, rubbed its smooth surface with her thumb. "Though I think it was more of an order than a challenge."

He chuckled, throwing his rock into the water. "In that case, you'll be happy to know that I followed your orders." Hands slung low on his hips, he moved toward her. "Funny thing happened."

"What's that?"

"I'm actually enjoying the ranch, perhaps for the first time in my life."

She couldn't help but grin.

"Being here and talking with my brothers has brought back a lot of memories that have helped me realize that the hardships we endured while I was growing up were what bonded us together as a family and made us stronger. Not the other way around." He moved a step closer. "I know the ranch had nothing to do with my mother's death." He shrugged. "I was just looking for a scapegoat instead of taking responsibility for my actions."

Amid the soothing backdrop of the water, Carly's heart swelled. She'd been praying that God would help Andrew realize the truth. Now she could only pray that he would decide to stay in Ouray. Because despite trying to convince herself otherwise, she wanted him in her life.

Andrew drilled another screw into the hinge leaf for Carly's new pantry door, amazed at how quickly things had progressed.

It was only Tuesday, yet Dad was celebrating a clean bill of health by reclaiming his freedom as a rancher, and Carly's kitchen was nearing completion. Andrew wasn't sure how he felt about either one. Dad couldn't just pick up where he left off. He'd need to ease back into things after being laid up for two weeks. And as for Carly, Andrew would be fine with her project going into perpetuity.

Unfortunately, it didn't look like that was going to

happen. The appliances had been delivered and installed yesterday, and thanks to Marianne's help and persistence in following up with their order, the marble countertops were set to be installed tomorrow. All he had left to do then was install the subway tile backsplash and hang the pendant lights over the island. Carly should be able to move back in before the weekend.

And he'd be on his way to Denver.

The thought making his heart ache, he leaned back against the doorjamb. He was in love with Carly again. Perhaps he'd never stopped. All these years and he'd never forgotten her. She was the standard by which all other women were judged. Not that he ever dated that much. Finding someone who even remotely understood him the way Carly did was next to impossible.

But he'd made a commitment to purchase Magnum Homes. Signed a contract. And he was nothing if not a man of his word.

He glanced around the space, pleased with how everything had come together. He and Carly made a good team. Now if they could just figure out what to do about his grandmother's house. Neither had broached the topic in weeks, and he was still clueless about how they were going to find a compromise.

He slid the screwdriver into his tool belt, grinning. He supposed he could marry her. That would keep the house in the family.

Yeah, right. If there's one thing he knew for sure, it was that Carly would never leave Ouray.

Still, if they couldn't come to some sort of agreement on what to do with Grandma's house, owning just half of it did neither one of them any good.

Movement outside the window on the opposite end of the kitchen drew his attention. Carly was just crossing the drive, bringing him lunch. Now that his father had been cleared, there was no reason for her to hang out at the ranch all day. Perhaps this would give them an opportunity to discuss his grandmother's house.

He hurried across the paper-covered floors to meet her at the door. At this point, he no longer wanted her to see the space until it was complete. Which reminded him, he needed to put paper over the windows, too, so she couldn't peek inside.

He swung open the door, quickly closing it behind him. "Why didn't you just text me? I could have come next door."

She sent him a shy smile. "Well, I was hoping to get a peek at any progress."

"Sorry." Hands on his hips, he blocked the door. "No more peeking until it's finished."

"But—"

He descended a couple of steps, then sat down. "Nice weather we're having today." Grinning, he perused the cloudless sky. "Good day for a picnic, don't you think?" He glanced back at her now. "And since you happen to be carrying a picnic basket…"

She sent him a pleading look. "Not even a little peek?"

"Nope."

Squaring her shoulders, she narrowed her gaze. "What if I said I'd withhold your lunch?"

He shrugged. "I have protein bars." Though they held about as much appeal as a brick compared to one of Carly's homemade meals. Still, he wasn't about to give in on this one.

"Okay, fine." She set the basket on the step in front of him with a thud.

"Hey—" leaning forward, he touched her cheek "—just think how exciting it will be to see everything done."

"I know." She lifted the basket lid. "But patience isn't my virtue." Reaching inside, she pulled out a foil-covered plate and handed it to him. "Hope you don't mind leftover fried chicken."

"Are you kidding?" He lifted the foil off the warm plate to discover mashed potatoes, corn and green beans, too. "There's no such thing as bad fried chicken."

She pulled out a plate for herself. "I was craving it last night, and since I'm alone, there's no way I could eat it all."

"And I get to reap the benefits." He bit into a drumstick. "This is delicious." He took hold of the napkin she offered and wiped his chin. "Seriously, you know you're spoiling me, don't you? I don't know what we're going to do at the ranch now that you're not there helping Dad."

"What can I say? I like to cook and take care of people."

"Well, your husband was a blessed man."

Carly's smile all but evaporated, and her pretty blue eyes clouded over. She set her plate on top of the closed basket, then dropped onto the bottom step.

Only then did he realize what he'd said. He set his plate next to hers and moved beside her. "I'm sorry. I shouldn't have said that. I wasn't trying to open old wounds."

"You didn't." She stared at her clasped hands in

her lap. "It's just that I don't think Dennis would have agreed with you."

"What do you mean?"

She drew in a deep breath before looking at him. "My marriage was a sham. Everybody thought Dennis and I were the perfect couple, but we were barely more than friends."

He could see the pain in her eyes and wished that he could make it go away. "Surely it wasn't always that way."

"No." She again looked at her hands as though she was too embarrassed to look at him. "I wouldn't have married him if it had been. But over time, his job took on a higher priority. He worked longer hours, and even when he was home, he was always tethered to his work."

Standing, she started to pace. "One day he announced that he wanted to move to Grand Junction. Said he could make more money there." She sighed. "Perhaps I should have heard him out. Instead, I told him no. We didn't need more money. That wasn't the real reason, though. Inside—" she laid a hand against her chest "—I kept thinking how lonely Megan and I would be in a strange place, not knowing anyone."

She stopped pacing then. "Dennis told me I was being selfish. That the only reason I didn't want to move was because I was afraid of change." Finally she met his gaze. "Then he slammed the door behind him. Two hours later, the police were at my door telling me he was dead."

Andrew's eyes fell closed as he processed her words. He understood just how she felt. He knew all too well what it was like to live with that kind of regret.

"Carly…" Standing, he wrapped his arms around her and pulled her against him, trying to decide who was the bigger jerk. Her husband for not giving his family the respect he should have, or him for bringing up the subject. "I'm so sorry."

She shook her head, tears falling. "I don't know. Maybe Dennis was right. Maybe I am afraid of change."

"Are you kidding?" Andrew set her away from him but still held onto her. "Look at how many changes you've not only faced but also overcome. You're a single mom, a business owner, and what about this fire?" He let go just long enough to gesture to the house. "You're stronger than you think, Carly. And you've tackled everything far better than most people."

"Thank you for saying that."

"I'm not just saying it. I know it."

Peering up at him, she smiled. "You need to eat before your food gets cold."

"Only if you'll join me."

She did, and as she started talking about her most recent phone call with Megan, he realized just how much grace this woman before him demonstrated under pressure. Like the night of the blizzard, when she climbed into a crumbling building to save those foals.

Carly was one in a million, all right. And he couldn't help wondering if she just might be the only one for him.

Chapter Sixteen

First thing Wednesday morning, Carly was busy in Livie's kitchen. Megan was on her way home, so her favorite foods were the order of the day. Peanut butter cookies with the chocolate Kiss in the middle, brownies, Carly's special four-cheese mac and cheese, and, tonight, Salisbury steak. Top that all off with the news that they'd be able to move back into Granger House on Friday and her daughter was going to be ecstatic. This would be a very good Good Friday.

Which reminded her, she needed to make some purchases. A new Easter dress for Megan. A ham. And probably some more replacement items for the kitchen. She'd ordered a lot of stuff online. Things that were now stored in Livie's laundry room. Then again, it had taken her a lifetime to collect all that kitchenware. She just hoped it didn't take that long to replace it.

Maybe they could run to Montrose tomorrow. Nothing better than a little retail therapy to kill time. Besides, Andrew would be too busy putting the finishing touches on things next door to spend a moment with them.

The thought of moving back into Granger House was a bittersweet one, though. She'd soon be saying goodbye to Andrew. Too soon, as far as she was concerned.

I'd like you to help me keep Andrew in Ouray.

Lately she found herself wanting him to stay, too. If only she knew how to make Clint's—and her—wish come true.

She put the lid on the casserole dish and tucked the mac and cheese in the fridge for either lunch or a side with dinner tonight. She went through the motions of her chores, but Andrew was never far from her mind. No one except her parents had ever encouraged her the way Andrew did. Not even Dennis. Andrew listened to her and was honest with her, not simply placating her with what he thought she wanted to hear.

Like yesterday, when he pointed out all of the changes she'd actually faced and lived to tell about. She'd merely thought of it as overcoming what life threw her way. Perhaps he was right. Perhaps she was stronger than she thought.

With her baking complete, she scanned the functional yet less than appealing seventies-era kitchen. If she were to use this place as an extension of Granger House, the first thing she'd do was paint the dark wooden cabinets a lighter color. Maybe a light gray or white, like in her new kitchen. That would depend on the flooring, though. Given that the house was a hundred years old, she assumed there were hardwoods under this ugly vinyl. If that was the case, she'd have them refinished, perhaps even the same color Andrew used in the kitchen at Granger…

Oh, why was she wasting her time daydreaming?

Because unless she could talk Andrew into selling her his half, it was pointless. And until she got the final bill for the repairs to Granger House, she wasn't even sure she could afford it.

She needed to focus on something productive while she waited for Megan.

Like Mona's scrapbooks. She'd already completed Noah's book and was ready to start on Andrew's.

She locked the back door and tilted the blinds so no one could see in before retrieving the stuff from the bedroom. The last thing she'd want was Andrew to come wandering in and spoil the surprise.

After laying out each small stack of photos, she found the handwritten note Mona had penned for her second-born. Did Carly dare look at it? No, not today. It would only make her cry.

She placed it back inside the box and began sorting the photos, putting them in chronological order. What a cute baby he was. And a mischievous-looking young boy. The next group of pictures was of his teen years. That playful gleam in his eyes wasn't nearly as prominent in his ninth grade school picture.

Shuffling to the next image, she smiled. What a handsome cowboy he was, though rather serious. She turned it over to read the note on the back.

Andrew, age 15. Working the ranch with Noah. My boys worked so hard to be men while their daddy was sick.

Carly flipped the picture back over and stared at the image. That was the summer of the horrible drought.

His father had pneumonia then, too, as she recalled. Except it was much worse and included a lengthy stay in the hospital.

She and Andrew were only friends at that point, but close enough for her to know that he and Noah poured all their efforts into helping their parents that year. They'd not only done all of the work at the ranch but also spent the summer building fences for a rancher down the road who had offered to pay them. All in an effort to spare their parents the humiliation of having an adjoining piece of land they'd recently purchased foreclosed on by the bank.

In the end, the boys' hard work wasn't enough, and their parents lost that land anyway. She'd never forget the look on Andrew's face when he came to visit his grandmother shortly thereafter. He was so broken. That was probably when she'd first fallen in love with him.

The doorbell rang, jarring her from her thoughts.

She glanced at the starburst clock on the kitchen wall. Was it really almost noon? If so, then that would be her baby.

She set the stacks of photos in the box and tucked it back in the bedroom before rushing to open the front door to Megan and her grandparents.

"Oh, I'm so glad to see you." She hugged her daughter for all she was worth the moment she stepped inside.

"Mom, you're squishing me."

There was that word again. After five days apart, she would have thought she'd be Mommy once again.

Carly released her. "Guess what?"

"You made cookies? I can smell them."

"Yes, but that's not what I was going to tell you."

"Oh. Okay. What, then?" At least Megan's smile had an anticipatory air to it.

"We get to move back into Granger House on Friday."

The girl's eyes went wide. "Really?"

"Unless Andrew changes his mind."

Megan jumped up and down. "I can't wait to have my room back."

"Any chance we could see the finished product?" Beverly watched her with great expectation.

"I wish you could, but unfortunately, Andrew won't even let me see it. He's got the windows covered and everything. Says he wants to do one of those big reveals like they do on TV."

"He'll let me see it." Megan was too confident.

"Probably not. But you're welcome to try."

Her daughter started for the door.

"After you unpack your suitcase and have some lunch."

"Aw, man." Megan grabbed her suitcase and dragged it down the hall.

Chuck smiled at Carly. "We've heard a lot about this Andrew in recent days."

"Indeed." Beverly looked as though she was accusing her. "Seems Megan is quite taken with him."

"Andrew and I have known each other since we were kids. He's a good friend."

Beverly's brow arched. "A *very* good friend, according to Megan."

Carly loathed the heat she felt rising into her cheeks.

Her mother-in-law stepped closer then and took hold of her hands. "And that's okay."

What?

She jerked her gaze to Beverly's. The woman was smiling. Really smiling. At her, no less.

"Dennis has been gone for five years, Carly. It's time to move on."

Chuck came beside them, laying a hand on each of their shoulders. "We just want you and Megan to be happy."

A lump formed in Carly's throat. She could hardly believe the words she was hearing. Obviously she had misjudged the woman. Perhaps she should start thinking of her as a friend instead of her mother-in law.

She hugged both Wagners. "I appreciate that. But don't worry." She looked at them now. "I have no plans to head to the altar anytime soon."

Andrew was still in shock. He never would have believed he could have put Carly's kitchen and family room back together in just four weeks. Yet by the grace of God, he'd managed to pull it off.

He was more than pleased with the way things had turned out. He'd even thrown in a few details she wasn't expecting. Now he couldn't wait to see her reaction.

"I didn't think this day would ever come." Carly moved through the front door of Granger House early Friday afternoon, hands clasped against her chest, a big smile on her beautiful face.

"It's so clean." Megan moved into the parlor, sniffing the air. "Smells clean, too."

"I know." Though she'd seen it before, Carly strolled through the space, examining everything from floor to ceiling. "I was skeptical when they said they'd be able to restore stuff to the way it was before the fire." Pausing, she bent over and sniffed one of the antique chairs, then straightened and smiled. "But they did a great job."

"I'm gonna check out my room." Megan ran across the wooden floor, taking a left at the dining room. "It smells good in here, too," she hollered a second later.

Shaking her head, Carly chuckled as she continued into the dining room, still taking in every nuance. "It's amazing how they were able to freshen everything."

Andrew stopped at the entrance to the kitchen. "Wait until you see what's in here."

Carly's smile had never been bigger. She practically wiggled with excitement as she approached.

"Don't you want to wait for Megan?"

"Megan," she called over her shoulder. "Hurry up so we can see our new kitchen."

"Coming." Her daughter was at her side in no time, both of them looking up at Andrew with those blue eyes filled with anticipation.

"Are you ladies ready to see your new kitchen and family room?"

"Yes," they responded collectively.

"You're sure?"

"Andrew…" Carly ground out the word.

"Okay, okay." Having replaced the old swinging door with a more practical pocket door, he slid it aside, allowing them to enter. "Welcome home."

Just like on those HGTV shows, Carly gasped, her eyes going wide as her hands moved to her mouth.

"Whoa…" Megan moved across the newly refinished floors, turning in circles.

Continuing toward the large island, Carly looked

left, right, up and down as if trying to take it all in. "Is this really mine?" She touched the apron-front sink.

"Yep." Watching her, seeing her so happy, filled his heart to overflowing.

Megan climbed onto one of the high-backed stools that sat along the far side of the island. "This is the best kitchen ever." She laid her cheek against the marble, her arms spreading across the expanse as though she were hugging it.

"It's so much brighter." Walking between the island and the stove, Carly smoothed a hand across the marble. Suddenly she stopped and whirled to face him. "Glass knobs? I told you I couldn't afford them."

"I know. But you wanted them." Hands shoved in his pockets, he rocked back on his heels. "My way of saying thank you for all the help you gave us at the ranch."

She opened her mouth slightly, then closed it without saying a word. She didn't need to, though. The tears welling her in eyes said it all.

"What's that?" Megan hopped down from the stool and hurried to the far corner of the room.

"That's your mom's new pantry." He moved beside Carly, gesturing toward her daughter. "Let's check it out."

Megan opened the door and moved inside. "This is so cool."

"I love the door." Carly caressed the frosted glass that read Pantry as they passed. She poked her head inside. "Holy cow." She looked back at him now. "I can't believe all this storage."

"I know. And all we did was utilize a corner that had been wasted space anyway."

Smiling, she said, "How did you get so smart?"

"It's a gift."

Megan squeezed past her mother. "Hey, cool table." She dodged toward his other surprise, positioned near the opening to the family room, beside the wall where the stove had once been.

Placing his hand against the small of Carly's back, he urged her that way.

Her eyes grew bigger with every step. "Is that what I think it is?"

He nodded. "It took forever, but I was able to sand down the old butcher block to use as the tabletop, and Jude turned the legs for me." He looked at Carly now. "He's quite the woodworker. And his specialty is custom millwork. He helped me with some of the window casings that were damaged."

"So that's why you kept telling me to stay away from the shop while you were hanging out at the ranch, waiting for the floors to dry." She fingered the satin finish. "This butcher block was one of the original countertops in Granger House."

"I remembered you saying that. Which is why I couldn't let it go to waste."

She reached for his hand, entwining their fingers. "I can't tell you how much I appreciate this. The table, the knobs, everything. This kitchen exceeds my wildest dreams, Andrew. And I'm glad it was you who made them come true." Pushing up on her toes, she kissed his cheek. "Thank you."

He stared into her blue eyes brimming with gratitude. He longed to take her into his arms and tell her how he felt. That he loved her. But considering Megan was here, he should probably wait.

Instead, he gently cupped Carly's cheek. "I'm glad I was here to do it. However—" He tugged her toward the family room. "There's more to see."

He led them into the cozy space with its warm gray walls, white-slipcovered furniture and natural wood entertainment center that surrounded their new 55-inch flat screen TV.

"This looks like something out of a magazine." Carly continued into the space. "I love the wood accents."

"The TV is huge!" Megan rushed to the opposite side of the room and picked up the remote. "Can I turn it on?"

"Not yet." Carly started back toward the kitchen. "We still have plenty of work to do."

After a little more exploring, they headed back to his grandmother's to gather their things.

He picked up a box from the kitchen counter that contained several shoe boxes. "What's this?"

"Oh!" Carly immediately turned away from the groceries she'd been bagging, hurried toward him and intercepted the box. "It's nothing you'd be interested in."

Then why did she look so sheepish?

"Why don't you take some of the heavier stuff I stored in the laundry room? Like my new pots and pans and that pretty purple stand mixer." Lately it seemed a day hadn't gone by without a deliveryman showing up at his grandmother's door or Carly running to Montrose to pick up replacement items for those she'd lost in the fire. Nothing like giving a woman a reason to shop.

"Purple, huh?" He opened the door to the laundry

room off his grandmother's kitchen. "Let me guess. Megan picked it out."

Carly smiled over the box she was still holding. "Yes. I think it'll be a nice pop of color in my new kitchen."

They trudged back and forth between the two houses for the next couple of hours until they'd gotten everything.

"I don't know about you two, but I'm famished." He dropped the final box on the kitchen counter. "What do you ladies say I go grab us some pizza?"

"Pizza?" Who knew it was so easy to get Megan's attention? "Can we?" She deferred to her mother.

Carly glanced around the space that was now brimming with bags and boxes of all kinds. "I don't think I'll be doing any cooking tonight, so go for it."

They ate at her new table, and later, after Megan had gone to bed and he convinced Carly she didn't have to unpack everything tonight, the two of them sat down on her comfy new sofa.

"It all feels so new." She snuggled beside him as he put his arm around her. "Like it's a brand-new house."

"In many ways, it is. New walls, new flooring, new furniture…"

"I love the glass knobs." She peered up at him, her smile making him want to do even more for her. "And you said I was spoiling you."

He chuckled. "You haven't gotten my bill yet."

She playfully swatted him.

"Seriously, though, I'm not going to charge you for any labor."

"Wha—?" She twisted to face him. "That's crazy. Why would you do that?"

"After all you've done for us? Helping with Dad and the foals. You gave up your day-to-day life. I think it's a pretty fair trade."

Brow furrowing, she seemed to ponder his words. "I'm not so sure about that. I mean, how would I have gotten through this craziness without you? The fire, redoing the kitchen… It was all so overwhelming."

He touched her cheek with the back of his hand. "I'm glad God put me in Ouray when He did."

There was that smile again. "Me, too."

Threading his fingers into her curls, he drew her closer. Breathed in the tropical scent of her shampoo, staring into her eyes for a moment and seeing eternity. The life he wanted. A life he wanted with her. She was the only woman he'd ever loved. The only one he could imagine giving his heart to. And boy, did she have it. Lowering his head, he claimed her lips. Tasted the spiciness of pizza, the sweetness of forever. He didn't know he was capable of loving one person so much.

But he did. And there was only one thing he could do about it.

Talk Carly into coming to Denver with him.

Chapter Seventeen

Carly never imagined there would be so much to do by simply moving back into her own home. But while most of Granger House remained the same, the heart of it, the kitchen and family room, was a complete do-over. Even the simplest things were gone, and it hadn't crossed her mind to add them to her inventory list. Things like a paper towel holder, dishrags and containers to hold flour and sugar. Probably because she'd had those things at Livie's house. Whatever the case, she was looking at either another shopping trip or more boxes arriving at her door.

For now, she'd started a list. Something that was likely to be ongoing as she worked to make her house a home again and an inviting retreat for guests.

Taking a sip of her second cup of tea from the Adventures in Pink Jeep Tours mug Blakely had given her from her tour company, she leaned back in one of the padded bar stools at her delightfully large island and admired her new kitchen. Yet as magnificent as it was, it couldn't dim the memory of Andrew and his kiss. *His* kiss.

Looking back, she sheepishly realized that she was the one who'd made the first move when they'd kissed before. But not last night. That was a curl-your-toes, make-you-sigh kind of kiss.

The mere memory had her cheeks warming.

Banishing the wayward thoughts from her mind, she focused on today. Since tomorrow was Easter, this was the perfect opportunity to break in her new stove. She'd have to boil some eggs to be colored later, decide on and make the dessert—maybe a fluffy coconut cake—and bake the ham. Even though she still had plenty to get back in order before she could host any B and B guests, she'd invited the Stephens men to join her and Megan for dinner tomorrow. Plus it would give Andrew the opportunity to show them all what he'd been working on this past month.

A few silent moments later, she discovered the best thing about sitting at her new island. From this vantage point, she was able to catch that first glimpse of her sleepy-headed daughter as she shuffled into the kitchen in her pajamas, rubbing her eyes, unaware that anyone was watching her. Like when Megan was a toddler. Only her blankie was missing.

"Good morning, sweetie." She hugged Megan, assisting her as she climbed onto the next stool.

"Morning." She yawned. "What's for breakfast?"

"I don't know. Cereal, may—"

A knock sounded at the back door.

Turning, she saw Andrew on the other side, waving.

"Anybody in the mood for some hot, fresh cinnamon rolls?" he asked as she swung open the door.

She glanced back at Megan. "Guess that answers your question."

Carly pulled three new plates and forks from the dishwasher and set them on the other side of the island as Andrew served up the rolls.

Finished, he licked the icing from his fingers. "There's a great doughnut shop just down the street from my place in Denver. Their doughnuts are so light and fluffy they practically melt in your mouth."

"I like doughnuts." Megan turned to Carly. "Don't you, Mommy?"

"On occasion. I much prefer one of Celeste's cinnamon rolls, though."

After breakfast, while she cleared off the island and counters on either side of the stove so she could start cooking, Andrew brought in the boxes from the garage. Items they'd salvaged from the fire, things like casserole dishes and cast iron skillets, as well as other belongings that had been stored there while the house was being worked on.

"You know, since reworking your kitchen—" he dropped another box on the long counter in front of the window "—I've been thinking about expanding Magnum Custom Homes."

"That's your new company, right?" She filled the large pot with enough water to cover the eggs and set it on the stove.

"Yes." He grinned. "Or will be in a few days, anyway." Approaching the island, he continued. "But what if someone doesn't necessarily want a new home? What if they just want to improve the one they're in?"

Eyeing two glass casseroles that needed to go into the dishwasher, she crossed to get them. "Like remodeling?"

"Sort of. But we're talking luxury homes—" his eyes followed her as she returned to the sink "—so let's call it…reimagining."

"Catchy." She added the items to the dishwasher.

"Right? So what if, in addition to new homes, we offer custom redesigns to help people *reimagine* the home they're in? And we wouldn't limit ourselves to just kitchens and baths. Not when there's so much more out there. Theater rooms and outdoor spaces are hot right now."

She closed the door to the machine, giving him her full attention. "Sounds like a good way to increase business."

"I know it'll take time to get things up to speed and on the path to growth, but I'm used to that. Trying new things is part of the freedom that comes with owning my own business."

"Kind of like when I try a new recipe for the B and B?"

"That's right. If they work, great. If not—" he shrugged "—we move on to the next idea. That's how I was able to grow Pinnacle Construction so quickly. I kept challenging myself to do things better than the other guy." The excitement in his voice had her feeling somewhat dismayed.

Listening to him, she realized how little she really knew about his world outside Ouray. He wasn't some small-town builder. He'd grown a major construction company from the ground up and then sold it for more money than she could imagine.

And hearing him now, she had no doubt he would put every bit as much of himself into this new business. Leaving little time for anything else.

An ache filled her heart. Which was foolish. There were no promises between her and Andrew. No commitment. She knew all along he'd be leaving.

As the day progressed, she tried not to think too much about that aspect of things and simply focused on her house and savoring what time she and Megan had left with him. They all colored Easter eggs, each of them trying to outdo the other two when it came to color and style. She genuinely enjoyed Andrew's company and the way he made her feel as though she could do anything.

Yet the more he talked about Denver and all it had to offer, the more she realized how much she'd come to hope he would stay. But that wasn't going to happen. No matter how badly she and Clint wanted it to.

For the second night in a row, Andrew joined her on the couch in the family room after Megan went to bed. Though for Carly, things didn't feel near as cozy as they had last night.

"You know, I'm going to have to leave Monday to head back to Denver," he said.

She nodded, not wanting to face reality. Why had she allowed herself to believe that maybe this was their second chance?

Taking hold of her hand, he faced her. "These weeks

with you have reminded me how good life can be." His dark gaze bore into hers. "I don't want to lose that."

Her heart leaped for joy, excitement spreading through her entire body. This connection between them hadn't been all in her mind. He felt it, too.

He looked at their entwined fingers, his thumb caressing the back of her hand, before he smiled at her. "I'd like you to come to Denver with me. You and Megan."

Just as quickly as her spirits had taken flight, they crashed and burned.

Did he even realize what he was asking? What about Granger House? What about Megan's school? She couldn't just uproot her, take her away from everything she'd ever known.

She thought back to that first and only semester she'd spent in Denver. All those lonely nights in her dorm room while Andrew worked. He said he was saving for their future. What kind of future could they have if they were never together?

None.

I know it'll take time to get things up to speed and on the path to growth, but I'm used to that.

Andrew might be used to devoting himself to his work, but where did that leave her and Megan?

Playing second fiddle, that's where. Just like they had with Dennis. And she'd vowed she would never put herself or her daughter through that again.

Slowly withdrawing her hand from his, she tried hard to keep the tears that threatened from falling. "I'm sorry. I—I can't do that."

He looked confused at first. Then upset. "Can't or won't?"

"Andrew, running your business is your top priority."

"Of course it is. It has to be."

"And I get that. But what about my business? Granger House is important to me."

His gaze searched hers. "But, I—" He shook his head. "Then where does that leave us?"

God, give me strength.

"There is no us." She stood, unable to look at him for fear she'd break down and cry. "We're too different, Andrew. You're driven to succeed. And I refuse to take second place in someone's life ever again."

He was silent for a long time, just sitting there with his forearms resting on his thighs, his head hung low. She'd hurt him. But what was she supposed to do? He hadn't even said he loved her.

"I guess it's time for me to go, then," he finally said.

She drew in a deep breath as he stood. "I'll walk you out."

They moved silently through the house and out onto the front porch. The night air was unusually warm, but she was chilled nonetheless. Still, there was one more thing they needed to discuss.

"So, what are we going to do about your grandmother's?"

"I told you, I'm not selling, Carly. Not to you or anyone else. However, my offer still stands, if you'd like to reconsider."

"But that would mean giving up my dream of expanding."

He shrugged. "The choice is yours." He stared at her

for what seemed like forever. There in those eyes she loved so much, she could see her own pain reflected.

Then, as though resigning himself, his body drooped. He stepped toward her, cupped her right cheek, then kissed the other. "You're the only woman I've ever loved." His words were a whisper on her ear, but they echoed through her heart and mind like an agonizing shout. He did love her. It didn't matter, though. He'd made his decision.

"Goodbye, Carly."

Arms crossed over her chest, she managed to keep her feet riveted to the porch until he pulled out of the drive. Once he was out of sight, she hurried inside, collapsed on her bed and cried until she fell asleep.

The first time Andrew lost Carly, he started Pinnacle Construction and threw himself into his work. When Mama died, he was too busy living his dream to be there to tell her goodbye. The ache of what he'd done nearly killed him. Instead of pulling back, though, he worked even harder, trying desperately to forget. But it was impossible.

Then Crawford Construction made him an offer. He figured God was trying to tell him something. To slow down. So he came back to Ouray and, for the first time, experienced firsthand all that his life had been missing.

Now here he was again, about to embark on a new business with a busted-up heart throbbing in his chest.

Driving back to the ranch, he swallowed the bitter taste stinging the back of his throat. He'd wanted to argue his case against Carly's protests. Yes, he was driven. Yes, he was a hard worker. But he wasn't her late husband. And if there's one thing he'd learned, it was how important family was to him. He'd never squander that.

Yet he'd heard the pain in her voice, seen it in her eyes, when she talked about her marriage that day over lunch. He could have made her all the promises in the world tonight and she still wouldn't have believed him.

He needed to get away from Ouray. Go back to Denver, close the deal with Magnum, throw himself into his work and forget about love, because it obviously wasn't meant for him.

When he pulled up to the ranch house, there was a white SUV parked beside his father's dually. What would Hillary be doing here this time of night? It was almost ten o'clock.

He heard laughter coming from the kitchen as he entered the mudroom. Following the voices, he spotted his father and Hillary sitting at the kitchen table.

If he was quiet and kept moving, they'd never notice him.

He started through the family room.

"Hello, Andrew," said Hillary.

He cringed.

"Pull up a chair and join us, son." Dad scraped the wooden chair closest to him across the vinyl floor.

The last thing Andrew was in the mood for was conversation. Though he was staring. While he knew there was nothing romantic going on, seeing his father sitting across the table from a woman other than Mama was downright strange.

"I had dinner at Granny's Kitchen tonight," Dad continued, as though he'd read Andrew's mind. "Ran into

Hillary, so we decided to come back here for some coffee."

"Thanks, Dad, but I'm going to go pack. I need to leave in the morning."

"In the morning? But it's Easter. We're supposed to have dinner at Carly's." His father stood, his voice holding both surprise and disappointment. "Are you sure this is what you want to do, son?"

"Yes, sir." If only his heart was as certain as his head.

"Did the two of you decide what you're going to do about Livie's house?"

"No. No decision yet." He could only pray Carly would accept his offer, because as long as they both owned that house, they'd be connected. And right now, he wasn't sure he could handle that.

"You like living in Denver?" Hillary peered at him over the rim of her coffee cup.

"Yes, ma'am. I've built one successful business and am about to close on another. Guess you'd say I'm living my dream." At least that's what he used to think. Until Carly came back into his life.

"Or having fun chasing them, anyway." She smiled.

Had he heard her correctly? "I'm sorry. What?"

She stood now, rounded the table. "I was like you. Growing up, I couldn't wait to get out of Ouray. Vowed I'd never come back." Arms crossed, she leaned against the counter. "I wanted to travel the world and be somebody. You know? Successful. And that's exactly what I did."

"Oh. I guess I was under the impression that you lived in Ouray."

"I do. Now. But I should have done it a lot sooner. I was just too hardheaded and stubborn."

"You, stubborn?" His father sent her a curious look.

"Oh, you hush, Clint." She turned her attention back to Andrew. "I had a beautiful home, a nice car, expensive clothes and more money than I could possibly spend. But I was alone. And it was the pits."

Why was she telling him this? He glanced at his father. Or, what had Dad been telling her?

"Well, I'm glad you're here now, Hillary." He pointed toward his father. "This guy needs a good sparring partner."

After bidding them good-night, he went to Daniel's room and closed the door, grateful his brother was nowhere to be found. He didn't feel like talking. Yet as he crawled into the second of the two twin beds, sleep evaded him.

But what about my business? Granger House is important to me.

He understood Carly's commitment. It's one of the things he admired about her. But his hands were tied with Magnum. He was contractually obligated to move forward with the purchase or risk being sued. Leaving him no choice but to go back to Denver. No matter how much he wished he could stay.

He tossed and turned most of the night, thoughts of Carly plaguing his mind. By morning, he knew what he had to do.

He said goodbye to his father then headed into town before the sun topped the Amphitheater, the curved volcanic formation on Ouray's eastern edge. While daylight invaded the sky, Ouray would remain bathed in shadows until the sun topped the mountain almost an hour from now.

Pulling into his grandmother's drive, he couldn't take his eyes off Granger House. From here he could see through Carly's kitchen window. The two pendant lights over the island glowed, telling him she was awake.

He drew in a deep breath as he exited his truck and made his way to her back door. *God, I know this is the right thing to do. Just please help me do it.*

He climbed the few steps and gently knocked on the door.

When it opened a moment later, Carly stood there in her fuzzy robe, mug in hand, her curls going every which way. She was the most beautiful woman he'd ever seen. What he wouldn't have given to wake up to that every morning.

But that wasn't going to happen.

"Andrew." She ran a self-conscious hand through her hair.

"I'm on my way back to Denver. But there's something I need to talk to you about."

"Okay." She moved out of the way, holding the door so he could enter.

He took in the space he'd worked so hard on, hoping to make Carly's dreams come true. And he believed he had. If only he could be a part of those dreams.

"I won't keep you," he said. "I just wanted to let you know that I'm giving you my half of my grandmother's house."

Her blue eyes went wide.

"You can do with it as you please. Renovate it, use it for the B and B or whatever, with the stipulation that if you ever decide you no longer want it, you will give me back my half and let me purchase yours."

"Wow. That's...that's very generous of you. But... why?"

He gazed at her, unable to deny the longing in his heart. "Because I can't think of anyone who would take better care of it."

She smiled now, but not the big, vivacious sort he was used to seeing. This one was more tentative. Sad, even. The kind that made him want to wrap his arms around her and tell her everything would be okay.

"I promise I will. Thank you."

"I'll have my attorney draw up the papers and get them to you as soon as possible."

She nodded, looking as though she wanted to say something more. When she didn't—

"I need to be going." He turned for the door.

"Andrew?"

He turned back, his heart hopeful.

She hesitated a moment. Then— "Drive safely."

He forced a smile, wondering if he'd ever see her again. "I will."

Chapter Eighteen

❧

For the second time in less than twelve hours, Carly watched Andrew pull out of the drive. He was gone. Forever.

She missed him already.

Still, she'd made the right choice, hadn't she? After all, he'd even said that his business was his top priority. Not her, not family. Business. She couldn't live like that again. Watching their relationship dissolve into nothing. Her heart wouldn't be able to take it.

Despite everything, though, he'd given her his half of Livie's house. Making her dream of expanding Granger House Inn possible. So why wasn't she jumping up and down, cheering at the top of her lungs? Wasn't that what she'd wanted all along? Where was the excitement?

Gone with Andrew.

Though he'd never even been a part of the equation, without him, turning Livie's house into an extension of the B and B just didn't feel right.

She downed what remained of her lukewarm tea and

set the mug on the island beside the pretty basket containing the colorful eggs they'd decorated. After crying much of the night, she must look like a mess.

She went into her bedroom, knowing she needed to get ready for church. She looked at herself in her bathroom mirror. Puffy, red eyes stared back at her. No wonder Andrew had been so eager to leave.

Turning, she slumped against the vanity. Who was she trying to kid? He left because there was nothing more to say. Their relationship was over. And still he'd given her his half of Livie's house. A move that made her love him all the more.

Tears threatened again, but she blinked them away. Tea. She needed more tea.

Returning to the kitchen, she grabbed another tea bag from the box on the counter, put it in her mug, added some water and put the cup in the microwave. She still couldn't believe she'd forgotten to buy a kettle. Since there was one at Livie's, it had completely slipped her mind. Add that to her ever-growing list of items that needed to be replaced.

Perhaps she should make a run into Montrose tomorrow and see what she could pick up. Hanging out in her new kitchen would only make her think of Andrew. She needed something to distract her. At least for a while.

She glanced at the clock. Almost eight o'clock and still no sign of Megan. She must be worn out from helping them yesterday. Unpacking, moving stuff around in her room.

Mug in hand, Carly moved to the beautiful table Andrew had made her out of the old butcher block. She smoothed her palm over the satiny surface. What a fun surprise this had been. Her gaze shifted to the family room before taking in the kitchen once again. Memories of Andrew seemed to be everywhere she looked.

She eyed the cardboard container of scrapbooks and shoe boxes she'd tucked in one of the four chairs. Whether Andrew was in her life or not, she would still complete them. She'd made a promise to both Clint and Mona.

She placed her cup on the table and picked up the shoe box belonging to Andrew. She knew it was foolish. Why torture herself?

But that wasn't enough to stop her from lifting the lid. There, on top, was the note Mona had written.

Carly picked it up, more curious than ever. What had Mona wanted to say to her second-born son? And though she knew she shouldn't look, Carly desperately wanted to know.

She fingered open the flap on the envelope, pulled out the note card adorned with columbines and read.

My sweet Andrew,
You were always my ambitious one. And so much like your father. You work hard and love even harder. Some think you're a workaholic. Inside, though, you long to be a family man. Or did, anyway. Until your heart was broken.

Carly's hand went to her mouth. Was Mona referring to her? Was she the one who broke Andrew's heart?

Instead of dusting yourself off and moving on, you channeled all of your energy and passion into your business, and it's paid off. But a mother longs to see her children happy. And despite your success, I don't believe you are.

An image of Andrew sprang to her mind. That day six weeks ago when she first saw him at Livie's. He was so intense. Not at all like the man she once knew. Or the man he'd been these past weeks.

Andrew, I pray that you will one day find the strength to let go of the pain of the past and allow yourself to love again. Open your heart to the future God has planned for you. You never know where it may lead.

A tear trailed down Carly's cheek. How could she have been so stupid? Andrew was the kind of man she'd always wanted. Yet she'd let him walk out of her life. Not just once, but twice. All because she was afraid.

Andrew was not Dennis. He'd demonstrated more love and understanding in this past month than she'd experienced in most of her marriage. Andrew went out of his way to show how much he cared for both her and Megan. Like that day he took her to the movies in Montrose and that first night when he taught Megan to play cards.

She tucked Mona's card back into the envelope and set it inside the box, her fingers brushing that photo of Andrew at fifteen. She picked it up. "Oh, Andrew, I do love you."

Enough to leave Ouray and risk a future with him in Denver?

Smiling, she swiped another tear from her face. Mona was right. It was time to let go of the past and see what God had planned for her future. To do that, though, she had to find Andrew.

But how? It wasn't like she could just call him and say, "I've had a change of heart. Would you mind turning around?" No, she had to prove she loved him and was committed to their relationship, no matter where they lived. That meant she had to go to him.

She hurried into her bedroom, threw on a pair of jeans and a sweater, then gathered a few things and threw them into her tote. Clint would know where she could find him. Where he lived. She and Megan could stop by the ranch on their way out of town.

Finished, she set her bag by the back door and went into Megan's room. "Wake up, baby. We need to—"

Megan's bed was empty.

"Megan!" she hollered as she left her daughter's bedroom, then again as she headed into the family room. Where could she be?

She searched the kitchen, her bedroom, the dining room and the parlor before heading upstairs. "Megan!"

Her sweaty palms skimmed across the banister as panic rose in her gut. She'd heard of children being taken from their beds, never to be seen again.

Finding nothing in the three bedrooms upstairs, she rushed back downstairs and searched Megan's room for any sign of foul play, any hint where her daughter could have gone. The windows were still locked with the blinds closed, and nothing was out of place.

"Megan!"

She went to the front door. It was unlocked and ajar.

Her heart sank into her stomach. She always locked up at night.

Pushing through the storm door, she checked the porch. "Megan?"

The silence reverberated in her ears.

She glanced left, then right. Spotting Livie's house, she darted down the steps. Maybe Megan forgot something and had gone back to retrieve it. She tried the front door. Locked. She rushed to the back. Locked again.

The key. She needed the key.

She hurried across the drive, into the kitchen, grabbed the key and went back to Livie's. Pushed through the back door. "Megan?"

She searched this house, too, her anxiety ratcheting up a notch with every empty room. Her stomach churned, her breaths coming so quickly she was getting light-headed. Where was she?

God, help me.

Pulling her cell phone from her pocket, she dialed 911 and choked back the tears that threatened to consume her.

"Ouray 9—"

"My daughter's missing."

Andrew continued north on Highway 550 on his way back to Denver, staring out over the open range without ever really seeing anything. When he'd arrived in Ouray almost five weeks ago, his plan had been to do the renovations at his grandmother's house as quickly as possible and then move on down the road with the possibility of some rental income. But all that changed when Carly walked in.

Now he wasn't sure if his life would ever be the same. If he'd ever be the same. Because for the first time in his adult life, he wasn't thinking about sales numbers or the next big deal. All he could think about was Carly. What was she doing? Was she already planning what to do with his grandmother's house, or was she sitting there with her cup of tea, missing him, too? And had she tamed those wayward curls?

The thought made him smile.

He was halfway to Montrose when he'd reigned in his emotions enough to call his attorney. So what if it was Easter? Ned would understand. He pressed the button on his steering wheel for the hands-free calling feature.

"Call Ned." The sooner they got the legalities squared away, the sooner Carly could incorporate his grandmother's house into the B and B.

"Hey, buddy." Ned's voice boomed through the speakers.

"I need you to do something for me." He went over what he wanted.

"Sure. Since you're both in agreement, it shouldn't take long at all. So, are you looking forward to getting back to the real world again?"

Strangely, he found life to be more real in Ouray than it had ever been in Denver. Between the fire, the foals, his dad and the blizzard, it had been an eventful few weeks. "I suppose."

"You don't sound very excited."

"Let's just say things in Denver don't hold the same allure as they once did."

"I see. This sudden change of heart wouldn't have anything to do with this Carly person, would it?"

He blew out a breath. "She helped me to see how much of life I've been missing out on."

"Then why are you leaving us?"

Andrew jerked his head toward the backseat, causing his vehicle to swerve.

"Megan?" He overcorrected, veering into the other lane.

A horn sounded from an oncoming car.

"What's going on, Andrew?" Ned asked through the speaker.

Heart pounding, Andrew put on his blinker and eased onto the shoulder. "I'll call you back, Ned." He ended the call and turned around.

"Megan, what are you doing here?" The poor kid was crying. No wonder. He could have killed them both. "Does your mother know where you are?"

"No." Shaking her head, she tearfully climbed over the leather console and into the passenger seat. Only then did he realize she was still wearing her pajamas.

He willed his heart rate to a normal rhythm. "Okay, sweetheart, what gives?"

"You can't leave us." Her bottom lip quivered.

"I don't have a choice, Megan."

"Yes, you do!" she yelled. "We love you and I know you love us, too."

He let go a sigh. Out of the mouths of babes.

Even Megan got it. How come he didn't?

Because until recently, all of his hopes and dreams had been in Denver.

He eyed the child he'd grown to love. Could God have put her here for a reason?

Yeah, to show him what a giant mistake he was making.

"Come here." He took the sobbing girl into his arms, feeling like the biggest jerk in the world. He couldn't have cared for her more if she were his own daughter. He wanted to watch her grow, to teach her how to drive and protect her from all those dates she was bound to have in a few years.

Most of all, he didn't want to go through life alone anymore. Hillary was right. It was the pits. He wanted to be closer to his father and brothers. And he wanted to be with Carly and Megan. Maybe Colorado's western slope was in need of a good construction/remodeling company.

Whatever the case, he knew in his heart that staying in Ouray was not only the right thing to do but also what God had been trying to tell him the entire time he was there. *Thank You, Lord.*

When Megan had calmed down, he set her away from him. "You're a pretty perceptive kid, you know that?"

"What does that mean?" She sniffed.

Lifting the lid on the console, he pulled out a napkin and handed it to her. "It means that you're right. I do love you. And your mama, too." Except he hadn't told Carly until he'd been walking away. What kind of guy did that?

His cell rang then, his dad's name appearing on the dashboard screen.

He pressed the button on the steering wheel to answer. "What's up, Dad?"

"Jude just called. Megan is missing."

Megan's eyes were wide as she looked up at him.

"I'm on my way to—"

"She's with me, Dad."

"Megan?"

"Yes." He continued to watch a silent, perhaps terrified, Megan. "Tell Carly not to worry. We'll be there shortly to explain."

"I wasn't trying to make Mommy sad," she said as he ended the call. "I just wanted—"

He touched her cheek. "I know. Now buckle up." He waited for the traffic to clear, then made a U-turn and headed back toward Ouray. "We don't want to be late for Easter service."

When they arrived at Carly's, she was out of the house and in the drive with his dad and Jude right behind her before he brought the truck to a stop.

She opened the passenger door and scooped her daughter into her arms. "Baby, you scared me to death. What were you thinking?"

Megan didn't respond. She simply twisted her head to look at him as he rounded the front of the vehicle.

He looked at Carly now. He could tell she'd been crying. Still, she was beautiful. Why had he ever thought he could walk away from her again?

"Would you guys mind taking Megan into the house while I talk to Carly?"

"Not a problem," said his brother, already making his departure.

"Come on, darlin'." The old man held out his hand as Carly set Megan on the ground. A few moments later, the three of them disappeared into the kitchen.

"Thank you for bringing her back." Carly crossed her arms over her chest. "But I don't understand how she ended up with you in the first place."

"She stowed away in my truck."

"What?" Her brow puckered. "Why would she do that?"

"Megan said she overheard us talking last night and then again this morning."

Carly winced, the morning breeze gently tossing those crazy curls of hers.

"Let's just say she thought I needed a little friendly advice."

Carly's mouth twitched, her arms dropping to her sides. "I'm sorry she caused you so much trouble."

He took a step closer. "She wasn't any trouble. At least, not once I got the truck under control again."

"Oh, no." She did smile then.

"Hey, we're both in one piece, and she's home safe and sound."

Carly nodded but wouldn't look at him.

So he forced her to do just that by erasing what little space remained between them and touching a finger to her chin. To his surprise, she didn't pull away.

"I love you, Carly. And I love your daughter, too."

Her body relaxed as though she was relieved. Then she laid a hand to his chest, staring up at him with those blue eyes. "I love you, too. And I'm willing to go to Denver or anywhere else with you, if you still want me to."

Being with her was what he wanted more than anything. But hearing her say those words made him realize how selfish he was even to have asked. She had built a successful business here, and she was an integral part of the community. A community he'd grown to care about a great deal these past few weeks.

Shaking his head ever so slightly, he slid his arms around her waist. "I don't belong in Denver. Ouray is my home, and home is where I need to be."

"What about Magnum Homes?"

"I'm still bound to the purchase. However, I might have to see about getting someone else to run it, because I plan to spend my time here with you."

Lowering his head, he kissed her. This amazing woman who had taught him more about himself than he'd ever known. She was his past, his present and his future.

Still holding her, he looked into the eyes of the woman he loved. "I guess we'd better get ready for church." He stroked her arms. "After all, Easter is a time of renewal and new beginnings."

"A new kitchen, new directions…"

"New life." He smiled, pulling her to him once again. "I guess my parents named the ranch correctly after all. Because I am abundantly blessed, indeed."

Epilogue

Carly couldn't think of any better time than Mother's Day to give the Stephens brothers the scrapbooks their mother had so lovingly planned for them. Mona was an amazing woman who'd raised five wonderful sons, and she deserved to be celebrated.

Of course, the guys didn't know anything about the scrapbooks. They simply thought they were treating Carly to lunch at the ranch because, as Andrew told her, "You're a mom, so it's our turn to celebrate you."

A day at the ranch would be a nice break. Since its reopening, Granger House Inn had enjoyed two fully booked weekends in a row, and she already had bookings all the way into August. By the time Andrew finished the renovations at Livie's house later this summer and they started hosting guests there, this could end up being one of the B and B's best years ever.

With her guests checked out by noon and the kitchen clean, she packaged up some of the leftover lemon cheesecake tarts and fudgy hazelnut cream cookies and headed out to the ranch. She knew the guys would have plenty of good food, but they always appreciated her leftovers. Especially the sweets.

Andrew had picked Megan up earlier from church and brought her back with him. Carly had a suspicion they were working on a surprise of their own. It was Mother's Day, after all.

Turning into the ranch, she noticed a dark gray Jeep pulling in behind her. Another glance in her rearview mirror revealed the driver as the third Stephens boy, Matt.

It had been a while since Carly had a chance to talk with him. She'd seen him in passing around town, but according to Andrew, Matt tended to steer clear of the ranch due to a strained relationship with his father. However, he was here, which meant he'd at least responded to Clint's request.

"Long time, no see," she said when they simultaneously emerged from their vehicles in front of the ranch house.

Matt, who was a couple of years younger than her, smiled as he came toward her. Like Noah, Andrew and Jude, he had the same dark hair and eyes as their father, though she could see a little Mona in him, too. His nose and the shape of his mouth definitely belonged to his mother.

"Sheriff's been working me too hard." He hugged her. "Good to see you, Carly." Releasing her, he nodded in the direction of the new barn. "Looks like Andrew's making some headway."

"Are you kidding? That's been his top priority." In the five weeks since Magnum Homes' owner's son backed out at the closing, deciding he couldn't let go of his father's legacy, Andrew had devoted most of his time to clearing away the old barn and starting the framework on the new. That is, between weekend trips to Denver to empty out his house so he could put it on the market.

"Well, we were long overdue for a new one."

She laid a hand on his shoulder. "I hear you're pretty good with a hammer. I'm sure he'd welcome the help."

He stared down at her. Nodded. "I'll think about it."

"Good." At least he hadn't said no. "Mind helping me carry in some stuff?"

"Not at all."

She opened the back door of her SUV and pointed to the large box that contained all five of the gift-bagged scrapbooks. To ensure there would be no peeking, she'd not only closed the flaps on the box but also sealed it with packing tape.

"This it?" he asked, hoisting the box into his capable arms.

"Yes, sir. Just let me grab these desserts and we'll head inside."

"Sweets, you say? That sounds promising."

She closed the passenger door and started up the steps of the deck. "One of the perks of owning a bed-and-breakfast. I almost always have sweets on hand." As she opened the door to the mudroom, it dawned on her that Matt lived only a couple of blocks from her. "You know, I'm always trying out new recipes. Would you mind if I dropped some samples by your place?"

"Mind? Carly, you're talking to a bachelor. We never turn down food."

She could hear a bustle of activity coming from the kitchen as soon as they stepped inside.

"No. The fork goes on the left and the knife goes on the right." Megan was giving somebody orders.

Matt looked at her over his shoulder. "Where would you like me to put this?"

"Anywhere in the family room is fine."

A lunch of prime rib, twice-baked potatoes and broccoli exceeded anything Carly might have anticipated. Given that they were cattle ranchers, she'd come to expect beef, but prime rib was definitely a special treat. And this one was cooked to perfection.

In addition to the meal, they'd given her a lovely bouquet of flowers and box of truffles from Mouse's. Those two things alone had made her day. But now, as everyone relaxed in the family room—Noah, Andrew and Matt on the couch, Jude and Daniel on the love seat—it was time for Clint and her to make their presentation.

Clint sat on the edge of his recliner, smiling, looking like the healthy rancher she was used to seeing. "You boys might remember how your mama always liked to give you one sentimental Christmas present."

"Like the Bibles with our names engraved on the front," said Noah.

His brothers nodded.

"And those hand-painted signs with our names and the meanings," said Jude.

More nodding.

"Your mother had one more gift planned for you boys." He looked at each of his sons. "Though she never got to finish them." He cleared his throat. "Matter of fact, I'd forgotten all about them until Carly came across the box in Mona's craft room. She agreed to pick up where your mama left off so you could have them."

Carly found herself blinking away tears as she cut through the packing tape with Clint's pocketknife. "Come help me, Megan."

After lifting the flaps, Carly pulled out the red, blue, yellow, green and orange bags one by one, each color a reminder for her of which brother's scrapbook was inside.

She handed her daughter the red one. "Give this to Noah." Then she grabbed the blue one for Andrew and the yellow one for Matt and presented them.

Megan returned for the orange one. "Whose is this?"

"That's Daniel's." She took hold of the green bag. "And this is for you, Jude." She returned to Clint's side. "You can open them now."

Colorful tissue paper flew through the air until each of the brothers had pulled out his scrapbook. When they opened the front covers, the first things they saw were the handwritten notes their mother had penned especially for them.

As she'd expected, tears fell from each man's eyes as they read her final words.

Finally, after a long silence, Noah said, "That's our mama." He sniffed, tucking his note back into the envelope. "Always trying to make us cry." He glanced heavenward. "I hope you're happy, Mama. We're blubbering like babies."

That caused them all to laugh.

Over the next few hours, they shared laughter and memories as each man went through his scrapbook. Carly couldn't remember the last time she'd cried so much.

"Would anyone care for some more cookies?" Still

wiping her eyes, she brought the plastic container from the kitchen.

"Oh, no you don't." Andrew intercepted her, taking the container and passing it off to Noah. "We're not done in here yet."

Not done?

"I have something I'd like to say."

"Oh. Sorry." Heat rose to her cheeks. "Didn't mean to steal your thunder."

He took hold of her hand. "On behalf of my brothers, I want to thank you for completing these scrapbooks for us. It means a lot to us. You mean a lot to us. Especially to me."

Boy, if she thought her cheeks were warm before, the look in Andrew's eyes had them downright flaming.

"Carly, when I'm with you, life makes more sense. You're my best friend and the love of my life." Letting go of her hand, he dropped to one knee and pulled something from his pocket.

Oh, my. He was going to…

Her heart felt as though it might burst with anticipation as he opened the black velvet box and held it out to her.

"Carly Wagner, will you marry me?"

"Um…" She held up a finger. "Hold on one second." She turned toward Megan, who was standing beside Clint. "What do you think, sweetie?"

As if her daughter's smile wasn't enough, she shot Carly two thumbs-up. "Go for it, Mom."

Unable to contain her own smile, Carly looked down at the man before her. The one she loved beyond question and couldn't wait to spend the rest of her life with. "Would you mind repeating the question?"

"You're really going to make me work for this, aren't you?"

"You ain't seen nothin' yet," said Noah.

Everyone laughed.

Again, Andrew looked up at her, his brown eyes alight with love. "Will you please do me the honor of becoming my wife, Carly?"

"Yes!"

He slipped the ring on her finger so quickly she didn't even have a chance to see what it looked like before he took her in his arms and kissed her.

She didn't care, though. She had the rest of her life to do that. With God's help, they had finally put their pasts behind them and allowed Him to open their eyes to the future He had planned for them. A future they would now share together.

And she couldn't think of anything better.

* * * * *

Get 4 FREE REWARDS!

We'll send you 2 FREE Books plus 2 FREE Mystery Gifts.

FREE
Value Over
$20

Both the **Love Inspired®** and **Love Inspired® Suspense** series feature compelling novels filled with inspirational romance, faith, forgiveness and hope.

HARLEQUIN
PLUS

Try the best multimedia
subscription service for romance
readers like you!

Read, Watch and Play.

Experience the easiest way to get
the romance content you crave.

Start your **FREE TRIAL** at
<u>www.harlequinplus.com/freetrial</u>.